Eric Wilder

Sisters of the Mist

Gondwana Press

Edmond, Oklahoma

Other books by Eric Wilder

Ghost of a Chance
Murder Etouffee
Name of the Game
A Gathering of Diamonds
Over the Rainbow
Big Easy
Just East of Eden
Lily's Little Cajun Cookbook
Of Love and Magic
Bones of Skeleton Creek
City of Spirits
Primal Creatures
Black Magic Woman
River Road
Blink of an Eye

Gondwana Press
1802 Canyon Park Cir. Ste C
Edmond, OK 73013

For information on books by Eric Wilder
www.ericwilder.com

Front Cover by Andres Grau

ISBN: 978-1-946576-04-0

Acknowledgments

I wish to thank Don Yaw for providing hours of editing and structural advice. I would also like to thank beta readers Michael Redd, Ray Roush, and Linda Hartle Bergeron for all their helpful recommendations.

For Marilyn

Sisters
of the Mist

A novel by
Eric Wilder

Chapter I

A silent moan died in my throat as my cat Kisses awoke me from a recurrent nightmare. She was standing on me, kneading dough on my chest as she licked my face with her emery board tongue. My heart raced, and I wondered if she could feel it. When I'd regained my senses, I gave her a full-body stroke that ended with the tip of her mostly missing tail.

"Did I wake you?" I said.

After arching her back to maximize my caress, she stopped licking and kneading and jumped off the bed. Grabbing my old robe, I followed her to the door leading to my second-floor balcony. The wind had blown it open sometime during the night, and a chill breeze greeted me as I stepped out onto the little terrace overlooking Chartres Street. Though it was dark, the lack of visibility resulted from more than just a power outage.

Thick fog rolling in from the river had all but engulfed the French Quarter thoroughfare. Headlights penetrated dark gloom as I stared up the street. A slow moving taxi, searching for one last fare, passed beneath me, honking its horn at a stray dog. The taxi swerved to miss the dog, and then disappeared into murky darkness. The foghorn of a passing freighter on the nearby river sounded muted and far away. Feeling a damp chill in the air, I pulled the robe tightly up around my neck.

Kisses stood at the edge of the balcony, her head protruding through the wrought iron railing, staring at something I couldn't see.

"What is it, girl?"

Whatever she was staring at was invisible to me because of the dimly illuminated rolling fog. It didn't matter. Cats see in the dark. I had no doubt something had focused Kisses' attention. It was then I saw it: another set of headlights shining through the fog as it moved toward us.

Unlike the glare from the taxi, this was as dim as the fog itself. I watched, transfixed as the long hood of a ghostly white limousine penetrated the fog. It passed beneath me on the street. More vehicles followed. Except for one, all were ghostly white, their passengers but gray outlines through the smoky windows.

A black carriage pulled by a prancing stallion, tendrils of steam wafting from its nostrils, appeared through the dense fog. In the back of the carriage, wreaths and garlands of white roses draped a gold coffin. The carriage was a funeral hearse. It had no driver.

One last vehicle followed the black hearse: a pearly white, stretch limo. Its tinted windows, all except for one, were closed. As I stared at the passing vehicle, the young woman in the window with snowy white hair gazed up at me. It was a person I recognized. Rushing to the railing, I leaned over and called to her.

"Desire, is that you?"

She followed me with her eyes; bewitching eyes I could never forget. Sadness masked her face, and she didn't answer. The limo had disappeared down the street when I realized the passing funeral procession had never made a sound.

Chapter 2

A gloomy day had turned rainy and overcast as Eddie Toledo waited in the drizzle outside the main building of the racetrack. Rain had begun dampening his long hair. Pulling the trench coat over his head, he gave up his grandstand seat and made a run for the entrance. After a quick glance at his watch, he let the door shut behind him.

His friend, Wyatt Thomas was thirty minutes late. It was still an hour before the first race. Plenty of time to lay a bet or two. He double-stepped up the escalator to an upstairs bar he liked, planning to settle in at a table overlooking the track.

Eddie had invited two attractive women he'd met at Bertram Picou's Chartres Street bar. They hadn't shown, and he was miffed. He needed a stiff drink and a racing form. The racing form could wait, and he could get a scotch in the dark bar. As he approached the bar, a familiar voice called to him.

"Trying to ignore us, Mr. D.A.?"

Eddie could barely see the person who had just spoken, though he recognized the gravelly voice in an instant.

"Mr. Castellano," he said, shaking the older man's hand.

"It's Frankie," the man said. "My dad was Mr.

4

Castellano."

Castellano was probably mid-sixties with dark hair just beginning to gray around the edges. A red carnation matching the silk handkerchief in his coat pocket protruded from the lapel of his suit. Had it not been so dark in the cozy fern bar overlooking the expansive racetrack, you could have seen your reflection in his thousand dollar shoes. Frankie wasn't alone. His companion, a very attractive, middle-aged woman, bounded from her seat and hugged Eddie.

"How you been?" she said in her Italian-laced, old Metairie accent.

"Adele! Been missing you, babe. How's marriage treating you?"

"Frankie swept me off my feet the first time I met him. Things haven't changed. We been to Italy twice, Bermuda and two cruises. Believe me when I tell you I'm ready to stay home awhile and cook cannolis and lasagna for my wonderful husband."

Adele had dark hair and eyes, and a perfect olive complexion. Her welcoming smile left no doubt about how much she liked Eddie. Another woman was with the happy couple. When Eddie's eyes adjusted to the dimness of the room, he saw she looked like a young Sophia Loren. Their eyes locked. For the first time in his life, he was speechless. Frankie rescued him.

"Don't have a coronary. This is my daughter, Josie."

"Then you better shoot me now because I think I'm in love."

The comment brought a frown to Frankie's face, and a smile to the young woman as Eddie grasped her hand. He was wrong. She didn't look like Sophia Loren. More like a Greek goddess with dark liquid eyes and black hair braided in intricate cornrows. Her black dress matched Adele's, and he could only catch his breath.

5

Adele bumped his shoulder with the palm of her hand. "What's the matter, Eddie? Never seen a pretty girl before?"

"Sorry," he said, regaining his senses. "It's just I didn't expect to be in the presence of the two most gorgeous women in New Orleans."

"You haven't changed a bit," Adele said, hugging him again.

"Watch it," Frankie said. "Don't be disrespectful or I may have to bump you off."

"Something I would never do," Eddie said. "But you'd kill me now if you knew the thoughts I'm having about your beautiful daughter."

When Frankie frowned and started to stand, Josie grabbed his arm. She was laughing, her eyes dancing.

"He's just kidding, Papa. Isn't someone going to introduce us?"

"This pretty boy with the big mouth is Eddie Toledo. A Federal D.A. who works with the G-men downtown."

Josie ignored her dad's sarcasm. "Happy to meet you, Eddie," she said. "Will you join us?"

Frankie grumbled as Eddie grabbed the chair beside Josie. His daughter's laughter had stemmed his anger. It helped when Adele kissed his forehead, sat in his lap, and squeezed him to her ample breasts.

With the races nearing, patrons had begun pouring into the bar. Frankie's table was the best seat in the house with a panoramic view of the track through the wall-sized window fronting the room. Frankie's frown returned.

"What's the matter?" Eddie asked. "Your horse throw a shoe before the big race?"

"I don't own quarter horses," Frankie said.

"Oh, why not?"

"Thoroughbred racing is the sport of kings. Nobody likes quarter horses except a bunch of damn

Mexicans."

"You kidding me?" Eddie said. "Quarter horses are among the fastest animals on earth. It's still misting rain, and just take a gander at all those people filling the outside grandstand. What do you have against Mexicans?"

"They been flooding the place ever since Katrina. Taking jobs that should go to Americans, living off welfare and paying no taxes. They also control the quarter horse business around here, and it's time someone investigated."

"Is that a hint?" Eddie asked.

"Someone needs to stop their nonsense."

"Most Mexicans I know are hard-working, church-going, law-abiding citizens," Eddie said.

Frankie snickered. "Now I get it. You're a tree-hugging, bleeding heart liberal. I hope, at least, you're not on their payroll."

Eddie let the thinly veiled accusation of corruption pass without replying to it.

"I'm here to watch the ponies run, not to talk politics," he said. "If you don't like quarter horses, why are you here?"

Josie raised a hand. "Blame me. They're my favorite. I wanted to see the races today, so I dragged Dad and Adele along. He couldn't come to a horse race without an entry, so he bought one."

"You're running a horse today?" Eddie asked. "Thought you said you don't own quarter horses."

"For Josie, I made an exception."

"And where did you get the horse?"

"Just an old nag I picked up for next to nothing. Like Josie said, I hate watching a horse race unless I have one running."

"Uh huh. How'd you get a trainer and a jockey so fast?"

Josie answered the question for him. "Dad has a horse farm north of Covington. Murky Bayou Farms.

7

One hundred eighty acre working horse facility. All pasture under fence with pipe on three sides. Three stock ponds, sixteen-thousand square foot metal barn with twenty-four twelve by twelve stalls, tack room, feed room, wash rack, stocks, and storage galore. Exceptional apartment above barn with three bedrooms and two baths. Ten loafing sheds in the pasture."

"You sound like a real estate agent," Eddie said.

Josie nodded. "Because that's what I am."

"Josie's been in the ten million dollar club three years in a row," Adele said.

"Impressive," Eddie said.

"Are you in the market for a horse farm, Eddie?" Josie asked.

He laughed. "Never gonna happen on my salary," he said.

Frankie frowned when Josie said, "You can visit Murky Bayou Farms anytime you like."

"Sounds like a great place," Eddie said.

"And so secluded. On the banks of a scenic bayou and ten miles from the nearest town. It's like a slice of heaven on earth. Dad's not a fan."

"Give me the city anytime. I don't like having to drive twenty miles for a decent plate of spaghetti," Eddie said.

"You don't have to drive anywhere," Josie said. "Your very own world-class chef works full-time at the farm, and cooks you anything you like."

"That just ain't the same," Frankie said.

"Sounds like heaven to me. Josie, I'll take you up on that offer," Eddie said. "I love horses."

"Want to see Dad's quarter horse?" Josie asked.

"Love to."

"You'll miss the first race," Frankie said. "Who you betting on?"

"I don't even have a racing form yet. You betting?"

"Always, even if they are quarter horses."

"Then here's a twenty. Can you pick a winner for me?"

"You trust me with your money?" Frankie said.

"You kidding? If I had your money, I'd burn mine."

Josie grabbed Eddie's hand. "We'll be back," she said.

She led him through the crowd starting to gather for the first race. It was still misting rain when they reached the paddock. Eddie didn't care, too enthralled by the gorgeous young woman pulling him through the throng of spectators viewing the horses parading out for the first race. The crowd abated when they reached the stalls.

"That's Lightning Bolt," she said.

She petted the mane of the black stallion, its head protruding from the stall.

"This is your dad's horse?" Eddie asked.

"Isn't he beautiful?"

"Doesn't look like a nag to me. Check out his muscular hindquarters and barrel chest. He's the best looking horse in the paddock area."

"He's gorgeous," Josie said. "I love the lightning-shaped blaze on his face. That's how he got his name."

Eddie glanced at the horse. "What blaze?"

Josie touched the wet dye on Lightning Bolt's forehead.

"Someone must have used shoe polish to cover it up."

"Why would they do that?"

"No idea. You'll have to ask Dad," she said,

Even without the distinctive blaze, the horse was gorgeous. Someone had braided its mane and tail with a red ribbon and decorated his fetlocks with bright red tape. He looked ready for a horse show competition.

9

"The way he's all dolled up, someone must expect him to win."

"Dad says he's never won a race. Precisely the reason he was able to buy him so cheaply. He's forty-to-one in the morning line."

"Guess looks are deceiving," Eddie said. "We better head back. From the sound of the crowd, the first race just finished. If we stay away much longer, your dad will come looking for me with a gun."

"He wouldn't do that, silly. He's a pussycat."

Eddie knew differently, though refrained from voicing his opinion. He followed her through the crowd of people, some with smiles, others with frowns, returning from the betting windows.

"If you say so," he said.

Adele was back in Frankie's lap, and both were smiling when Josie and Eddie joined them at the table overlooking the track. Frankie handed Eddie a wad of cash.

"You won," he said.

"Wow! Must have been a long shot."

"Can't make any money betting on the favorite," Frankie said.

"How'd you know it would win?"

"Betters' luck," Eddie said. "There's no other way to bet on these damn quarter horses."

A waitress in a revealing skirt and skimpy blouse brought everyone fresh drinks. Josie saw Eddie glancing at the young woman's long legs clad sexily in black mesh stockings. She smiled at him when he realized she'd caught him looking. He grinned back at her and shrugged his shoulders. Adele also noticed.

"Eddie likes the ladies," she said.

"Guilty as charged, your Honor," he said.

"At least he ain't looking at my legs," Frankie said. The comment caused both Josie and Adele to erupt into laughter. "What's so funny?" he demanded.

Neither of them answered, or stopped laughing. Frankie rolled his eyes as he sipped his drink.

"Can I have a look at your racing form?" Eddie said.

Frankie handed it to him. "For all the good it'll do you," he said.

Eddie thumbed through the magazine. "Is pure speed all you look at?" he asked.

"Lots more than that," Josie said.

"Please tell me."

"The races are short. Most are less than a quarter mile and last only twenty seconds, or so."

"What's your point?"

"There isn't much time to correct a mistake made coming out of the gate. A bump can end a horse's race before it starts. There's also the matter of track bias."

"Most of the races have no turns," Eddie said. "How can there be a track bias?"

Josie handed him a pair of powerful binoculars. "Look at the turf directly in front of the gate. Specifically, the fifth through the tenth spots. What do you see?"

"The dirt's not as even," he said.

"Whoever smoothed the track left the turf in front of the last five slots deeper and more furrowed than the first five."

"That can't make that much of a difference," Eddie said.

"In a race that takes only twenty seconds to complete, every tenth is critical. Trust me. In this race, horses one through five have a definite advantage. Gate three has the smoothest exit from the gate."

Eddie glanced at the racing form. "The number three horse is a twelve to one long shot."

"And it's the horse I'm betting on," Josie said.

Frankie didn't comment, though Eddie noticed

11

his wry smile.

"Tell us who you're betting on, Frankie," he said.

"Not the three horse."

"You think he's too much of a long shot, even with the favorable track bias?" Eddie asked.

"Nope," he said. "I think an even bigger long shot will win."

"You know something you're not telling us?"

"The number three is a plant. Everyone in the paddock knows he's supposed to win. He'll be bet down to less than three to one by the time they come out of the gate."

"This is all sounding complicated," Eddie said. "How do you know so much?"

"The four horse is gonna come across the track and bump the three," Frankie said. "He'll veer to the left and take out the one and two. The six-horse is a twenty to one that's never won a race. It'll win this one."

"How do you know that?" Eddie demanded.

"His owner is Diego Contrado, the nephew of Chuy Delgado."

Chuy Delgado, the Mexican drug lord?" Eddie asked. Frankie nodded. "Should I believe you?"

"I'm not making it up."

"Who owns the number four?" Eddie asked.

"Angus Anderson. He owns the three and the four."

"Angus Anderson, the president of Anderson Energy Corporation?"

"Probably the richest man in New Orleans. He's also a media mogul and owns more radio and TV stations, newspapers, and Internet properties than you can count."

"The four is the favorite to win. Why would he ruin his own horse's chance to help Chuy Delgado?" Eddie asked.

"Maybe he owes him a favor."

"If what you say is true, your sources are better than those we have downtown. Who are your sources?"

"I didn't say," Frankie said.

"You know I can subpoena you and get all the answers I need," Eddie said.

Frankie smiled again. "Answers to what?" I can't even remember what we were talking about."

Eddie took a deep breath as he stared at Frankie. "I gotcha," he said. "You're probably pulling my leg, anyway. Horses one and two are both good bets. If the four doesn't win, my money says it'll be the one or the two."

"You're a smart man, Eddie. I wouldn't bet all my money on it if I were you."

"Stop it, you two," Adele said. "We're here to have fun."

"She's right, you know?" Josie said. "You shouldn't disrespect your new bride by arguing in front of her."

Frankie grabbed Adele's hand and kissed it. "My wonderful daughter speaks the truth. Please accept my humble apology. There'll be no more harsh words out of my mouth the rest of the day. Forgive me?"

Adele hugged his neck. "You big galoot, you know I do."

"I'm also sorry," Eddie said. "Let me buy the next round of drinks. I'm on vacation for the whole week. I intend to quit thinking about work, and I promise to keep my big mouth shut."

"Good idea," Frankie said. "I'm gonna place my bet. You coming, Josie?"

Josie grabbed Eddie's wrist again. "Come with me to the betting window?"

"Why not? I have money burning a hole in my pocket."

"Not for very long unless you take my advice," Frankie said.

Frankie hurried ahead through the crowd, Josie and Eddie holding hands as they followed him.

"No matter what your dad thinks, I'm betting with you, babe."

"I was going to bet a hundred to win on the three-horse," she said. "Dad sounded pretty sure of himself. I'm putting the hundred on the six-horse instead."

"You think your dad has inside information?"

"Don't be silly. He has excellent instincts when it comes to horse racing, though from the absolutely crazy story he told us, I'd say he has a bit of fiction writer in him."

"Then I'm betting with you," Eddie said.

Fresh drinks waited for them when they returned to their table. Frankie and Adele were standing outside on the balcony, preparing for the start of the next race. Eddie and Josie joined them.

"Hope your prediction proves correct, Frankie. I put all my money on the six horse. If it doesn't win, I'll be living off my credit card for the rest of my vacation."

"Hey, no guarantees," Frankie said.

The starting bell rang as they watched the horses bound out of the gate. The three horse was almost too fast for Frankie's scenario to occur. Almost. The four veered toward the rail, bumping into the three horse. The collision caused the three to impede the path of the one and the two. Taking advantage of the chaos, the six-horse raced into the lead, holding it all the way through to the finish line. Josie and Eddie were going wild.

Eddie clutched Josie to him, twirling her twice before returning her feet to the balcony.

"Oh my God!" he said. "We won."

The other spectators on the balcony weren't so happy, most of them frowning as they wadded their tickets and tossed them into the trash. Eddie and

Josie, smiling as they counted their money, were soon back at their table overlooking the track.

"How much did you win?" Adele asked.

"Almost three grand," Eddie said. "Gonna be a hot time in the old town tonight."

"Yeah, yeah," Frankie said. "You amateur betters are all the same. You'll be penniless when you leave the track."

"No more tips?"

Frankie crossed his arms. "You're on your own, big boy. My horse is running in the next race. Hold the fort down up here. Josie, Adele and me are gonna watch from the owner's box near the track."

Eddie blew Josie a kiss as she, her dad and Adele disappeared down the escalator. He wasn't alone for long.

Chapter 3

I'd almost forgotten about attending the races with Eddie Toledo. Bertram Picou, my landlord, and owner of the French Quarter bar I lived above, reminded me when I wandered downstairs.

"Kinda running a little late," he said.

A gloomy fall day outside, the bar was practically empty, Bertram sitting on a barstool, rubbing Lady, his dog's head.

"What?" I said.

"Eddie left here more than an hour ago. Said you were meeting him at the track to watch the ponies run."

"Damn," I said. "Can I borrow an umbrella?"

Bertram reached behind the bar, handing me a Mardi Gras colored umbrella complete with fleur de lis. He called to me as I rushed out the door.

"Hey, don't forget where you got it."

When Eddie wasn't in the grandstand, I knew I'd find him in his favorite track bar. Instead of the two beautiful women he'd told me who'd be joining us, he was sitting alone at the best table in the house.

"Where you been?" he asked. "The races are half over."

"Sorry. Where are the two babes you promised,

and how did you manage to snag the best table in the place?"

"The two ditzy blonds were no-shows. Just as well because I ran into Adele and Frankie Castellano, and Frankie's daughter Josie. I gotta tell you, Wyatt, I think I'm in love."

"First time this week?"

"Don't make fun. This time, I'm serious."

"Sitting with the Castellanos explains the table. Where are they?"

"Frankie has a horse running in the next race. They're watching it from the owner's box down by the track."

"Aren't you afraid that some of your cohorts might see you with the Don of the Bayou?"

"I have clearance, as long as I report anything suspicious I learn to my boss."

"If you go to hell for lying, seems to me you'd already have one foot pointed south," I said.

"All in the way you spin a tale," he said.

I could only shake my head as I grabbed the binoculars resting on the table.

"You mind?"

"Knock yourself out. Take a look and give me your best pick."

The horses were parading up to the starting gate, a spotted bay bucking and kicking up turf.

"I don't even have to think twice about this one," I said. "The big black horse will win by a length or two."

"Hardly. It's a forty to one long shot."

"No way. Let me see your program."

Eddie sipped his scotch as I studied the racing form.

"This says the name of the black horse is Warmonger. I don't think so. Looks like another quarter horse to me," I said.

"I doubt it," Eddie said. "Frankie bought the nag

17

for next to nothing so he'd have a horse running today. Josie says it's never won a race."

"That horse isn't Warmonger, and he's won lots of races."

"How do you know that?" Eddie asked.

"You know I never forget a face."

"That's a horse, not a person."

"You have a short memory," I said. "We both won money on him last time we hung out at the off-track betting site in the Quarter."

"Let me see," he said.

Handing him the binoculars, I watched as he studied the horses.

"Now that you mention it, he does look familiar," he said. "Except that horse had a . . ."

"Lightning blaze on his forehead. His name was Lightning Bolt. Undefeated in ten races."

"That's the name Josie called him. Shit!" he said, suddenly remembering something. "The blaze is gone because Frankie used shoe polish to dye it. Why would he do that?"

"Shenanigans," I said.

Eddie glanced at the time on his cell phone. "Let's place a bet. We still have a few minutes before they load."

"You're a Federal D.A. You can't bet on this race if you know it's rigged."

"Nothing is stopping you from betting the farm," he said, counting out almost three thousand dollars in cash. "I'm lending you half of this. Bet it all on Lightning Bolt. You can pay me back with the winnings."

"Where'd you get so much money?" I asked.

"Frankie placed a bet for me while his daughter was showing me his new horse. It won."

"Must have been a long shot," I said. "You think Frankie had insider information?"

"Hell, he's the Don of the Bayou. What do you

think?"

I didn't bother responding to Eddie's question because we both knew what the likely answer was.

"What difference does it make who places the bet? If they find out about it, won't your employers see it as the same difference?"

"If you do it, then I'll have plausible deniability," he said.

"You lawyers are all a sorry bunch," I said.

He was grinning as I took the money and headed toward the cashier.

"Yes we are, Mr. Disbarred Attorney."

I let the remark pass as I headed toward the betting window. Eddie had a pitcher of lemonade waiting for me when I returned to the table.

"Don't worry about the drinks," he said. "I'm buying."

"Thanks, moneybags," I said, showing him the betting voucher. "Where do you think Frankie got the horse?"

"Wasn't it running at a track in Oklahoma when we bet on it?"

"You're right. I can see how the locals might not recognize the horse as a plant. What about the jockey and the trainer?"

Eddie tapped his glass against mine. "Don't know. If Lightning Bolt wins, we'll be rich and won't have to worry about it."

"And if he doesn't, we'll each be out almost fifteen hundred dollars."

"C'est la vie," he said. "I didn't have it when I walked in the door."

"No, but I'll still owe you my half."

"I'll worry about that if it happens," he said. "Meanwhile, let's enjoy the moment."

"Better enjoy it fast," I said. "They're starting to load."

"Then let's go out on the balcony."

"You can't see any better from out there than you can from here."

"No, but if we lose, I can jump over the edge."

"Shut the hell up, Eddie," I said as I followed him out to the balcony.

This was the big race of the day, the balcony crowded with spectators. The starting bell rang as we tried to get closer to the railing. We didn't quite make it as Lightning Bolt broke cleanly from the gate, a full half-length ahead before he'd gone a hundred yards. He won by three lengths, everyone giving Eddie and me dirty looks as we screamed and cheered. Finally realizing we were a minority in the crowd, I grabbed Eddie's arm and pulled him back into the dimly lit bar.

"Wait for me," I said. "I'm going to cash this before I lose it."

Eddie, a big grin still on his face, was motioning our waitress for more drinks.

"Go for it," he said.

I returned with a check for sixty-six thousand dollars. "Got it," I said.

"What took you so long?"

"Had to fill out a butt-load of paperwork for the I.R.S. I'm getting thirty-three thousand dollars less the fifteen-hundred I owe you, but it's me that's going to get a W2-G for sixty-six thousand dollars."

"Deal with it, loser," he said. "And keep the fifteen-hundred. You deserve a fifty-fifty split seeing as you were the one that recognized the horse."

"Let's hope we don't get mugged before we leave the place. I'd hate to lose my share before I have a chance to pay Bertram his rent this month."

"There's a mail drop in the gift shop. I'll bet they have stamps there. Put the check in a birthday card and send it to yourself in the mail."

"You trust the U.S. mail?"

"More than I trust you and me. You were causing

20

quite a scene on the balcony."

"Me?" I said. "You were pounding an old man's back so hard you practically knocked him over the railing."

"Then hurry up and go to the gift shop. You may have jinxed us by blabbering about being mugged."

They did have stamps in the shop. The cashier smiled when she rang up the birthday card I'd bought.

"That one's very funny," she said. "Who's having a birthday?"

"Friend of mine," I said, paying for the card. "Better also ring up one of those souvenir pens."

"Surely that's not the present you're buying," she said.

"No way. This is for me."

"To remember your day at the track?"

"Don't need a souvenir pen for that. I just need it to address the envelope."

After stuffing the check into the birthday card, I kissed it before dropping it into the mailbox. I was halfway out the door when I returned to see what time the mail would go out. Smiling at the nosy cashier, I waved and hurried back out the door.

"Well?" Eddie said when I rejoined him.

"Check's in the mail," I said.

Eddie had the binoculars in his hand. "Funny. The Castellanos just left the winner's circle. Looks like they got one big trophy."

"Bet that isn't all he's collecting. If we made sixty-six grand, I can only imagine how much he's going to get."

"At least ten times as much," Eddie said.

"Can't imagine he'd be so blatant. If we figured out the scam, how many others did as well?"

"Maybe that's the point. He told me before you got here that Mexican drug lords are pretty much running the quarter horse game right now. Maybe he's trying to pick a fight with them."

"And the authorities?"

Eddie pushed the binoculars across the table. "They're probably already in Frankie's pocket. I doubt he has anything to worry about there."

"Sounds like the opening salvo of an old-fashioned turf fight. Maybe you better sever your connections with Frankie's daughter before you get in too deep."

"I know this may sound crazy. I'm sensing Josie doesn't have a clue her father is a gangster."

"What makes you think so?" I asked.

"Some of the things she's said. Either she's the best actress in the world, or else doesn't know what business her father's in."

"Surely someone would have told her by now. She can't be that naïve."

Eddie fidgeted with the straw in his drink. "You really think I should forget about her and move on down the road?"

"That's what I'd do if I were you. You know lots of women. This one can't be that much more special."

"You're about to see for yourself. Here they come. And Wyatt, I think we should keep it to ourselves about winning big money on Frankie's horse."

"Probably a good idea."

Frankie had a large silver trophy in his arms. When they joined us, I was too stunned to react, other than to stare at the gorgeous young woman like a bumbling fool.

"Told you she was a knockout," Eddie said.

"I'm Josie," the woman said. "Frankie's daughter."

Adele grabbed me around the waist and hugged me. "You look like you seen a ghost," she said.

Frankie had a smug grin on his face as he put the trophy in the center of our table, and then shook my hand.

"My beautiful daughter has that effect on men."

"Please, Dad," Josie said.

With my arm around Adele, I shook Josie's hand. "I'm Wyatt. Hope I'm not disturbing your party."

"It's just beginning," Adele said. "Frankie's horse won its first race."

"I know. We watched it from the balcony," I said.

"You don't look very happy," Eddie said.

"Because some clown bet big on Warmonger just before the race started. It lowered the odds from forty to one down to twenty-two to one," Frankie said. "Cost me big time. Wasn't you, was it?" he asked, looking at Eddie.

Eddie showed them his empty wallet. "No way. I'm leaving with no money, just like you said I would. You'll have to take a rain check on those drinks I was gonna buy."

"Your money's no good today. Like my wonderful wife said, we just won big time."

Adele pulled me to the table, directing me to sit between her and Josie. It must have been Eddie's chair because he gave me a dirty look.

Josie was drinking Manhattans, one of my favorite drinks from my alcoholic past.

"You're drinking lemonade?" she said.

"Long story. I'm a recovering alcoholic."

She pushed her drink aside. "Then I'll drink lemonade with you. I know how hard it must be to break an addiction."

I grabbed the drink, smiling as I returned it to her. "You're an angel. Drink your Manhattan and enjoy yourself. You can't live in New Orleans without being around people consuming adult beverages. I'm used to it."

Adele rested her hand on my shoulder. "I wasn't lying when I said you look like you seen a ghost. Everything okay?"

"When I first saw Josie, I thought she was

23

someone else."

"Who?"

"A woman I knew. Her name was Desire."

"We're trying to have a party here," Eddie said. "None of us want to hear your heartbreak story."

"I do," Josie said, grasping my hand. "Was Desire someone you loved?"

"Very much so," I said.

By now, Eddie's body language left little doubt that he was growing increasingly angry. His legs and arms were tightly crossed, and he'd pushed his scotch an arm's length in front of him. I could also feel the chill radiating from Frankie's eyes.

"Please tell me about it," Josie said.

I smiled and took a sip from my lemonade. "It was a while back. I'm over it now and don't want to spoil the party."

Josie glanced first at Eddie, and then at her dad. "I sense Wyatt has something important to tell us. Do you mind?"

"Not me," Eddie said.

"Go right ahead," Frankie said.

"Wyatt, tell us what's bothering you?" Josie said.

"You're very perceptive. I didn't realize I was broadcasting my feelings."

"Like a beacon," Adele said. "I'm with Josie. I want to hear your story."

"Did Desire die?" Josie asked.

"I'll make it short and sweet, and then we can celebrate your dad's victory. She didn't die. When her twin sister committed suicide, Desire became a nun and cloistered herself for life in a nunnery. She somehow felt that I was responsible for her sister's death. I never had a chance to explain that I didn't."

Josie hadn't released the grip on my hand. "Oh, Wyatt, that's so tragic."

"Like I said, it was a while back. I've moved on with my life, except . . ."

24

"Except what?" Adele said.

"Early this morning, I saw her again for the first time since she went away."

Chapter 4

Suddenly interested in what I had to say, Eddie leaned across the table.

"You didn't tell me you saw Desire."

"Because it was almost like a dream, except it wasn't."

Frankie held up a palm, waving it to get my attention.

"I need a drink first," he said, motioning our waitress. "Doll, bring us fresh drinks, six dozen raw oysters and keep them coming till we tell you different. You can go ahead now," he said after she'd left the table with the order.

"Yes, Wyatt, please," Josie said.

A roar went up from the people in the bar, and the crowd outside. We'd missed the last race of the day. Patrons began clearing their tabs and filing out. Josie and Adele didn't seem to notice. Frankie frowned as he glanced at his watch.

"My cat woke me this morning, and I followed her out to the balcony of my apartment. I live over Bertram Picou's bar on Chartres Street. The door was ajar, ground fog outside so thick, it was rolling across the floor. I know this sounds strange, but I think Kisses saw something that spooked her and came in to wake me up."

"Get outta here," Eddie said. "Cats aren't that smart."

"You've apparently never owned cats," I said. "They're intelligent creatures."

"I'm a dog person," Frankie said. "I'll take your word for it."

"Go on with the story," Josie said.

"The fog was like proverbial pea soup. I couldn't even see the railing. I don't know what time it was. A cab drove past. It was the only vehicle on the road. At least until . . ."

"Until what?" Josie said."

"Kisses' attention was focused on something I couldn't see, at least until a pair of approaching headlights appeared through the fog."

"Another car?"

"Yes, and unlike any car I'd ever seen. A limousine, colorless and almost indiscernible from the fog."

Adele was staring at me. "You mean like a ghost car?" she asked.

"Yes. As I watched, more cars passed on the street below, all ghostly and none with any engine noise. Ephemeral light glowed from inside each vehicle, and I could see blurry shapes of people inside them. All except one."

I stopped for a moment to take a sip of lemonade. Eddie's grin was gone, as was Frankie's.

"Don't stop now," Frankie said.

"A black, horse-drawn hearse carrying a gold coffin trotted past. There was no driver. Another limousine followed close behind, its back window open. The person inside stared up at me. It was Desire."

The retelling of the story affected me more than I cared to believe. My hand trembled as I reached for the lemonade. When I returned the glass to the table, Josie clutched my hand. Adele stood behind me and began massaging my shoulders.

"You were dreaming," Frankie said.

"Maybe, maybe not. A dream doesn't explain this," I said, taking something from my pocket.

Everyone's attention focused on the object in my hand.

"What is it?" Frankie asked.

"A diamond and opal bracelet. There's an inscription engraved on the back. It says, 'For my two precious daughters.' I found it on the edge of my balcony after Kisses pointed it out to me."

"What makes you think it was Desire's bracelet?" Eddie asked.

"Desire and Dauphine were born in October, opal their birthstone. I saw this bracelet on Desire many times. This is October. Maybe there's a reason I'm getting it now."

"She wore that particular bracelet, or maybe one that looked like it?" Eddie asked.

"Don't know. She never took it off."

"Your cat showed you the bracelet?" Frankie said.

I could tell by Frankie's tone that he was skeptical.

"Please, Dad," Josie said. "Don't be so negative."

"Kisses was pawing at the bracelet, almost as if it were a mouse. She went back and forth between the bracelet and my leg until I decided to see what she'd found."

Frankie forked an oyster, dipped it in red sauce and popped it in his mouth.

"You're not talking about Gordon Vallee's daughters, are you?" he asked.

"Yes," I said.

"You know him, Dad?" Josie asked.

"I did. A wealthy socialite banker. Once was the crème de la crème of this town's top-tiered citizens. He's dead now."

"How did he die?" she asked.

"A cop blew him away when he tried to resist arrest. He'd just killed Claude Sonnier, his former best friend, and another wealthy banker. They lived in adjacent houses in the Garden District."

"Why on earth would he kill his best friend?" Josie said.

"Claude was bonking Junie Bug. Guess he'd finally had enough."

Josie looked at me. "Who is Junie Bug?" she asked.

"The mother of Desire and Dauphine," Adele said, answering for me. "They used to come eat at the Via Vittorio Veneto."

"Wyatt, was Desire's mother sleeping with another man?" Josie asked.

"There's lots more to the story, though that's the gist of it," I said.

"The Via Vittorio Veneto was the best Italian restaurant in the metro," Eddie said. "Haven't been there since you left. Is Pancho still at it?"

Adele smiled at the mention of Pancho, her father. They were running an Italian restaurant in old Metairie when she'd met Frankie. I knew because I'd met her the very same night.

"When I married Frankie and stopped cooking, he sold the place to a cousin of mine and retired. It's still mine and Frankie's favorite place to eat."

"Your cousin's almost as good a cook as you are," Frankie said. "Don't matter none. I wouldn't trade you for the world."

She was smiling when she shook a fist at him. "You better not."

Frankie grabbed her hand and pulled her into his lap. "I'd have to have my head examined if I ever did. You're the best woman on earth."

Having apparently witnessed the same scene many times before, Josie rolled her eyes. Eddie reached across the table and used a cocktail fork to spear an oyster.

"Leave a few for me," Frankie said. "I may need all I can eat before the night is over."

"Please," Josie said when Adele kissed him on the neck.

Adele finally pulled away from Frankie's grasp, though she didn't move far away.

Josie had the opal bracelet in her palm and was giving it a closer look.

"What happened to Junie Bug?" she asked.

"Still lives in the same house in the Garden District, though she became reclusive after the death of her daughter," Frankie said.

"How do you know that?" Josie asked.

"I still read the society page of the newspaper. The Vallees were the talk of New Orleans for awhile," he said.

"I wouldn't have taken you for the type that reads the society page," Eddie said.

"Why not? It's the best way to keep up with what the social elite in this fair city is doing. They don't like outsiders, and I'm at the top of their list. Don't matter none because they're some of my best clients."

"You said you knew Desire's father. Did you know Junie Bug?" Josie said.

"I knew her. Desire was a supermodel. I'd see her pictures on the front covers of magazines everytime I went through a check out line."

"Oh my God!" Josie said. "Now I know who you're talking about. You dated her? She had to be one of the most beautiful women on earth."

"Present company excluded," Frankie said. "You look enough like Desire to be her sister."

I nodded. "When you walked up, I thought you were her," I said.

Josie didn't comment. "Tell me about Junie Bug," she said.

"She was also a looker," Frankie said. "A famous runway model that got her daughter her first modeling job. Gordon married her when she was still in her teens. I remember because everyone in New Orleans was gossiping about it."

The place had emptied out after the races. Frankie frowned when two nattily dressed men came through the door and sat at the bar. Eddie didn't miss much, and couldn't contain his interest.

"Friends of yours?" he asked.

"Hardly. It's Diego Contrado and Angus Anderson. An odd couple if there ever was one."

"Dad, they're staring at us," Josie said.

"I'm sure they're pissed about losing the race. I'm going over there."

Frankie walked over to the two men at the bar. We watched as he patted their shoulders and shook their hands. Motioning the bartender, he directed him to put Contrado and Anderson's drinks on his tab. He wasn't smiling when he returned to our table.

"Spineless bastards," he said.

"Don't sugar coat it, Frankie," Eddie said. "Tell us how you really feel."

"That, I'd like to do. Not with ladies present, though. We gotta go now. I left the tab open for you. Eat and drink as much as you like."

Eddie grabbed Josie's hand. "Stay and celebrate with us?"

"Love to, but I'm showing a luxury condo over on Riverfront. Where will you be later on?"

"Picou's Bar on Chartres."

"My appointment could take several hours, especially if I close the deal. Wait on me?"

"I'll stay until you get there," he said. "Even if it's the middle of next week."

"You're so sweet," she said. "And Wyatt, what about you?"

"I'll be there if I can," I said. "I have something I

need to do first."

"Bye guys," Adele said, giving us both a hug.

Frankie was already halfway out the door as she hurried after him.

"I'm going with them," Josie said. "It's getting dark outside, and they'll walk me to my car."

They were already out the door when Eddie noticed the trophy still sitting on the table.

"They forgot something," he said.

"We'll take it to Bertram's. They can get it later."

"Feeling better now?" he asked.

"I'm fine. Do I look sick?"

"When Josie walked in the door, I thought you had a heart attack. She does look like Desire."

"Like I said, I thought she was when I first saw her. It shook me after what I saw last night."

Eddie began mixing horseradish and cocktail sauce, and opening packets of crackers. He was soon consuming the succulent mollusks at an alarming rate.

"I can't eat six dozen oysters by myself. Dig in," he said.

We'd managed to work our way through most of the oysters when a Hispanic-looking man entered the room, joining Anderson and Contrado at the bar. After a whispered conversation, they glanced at us and the trophy on the table.

"Bet he's packing heat beneath that fancy black sports coat," Eddie said.

"We might find out. He's coming our way."

The man didn't look happy when he stopped at our table, though he sported a false smile. He'd brought his bottle of Mexican beer with him.

"Hola mi amigos. You work for Senor Castellano?"

"Not us," Eddie said.

"You got his trophy," he said, his smile disappearing.

32

When he leaned over our table, supporting his weight with his hands, we could see the skull and crossbones tattoos on his knuckles. The tats looked amateurish as if he'd used a sharp pencil to do the work himself.

"He forgot to take it with him," I said.

The man grabbed the trophy off the table and put it under his arm.

"I'll take care of it."

"No need," Eddie said. "We can handle it."

"Thought you said you don't work for him," he said.

"We don't."

"You a liar," the man said. "I don't like liars."

Turning his beer upside down, he began emptying it over Eddie's head. As cold Corona rolled down Eddie's face, the lime dropped into his lap. The thug walked a few steps, then wheeled around and pointed his finger.

"Bang," he said.

The three men were laughing as they exited the door. Eddie's long hair was plastered to the back of his neck. I grabbed a couple of bar rags from the bartender and tossed them to Eddie.

"Frankie wasn't right about his assessment of all Mexicans," he said. "But I hate the hell outa that one."

I was grinning when I asked, "Why didn't you just kick the big mofo's ass?"

"I didn't notice you coming to my rescue," he said.

"Then forget about it. That guy's a pro."

"And packing heat, just like you said. I caught a glimpse of his pistol when he bent over to take the trophy."

"You're about my size. I have clean clothes at my place you can wear. You can dry off and clean up for your meeting with pretty Miss Josie."

"You think she'll show?"

"She doesn't strike me as a tease," I said. "She'll show."

"Then let's get the hell outa here. My shirt is drenched."

Bertram's wasn't far from the track, and Eddie managed to find a parking place on a side street. I handed him the keys to my room.

"Grab some clothes from the closet. I'm not going with you."

"You kidding? We got celebrating to do. You haven't forgotten about the sixty-six grand, have you?"

"There's something I need to do first."

"Like what?" he asked.

"I wasn't looking for answers when I went to the track, but you and Josie gave them to me."

"Which is?"

"Pay Junie Bug Vallee a visit and find out what this means," I said, turning the bracelet in my hand so he could see it.

"Desire and Junie Bug, as I recall, weren't really happy about what they perceived as your involvement in the murder."

"I did my best to stop it. You know that, and so will Junie Bug when I have a chance to explain."

"How you gonna get in the front door?"

I flashed the opal heirloom. "She'll let me in when she sees this."

"Then wait for me while I change out of these wet clothes. I'm going with you to Junie Bug's."

"No way. I don't want to be responsible for causing you to miss seeing Josie again. I can catch the streetcar on Canal."

"If she shows up before we get there, Bertram won't let her leave. You brought me luck today. I know how much you loved Desire. Now, I'm going with you."

Chapter 5

During the fall of every year, it often rains bucket loads in New Orleans. Heavy rain had fallen in relentless waves for the past three days. It had finally stopped, fog forming on St. Charles blacktop as we headed toward the Garden District and the mansion of Junie Bug Vallee.

"You'd think we were in London," Eddie said. "Wish this tub had fog lights."

The street was damp. When a cat ran across the road in front of us, the big Ford skidded as Eddie tapped the brakes.

"Want me to drive?" I asked.

"Didn't know you could," he said.

"Funny."

"Thanks for letting me use your shower, and for the dry clothes," he said. "My hair was a little sticky."

"Getting drenched with beer isn't the worst thing that could have happened with that big goon."

"Got that right. Hope you got a good look at him."

"Not to worry," I said. "I'd never forget that pug-ugly face."

"Good, because I want you to ID him so I can determine if he's legal."

"Or wanted for some crime, maybe even murder," I said.

35

"Wouldn't that be sweet? I'd love to have a reason to install that thug in a Federal maximum security prison."

"Hell, Eddie, what's wrong with Angola."

"Why not? He'd probably fit in well," he said. "How old do you think Junie Bug is?"

"She was only eighteen when she got pregnant with the twins. Desire isn't thirty yet. I'd say Junie Bug is in her late forties. Why do you ask?"

"Just wondering," he said.

"You remember the way to her house?"

"I'd better. There's no GPS in this government rumble bucket."

Eddie remembered, parking beneath a giant live oak across the street from her house. The old mansion was dark, not another car in sight. We kicked up wafting ground fog as we shut the iron gate behind us and knocked on the front door. Someone answered almost immediately. It was a young woman dressed, in jeans and tee shirt.

"I'm Abba, Dr. Morrison," she said. "Thanks for arriving so quickly. Please come with me, and hurry."

Eddie and I followed her through the house, a smell of must and age I hadn't noticed during my previous visit. Dim lighting barely illuminated the resplendent ballroom I remembered from the Mardi Gras party I'd once attended there. Dust covers draped all the furniture I could see through the gloom. Abba led us to a large bedroom; the same room where the police had shot Gordon Vallee dead as Desire and I watched.

Junie Bug was lying in bed, her face ashen, eyes closed. At first, I thought she was dead. Eddie put his face close to hers, then began performing CPR, stopping only briefly to slap her cheeks, pump her chest, and then began the routine anew as Abba and I watched in frozen horror.

36

"Wake up, Junie Bug," he said, shaking her like a rag doll.

Abba dropped to her knees, her hands clasped together. Tears streamed down her face in rivulets as Eddie worked on Junie Bug at a fevered pace.

"Don't die on me. God damn it, don't do it. Get me some water," he said, staring up at me.

An empty tumbler and an antique porcelain ewer sat on a nightstand beside the four-poster bed. I quickly filled the glass and handed it to him. Halting his CPR, he trickled a few drops between her lips as a man with a goatee and doctor's bag came rushing into the room. He prepared a large syringe from his black bag, injecting directly into her heart without hesitation.

Junie Bug's eyes opened immediately, and I was the first person she saw. Her words were groggy as if she'd just awoken from a deep sleep.

"Wyatt, is that you?"

"It's me," I said, grasping her hand.

"Are you Dr. Morrison?" Abba asked.

The older man dressed in a seersucker suit with a bright yellow bowtie nodded. His goatee, like the sparse hair left on his head, was snowy white.

"I am," he said.

Abba's tears turned quickly to anger. After glancing at Dr. Morrison, she shoved Eddie.

"Then who are you and what right do you have pretending to be the doctor?"

"I'm Eddie Toledo, and this is my friend Wyatt Thomas. You let us in the door," he said.

"It doesn't matter," she said. "You aren't supposed to be here."

"Stop it," Dr. Morrison said. "Junie Bug would be dead now if this man hadn't gotten here before me. He saved her life, not me."

"Why didn't you call 9-1-1?" I asked.

Dr. Morrison glanced first at Abba, then at Junie Bug. He was glaring.

"I was given no choice in the matter. You pull this stunt one more time Junie Bug, I'll see that you're placed in a rehab facility. You almost didn't make it tonight. If it weren't for Mr. Toledo, you'd be dead now."

Junie Bug dismissed his rebuke with a toss of her head. "I'm fine, Reggie," she said. "You did your job, and I thank you. You can go home now."

"Not so fast. I want to check you into the hospital for observation," he said.

"I'm going nowhere," she said, throwing off the sheet and bounding out of bed.

She was stark naked and didn't try to cover herself as she hurried to the bathroom, slamming the door behind her. She reemerged dressed in a shiny gold robe that must have cost a fortune. Pouring herself a shot of vodka from the cut glass decanter on the nightstand, she downed it before facing off Dr. Morrison.

"Thanks for coming, Reggie, now get the hell out of here," she said. "I'm fine now."

"Don't put me in this position again, Junie Bug," he said as he scurried out the door.

Junie Bug sat on the side of the bed. "Abba, this is Wyatt and Eddie. They're friends of mine. I need to speak with them. Alone," she said.

Abba looked at me, and then at Eddie before leaving the bedroom and shutting it behind her without saying another word.

"She works for you?" Eddie asked.

"Personal assistant," she said. "Headstrong and smart as a whip." She began to smile. "I haven't needed much assistance lately except for someone to keep me stocked with vodka."

"You were on death's door," I said. "Why didn't she call 9-1-1?"

"She and Reggie have their orders. I don't want to die in a hospital," she said.

"You're too young to die," Eddie said. "Why are you doing this to yourself?"

"Have you ever lost your husband, your lover, and your two twin daughters the same day, Eddie?"

"No."

"Then shut the fuck up," she said, pouring another shot of vodka.

"Fine," he said. "If you'll share your hooch with me."

"Why not," she said, pouring him a shot.

"What's with all the dust covers?" I asked. "Last time I was here this place was alive with people. You had at least a dozen servants. Where are they?"

"They all quit."

"Because you didn't pay them?"

Junie Bug grinned. "Gordon died, but he didn't take his money with him. The staff was afraid of ghosts. One by one, they quit, finally leaving me all alone."

"Because?" I asked.

"The house is haunted."

"Claude and Gordon?"

"Among others, most I don't even recognize. Everyone except Dauphine."

"They've accosted you?" I asked.

"They're harmless. I even enjoy knowing I'm not alone here, though that hasn't worked for everyone else."

"And Abba?"

"A student at Tulane. She needs the money and is trying her best to deny her own eyes."

"What'll you do if she quits?" Eddie asked.

"Be totally fucked," she said.

"Then why don't you move?" I asked.

She hesitated a moment before answering. "Because I'm trapped in this house; just as Claude and Gordon are trapped here."

"You came damn close to joining them a few minutes ago," Eddie said.

For a moment, the room grew quiet, and I could almost feel the icy presence of Claude and Gordon. Eddie must have felt it too because he poured himself another shot of vodka, downing it in one slug.

Realizing I was still standing in the same spot as when I'd entered the room, I sat on the bed beside Junie Bug and squeezed her hand.

"You could at least call some of your friends," I said. "Go to a movie, maybe. You can't just lie around here and drink and drug yourself to death," I said.

"What friends? Instead of embracing me during my time of need, they ousted me from the country club and from their lives. None of my girlfriends would take my call. I finally gave up trying. It's as if I no longer even exist."

"Because of the murder?" Eddie asked.

"Because Gordon was black, and had been passing as white his entire life. The crowd we ran with could have forgiven him for murder. Not for being a nigger," she said, spewing the hateful racial slur.

"Neither you nor Desire have a racist bone in your bodies," I said.

"I can't say as much for Gordon, Claude, and Dauphine, or the socialite crowd we ran with. I miss Claude and Dauphine, and even Gordon, though not my fake friends. I'm glad they're gone. It's just hard living with such loneliness."

Eddie embraced her again. "You're still young, Junie Bug, and still a very attractive woman. Get out of the house. Meet some new people. With your personality, it won't take long."

Pulling away from Eddie's embrace, she turned to me. "I wish I could. What brings you two here on this utterly dreadful night?"

Her somber expression faded into a smile of recognition when I handed her the opal bracelet.

"I found this on my balcony."

"Impossible," she said.

"Obviously not."

"This was Dauphine's bracelet. She always wore Desire's and Desire hers. It was a statement to the strength of the bond between them. This can't be the bracelet I remember because Dauphine was buried with it on her wrist."

Eddie poured her another shot of vodka when she began weeping.

"It's okay," he said.

"Oh Wyatt, do you think it was stolen by grave robbers?"

I could only shake my head. "I think Dauphine left it on my balcony."

"But Dauphine's dead."

"Mama Mulate would tell you that she's only crossed over into a different state of cosmic awareness."

Junie Bug stared at the bracelet as I told her about watching the ghostly funeral procession pass beneath my balcony. She waited in silence until I'd finished the story.

"Why would Dauphine give you the bracelet?" she asked.

"Maybe she wanted to warn me about something."

"Desire?" Junie Bug said.

"That very idea has been percolating in my brain. Have you heard from her since she became cloistered?"

"No," she said. "I don't even know where she's at. You think she's in danger?"

"I don't see any other possibility."

"I have something to show you."

She disappeared into another room, returning with a photo album in her arms. Sitting on the side of the bed, she began thumbing through it. Finding what she was looking for, she removed a photo from its plastic pocket. I stared at it in disbelief.

"Let me see," Eddie said.

It was an old black and white photo of Desire and Dauphine taken when they were about five. Someone had written the girls names in ink to distinguish one from the other. The photo was curled and yellowing at the edges, over Desire's face the faint image of a superimposed skull.

"The ghosts move things around at night. I found this album on the floor, the photo sticking out like a bookmarker. It's a sign; God forbid, Desire may already be dead."

"That's why I'm here. I'll tear this town apart if I have to to find out. I just need a place to start. Can't you tell me anything about where she might be?"

Junie Bug buried her face in her hands and shook her head.

"Desire forbade me from being present when the people came to get her. Doesn't matter because I was peeking through the door. She left here with two people: an older woman dressed in a nun's habit, and a little man dressed in an awful-fitting black suit."

"A priest?" I asked.

"I'm not sure," she said. "A funny looking little man. The woman introduced herself as Sister Gertrude. She called the man Father Fred."

"Can I take the photo with me? I have someone I can show it to. It may be a clue. At any rate, we have to go now."

She handed it to me, draped her arms around my neck, buried her face against my shoulder and began to sob. There was little I could do except gently pat her back.

"Wyatt and I are meeting someone at Bertram's Bar on Chartres. Why don't you come with us? We'll bring you back home."

"I can't. I haven't been out of the house in almost a year. I'm not dressed, and my hair's a mess."

"No excuses," he said. "Get cleaned up and dressed. Wyatt and I will wait on you."

Junie Bug's expression brightened as she sprang up from the bed.

"Abba," she said, calling from the door. "Come help me. We're going out."

Chapter 6

Eddie and I waited in the parlor for Abba and Junie Bug to get ready, Eddie drumming the arm of his chair with a nervous forefinger to pass the time. They didn't disappoint when they finally came out to join us.

"You two look great," I said.

I wasn't kidding. Eddie couldn't stop staring, earning laughter from Junie Bug. Abba was wearing either Dauphine or Desire's dress. While both tall, neither was as tall as Abba, the seam of the skirt rising at least twelve inches above her knees.

Though Junie Bug was old enough to be Abba's mother, she still had the face and body of the runway model she'd once been. Abba was slender, stood six inches taller than Junie Bugg, and had the shapely legs of a dedicated runner. Unlike Eddie, I tried not to stare.

As we left the Garden District and headed toward Bertram's, we learned the weather conditions had only grown worse. Rampant fog and the resultant visibility problems it brought with it had kept his normal patrons at home, and the tourists already asleep in their hotel rooms waiting for morning. Bertram was sitting at the bar with Josie. They didn't see us come in the door.

Junie Bug was laughing, not yet paying attention to Josie as we approached. When Eddie tapped Josie's shoulder, and she turned around, Junie Bug's smile disappeared. Clutching her heart, she collapsed to the floor.

"What the hell!" Bertram said, wheeling around when he heard the thump.

Eddie had already dropped to his knees, preparing to perform CPR for the second time the same night. Before he could proceed, Bertram stuck smelling salts beneath Junie Bug's nose. In a moment, her eyes popped open.

Josie was on her knees beside Eddie. When Junie Bug realized she wasn't who she'd thought she was, she relaxed.

"You okay?" Josie asked.

"When I first saw you, I thought you were my daughter," Junie Bug said. "It gave me quite a start."

Eddie explained when Josie cast him a puzzled glance. "This is Junie Bug Vallee, mother of Dauphine and Desire, the two twins we told you about at the track. Junie Bug, this is Josie Castellano."

"Josie Tanner," Josie said. "Though I'm divorced, I still use my former husband's last name in deference to my son."

"You have a son?" Junie Bug asked.

Josie squeezed Junie Bug's hand. "Yes, and I don't know what I'd do if anything ever happened to him. I'm so sorry about your daughters."

"I didn't know you have a son," Eddie said.

"Franklin Joseph. Everyone calls him Jojo because there's already a Frankie in the family."

"You didn't tell me you have a son, or that you're divorced," Eddie said.

"What difference does it make?" Josie asked.

"Nothing, I guess," he said.

Josie handled Eddie's look of concern with a

dismissive frown. "We'll talk about it later," she said. "Junie Bug and I need to go to the ladies room so I can help her clean Bertram's dirty floor off her pretty dress."

"Thanks, baby," Junie Bug said when Josie and Abba gave her a hand. "These gentlemen would have left me sitting on the floor all night."

Josie, Abba and Junie Bug were chattering like old friends as they headed toward the ladies room. Bertram twisted his mustache.

"Where you boys been," he asked in his bayou-flavored Cajun drawl.

"Not where we been," Eddie said. "Where we are now. Drinks are on me tonight. We're celebrating."

"Oh hell! Musta hit the big one at the track," Bertram said. "How much you win? Hundred, two hundred, a thousand?"

"Try sixty-six thousand," Eddie said. "Half for me and the other half for Wyatt."

Bertram held out his hand. "Good," he said. "Now you can pay me the six months rent you owe me."

"When the check clears the bank I'll pay you, along with another six months in advance."

"Yeah, yeah," he said. "Check's in the mail. Same song, second verse."

"That's where it is," I said. "I mailed it to myself, so Eddie and I wouldn't lose it before the banks open tomorrow."

Bertram turned to Eddie. "Is he pulling this old Cajun's leg?"

"Not this time," he said. "Break out the hooch and put it on my tab."

Eddie and Bertram had already had a round when Abba, Josie, and Junie Bug returned from the ladies room. Abba pulled up a stool beside me at the bar. Josie and Junie Bug kept walking to an empty booth in the back.

"Looks like those two hit it off," I said. "Eddie's

buying. Want something to drink."

"A glass of Chardonnay would be nice," she said.

The bar was empty of customers, Eddie and Bertram deep in conversation as they joined us.

"I'll get it for you," I said, ducking under the entrance.

Bertram was cheap, though he didn't serve cheap booze, or wine, in his bar. I found a nice bottle of chardonnay in the wine cooler, uncorked it and poured Abba a glass. She smiled and licked her lips after taking a sip.

"Absolutely wonderful. Join me in a glass?"

"Love to," I said. "I could never stop at one, so I had to stop drinking altogether." I tapped her glass with my own glass of lemonade. "Cheers."

"I love this place," she said. "It's so . . ."

"Eclectic?"

"Not exactly the word I was looking for, though close. How in the world did all those bras, panties and undergarments end up hanging over the bar?"

"A testament to lost inhibitions; a common malady for first time French Quarter visitors."

"I've lived here all my life. It's not just the visitors."

"That's a fact," I said. "New Orleans casts spells on people that are impossible to break."

"What's your last name, Wyatt, and what's your story?"

"Thomas is my name, snooping my game. I'm a disbarred attorney turned private investigator."

"Is there big money doing that?"

"More often than not, I'm broker than a church mouse. I won big today at the track. Right now I'm rolling in dough."

"Are you pulling my leg?" she asked.

"No, but I'd like to."

Abba was quite handsome, her deep brown eyes matching the curly hair that draped her bare

47

shoulders. She was at least ten years younger than me, and my comment made her grin.

"You're quite the flirtatious one," she said.

"A bad habit that gets me into trouble every time I sit beside a pretty girl."

"How do you know I'm not married?"

"I don't see a ring."

"Some people don't wear rings," she said.

"Are you married?"

"No. Are you?"

"No."

"Have you ever been?"

"Once."

"What happened?"

"Didn't work out."

"Your fault or hers?"

It was my turn to smile. "Are you in law school?" I asked.

"Why is that?"

"Because if you're not, you're missing a good bet."

"I'm in medical school at Tulane."

"A doctor," I said. "You'll soon be driving a Lexus."

"I don't think so. I'm contemplating working at some disadvantaged hospital in Africa."

"Very noble of you," I said. "A close friend and business associate teaches at Tulane."

"Oh, and who is that?"

"Dr. Mulate."

"You know Dr. Mulate?" she asked, her gorgeous brown eyes beaming.

"Yes, I do."

"Then you also know she's an honest-to-God voodoo mambo."

"How do you know Mama Mulate so well?" I asked.

"I was on the track team until I graduated. I still work out every day. Mama's one of my running buds.

Neither of us has ever competed in a marathon, and we're training to run one together."

"Mama was on the track team at the University of South Carolina," I said. "She doesn't talk about it, though I think she may have competed professionally for a while."

"Get out of here," she said. "Mama never told me that."

"We've run together many times. She hates to lose."

"You're a runner?" she asked.

"Almost every day. I can still run a five-minute mile," I said.

"You're bragging," she said.

"Nope. Lying."

"You're funny," she said as I topped up her glass. "You smoke?"

"One vice I've never partaken of. You?"

"My mother smoked herself to death. Lung cancer. I would never touch those nasty things, although I used to have to light them for my grandmother, Marlene."

"Your last name wouldn't be Gigoux, would it?"

Abba stopped sipping her wine, her eyes narrowing as she stared at me.

"How did you know that?" she asked.

"I was working on an investigation for Junie Bug's husband when I met Mama Marlene. How's your dad doing?"

"He's doing well, thank you." After a pause, she said, "What else do you know about Mama Marlene and my father?"

Abba's smile disappeared as she drained the rest of her wine.

"I'm disbarred though I'm still an attorney," I said. "I promise you I haven't discussed your family's business with anyone."

"Then you know my father is really Gordon

49

Vallee."

I nodded, and when she drained her wine, I poured her more. "Does Junie Bug know your real identity?"

Abba shook her head slowly. "Dad refused to acknowledge that he was switched at birth with another baby. It's strange, now that I think about it."

"What's strange?"

"My mom's color wasn't just chocolate brown. She was black as a well-used cast iron skillet. Mama Marlene could have passed as white or black. Dad has blond hair and blue eyes and is as lily white as if he'd come from Sweden."

She smiled when I said, "Maybe why he and your mom named you Abba."

"Maybe so. My skin is somewhere in between Mom's and Dad's. Doesn't matter because all my life I've thought of myself as black. So has Dad."

"Your grandmother Marlene was a great lady. 'There's a lot of both black and white in all of us,' she once told me."

Her smile turned into a grin and then she began to laugh.

"What's so funny?" I asked.

"Dad doesn't have an ounce of black blood in his body. He's white as the Pope."

"And Gordon Vallee, a black man by birth, spent his entire life pretending he was white. Are you ever going to tell Junie Bug who you really are?"

"That was my intention when I went to her house. She thought I was there applying for a job as her assistant. I needed the job, and she pays very well. She was so sad and helpless, I just couldn't tell her who I am."

"The house and everything she owns is rightfully yours and your dad's. Mama Marlene wasn't your blood grandmother."

"I know that," she said.

"You could do DNA and prove it."

"That's what I intended to do, but . . ."

"But what?"

"I saw what all that money did to corrupt Mama Marlene's real son, and how it destroyed his family. Every day, I see how happy my dad is. I decided to choose happiness."

"You may someday change your mind. If and when that day arrives, I'll back you up," I said.

Josie and Junie Bug had finished their conversation and were holding hands as they joined us at the bar.

"Thank you for bringing me with you," she said. "I haven't been out of that dreadful house in so long, I'd forgotten there are real people in the world."

"Our pleasure," Eddie said.

"Sorry the place is so dead tonight," Bertram said. "Damn fog's ruining my bidness."

"You'd complain about a sharp stick in the eye," Eddie said.

Bertram had no chance to reply, fog rolling through the door when someone opened it and entered. The tall man joined us at the bar. It was Rafael Romanov, a friend of mine.

"Well look what the cat drug in," Bertram said. "Pull up a stool and start drinking. Eddie's buying tonight."

"Lucky me," Rafael said. "What's the occasion?"

"Wyatt and I won a small fortune at the track today," Eddie said.

"Lucky you, and lucky for you to be in the company of three beautiful women. Please introduce me to these lovely damsels."

Rafael stood six-three or four, his slender frame resplendent in khakis, blue blazer and gold cufflinks. His silk shirt splayed open to show his hairy chest and the heavy gold chain around his neck. Thinning hair, dark eyes, pointed nose and olive complexion did more than hint at his gypsy heritage. There were handshakes all around, and I noticed Junie Bug's curious glance when I introduced Abba as Abba Gigoux.

"Rafael and I were married to the same woman," I said. "We became friends when I met him at her wake."

Josie patted my shoulder. "I'm so sorry about your wife," she said.

"We were divorced, Rafael married to her when she died."

Bertram had put two ice cubes in a tumbler, handing it, and a bottle of scotch, to Rafael.

"Enough about the past," Rafael said. "Tonight, I intend to enjoy some of Eddie's generosity."

"Hot tip," Eddie said, winking at me.

"Yeah, yeah," Bertram said, pouring himself a shot of Cuervo and then downing it. "I predict you two yahoos will burn through all that money before the week's out."

"I'm going to try my best," Eddie said as he topped up his own tumbler.

Junie Bug was all smiles as she held Rafael's hand in both of hers.

"When I was a model in the New York rag trade I used to date all the drop-dead gorgeous male models. If that's not what you do for a living, then you're missing a good bet."

"Rafael's a priest," I said.

"Rent-a-priest," Rafael said. "The mother church defrocked me."

"What's a rent-a-priest?" Josie asked.

"I do weddings, special religious gigs, funerals, you name it. I also have an ongoing job on a cruise ship that sails out of New Orleans."

"If you were defrocked," Josie asked. "How can you still act as a priest?"

"Luckily for me, once a priest, always a priest,"

he said.

"Wyatt, show him the picture," Junie Bug said. "Maybe he can shed light on what it means."

I handed him the old photo of Desire and Dauphine. He squinted as he held it toward the light for a better look.

"My knowledge of the priesthood serves no benefit in interpreting this photo. My gypsy heritage does, however."

"You're a gypsy?" Abba said.

"Part of the reason I was defrocked; that and because my mother is a witch."

"A real witch?" Josie asked.

"Yes, my dear, a very real witch. Are these two young twins your daughters?" he asked, looking at Junie Bug.

"Desire and Dauphine, taken when they were five."

"Is it Desire with the web over her face?"

"How did you know?" Junie Bug asked.

Rafael squeezed her hand. "I know what happened to Dauphine. Desire is alive, though she's in grave peril."

"I just changed my opinion of you," Josie said. "Even if what you say is true, it was exceedingly mean of you to say it."

"No, dear," Junie Bug said. "Wyatt and I already suspected Desire is in danger, and I've known about my other daughter's death for some time now. Rafael just confirmed what we believed to be true."

"Did you know before answering the question?" Josie asked.

"Being a gypsy and the son of three generations of witches, I have certain senses most people don't possess. I knew when I first saw Junie Bug that she had a grave question that deserved an honest and direct answer."

"Then I'm sorry," Josie said. "Forgive me?"

"I could never be mad at you, my dear. Not even for a moment," he said.

I returned the picture to the pocket of my own sports coat. "You've answered a question as a gypsy. Now, we have a question about the church," I said.

"Hit me," he said."

"When Desire decided to become a nun she was secretive about where she was going. Junie Bug was peeking through the door when two people arrived at their house to take her away. A woman dressed as a nun and a strange looking little man in an ill-fitting black suit."

"Do you remember their names?"

"Yes, they introduced themselves as Father Fred and Sister Gertrude. Heard of them?"

Rafael's smile disappeared. "Yes."

"Why are you frowning?" Junie Bug asked.

"I should clarify a few things," he said. "The Catholic Church is more than a religion. It's one of the largest organizations on earth. There are those that make their living off the church. Custom letterhead, for example. Quite benevolent."

"And?" I said.

"There are others that feed off the church that aren't so benevolent. Father Fred and Sister Gertrude fall into that category."

"You're frightening me," Junie Bug said.

Eddie's back had been to us as he sat at the bar, nursing his drink. Because of something Rafael had said, he became suddenly interested.

"To what exactly are you referring, Padre?"

"Some provide services for Catholics such as adoption. They attempt to place Catholic children with Catholic families."

"I'm still not following you," Eddie said.

"Catholics have faults and commit sins like everyone else. I'm saying, there's someone out there catering to whatever whim a person might have."

"Like human trafficking?" Eddie said.

"Among other things," Rafael said.

"I'm Catholic, and I've never heard anything like that," I said. "Where are you getting your inside info."

"As part of the clergy, I was privy to lots of information not readily available to most members of the religion."

"Then tell us about Father Fred and Sister Gertrude," Eddie said.

"I'm afraid I don't know any of the particulars," Rafael said, silent for a moment to sip his drink. "I do, however, know a person that does. I can take you to see him tomorrow."

Suddenly animated, Abba grabbed my hand. "I'm going with you."

Chapter 7

Former N.O.P.D. homicide detective Tony Nicosia always slept with his cell phone and his handgun on the nightstand beside his bed. When his phone rang at three A.M., he answered it without even thinking twice. Old habits die hard.

"Lieutenant Nicosia here. What's up?"

It was Tommy Blackburn, Tony's old partner on the force. Tommy was still with the N.O.P.D.

"You awake?" Tommy asked.

"I sure as hell am now," Tony said, glancing at his watch. "Why are you calling me at three in the morning."

"I got promoted."

"Congratulations. Couldn't you have waited until daylight to tell me?"

"I'm on my first homicide as Chief Detective."

"Is this important?"

"Kinda," Tommy said.

"What the hell does that mean?"

"You'll know when you get here. Can you come look at this one for me?"

"You've seen hundreds of murder scenes. Why is this one any different, and why do I need to see it? You don't need me to hold your hand."

"I got my reasons. Can you come?"

When Tony switched on the nightstand lamp, his little white dog bounded off the foot of the bed where he always slept.

"Come on, Patchy boy. No rest for the wicked. We got work to do."

Tony was pulling on his trousers when his wife Lil awoke.

"Where you going?" she asked.

"A murder scene."

"Have you lost your mind, Tony? You're not a homicide detective anymore. Come back to bed and go to sleep."

"Maybe I'm retired from the force. Don't matter cause tonight, I'm a homicide detective," he said.

"You sleepwalking again? Please come back to bed."

"Tommy just called. He's on his first case as Chief Homicide Detective and needs my help."

"Call him back and tell him no. It's three in the morning, and he's a big boy."

"And it'll be four before I get there unless I leave now."

Lil got out of bed, pulling on her robe as she headed for their little kitchen. Tony was coming out of the bathroom when the aroma of bacon and eggs caused his stomach to growl. Lil was putting breakfast on the table for him when he entered the kitchen.

"This is just a one-time deal," he said. "You didn't have to make me breakfast."

"Lord knows, I don't have to do anything, Tony. No matter how much I hate this, I can't let you start the day hungry."

Tony kissed her, and then pinched her butt. "You're a wonderful woman, Lil," he said.

"No, I'm not. If you're going out in the middle of the night, then keep your hands off my ass."

Tony grinned and kissed her again.

When Tony had left the police force, he'd bought a Mustang convertible with the severance money he'd received. The sleek, red car remained his all-time favorite possession. He usually drove it with the top down and his dog Patch in the front seat beside him. Tonight was different, thick ground fog making visibility almost nil.

As always, Patch occupied the passenger seat, wanting to stick his head out the window though restrained because Tony wouldn't open it. Tony reached across the console and gave his head a rub.

"You excited, boy? Feels like old times for me," he said.

Tommy had called from City Park, the sprawling public recreational area within the city limits of New Orleans. Left in a state of disarray after Hurricane Katrina, the scenic park had been reclaimed by the diligent work of volunteers and citizens of the city. Now, it was again the showplace that it had been before the killer hurricane had devastated New Orleans.

Happy that he'd had fog lights installed the previous spring, Tony entered the park, driving cautiously through the damp mist. Tommy had given him the coordinates of the murder scene, and he'd programmed them into his car's GPS. A good thing because once inside the park, the visibility had become almost negligible.

Tony couldn't see what was beneath the wheels of the car though he could tell it wasn't pavement. He hoped he'd make it to the murder scene and out again without becoming mired in the mud. On a couple of occasions, he wasn't sure that it was in the cards. His fingers finally relaxed on the wheel when he saw rays of ghostly light piercing the cloud of fog in front of him. Tony parked the car, got out and stretched.

When his headlights finally went out, he saw dim

figures moving in the distance. It was the murder scene crew, their appearance altered by fog swirling as it was blown by a slight breeze. He called out to them before entering the clearing.

"Tommy, it's me, Tony."

"Over here," Tommy said, his voice muffled by the atmosphere. "I was beginning to think you weren't going to make it. Did Lil make you eat breakfast before letting you leave the house?"

"You know Lil too well," Tony said. "What you got here?"

"Double homicide," Tommy said.

The gasoline motor of a portable light plant droned in the background, working hard to penetrate the misty haze, though doing little more than casting an eerie glow on the surroundings. Technicians, on their knees by the bank of a lagoon, were searching for evidence. A tow truck was pulling something from the water.

"Who reported the homicide?" Tony asked.

"Two teenage couples were parking near here. One of the couples apparently wanted some privacy. The kids in the back seat decided to take a walk and got lost. They tripped over one of the bodies."

"Hope it wasn't their first date," Tony said.

"Probably their last, I'm betting," Tommy said. "They called 9-1-1 on their cell phone, and we used their signal to track them here."

"You don't think they might have done the killing?"

Tommy shook his head. "No chance in hell. The only murder those two kids know about is what they seen on TV. They didn't kill nobody."

"You said it's a double homicide."

"That's right," Tommy said. "One of the victims was shot in the back of the head. The other man apparently made a run for it and got as far as the lagoon before the killer put a slug in him."

As they watched, the front end of a large trailer made for transporting horses popped out of the water. The sign on its side said Murky Bayou Stables. When a policeman opened the back of the trailer, he jumped aside as water, and the body of a dead horse came pouring out.

"Jesus!" Tommy said. "Two murder victims and a dead damned horse. What next?"

"Hopefully not another body in there with it," Tony said. "Who owns the trailer?"

"Murky Bayou is Frankie Castellano's horse farm."

"Who are the victims and how are they connected to Castellano?"

"A trainer and jockey that worked for him. The jockey was still dressed in his colors. He was holding a trophy he'd won in a quarter horse race on one of Castellano's horses. The trophy had a couple of bullet holes in it and was filled with horse shit."

"So why did you call me out here in the middle of the night if you already have all the answers? You got a gangland hit on your hands. You know that. Frankie has so many enemies, the killer could have been anyone."

"You been off the force a while now," Tommy said.

"So?"

"Things have changed."

"Like what?"

"That's what I'm getting at. There was another murder tonight outside a local restaurant."

"And?"

"The victim was Diego Contrado. Gunned down as he walked out the door. The killer was gone before his bodyguards got to him."

"He had bodyguards?"

"And his mistress was with him, not his wife. You know who he is, don't you?"

"Just that it's rumored he's somehow associated with the Mexican cartel," Tony said.

"Fact, not a rumor. He was Chuy Delgado's nephew and ran the cartel's racehorse business for him."

"Another gangland hit," Tony said. "So what?"

"Our evidence points to one person."

"Who?"

"Frankie Castellano. The way the murders went down, it looks like Frankie had Contrado popped, and then Delgado's people retaliated by killing Frankie's jockey and trainer."

"Frankie ain't stupid. If he'd put a hit out on someone, and I don't say he hasn't, he would have made sure there was no way to connect the dots to him."

"Me and you both know that. Don't matter none. The killing has got the attention of our fair city's holier-than-thou mayor, and he's been after Frankie for awhile now."

"Don't Frankie grease his palm enough?"

"Not as much as he's used to having them greased now. The Mexican drug cartel has arrived in town. They're paying top under-the-table dollar for our crooked local politician's goodwill."

"I thought things had gotten better," Tony said.

"Worse. On the outside, the mayor's doing all sorts of social reform. You musta heard he's got the city divided because of his crazy politics."

"Oh, I've heard all right. You can't read the papers or watch TV around here without hearing about it."

"Well, taking down statues isn't his only agenda. One of his other goals is getting rid of Frankie Castellano. Now, he has all the ammo he needs."

"More powerful men then the mayor have tried taking down Frankie," Tony said. "Last time I checked, he was still big business in this town."

61

"Not for long if Mayor Portie has his way," Tommy said.

"Why did I have to come all the way out here for you to tell me this? Couldn't we have talked about it over breakfast at Culotta's?"

"Like I said, things are changing. The department's different now than it was when you was there. Way different."

"Maybe you better spell it out for me," Tony said.

"It started with the Mexican cartel spreading big influence bucks to anyone that would take it. Those that didn't were drummed out of the force, or worse. Our greedy politicians didn't take much convincing."

"You ain't gone over to the dark side, have you, Tommy?"

"It's gotten so bad, you got to be careful who you tell what. Almost everyone has dirty hands."

"You didn't answer my question," Tony said. "Are you taking money under the table?"

"I don't like it. Don't matter what I like cause I got no choice in the matter."

"Dammit, Tommy, you don't have a dishonest bone in your body. What in the hell do you think you're doing?"

"Staying alive until I can change things. It's either that or quit and leave town."

"It can't be that bad."

"Worse. One of the officers you don't know was killed because he threatened to talk to the Feds. You don't hate me now, do you, Tony?"

Tony put his hand on the big man's shoulder.

"I broke you out on the force and worked with you for ten years. I could never hate you. I just don't want to see you go down on a corruption charge."

"Better than a bullet through the back of the head like that poor slob on the ground over there. That's why I called you tonight, and that's why I need your help."

"What do you want me to do?" Tony asked.

"You know Castellano. You've worked for him. Tell him what's going down."

"Why do you give a shit about Castellano? He's one of the bad guys. You know that."

"Because his family always did as much to stop neighborhood crime as the police did."

"That's a fact," Tony said. "Frankie's probably done more good for New Orleans than we'll ever know. He's still a bad guy."

"You told me yourself that sometimes your worst enemy can be your best friend. When it comes to getting these bastards out of power, he wants the same thing you and I want. You think you can swing his help?"

"Maybe. When it comes to organized crime, Frankie's hands are as dirty as they come. Still, he's never lied to me. And like you say, we're working the same side of the fence on this little problem."

"Will you ask him?"

"He wouldn't piss on us if we was on fire. Unless that is, he needed us to help him. Frankie's a smart man, and we got something he needs."

"And I'm betting he's smarter than that pack of jackals down at City Hall," Tommy said.

"The problem is with you and me. We gotta stay one step ahead of Frankie, or we'll wind up like those two stiffs your boys are slipping into body bags."

"You up to it?"

"Maybe. Siding with Frankie is kinda like keeping a rattlesnake for a pet," Tony said.

"Then don't get bit," Tommy said.

A big fish broke the dark surface of the lagoon, the sound echoing through the fog. Patch was sitting at Tommy and Tony's feet. His low whine ceased when Tony scratched his ears.

"Since I'm poison to your career," Tony said. "How are we gonna keep in touch?"

A smile lit Tommy's expression for the first time.

"Hell, Tony, N'awlins is the murder capital of the country. I could call you out to join me most any night."

Tony slapped Tommy's broad shoulders before turning back to his car.

"Then try not to make it so late next time," he said as he turned to walk away. He stopped before he and Patch had gone ten feet. "Lil misses you. Sneak by for a bowl of her gumbo sometime. And Tommy, don't get yourself shot. I've sorta grown fond of your homely chops."

Chapter 8

Tony was sleeping late the next morning when his cell phone began ringing. Thinking he was dreaming, he rolled over without awakening. Lil shook his shoulder until he opened his eyes. When he did, she handed him the phone.

"That you, Tony?" the coarse voice on the other end said.

"It's me. Who is this?"

"Your voice sounds a little weak. Did I wake you up?"

"Had a late night. Who is this?"

"Frankie Castellano. We need to talk."

"I'm awake now. Go ahead."

"I don't mean over the phone. In private."

Tony was rubbing his eyes when Lil handed him a cup of steaming coffee. He took a sip, wishing the caffeine would take effect before he had to respond, though knowing it wouldn't.

"Sure, Frankie. At your house on the lake?"

"I have a place a little further away from New Orleans in mind."

"You tell me," Tony said. "I'll be there."

"My horse farm, about a half-hour north of Covington. Can you come right now?"

Tony set his cup on the nightstand and glanced

at his watch.

"It's already two. I probably can't get there before five."

"I'll text you directions. Come as soon as you can. And Tony, bring that dog of yours I like."

Frankie hung up the phone without saying goodbye. Lil was standing at the foot of the bed, her arms folded.

"Want to explain what was so important that you had to meet Tommy at three in the morning?"

"I ain't gotta girlfriend if that's what you mean," Tony said.

"Sure about that?" Lil asked.

Tony popped out of bed, kissing her square on the mouth before proceeding to the bathroom. Lil was still standing at the door, waiting for him when he exited.

"Like I said, I got no girlfriend. I learned my lesson on that one. I promise you're the only woman in my life," he said.

"And Patch?"

"He pinched her chin. "I like you every bit as much as I do Patchy."

She was smiling when she shook her fist at him. "Who was that on the phone?"

"Frankie Castellano."

"What did he want?"

"He didn't tell me. Wants me to meet him at his horse farm north of Covington."

"He didn't tell you for what?"

"Not over the phone," Tony said. "I have an idea, though. Two of his men got popped last night. The murder case I was helping Tommy on."

"You think it means he has another job for you?" she asked.

"Wouldn't that be nice? Last job I did for him paid for our trip to Italy."

Hearing about the prospect of a new, high-paying

detective job for her husband changed Lil's demeanor immediately.

"Why does he want you to meet him that far away from New Orleans?" she asked.

"Frankie's as secretive and paranoid as they come. In his line of work, he has to be. If I was in his shoes, I'd be the same way."

"You won't be involved in any of that, will you?" She asked.

"Hell no," he said. "In my whole life, I never even had a traffic ticket."

"Sometimes, you're a little too honest," she said.

"Can't be too honest."

"I got a pot of gumbo simmering on the stove. You need to eat something before you go."

Tony kissed her again. "Lil, you're the most wonderful woman on the face of the earth."

"Tell it to one of your girlfriends."

As Tony entered the Causeway spanning Lake Pontchartrain, he wondered if Lil would ever really forgive him for the affair he'd had with a younger woman. When Patch barked at a passing vehicle, his attention returned to the road.

The late October day had turned dull, gray clouds hanging overhead like damp cotton balls. Except for the pickup he'd passed after entering the bridge, the road in front of him was empty. Almost thirty miles long, the Causeway was one of the longest bridges in the world to cross a body of water. Reaching across the console, he rubbed Patch's head, feeling glad he wasn't alone.

Frankie's horse farm lay in the rolling countryside north of Covington. Tony knew before reaching it that any place owned by the mob boss Frankie Castellano would be quite spectacular. As he entered the majestic front gate and followed the narrow brick-lined road cutting through acres of manicured grass, regal barns and stalls, he wasn't disappointed.

Many beautiful horses were grazing in the fields. Starting at the front gate, he also passed several brand new Tahoes with matching black paint jobs. Their occupants were keeping vigilant eyes on the comings and goings of the farm. It didn't take Tony long to realize the place was on high alert.

The main residence was a sprawling, single-storied house; a cross between a Texas ranch house and a Louisiana plantation home. A banistered veranda encircled the house, a man with a shotgun in his lap guarding the front door.

"I'm Tony Nicosia. Frankie's expecting me."

The rough-looking little man with a pock-marked face glanced at Tony's driver's license before signaling him to go into the house. Frankie met him inside the door, handing him an icy tumbler of scotch.

"What took you?" he said.

"Plane's in the shop. Had to come in the car."

Frankie grinned. "Glad to see you. How's that dog of yours?"

"From the way he's wagging his tail, I'd say he's glad to see you."

Frankie had a dog treat hidden in his hand and Patch gobbled it up.

"This is quite a place," Tony said. "I didn't know until yesterday that you raise horses."

"Some of the best Louisiana-bred thoroughbreds going," Frankie said.

Like the inside of a Garden District mansion, the floors were done in marble and polished hardwood and covered with Persian rugs. Paintings of champion horses decorated the walls. Slow-moving fans graced the ceilings.

"Real nice," Tony said.

"My daughter Josie found it for me."

"How she doing?" Tony asked. "And your

68

grandson Jojo?"

"Thanks for remembering," Frankie said. "Jojo's outside in the pool with Adele. Josie met your buddy yesterday and they been inseparable ever since."

"Oh, who's that?"

"Eddie Toledo. We met him and Wyatt at the track yesterday. Eddie was on Josie like a hound on fresh meat."

"You don't sound too happy about it."

"Because I told her to get her butt out here. Things are dangerous right now in the city. She's about a hard-headed one, her. Said she was too old for me to tell her what to do."

"Eddie has that effect on women," Tony said. "I noticed your farm is like an armed camp. Something to do with last night's murder?"

"Hell, Tony, let's go to my office. I'll tell you all about it," Frankie said.

Tony followed Frankie down an elegant hallway to his office. The dapper mob boss bypassed the massive oak desk and sat on an expensive leather couch instead, motioning Tony to join him.

"Nice," Tony said.

"My little home away from home; a country retreat when the pressures of the city become too great. Now tell me, what do you know about last night's murders?"

"Probably more than you do," Tony said. "Just so happens I was at the murder scene."

Unsure of what Tony had just told him, Frankie could only stare at him for a moment.

"What did you just say?"

"I was at the murder scene. My old partner Tommy Blackburn wanted to talk. He woke me up. Asked if I would join him."

"Blackburn was your partner?"

"Yes sir, he was," Tony said.

"I've heard good things about him."

"He wanted my opinion on something. He says things are getting dirty in the department, and down at City Hall."

"Tommy's right. Damn Mexicans are ruining things for everybody," Frankie said.

"He also said the mayor is out to get you and won't stop till he does."

Light jazz began emanating from hidden speakers when Frankie strolled over to the well-stocked wet bar and poured himself another drink. He returned to the couch with scotch, tongs and ice bucket in hand. After refreshing Tony's drink, they tapped tumblers.

"Cheers," Frankie said.

"I'd almost forgotten that you're a jazz fan, not to mention one of the best trumpet players in New Orleans."

"Thanks for remembering. The mayor's a certifiable headcase, even without the bottomless pit of Mexican drug money corrupting him. And you're right. He will get me unless I get him first."

"I'm wondering how he ever got elected," Tony said. "He's managed to piss off practically every person in town."

"Like I said, his agenda includes getting rid of me. Problem is, I'm not as easily removed as a Confederate statue."

"Hope not. I don't think our city can survive a human Katrina. Why did you call me here? From the looks of the firepower you're sporting, I'd say you have things well in hand."

"You'd think," Frankie said. "There's one small problem my men aren't equipped to handle. You are."

"Such as?"

"The assassins did more than kill two of my men last night; they stole my grandson's horse. Though I don't need the cops to help me settle a score, my boys aren't up to finding and recovering the horse."

"The horse seems like the least of your problems," Tony said.

"You got kids. Sometimes the most important things in life are making sure you keep your promises to the ones you love."

"Which horse are you talking about, and how is it connected to the deaths of your two men?"

"Long story," Frankie said.

"I got scotch in my hand and my butt's planted on this comfortable couch," Tony said. "Start from the beginning."

"I told you I like thoroughbreds, and that I've never cared much for quarter horse racing. Josie loves it, and everything about it. She talked Adele and me into going to the quarter horse races at the track."

"They still running quarter horses? I thought the meet was over," Tony said.

"Yesterday was the final day of the meet. Anyway, I hate going to the races without a horse of my own entered. A trainer that works for me from time to time called someone he knew in Oklahoma. He found a horse of championship caliber. He'd already won ten races in a row. I had him transported here and flew in his regular jockey to ride him for me. Believe me when I tell you he cost me an arm and a leg."

"You bought an expensive racehorse for one race, sight unseen?" Tony asked.

"That's right."

"I understand that you wanted to have a horse running. Was that the only reason?"

Frankie slugged his scotch and poured himself another before answering. The overhead fans seemed to be keeping time with the clarinet solo coming through the speakers.

"The damn Mexicans have been getting in my back pocket ever since they started arriving in town

71

after Katrina. Since I was going to the quarter horse races, I decided to beat them at their own game. Show them who's still boss around here."

"Pour me another shot, if you don't mind, and then tell me how you planned to do that," Tony said.

"I didn't just plan to do it, I pulled it off."

"Explain it to me."

"I forged some pedigree papers on the horse. His real name is Lightning Bolt. I give him the name Warmonger. Even went so far as to fake his starts. According to the records, he'd never even come close to winning a race."

"Let me guess. You entered him in a race yesterday, and he went off as a thirty to one longshot."

"Almost," Frankie said. "Some asshole bet big on him to win and it lowered the odds a bunch, though not enough for me not to recoup my investment first."

"I guess there were lots of pissed off bettors," Tony said.

"And owners," Frankie said. "Chuy Alvarado was staring a hole through me when I hoisted the trophy in the winner's circle."

"Surely you weren't planning to ever race the horse again," Tony said.

"Right about that. I give him to my grandson Jojo after the race. Adele and I put him on Lightning Bolt's back and let him ride around the paddock before the races started yesterday. It was Jojo's first time on a horse, and that big stallion loved it as much as my grandson did."

"Your grandson was at the track with you?"

"With his nanny. She brought him back to the farm after leaving the races. Said he talked about the horse all the way here."

"Can't you just give him another horse, or a pony, maybe?" Tony asked.

"Adele took their picture at the track. When Jojo

got here, he hung it on the wall in his bedroom. First thing he did when he got up this morning was to go looking for the horse. Hardest thing I ever did was to explain to him that someone had stolen Lightning Bolt."

"Doesn't sound like he took the news very well," Tony said.

"He said, 'Papaw, please find Lightning Bolt.' I was on the phone to you ten minutes later. It'll be worth the world to me to get that horse back for JoJo."

"You know I'd do my best," Tony said. "But . . ."

"I know," Frankie said, holding up a palm. "Those damn Mexican mobsters have probably already cut him up to sell as dog food in Mexico. I been waiting for a video showing those bastards killing him."

"I think you're too late," Tony said. "There was a dead horse in your trailer last night. My guess is that it was probably your horse."

Frankie's hand went to his forehead. "Dammit!" he said. "You absolutely sure about that?"

"Nobody identified the horse, far as I know."

"Then it's possible it wasn't Lightning Bolt."

Tony sipped his scotch before answering. "Anything's possible."

Frankie got up from the couch and began pacing in circles. Finally, he sat back down.

"I want you to assume Lightning Bolt is still alive. Start your investigation. If nothing else, it'll buy me some time to think of an explanation for Jojo."

"I can do that," Tony said.

"While you're at it, find out who ordered the killing of my men and get me a name of the shooter. Think you can handle it?"

"I'll do my best," Tony said. "I'll conduct a thorough investigation as if I had never seen the dead horse slide out of the trailer."

73

"Thank you, Tony. I feel better already. Where do you intend to start?"

"Lightning Bolt's stable at the racetrack. Whoever killed the jockey and the trainer no doubt took your horse at the same time."

Frankie smiled and slapped Tony's shoulder. "I knew I could count on you."

"I'll do what I can," Tony said.

"The farm's under surveillance. My men will follow you to the Causeway. After that, you're on your own." Tony was half-way to the door when Frankie stopped him. "If you see that daughter of mine, tell her she needs to get her ass out of Nawlins, and join me, Adele and Jojo until things cool down."

"Hell, Frankie, just call and tell her to bring Eddie with her. He's on vacation and has time on his hands. You know he's a Federal D.A. Maybe he can pull some strings and help you with your problem with the mayor."

"Good idea, Tony. Guess that's why I pay you the big bucks. Speaking of which, here's your retainer," he said, handing Tony a check.

Without bothering to look and see how much Frankie had given him, Tony grinned and kept walking.

Chapter 9

Bertram's watering hole was empty when I came down from my upstairs room the next morning. All except for Rafael Romanov. He was alone at the bar, sipping from a mug of steaming coffee.

"Stay up all night drinking, Padre?" I asked.

"Eddie's free liquor was tempting. I went home after dropping off Abba and Junie Bug." He grinned. "I half expected to see Eddie still here when I arrived."

"Not a chance. He's too enamored over Josie, the new woman in his life."

"Did she take him home?" he asked.

"Lawyer-client privilege," I said. "I couldn't tell you even if I knew the answer."

"Damn those professional obligations," he said.

Bertram's mailman came through the door, still wearing his summer uniform. He saluted when he saw me at the bar, and then handed me a letter.

"Send this one to yourself, Wyatt?" he asked.

"That I did, Steve. I'd almost forgotten about it till I saw you come through the door. Kind of nippy out there for summer shorts."

"With the miles I put in, I usually don't notice the chill, even in late October," he said.

"Then don't get transferred to Chicago," Rafael

said.

"Hope not. Bertram, you got mail," Steve said.

Bertram stuck his head through the kitchen door. "Probably not a damn thing but bills and advertisements," he said, taking the handful of mail from Steve.

"You going to the bank today?" I asked.

"Don't I always?" Bertram said.

"With the money you make in this cash cow, you probably have to go twice."

"Yah, yah," he said. "What you need?"

"Will you put this in my account for me?" I said, handing him the check for sixty-six thousand dollars and a deposit slip.

"You and Eddie weren't kidding when you said you won big at the track. Sure you trust me with this?" he said.

"More than I trust myself. If you lose it, I'm staying here free for the next five years."

He snickered. "What else is new? Next thing I know, you'll be wanting me to pay you."

"Now that's an idea," I said.

"Lots of money you got there," Rafael said. "Most I ever won at the track is a few hundred dollars. Don't ask me how much I've lost."

"Let's just say Eddie and I had a hot tip on a longshot."

"Call me next time you get another hot tip like that," he said.

"Me too," Bertram said, shouting through the open door of the kitchen.

Before we had time to further discuss the horses, Abba popped through the door looking stylish in jeans, ankle-length boots, and a down parka over her white braided sweater. She tapped a foot when she saw us sitting at the bar.

"You two at it already?" she said.

"Just mugs of Bertram's coffee and chicory,"

Rafael said. "Join us?"

"Don't mind if I do," she said.

Bertram was already on his way out of the kitchen, an empty mug in one hand and a steaming pot of coffee in the other.

"Why so glum, Bertram?" I asked. "Didn't make enough money off Eddie last night?"

"If I hadn't, I'd have had to pad the boy's bill," he said.

Bertram was lots of things. Dishonest wasn't one of them.

"We both know better than that," I said.

As he poured coffee for Abba, we all knew he'd been kidding about padding Eddie's tab.

"Smells wonderful," she said. Smacking her lips after taking a sip. "This is the best cup of coffee I've ever tasted. What's your secret?"

"If I told you, I'd have to kill you," he said. "It's a recipe my mama taught me that not many people in the world know."

"Whisper in my ear," she said. "I won't tell anyone."

Her eyes grew large when he whispered his secret into her ear.

"Now promise ol' Bertram you'll never tell nobody."

"You can trust me," she said.

"What'd he say?" Rafael asked once Bertram had disappeared back into the kitchen.

"Eggshell and a touch of salt mixed into the coffee grounds," she said.

"I heard that," Bertram said, sticking his head through the door. "Can't trust nobody these days."

"Everyone in town already knows your recipe," I said.

"Yeah, what other secrets of mine have you been spreading around?"

Bertram went into to the kitchen, not waiting for

my reply. He wasn't mad because he soon returned with crawfish omelets and Creole hashbrowns.

"Thanks, Bertram," Abba said.

She grinned when he said, "You're welcome, and no, I ain't giving you the recipe."

"I bumped into the mailman down the street," Abba said. "Did he bring your winnings from the track?"

"Thank God, yes," I said.

"Were you worried?" she asked.

"Tell you the truth I'd forgotten about it," I said.

"I'd never forget sixty-six grand," Rafael said.

"Me either," she said. "I saw a bit of early morning news on the Internet before leaving the house. I think you might be interested."

"Like what?" I asked, sipping the steaming cup of coffee.

"There was a murder in town last night," Abba said.

"In this town, what else is new?" I said.

"Double homicide," she said. "They found a body floating in a lagoon at City Park. Since you and Eddie were at the track yesterday, I thought you'd like to know."

She suddenly had my attention. "Go on," I said.

"The two victims were a jockey and trainer from the track. The jockey was still wearing his colors. Want to see a picture?"

The picture of a track trophy, riddled with bullet holes caused me to do a double-take as I held Abba's cell phone.

"Can you text me the link?" I asked.

My phone beeped as the file was transferred from Abba's to mine. I quickly forwarded it to Eddie's, along with a terse message.

"Problem?" Rafael asked.

"Maybe," I said. "That trophy was in our possession last night before a Hispanic thug took it from us. Eddie and I may be accessories to murder."

"Need to leave and take care of the situation?" he asked.

"Eddie will know what to do, and I'm not changing our plans," I said.

A gentle rain had replaced the fog from the previous night, a cool draft of air flooding the bar when a customer entered through the Chartres Street door. Abba zipped up her parka.

"Though I love these old French Quarter buildings, they can be drafty in the winter," she said.

"Then thank God we rarely ever get much of a winter here," Rafael said.

I finished my omelet and pushed the plate aside. "Who are you taking us to see, Raf?" I asked.

"An acquaintance. We'll need to leave soon because we're meeting him in thirty minutes," he said.

"Then wherever we're going must not be far from here," Abba said.

"St. Roch Cemetery and Chapel," he said.

"Seems a strange place to meet someone," Abba said.

"You'll understand why when we get there."

Bertram waved Rafael off when he called for the tab.

"I make a decent living selling alcohol to lost souls. Least I can do is provide them an occasional free meal," he said.

He blushed when Abba reached over the bar and gave him a hug.

"Thanks, Bertram," she said as we walked out into the crisp autumn weather.

"My vehicle is in a parking lot not far from here," Rafael said.

"I parked on the street, outside the door," Abba said. "Let's take mine."

Misting rain had replaced last night's fog. When

Abba unlocked the front door of a bright orange crossover of questionable vintage, I quickly climbed into the rear seat.

"You take shotgun, Padre," I said. "I'll ride back here."

"What kind of car is this?" Rafael asked when we pulled away from the curb.

"Pontiac Aztek," she said.

Oblivious to the drizzle, a dozen pigeons fighting over the remains of a Lucky Dog someone had dropped in the street took flight in front of us. Abba swerved to miss the French Quarter specialty, and the pigeons landed behind us to finish their clean up duty.

"How old is it?" Rafael asked. "They don't make Pontiacs anymore, do they?"

"This is a 2005 model, the last year they made Azteks. My dad bought it for me when I started driving."

"As I recall, not many people bought Azteks. Is your dad . . . ?"

"A nerd? Very much so," she said, answering Rafael's question before he'd finished asking it. "Must have rubbed off on me because so am I."

"Looks to be in pristine condition," he said. "You apparently take excellent care of your possessions."

His comment made her laugh. "When you're a poor medical student, you have to make things last, or starve to death."

"You look neither broke nor starving," Rafael said.

"My job with Junie Bug pays well, and Dad helps with unexpected bills."

"Why are you taking such an interest in Junie Bug's daughter?" he asked.

Abba seemed miffed by Rafael's question. "Will you tell him?" she asked, glancing at me for a moment in the rearview mirror.

"Abba's father is Vincent Gigoux. He is the baby that was switched at birth with Gordon Vallee. Vincent is the real heir to the Vallee fortune, and not Gordon, Junie Bug's husband and the father of Desire."

Rafael's smile had disappeared when he turned to glance at me.

"Then are you trying to find Desire with ill intent?" he asked.

"I don't intend to ever tell Junie Bug, or her daughter if we find her, who I really am."

"Is that the way you've always felt?" Rafael asked.

"Dad would have no part of butting into Junie Bug's life. I approached her with the intention of telling her who I am. She thought I was interviewing for a job. I took the job and chickened out about telling her my story."

"And things have changed?"

"I've worked for that wonderful lady more than a year now and have real empathy for her. She trusts me, and I will never betray that trust."

"Sure about that?" Rafael asked.

Abba's smile returned, her hair moving in waves when she shook her head.

"You are a priest, aren't you? I haven't been grilled like that since I confessed to my parish priest about kissing a boy for the first time."

"Sorry, my dear," he said. "I try to stay in practice."

"You still haven't told us who we're meeting and how he can help us find Desire," I said, piping in from the backseat.

"His name is Lando Impeke. He's a Tutsi that immigrated from Rwanda after the conflict in the nineties. I've never met him though I understand he's quite a tragic figure."

"How so?" Abba asked.

81

"His entire family was slaughtered in the genocide resulting from the Hutu-Tutsi conflict. He was a broken man when he first came to New Orleans."

"And now?" I asked.

"We'll soon find out. We're entering the St. Roch neighborhood."

"Looks bleak," Abba said.

"Hurricane Katrina hammered this area. Flooded everything. Many of the abandoned board-framed houses have never been reoccupied. Crime here is off the charts."

A stray dog digging in an overturned garbage can that had blown into the street didn't bother moving when we drove past.

"What about the cemetery?" I asked.

"Also flooded, many of the graves destroyed or looted," Rafael said. "Thankfully, the two St. Roch cemeteries have been restored."

"What's the deal with the shrine?" Abba said.

"Many decades ago, during an outbreak of yellow fever, the priest of this parish prayed to St. Roch, the patron of good health. He promised to build a shrine if the people of his parish were spared. Not a single parishioner contracted the disease, and the priest made good on his promise. The chapel is famous all over the world."

"Because?"

"It's a place of healing. People coming there seeking intervention in their health problems have reported many miracle cures," he said.

"I'm a medical student," Abba said. "Pardon me if I'm a bit skeptical about faith healing."

"No problem, my dear. The world has become a skeptical place."

"Have either of you seen any such miracles in your lifetimes?" she asked.

"I'll readily admit I've never witnessed a miracle,

though others that I trust have," Rafael said.

"You, Wyatt?"

"I've seen lots of things I can't explain, though I've never witnessed what I'd consider a miracle."

We'd reached the entrance to the St. Roch Cemetery, and Abba quickly found a place to park. At least the drizzling rain had ceased as we stepped out of the car.

"It's spectacular," she said.

"Looks like a place where miracles could happen," Rafael said.

"Maybe so," Abba said. "Doesn't matter because I'm going to continue discounting the possibility of miracles until I see one with my own eyes."

Chapter 10

As Abba had said, the entrance to the cemetery was spectacular. The tall gate topped by an ornate cross said St. Roch Campo Santo. A smiling black man dressed in a colorful African-print shirt waited for us just inside the open gate.

"Lando Impeke?" Rafael asked.

"That is me," the man said. "Are you Father Rafael?"

"Yes, and this is Abba Gigoux and Wyatt Thomas. They have questions that maybe you can answer."

"I will do my very best," Impeke said. "Please follow me. I will give you a brief tour on our way to the chapel."

Impeke's skin was the color of dark chocolate, his hair cut short and snowy white. He spoke in a clipped, though discernible African accent.

A tiny man, he barely reached Abba's shoulder. Neither he nor Abba seemed to mind.

Some of the aboveground crypts were massive and ornate. Many were "oven" vaults meant for multiple interments. All were colorful. Standing in front of the entrance to the chapel was a statue of Jesus on the cross. In front of it was a marble carving of a sick girl lying on a bed. Impeke stopped to show us.

"This statue represents the reason so many people visit this cemetery from every place on earth."

"The little girl was healed of her affliction?" Rafael said.

Impeke nodded. "Along with many others. The recipient of a miracle."

"Have you ever seen such a miracle?" Abba asked.

"Many people enter these gates, helpless and broken. Always, when they leave, they are once again whole."

"Did you hear about St. Roch after settling in the neighborhood?" Rafael asked.

"I had heard of this place even when I was in Africa. The statue of the little girl is part of the reason I came to New Orleans."

"Part of the reason?" I said.

"Yes, though I had other considerations," he said.

Abba didn't let him explain. "You had an impairment that was healed?" she asked.

"My soul," Impeke said. "I prayed to St. Roch, and he restored me."

Afraid of insulting the passionate little man by saying something negative, Abba refrained from commenting. We followed him down the pathway to the chapel.

"The graves are hauntingly beautiful," Rafael said.

"You should see them at dusk," Impeke said. "It is when the spirits begin their nightly walk, and the colors of the graves and statues, and sounds of the dead come alive."

He smiled when Abba said, "You believe in ghosts?"

"Of course. There are more spirits in this city than can be counted."

"Then why haven't I seen them?" she asked.

Impeke stopped and touched her hand. "We see

only what we wish to see, and filter out the rest."

"But why?" she said.

"Fear of the unknown," he said.

She shook her head as we entered the chapel, a surreal little room filled with canes, wooden crutches, and artificial limbs hanging on wall pegs.

There was also a table covered with relics, a red plaster heart, leg braces, at least one set of false teeth, and many crosses. Plaster peeled off the walls, the small statue of the Virgin Mary almost seeming alive.

"Offerings," Impeke said. "Left by pilgrims searching for miracles. They are not the only ones to visit St. Roch," Impeke said.

"Who else?" Abba asked.

"The curious. People who wish to see another side of our Catholic faith."

"I'm sorry," Abba said. "I have no idea what you're talking about."

"Exotic Catholics; believers who push the charismatic element of our religion to the limits," Impeke said.

"It's the same in all Christian religions," Rafael said. "Some believers sit sedately in their pews and mouth the words to hymns sung by the choir. Other believers fall out of their pews, roll down the aisles, and speak in unknown tongues. Catholics are no different."

Impeke knelt in front of the statue of the Virgin Mary and began to pray. Abba waited for his prayer to end before speaking.

"We understand you know a man named Father Fred," she said. "I could find nothing about him when I did a search of the Internet and local documents. What can you tell us about him?"

Even in late October, humidity was high, plaster flaking off the ceiling as well as the walls. Impeke gazed up at it before answering.

"Sometimes the Devil walks in human shoes.

Such is the case for the man you know as Father Fred."

"Is he a priest?" Rafael asked.

Impeke nodded. "A rogue priest; a person that uses the priesthood to his own advantage; someone that deserves to burn in hell."

Rafael placed his hand on Impeke's shoulder. "I sense you have more to tell us about Father Fred than just where we can find him."

Tears had begun streaming down the man's face. Still on his knees, he lowered his head and began praying again. We watched, transfixed, the humidity high and the faint smell of mold lingering in the eclectic little chapel. His eyes remained closed, and his head bowed when he began to speak.

"Nearly twenty-five years have passed since I first laid eyes on the Devil himself. It was a hot night in my village. I awoke to the howl of a stray dog outside my hut. It was then I began hearing shouts and screams.

"My wife was asleep beside me, my two sons in pallets across the room. I wasn't fully awake when men with machetes came screaming through the door.

"Several of the men overpowered me, binding my hands behind me with steel cuffs. I could only struggle, scream, and cry as they hacked my two sons to death. My wife Aiella was with child, eight months pregnant. I tried to help as the men began raping her. They held me down, and I could do nothing except scream for them to stop the atrocity. They didn't.

"It was a damp night, humidity high and the cloying smell of sex, sweat, and blood hanging in the air. When they finished with Aiella, they hacked her to death with their machetes. Her eyes had closed, and she was no longer screaming.

"I begged them to kill me too. They did not. One of the men knocked me out with the butt of his machete. When I finally opened my eyes, I found myself chained by leg irons to a tree along with dozens of other men, boys, and girls. The next morning, we began a trek that lasted many days.

"They kept us in leg irons and neck chains and fed us slop once a day along with just enough water to keep us alive. We finally reached the coast. It was then that I saw Father Fred for the first time."

Impeke grew silent, his head bowed as tears continued streaming down his face. Rafael began softly patting his back, trying to comfort him.

"This is so painful for you. Spare yourself. We don't need to hear the rest of the story," he said.

"I must tell it," he said. "It's the only way you'll know the evil with which you are dealing."

"Then take your time," Rafael said. "We're going nowhere."

A flock of pigeons landed briefly outside the open door, raising a ruckus before flying away in a flap of many wings.

"The Hutus built half a dozen large bonfires. When darkness came, they slaughtered a young man, butchered, cooked, and feasted on him. Father Fred was with them, laughing and enjoying the meal along with them.

"They threw us leftover scraps and bones. Half-starved, many of the captives ate human flesh. After the feast, Father Fred joined the Hutus in the ceremonial revelry of rape and child molestation that followed."

I didn't ask Impeke if he had also consumed human flesh.

"What was he doing there?" I said.

"Purchasing slaves. Human contraband for buyers from all over the globe."

Abba's eyes had grown progressively larger, a hand covering her open mouth.

"Oh my God!" she said.

"Yes, the man is a slave trader, buying and selling human chattel for rich and powerful clients. God help them."

Rafael's hand hadn't moved from Impeke's shoulder. "And you?"

"Like many other captives, I had developed a tropical fever. They thought I was going to die."

"You escaped?" I asked.

Impeke shook his head. "They beat me and left me on the side of the road. When I came to from the beating, I was alone."

He pulled up the long sleeve of his colorful shirt and held up his arm. For the first time since meeting him, we realized that only a stump remained where his hand had been. He pointed to a porcelain prosthetic hanging on the wall.

"Before leaving me to die, the monsters cut off my right hand. They had already taken my soul. St. Roch restored my soul and gave me new life. In exchange, I left the prosthetic as an offering and have lived without it ever since."

Wind gusted through the portal we'd left open, sucking the air out of the small chapel and causing the door to slam shut with a bang.

"Enough of this place," Rafael said. "I've developed a splitting headache, and I badly need a drink. It's past lunch hour. You can tell us where we can find the monster as we break bread."

Impeke's tears had vanished, replaced by his original rosy smile.

"There are only a few places to eat and drink in this neighborhood. St. Roch Market is one of them, and it is near."

"Is it a good place to eat?" Abba asked.

"A marvelous place," Impeke said. "They have gumbo, po'boys, and even African beer."

"I can go for that," Abba said.

"Then let's go," Rafael said.

89

Clouds had begun gathering as we drove away from the cemetery. No one spoke as Abba pointed the Aztek toward the nearby St. Roch Market. Public money had transformed the old market building into a food court, the aroma of food intoxicating as we entered the building.

Upscale vendors sold exotic coffees, beer, and mixed drinks. The market's many vendors specialized in everything from oysters to traditional Korean cooking. As Impeke had said, there was even African beer on tap.

The rain had returned outside as we found a table near the front door of the market. It was my first visit, and I wasn't disappointed. Rafael had a chef salad with a glass of cabernet. Abba had a dozen raw oysters, a spicy plate of Kimchi, and, like Impeke, an icy glass of African beer. He and I had gumbo and red beans and rice, Impeke lacing his with lots of pepper sauce.

After his second beer, his smile had returned. I took it as an opening to quiz him.

"Did you come to New Orleans specifically to find Father Fred?"

"Yes. I had learned that he lived here and came to Louisiana with every intention of killing him."

"But your experience at St. Roch changed your mind?"

"Yes. I am at peace with myself and no longer dream about ripping his throat out." He smiled again. "It wouldn't bother me, though, if someone else killed him."

"We are looking for Father Fred because of a much different reason," Abba said. "He recruited a young woman we know, apparently convincing her she was going to become a nun and join a convent. If she's still alive, we want to rescue her."

"I'm so sorry for the young woman," Impeke said. "Father Fred preys on the weak. He runs his operation from an old orphanage in Mid-City. He keeps people he will sell as slaves, or worse. It is a prison disguised as a place of hope."

"Why haven't you reported this to the police?" Abba asked.

"Oh, but I have," he said. "Many times."

"What happened?"

"I was threatened with bodily harm if I persisted in harassing Father Fred."

"New Orleans politics," Rafael said. "Gotta love it."

"Greasing the palms of politicians didn't start in New Orleans," I said. "Local officials merely perfected the practice."

"The address where you will find Father Fred is on this slip of paper," Impeke said. "I wish you better luck than I had, and I pray that you find your friend alive and well."

"Thanks, Lando. We couldn't have located Father Fred without your help. Can I ask one more question."

"Yes?"

"What about Sister Gertrude? What can you tell us about her?"

Impeke downed the last of his beer, and then wiped his mouth with the sleeve of his shirt. The wind had picked up outside, rain blowing through the front door as a young couple hurriedly entered.

"If at all possible, Sister Gertrude is even eviler than Father Fred."

"How so?"

"She is the Head Mother of a very special Catholic convent."

"Tell me," Abba said.

"Most of the nuns there are little more than prostitutes, performing vile sex acts for those sick people with nun fetishes."

"Oh my God! Why would the victims allow them

to do such things?"

"They would not if they had the choice. They are beaten and coerced by mind control along with mind-altering drugs. I have heard some of the young women lapse into insanity, and that the suicide rate is high."

It was clear from her expression that Impeke's words had incensed Abba.

"What kind of horrible pervert would frequent such a place?"

"There are all kinds of crazy and perverted people in this world," Rafael said, clutching Abba's wrist. "Can you tell us where to find this convent?"

"Only that it is in another parish," Impeke said. "I wish I had more information for you. Now, you know as much as I do."

Before letting Lando Impeke out at the gates to St. Roch, Rafael shook his hand. Abba got out of the car and hugged him.

"I can't tell you how much I appreciate your help," she said.

"Young lady, you are so very welcome. I truly hope you find your friend."

"You are the one to thank," she said, kissing his forehead.

He took her hand when she started to pull away. "I sense you have serious questions that perhaps only God can answer. When they begin weighing on you too heavily, return to St. Roch. I will help you cast away the pain weighing on your soul."

Chapter II

Lando Impeke waved as Abba pulled away from the curb and headed toward Mid-City. The rain had finally ceased leaving the streets wet and potholes filled with water.

It was almost Halloween in the Big Easy, spooky bats, and monsters decorating the front of many of the houses. After seeing the chapel at St. Roch, I realized the creepy decorations could never compare to the real thing. After five minutes of silence, Abba glanced at me in the rearview mirror.

"You okay back there?" she said.

I glanced up as a car raced around us, my thoughts of Desire dissolving like the speeding vehicle's brake lights in the distance.

"Sorry," I said. "My mind was somewhere else."

"Please stop worrying about Desire," she said. "We'll find her. She'll be okay."

After listening to Lando Impeke's description of Sister Gertrude's convent, I wasn't so sure. Father Fred's address wasn't far away, though we had an unexpected shock when we reached it.

The old orphanage was a two-storied frame and plaster structure that had suffered through too many hot and wet Big Easy seasons without a fresh coat of paint. It was almost a given that the flat roof leaked.

The ten-foot fence surrounding the building and small compound surprised us, though not as much as the security vehicle parked at the entrance to the property. We could only presume the guard sitting behind the steering wheel was armed. Abba kept driving.

"What now?" she asked.

"I doubt they accept visitors at the front gate. Let's hunker down someplace and talk about it," I said.

Abba glanced at me in the rearview mirror. "Where do you suggest?"

"We're not far from City Park. It's so big, I'm sure we can find a secluded spot away from the crowds."

"There's a liquor store up ahead," Rafael said. "If we're going on a picnic, then I'll need sustenance. What are you drinking?" he asked Abba before exiting the car.

"Some of whatever you're having," she said.

Abba and I waited in the parking lot until Rafael returned, arms loaded with a large jug of Chianti and a bottle of processed lemonade.

"Don't turn up your nose," he said. "It's all they had, and you can always share our wine."

I took the lemonade and said, "Beggars can't be choosers."

After driving a short distance into City Park, Abba backed the Aztek up to the bank of a scenic lagoon, possibly the exact place where last night's murder had occurred. After opening the dual tailgate, she dug around for a picnic blanket.

"Voila," she said, spreading it on the grass in front of the open tailgate.

Abba and Rafael were soon sharing Chianti that they drank straight from the open bottle. A splash and resultant circular ripple of water marked the spot where a big fish broke the surface of the lagoon.

"Father Fred's place looked ominous," Abba said.

"Even if Desire is there, they won't let her come to the door for a chat."

"She's not there," I said.

"And how do you know that?" Rafael asked.

"It's probably the place they take their recruits for processing. I doubt anyone stays there very long."

"Then what do you expect to find?" Abba asked.

"Information. I'm betting it's where they keep their records. If so, we can find out where Desire is."

"Great," Rafael said. "We'll just knock on the front door and ask them if we can have a look at their records."

"Not funny," Abba said.

"What, then?" he said. "This is starting to feel like an exercise in futility."

"I have a plan," I said.

Rafael took a swig from the jug of Chianti. "Then don't keep us in suspense," he said.

"It'll be dark in a few hours. When the time is right, you can drop me off a block or so from the orphanage. I'll break in, get the records we need and then get out."

Abba was smiling when she said, "Better pass me the bottle, Padre."

Rafael was grinning as he handed the jug to Abba.

"And how do you plan to accomplish that particular feat?" he asked.

"Experience," I said. "I worked for the F.D.I.C. during my college years. We repossessed many houses. I became fairly proficient at breaking and entering."

"The F.D.I.C. hired you to break into houses?" Abba said.

"Believe me, they repossess lots of houses. If you don't want to go through the court system, then you send in a housebreaker."

"Are you making this up as you go along?" she

95

asked.

"I'd wait until the occupants left the house to go shopping, or to work. When they did, I'd break in, have the locks changed, and take control. Physical possession of the house precluded us from having to go through the court system. Worked like a charm."

"Nice man," Rafael said. "Think I'm reassessing my opinion of you."

"Never said I was perfect. I learned enough to have made it as a cat burglar. I haven't found a place yet I can't break into."

"Comforting to know," Abba said.

"Father Fred's compound isn't exactly your typical house," Rafael said. "More like an armed compound. How do you intend to get over the fence?"

"Easy," I said. "Climb one of those live oaks with draping limbs, and drop over to the other side."

"There's a guard at the gate. How do you know what you'll find once you get inside the compound?" Rafael said.

"Though I only had a quick look at the place as we drove past, my guess is they're more worried about someone breaking out than breaking in."

"Even if you get inside, you surely don't think you can find the records we need without someone spotting you."

"Cat burglars steal things all the time from occupied houses. I'm up to the task," I said. "I'll figure everything out on the fly."

Rafael's cool expression indicated he was less than confident about my boast.

"Fine," he said. "What about us?"

"We wait until after dark. I'll watch from across the street until activity in the compound tells me it's safe to go inside. If the documents are there, it should take me about twenty minutes to get in, find them, and then get out."

"You sound pretty sure of yourself," Rafael said.

"Have a better idea?"

"Can't think of one at the moment," he said.

"I sense your skepticism."

"It's your ass," Rafael said.

"And you?" I said, looking at Abba.

She smiled and winked. "Sure you don't want to get a little drunk on some of this cheap swill before you try?"

"Better stick to my soda pop," I said. "It's loaded with sugar, and I'll be buzzing for hours.

Katrina had felled many of the big trees in the neighborhood, though not all of them. During my two-block trek to Father Fred's compound, I followed a path through their shadows, and the ground fog beginning to kick up around my ankles. The red eyes of a Halloween witch in the front yard of a house down the street flashed off and on. The decorations weren't half as creepy as the old orphanage across the street from me.

No lights shined from the building's many windows. The floodlights on poles in the courtyard were also dark. Something was amiss at the compound. Staking out a spot across the street in the shadows of a giant live oak, I waited, hoping to determine what it was.

After half an hour, my eyes were popping as I stared at the security vehicle parked in the driveway. I finally convinced myself the driver must have fallen asleep. After walking a block down the street, I crossed to the other side and followed the sidewalk back to the compound. My brain told me the man in the car wasn't guarding anything. My better senses screamed for me to walk past, and then to keep on walking. I didn't listen to my better senses.

I decided to saunter up to the driver's window. If the guard was awake, I planned to tap on it, and ask him if I could bum a cigarette. If he were asleep, I would enter the compound through the front gate. If there were security cameras, then so be it.

When I reached the old black Ford beater with the word 'Security' painted in white on the door, I found the driver's window open, the driver neither awake nor asleep. He was dead.

Someone had cut his throat, the front of his shirt red with blood. The blood had already begun to dry, the man's body growing cold. A metal slug with a mysterious symbol scratched on it covered his right eye. I spent no time looking for a murder weapon, hurrying past the security vehicle and into the compound.

The place was eerily quiet, the compound dark. When I found the front door open and wafting in a gentle breeze, I wondered what else I'd find inside Father Fred's orphanage.

I always carry a keychain flashlight. The beam did little to light the empty hallway in which I found myself. It sufficed until my eyes dilated and adjusted to the shadows. Finding a hallway door ajar, I opened it and peeked inside.

The large room was where Father Fred and his staff housed prisoners waiting for someone to buy them. Leg irons and handcuffs draped from the metal frames of the dozen or more bunk beds. There was no air conditioning or even fans, and the large room reeked of sweat and urine.

Though I'd left the ground fog outside, a pervasive chill cooled the back of my neck. The room was empty of human life, yet I felt the presence of unhappy spirits. I backed out of the room, into the deserted hallway.

Down the hall, I found the building's control center. Several computers with dead screens populated a room that seemed more suited to a jailhouse than an orphanage. I also found my second corpse. Like the man in the car, this one also had a severed jugular and a slug over his right eye.

On the way out, I passed through a kitchen area and a small dining hall. A bowl of soup sat on one of the tables, the half-eaten contents still warm to the tip of my finger. Finding no books or records, I returned to the hallway and stood at the base of the stairway, the beam of my light briefly illuminating a strange scratching on the wooden banister. After reaching the top of the stairs, opening a door and peeking in, I dialed Rafael on my cell phone. He answered on the first ring.

"Wyatt, what'd you find?"

"You need to see for yourself," I said. "Can you join me?"

"Are you okay?" he asked.

"I'm fine," I said.

"Is it safe?"

"There's no one here except me," I said. "At least no one still alive."

Rafael and Abba parked the Aztek down the street and joined me. I was waiting for them beside the security vehicle, and they got a shock when they peered into its window. Rafael crossed himself, and Abba's hand went to her mouth as they stared at the body behind the wheel.

"Is he dead?" Abba asked.

Her question made me grin. "If you can't tell, I'd suggest you consider changing your college major."

"It was just a gut reaction. Don't be such a dick," she said.

"Sorry. You set me up for that one."

"Next time, cut me some slack."

Rafael was paying no attention to our banter as he lifted the slug from the man's eye, borrowing my flashlight for a closer look at the mysterious object.

"Any idea what it is?" I asked.

His reply was ominous. "I know exactly what it is. It's a death token."

"What the hell is a death token?"

"A witch thingy," he said. "This scratching on the metal was done by hand during some black magic ceremony that quite possibly included the sacrifice of some small animal."

"Who . . . ?" Abba said.

"A witch," Rafael said.

It was his turn to smile when she said, "A real witch?"

"Yes, my dear, a very real and deadly witch. One that practices the black arts and is very good at it."

Rafael put the token in his pocket. He stopped at the front door, again borrowing my flashlight. He pointed the beam at a scratching I hadn't seen, though it was similar to the one on the banister.

"A witches mark," he said.

He shook his head when Abba asked, "Put there by the witch?"

"By someone afraid of a witch," he said. "Apparently, there was good cause to be frightened."

I led them through the dormitory, control center, and dining area, and then up the stairs to the second floor. Abba gasped when she saw body number three situated in a sitting position at a table. A black candle flickered, smoking and about to go dead.

"Is that . . . ?"

"Father Fred," I said.

She held up her hand. "Don't say a word. The dagger in his heart tells me all I need to know."

Chapter 12

Tony had dropped his dog off at the house, his wife Lil miffed when he left again and headed for Bertram's bar. He was looking for someone in particular. Even if he didn't find him there, he needed a drink in the worst way, and Picou's was always a good place to quench one's thirst. Though it was just getting dark, ground fog was already forming outside on the street, Eddie Toledo sitting at the bar, nursing a tall scotch.

"Mind if I join you?"

"Pull up a stool, Lieutenant. I was looking for someone to buy me a drink."

"You're in luck. I'm working a case and on the payroll tonight. Your future father-in-law is paying for the drinks and information," Tony said.

"You working for . . . ?"

"Frankie Castellano," Tony said.

"How do you know about Josie and me?"

"Frankie says you're responsible for keeping her from joining him at his horse farm north of here."

"Not any longer," Eddie said. "He asked for her to bring me along. She left already. I'll join her later."

"How did you get her to leave without you?"

"I told her I have a dentist appointment tomorrow morning."

"Do you?"

"A little white lie. My appointment was last week."

"And your reason for lying?"

With a deadpan expression, Eddie said, "I'm a lawyer; that's what we're paid to do."

"I heard that," Bertram said, bringing Tony his own tall glass of scotch. "You know how to tell when a lawyer's lying, don't you?"

"When his lips start to move," Tony and Eddie said in unison.

"That's the oldest joke in the book, Bertram," Eddie said. "Get some new material, or I'll have to find a higher class place to drink."

"I doubt I got anything to worry about," Bertram said. "What are you doing out after dark, Lieutenant?"

"Working on a case, and you two need to stop calling me Lieutenant. I've been off the force a while now and I ain't ever going back."

"You'll always be Lieutenant Tony to me," Bertram said.

"Me too," Eddie said. "Get used to it."

Bertram left them to take a pitcher of beer to a couple of tourists that had tired of Bourbon Street.

"If your dentist's appointment was last week, why didn't you just go to the horse farm with Josie. You working tomorrow?"

"On vacation for another week now. I had a date with a cutie I met a while back. She called and canceled."

"Smart girl," Tony said. "Now what?"

"Join Josie tomorrow."

"Can you postpone for a while?"

"Maybe. For what reason?"

"Did you hear about the murder last night?"

"Wyatt texted me a link."

"Oh yeah? Why did he do that?" Tony asked.

"Because he thought there might be a chance

we'd be implicated."

Tony drank a healthy swig of his scotch, hoisting his glass as he glanced around the bar for Bertram.

"Hold your horses," Bertram said. "I'm coming."

Despite the rolling fog outside on the street, business inside had begun picking up. After delivering fresh drinks for Tony and Eddie, Bertram hurried away to pour a glass of wine for an attractive brunette in a short, red dress and her slightly tipsy boyfriend.

"What makes Wyatt think that you and him could be implicated in the murder?" Tony asked.

"The trophy in the news article. Wyatt and I were at the track yesterday, the trophy in our possession just a few hours before the murder occurred."

"That would make you two prime suspects."

"Or the killer's next victims," Eddie said. "A big, ugly Mexican goon took the trophy from us before we left the track."

"Can you I.D. him?"

"Lonzo Galvez; thirty-nine years old; born and raised right here in Louisiana; in and out of trouble most of his life though he's never been convicted of a major crime."

"How's he connected to Chuy Delgado?"

"He's not, at least directly. He's the bodyguard of Angus Anderson."

"You're shittin' me," Tony said.

"Nope. Anderson and Contrado were drinking in one of the track bars. Galvez took the trophy from Wyatt and me after talking with them."

"Hell, Eddie, your life might not be worth a plugged nickel right about now. What the hell are you still doing in town?"

"Wyatt and I won a sizeable amount of money at the track yesterday. Bertram deposited the check into Wyatt's account, and it doesn't clear until tomorrow."

"Can't you just wait to get your share? It ain't going no place."

Eddie grinned. "I've never had thirty-three grand in my checking account before. I wanted to see how it felt before I get whacked."

Tony whistled. "You won sixty-six thousand dollars?"

"Yes sir, we did."

"Hot tip?"

"Wyatt never forgets a face; even a horse's face. He realized Frankie had entered a sleeper in the race disguised as a nag. We bet the farm and the horse won going away."

"Lightning Bolt?" Tony said.

"That's his real name. Frankie was calling him Warmonger and had apparently falsified his pedigree."

"You must have bet big to win that much. If I was you, I wouldn't tell Frankie it was you and Wyatt that lowered the odds."

"We already figured that part out," Eddie said.

"What else do you know about the horse?"

"Frankie imported the jockey from Oklahoma so no one would know who he was."

"He paid the price for it," Tony said. "He was murdered last night, along with Frankie's trainer."

"How do you know so much about this case?" Eddie asked.

"I was at the murder scene."

"What the hell for?"

"I'm not sure I should tell you," Tony said. "You being a Fed and all."

"Well, then you better tell me now. You know I'll ferret it out if you don't."

"Tommy called me. Seems the normal graft and corruption downtown has taken on new proportions because of the influx of Mexican mob drug money."

"Tell me something I don't already know," Eddie

said.

"Then hear this and let it sink in a minute. Tommy's taking dirty money. Not because he wants to but because he'd out himself if he didn't."

"I didn't realize it had gotten that bad."

"It's bad. Can you promise Tommy some sort of immunity if he cooperates with the Feds?"

"You already know the answer to that. Did Tommy put you up to asking me for him?"

"Tommy don't have a clue how close he is to going to federal prison, and I ain't talking about one of the white collar varieties."

"I'd have to know he's willing to implicate anyone guilty, even if they were his close friends."

"You may have a problem there," Tony said.

"Then he'll go to jail just like everyone else."

"Don't be such a hard ass," Tony said. "If you want his help, you need to cut him a deal he can live with. If not, I guarantee you'll be no closer to accomplishing your goal this time next year."

"People have a tendency to change their minds when faced with the possibility of ten years hard time."

"Not Tommy. He'll never rat out his friends, no matter what."

"Sure about that?"

"As sure as a sharp knife buried in a warm heart," Tony said. "Does he get a guarantee?"

"I'll see what I can do," Eddie said.

"You speaking as a friend, or a lying lawyer?" Tony said.

"Friend," Eddie said. "Will you talk to him for me?"

"Nope, I'm gonna be recording the conversation when you tell him what he needs to do."

"Touche," Eddie said, clinking Tony's glass. "Nothing like a binding contract. I like your thinking."

"Ain't no such thing as a binding contract," Tony said.

"Don't trust me, Lieutenant?"

"I don't trust lawyers. Even my close friends that are lawyers. That includes you and Wyatt. You okay with that?"

Eddie grinned and raised his glass for more drinks. "Hell, Tony, if I were you, I wouldn't trust me either. Where do you suggest we meet Tommy?"

"My house. Lil has a pot of gumbo simmering on the stove, and is expecting us."

"Won't she be angry when you drag home two hard legs?"

"She was a cop's wife for twenty-five years. Nothing much shocks her anymore. And, I have a little surprise for her."

What's that?"

"Tell you on the way over. Tommy's already there."

There was a chill in the air, Tony, and Eddie both pulling their light jackets up around their necks when they stepped outside.

"Fog lights," Eddie said. "Smart man. When did you have them installed?"

"Over the summer. I don't know now how I ever drove in this pea soup without them."

"I know," Eddie said. "I tried to get the D.A.'s office to put them on our cars, but I was told it was an unnecessary expense."

"Gotta save the dough for those twenty-five hundred dollar toilet seats the government buys," Tony said.

"I hear that," Eddie said, miffed by Tony's verbal jab. "Seriously though, I'm going to have a hard time protecting Tommy."

"I know how you can do it with no problem."

"How?"

"Remember when the U.S. Marshal deputized me

and Marlon?"

"Yeah."

"Deputize Tommy as part of the Federal D.A.'s office as an undercover agent. Hell, he could even kill somebody if he had to and he'd be exempt from prosecution. You got the power to do that?"

"Yeah," Eddie said.

"Then what do you think?"

"I'll have to clear it with my boss."

"How long will that take?" Tony asked.

Eddie was punching a number on his cell phone and didn't answer. After a lengthy conversation, he smiled and showed Tony a thumbs up.

"He bought it," Eddie said. "He liked the idea so much, I may even get a raise."

"Wonderful."

"I'm not holding my breath. Raises have been about as scarce as those foglights lately. Thank God for my new-found wealth."

"If you live to see it before the Mexican cartel whacks you," Tony said.

"Don't remind me. Tell me what you're doing for Frankie Castellano."

"Whoever whacked his two men last night also stole his horse, Lightning Bolt. Frankie hired me to recover him."

"Frankie doesn't even like quarter horses."

"His grandson does. He gave the horse to JoJo after the race, and the kid is in love with the animal. Grandpa has given him his solemn vow that he'll find Lightning Bolt."

"Then I hope his middle name is Lazarus. The article Wyatt sent me said they found the horse's remains in the trailer they pulled from the lagoon."

"Maybe the horse in the trailer wasn't Lightning Bolt."

Eddie punched up the article he still had on his phone and glanced at it.

"Could be right. The article says the horse wasn't identified and suggests the police will probably have to use DNA to derive the answer."

"That's a new one on me," Tony said. "I didn't know you could DNA a horse."

"Who even gives a shit?" Eddie asked.

Tony could only shake his head. "Frankie, for one."

Eddie fidgeted with a swizzle stick someone had left on the bar. "Where do you start looking?"

"The track, tomorrow morning; the last place anyone saw the horse," Tony said.

"Mind if I tag along?" Eddie asked.

"If you like. Why the hell do you care?"

"Brownie points," Eddie said. "Frankie doesn't like me very much. I need all the goodwill I can accumulate."

"Sounds to me like you got yourself in a pickle," Tony said.

"What do you mean?"

"I doubt your boss would like it if he knew his Assistant Federal D.A. was dating the daughter of the biggest Don in New Orleans."

"Ted doesn't keep up with the women I date. When he finds out, I'll be three women down the road from Josie."

"You got a mighty high opinion of yourself," Tony said.

"I can't help it if gorgeous women find me attractive. I'm enjoying it as long as I can."

"Yeah, well one of them gorgeous women is gonna shoot you in your sleep some night, or worse, take a sharp razor to a part of your body you don't want to lose."

"Never gonna happen," Eddie said with a grin. "I don't do much sleeping when I'm in bed with a woman."

Tommy had already arrived when they reached

Tony's house. He was sitting at the kitchen table talking to Lil as he worked on his second bowl of gumbo. Eddie gave Lil a hug and joined them. Patch came sauntering in from another room.

Eddie and Tommy averted their eyes as Tony gave his wife an intimate kiss.

"What's all of this about?" she asked.

"I got private business to discuss with Eddie and Tommy. When we're done, I have a surprise for you."

"Should I be worried?"

"Not this time," he said. "Frankie and Adele asked us to spend a week, or so with them at their horse farm north of here."

"Does this have anything to do with last night's murder?" she asked.

"Lil, we been married too long. It does, but don't matter none. The farm is like a resort. You'll have a great time, and you can even take that cat of yours."

"I'll have a great time? What about you?"

"I'm working for Frankie and will be in and out," he said.

"Something dangerous?"

"Couldn't be safer," he said.

He ignored Eddie's amused grin he noticed from the corner of his eye.

"When are we leaving?" she asked.

"Soon as we finish our discussion," he said.

She served Eddie and Tony gumbo and ladled another helping into Tommy's bowl. She also gave them cold beers from the refrigerator.

"I'll start packing and leave you alone to discuss your important business," she said, kissing Tony's forehead before exiting the kitchen.

When the door shut behind her, Tony laced his gumbo with an extra helping of hot sauce, making a face after drinking some of his Dixie.

"Used to be my favorite beer when they made it here in Nawlins," he said. "Now that it's brewed in

Ohio, or wherever it's made, it just ain't the same."

Hurricane Katrina had decimated the Dixie Brewery in New Orleans, and the beer was now contract-brewed by out-of-state breweries. Tony had never gotten over the loss.

"Hell, Tony," Eddie said. "It always tasted like horse piss, even before Katrina."

"Yeah, but you gotta drink it if you're in New Orleans," Tommy said. "What's up, Tony?"

"Eddie has a proposition for you," Tony said.

"What kinda proposition?"

"Tell him, Eddie."

"Tony told me about your problem with the Mexican cartel. He asked me to help, and strongly suggested I might recruit you to work for me."

Tommy dabbed hot sauce off his lips and swigged his Dixie.

"I already work for somebody. The N.O.P.D. You know that, Eddie."

"You'll still work for the force. At the same time, you'll be undercover for the Federal D.A.'s office."

"My loyalty is with the N.O.P.D."

"Sorry to hear that," Eddie said. "Tony told me you're already dirty. My department is investigating alleged corruption in the city. He says you were concerned enough to talk to him about it last night."

Tony glanced away when Tommy gave him a dirty look.

"What else did he tell you?" Tommy asked.

"Pretty much what I already knew; that you're a good cop caught in a bad situation you'd like to rectify."

"I want to help. Don't matter none cause I can't take my friends down doing it."

"Most of your friends are probably a lot like you. They want to do the right thing. We're not after them. At best, they'll probably get a slap on the wrist. We want to catch the big fish, from the mayor's office on down, and prosecute them."

"Help me on this, Tony," Tommy said.

"Do it," Tony said. "It's the only way this town's ever gonna get back to normal."

"All right, then. I'm in. What now?" Tommy said.

Eddie gave him a nod. "Raise your right hand and repeat after me."

Chapter 13

When Eddie finished swearing in Tommy, Tony grabbed fresh cans of Dixie from the refrigerator and threw them each one. They were drinking in silence when Lil returned to the kitchen.

"With those smiles on your faces, I can only imagine what you're plotting," she said.

"We'll never tell," Eddie said.

Tommy glanced at his watch after chugging the last of his beer from the iconic green and white can.

"Love your gumbo. Gotta go now," he said, giving her a hug.

"Then don't wait so long next time before coming to get some," she said as the back door closed behind him. She glanced at Tony. "I packed for both of us. What now?"

"Road trip," he said.

"You sure I can take the cat?" she asked.

"I'm sure, Babe. Frankie said to bring the pets. Why don't you come with us, Eddie? We can follow you to your apartment. You can pack some clothes and drop off your car. I'll bring you back to town tomorrow morning."

"Sounds like a plan," he said. "Better call Josie first and make sure she still wants me to join her."

With Lil's cat Silky sleeping in his lap, Eddie rode in the backseat of Tony's Mustang on the way to Frankie Castellano's horse farm. Heavy fog began rolling across the Causeway in front of them as they crossed Lake Pontchartrain. It disappeared once they were well north of the giant, inland sea. Armed men in a black Navigator let them in the front gate when they reached the farm.

"Why all the security, Tony?" Lil asked.

"The murders last night, Frankie's men on high alert till all this blows over."

"Do the murders have anything to do with why Frankie hired you?"

"Whoever killed Frankie's men also stole his prize horse. Frankie hired me to recover it. Eddie here is helping me."

"You sure that's all he hired you to do?"

"Believe me, I'm too old to get shot at for anybody. Not even Frankie Castellano."

Frankie and Adele's house was as large as many small hotels, a staff of support personnel making sure their stay at the farm was no less than first class. Bellmen opened Tony's car door when they pulled up in front of the expansive veranda surrounding the house. Adele, Josie, Jojo, and Frankie, lounging in rustic but comfortable furniture, awaited their arrival.

"Tomasito, drive Tony's car to his bungalow and get them situated," Frankie said.

Adele and Lil were both all smiles. "How have you been, girlfriend?" Adele said, hugging Lil.

"Great. Tony told me you and Frankie just got back from Italy."

"Oh, Lil, I love that place," Adele said.

"Know what you mean," Lil said. "Tony and I celebrated our second honeymoon there awhile back."

"Have you ever met my step-daughter, Josie?"

113

Lil hugged her as if they'd known each other forever. "You're just as beautiful as Tony said. Is this your son?"

"I'm Jojo," the boy said.

"How old are you, Jojo?"

"Seven," he said. "Papaw just bought me a horse. It's the biggest, strongest, and best horse in the whole wide world."

Frankie's smile disappeared as he glanced at Tony. Eddie was still carrying Lil's cat when Adele introduced him to Jojo.

"This is Eddie, Jojo. He's your mother's friend, and he's going to stay with us a few days."

Eddie reached to shake the boy's hand. Jojo was paying no attention, stroking the cat instead.

"Oh, what a pretty cat," he said. "What's his name?"

"He's a she, and her name is Silky. Want to hold her?"

"Sure," Jojo said, taking the animal.

Lil's white cat rubbed its head against Jojo's neck, began purring, and closed his eyes as the boy stroked him.

"Think he likes you," Eddie said.

Jojo handed him back to Eddie. "Better take him. I don't want him disappearing like Lightning Bolt did."

Frankie had an icy tumbler of scotch in his hand and a wounded expression on his face. When Jojo hugged him, burying his face against his leg, his woeful look grew even worse. Tony knelt beside him.

"You probably don't remember me, Jojo. I'm Tony, and we met a while back. Your papaw hired me to find Lightning Bolt, and I promise you I'm going to do just that."

When Jojo looked at him, the hint of a smile appeared on the little boy's cherubic face. "You promise?" he said.

"I promise," Tony said, bumping fists with him.

"Now, big boy, it's past your bedtime," Josie said. Grabbing his hand, she started to lead him into the house. He tugged at her, causing her to stop in her tracks.

"Can Silky sleep with me tonight?"

"Of course she can," Lil said.

Eddie handed Silky to the little boy. He was smiling as he followed his mother into the house. Adele grabbed Lil's hand.

"Let's walk down to the bungalow where you and Tony will be staying. You're just not going to believe it."

Tomasito had returned from taking care of Tony's car and appeared on the veranda with a tray of mixed drinks. With icy beverages in hand, they plopped down in the veranda furniture to enjoy the cool night.

"Thought you didn't like Mexicans," Eddie said.

"Only ones I hate are in the Mexican cartel, and they aren't exactly stellar citizens."

"I hear that," Eddie said.

Frankie turned his attention to Tony. "You think you'll really find Lightning Bolt?" he asked.

"Eddie's on vacation and helping me. If the horse is alive, we'll find him. I promised Jojo, and I promise you."

"The newspapers say the horse is dead."

"Maybe so," Tony said. "All I know is the horse that died in City Park is yet to be identified."

Lil and Adele came chattering out of the darkness. "You are absolutely not going to believe where we're staying," she said.

"Is it nice?" Tony asked.

"Nice isn't the half of it. There's even a redwood hot tub on the deck with a great view of the barns and pastures. We may even have to go skinny dipping tonight."

She and Adele hurried into the house before
Tony had a chance to reply. There were no lights on
the veranda. Though he couldn't see Eddie's
ear-to-ear smile, he sensed both he and Frankie were
amused by Lil's comment.

"Sounds like you're in for a hot time in the old
town tonight, good buddy. In more ways than one."

Tony had to laugh. "Lil's a morning person, not to
mention she and Adele are drinking wine. I'll
probably have to carry her to the room and put her in
bed."

Tony, Frankie, and Eddie were working on fresh
drinks when Josie returned from Jojo's room. She
took Eddie's hand and kissed him on the forehead.

"Would you like to take a moonlight walk with
me?"

She didn't have to ask twice. "Lead the way,
pretty woman," he said.

Frankie stopped them before they stepped off the
veranda.

"Your room will be waiting when you get back
from your walk," he said. "It's on the other side of the
house from Josie's room; hint, hint."

"Really, Dad," Josie said. "Don't you think I'm old
enough to make my own decisions?"

"You do whatever you want, baby," he said.
"Eddie, you watch yourself with my daughter."

Eddie didn't reply as he followed Josie off the
veranda and into the darkness. A manicured
pathway led them through a labyrinth of ancient live
oaks, late fall flowers still blooming, and spreading
shrubbery. Discreet lighting illuminated their path to
a hill overlooking acres of pasture. Josie sat in the
grass, Eddie joining her.

"It's magical out here at night with only solitude
and stars," she said.

"It would be magical for me in a hot factory, long
as I was sitting beside you."

"You always know the right thing to say, don't you?"

"I was truthful."

"My son likes you."

"And how do you know that?"

"He told me when I was putting him to bed. He never knew his father."

"He doesn't have visitation?" Eddie asked.

"He died in Afghanistan."

Eddie squeezed her hand. "I'm so sorry. I just assumed you were divorced."

"I'm Catholic," she said. "I would never divorce my husband."

"Not for any reason?"

"Though I might leave him, my marriage will never end in divorce. I'd just finish out my life living all alone."

"I'm also Catholic," Eddie said. "Doesn't matter because I believe in birth control and lots of other things the Vatican says is verboten."

"Rules are rules," she said.

"And meant to be broken."

"You're an attorney. How can you be so indifferent when it comes to rules? Do you ever break the law?"

"Laws aren't hard and fast commandments from above. They are guidelines set by human lawmakers that are forever changing. That's why the law is interpreted and not set in stone."

"I'm not sure I agree with your opinion," she said.

"And that's the way it should be. In this world, few things are black or white. Almost everything is a shade of gray, somewhere in between."

A night bird sang in the distance as she turned and kissed his cheek.

"You are so intelligent. Maybe too intelligent for me," she said.

"You're the first person that ever told me that," he said.

His comment brought a grin to her face. "Now I know you're a liar. I'll bet people tell you every day how smart you are."

"Maybe," he said.

"You must be wondering how I justify my dad's profession if I'm so *holier than thou.*"

"How much do you know about what he does?" Eddie asked.

"He never talks about it, and I don't directly know anything about his business. I know that all my friends and the kids I knew growing up treated me differently than everyone else."

"Better or worse?"

"Much better. It was as if they were afraid to anger me. I can only imagine what their parents told them about Dad."

"Your dad has his fingers in lots of pies," Eddie said. "I know because I work for the justice system. He covers his tracks very well. I think you know he isn't a perfect citizen."

"He was just a normal dad to me growing up. When my mom died a few years back, he became a broken man. I was so happy when he met and married Adele."

"No jealousy there?"

Josie shook her head. "None whatsoever."

"You're not worried that Adele is a gold digger?"

"Besides my mother, she's one of the most caring and understanding women I've ever met. I can only hope to marry someone someday that will make me as happy as those two are."

"They do seem perfect for one another," Eddie said.

"They can't keep their hands off each other. It's embarrassing sometimes."

"I noticed," Eddie said.

"I hope you and Tony can find Lightning Bolt for Jojo. I think a horse would be good for him."

"Probably any pet. He liked Lil's cat."

"Yes he did," Josie said. "The cat seemed to take to him. I find it a bit strange because he's never shown any interest in owning a dog, much less a cat."

"Maybe your grandfather had something to do with it."

At the mention of her grandfather, she turned and stared into Eddie's eyes.

"What are you talking about?" she asked.

"Silky was your grandfather Paco's cat."

"What makes you think that? And even if she was, how could you possibly know?"

"Because Tony and I were with your grandfather the night he died. He handed Tony the cat before he passed and asked him to take care of it for him."

Josie wasn't smiling as she continued staring at Eddie.

"Are you making this up?"

"No, I'm not. Your dad hired Tony to find his lost cornet, and I was helping him. The search took us to a room on the second floor of one of Frankie's nightclubs in Fat City."

"Dad told me Gramps was alone when he died."

"We weren't supposed to be there, so we got the hell out. Your gramps wasn't alone when he died; we were with him, Tony holding his hand."

"Does Dad know this?" she asked.

"No, and please don't tell him."

"Why not?"

"Let's just say the relationship between Frankie and your gramps was less than ideal."

"Dad said Gramps had disappeared and he didn't know where he was."

"I've probably already said too much," Eddie said. "I'm sorry."

"This is crazy," Josie said. "And surely a coincidence. I don't believe in ghosts."

"Doesn't matter because I doubt Lil would give you the cat. From what Tony says, they are attached at the hip."

"I would never ask anyone to give up their favorite pet," she said. "Do you believe in signs?"

"I didn't a few years ago."

"You do now?"

Eddie nodded. "You can't live in the Big Easy for very long without realizing we're surrounded by spirits."

"Then maybe the cat is a sign from Gramps that he's watching over Jojo and me."

"I bet you're right about that," Eddie said. "Your dad isn't taking our relationship very well. Am I too forward to ask if you would pay me a visit later on tonight?"

"You're very blunt."

"Just asking," he said.

"As I told you, I'm Catholic. I don't believe in sex outside of marriage."

"Well, that's a bummer," Eddie said. "How do you really know if you like someone?"

"I already know, and I think you do too."

Chapter 14

The sight of the ornate dagger transfixed Rafael's attention. When he reached for it, intent on pulling it out of Father Fred's heart, I grabbed his wrist and stopped him.

"This is a murder scene. Cops will soon be swarming this place, looking for evidence. They may be on their way here already. You don't want your prints all over the murder weapon."

Pulling his hand away, he took a step backward.

"There are reasons we should take it with us," he said.

"Maybe so. Whatever those reasons are, they aren't good enough for us to face a charge of first degree murder. If the police show up, we don't have a good excuse for being here."

"What, then?" Rafael asked.

"Case this room for information, and do it fast. Otherwise, someone will soon be bailing us out of jail."

Abba was trying to reboot the laptop on the desk in front of Father Fred's body. Instead of a welcome message, a blue screen was the machine's only sign of life.

"Someone sabotaged the computer; probably erased the hard drive," she said. "I'm going

121

downstairs to check the one in the control room."

Rafael and I began opening and shutting drawers and cabinets with a purpose, searching for prisoner records but finding none. We split up and branched out to the other rooms. One by one, all empty handed, we returned to Father Fred's death scene.

"No use," Abba said. "Whoever killed Father Fred wrecked the computers and took the books with them."

"They also released the prisoners," I said.

"How did they get away and where did they go?" Abba asked. "We saw no one, in a group or otherwise on our way over here."

She smiled and tugged her earlobe when Rafael said, "Perhaps they were spirited away by magic."

Rafael wasn't smiling, and Abba frowned as she glanced around the room, searching for a place to begin.

"There's something in Father Fred's hand," she said.

We stopped what we were doing to see the small notepad clutched in the priest's right hand. His body was in the early stages of rigor mortis, the condition already beginning to stiffen his fingers. I had to force them open to remove the notepad from his grasp, and tried not to think about the eerie sensation it sent surging up my spine.

As I leafed through the notepad, we began to hear sirens wailing in the distance. Rafael glanced out the window before returning his attention to the notepad.

"Important?" he asked.

"Mostly just scribble-scratch Father Fred must have used to remind himself of appointments and things he needed to do," I said.

Rafael reached for the pad. "Let me see it."

He stopped thumbing when he reached the last

page.

"Find something important?" Abba asked. "What is it?"

"The last entry says, 'respond to the witch's demand by four p.m. today.' The date and time are double underlined."

When the notepad suddenly combusted in his hand, Rafael dropped it to the floor. Smoke began billowing from the sleeves and neck of Father Fred's black jacket. Within seconds, the jacket burst into flame.

"What the hell!" Abba said.

Rafael pulled her away from the suddenly flaming body as the desk and chair began smoking and then burning.

"Spontaneous combustion," he said.

"What's causing it?" she asked.

"Dark magic. We must exit this building. This whole place is going to burn to the ground."

Rafael clutched Abba's wrist, pulling her toward the door as the curtains in the room caught fire in an explosion of smoke and flame. I followed them, halfway to the ground floor before turning around and rushing back up the stairs.

"Wyatt, no! What the hell are you doing?"

"Forgot something," I said as I disappeared into the billowing smoke.

Toxic fumes belched from the room we'd just exited, walls and floors crackling and snapping as flames began to consume the dry wood. Covering my nose and mouth with my handkerchief, I dodged my way through the flames and smoke to Father Fred's body.

Skin had begun to blister and char, Father Fred's dead eyes open and glaring at me as I grabbed the hilt of the dagger and yanked, escaping gases sounding like the wail of an angry banshee.

Billowing smoke had set me to coughing, my eyes

red and watering. As I pulled the dagger from Father Fred's body, a surge of pure energy rushed up my fingertips.

Suddenly unable to see because of the acrid smoke and billowing flame, some unknown force began pulling me in the wrong direction. At least I thought it was the wrong direction. When I fought it, I tripped over a chair, skinning my knee. Thinking I was going to die, I let the force pull me through the smoke. Rafael grabbed my arms, yanking me from the building now fully aflame.

"You okay?" he asked as I handed him the dagger.

I was coughing too badly to answer. He hurried me to the front gate where Abba was waiting with the Aztek. Reaching over the seat, he tossed me the bottle of Chianti.

"Drink some," he said. "It'll stop your coughing. Otherwise, you're going to choke to death."

Without hesitation, I took his advice, the cheap red wine burning as it went down my throat, and halting my coughing jag. A few blocks from the compound, we heard the explosion and turned to see the smoke and flames licking skyward behind us. Abba kept driving until we were out of the neighborhood and well away from the fire.

"You don't sound good. Are you going to make it?" she asked, glancing at me in the rearview mirror.

"I'll make it," I said. "Just skinned knees, a few burns and blisters, and my eyes are burning like holy hell."

Finding a convenience store, she wheeled into the gravel and shell parking lot. Rafael hurried into the store, returning with peroxide, Band-Aids, rags and a jug of water to flush my eyes. I was soon feeling better, though I took an extra swig of the Chianti before returning it to Rafael.

"Were you trying to kill yourself back there?"

Abba asked.

"I decided we needed the dagger," I said.

"There was so much flame belching from the building, I thought you were surely dead," he said. "How in the world did you get out of that inferno?"

Rafael's question was one for which I had no answer.

"I'm not sure," I said. "What were you going to tell us about the dagger?"

Rafael studied the ornate weapon engraved with undecipherable symbols as he turned it in his hands.

"It's a one-of-a-kind weapon. Probably used in specific ceremonies."

"So?"

"I've seen knives like this at a shop in the Quarter. Maybe the people there will tell us who made it and where we can find him."

"I don't get it," Abba said.

"Someone paid lots of money for the dagger maker's expertise. I'm sure he knows exactly for whom he made it for," Rafael said.

"I still don't get it," she said.

"It's the killer's knife," I said.

"You intend to confront the killer? If so, what's to stop that person from killing us as well?" she asked.

"No ordinary person dispatched Father Fred and his guards, and then released and spirited away the prisoners into thin air. The killer is a witch," Rafael said. "Not an old hag with a big hat riding a broom, but a real live, honest-to-goodness witch that practices dark magic, and does absolutely nothing without cause or provocation."

"Even if she had reason to kill Father Fred, it doesn't mean she knows anything about where we can find Desire," Abba said.

"Maybe not. At this point we have nothing else to go on," I said. "We have to play this out and see where it leads us, or else pack up and go to the house. Where is this place in the Quarter you're talking about?"

"On Bourbon Street."

"Great," I said. "It's still early by Bourbon Street standards, and it'll be rocking this time of night."

"I'm not so sure about that," Rafael said. "Fog is starting to roll in off the river, and it may deter some of the crazies."

Abba was already heading toward the Quarter. When a cop car went racing past us, its sirens blasting, she tapped the brakes a little too hard.

"You okay?" I asked.

"Worried," she said. "When I saw the flashing lights in the mirror, my first thought was they were going to pull us over, rip us out of the car and take us to jail."

"Stop worrying. The fire destroyed any evidence we may have left. No matter how good the investigators are, they'll be years trying to figure out what happened."

"Sure about that?" she asked.

"I used to be a criminal lawyer," I said. "The police regularly botched cases they had ironclad evidence on. Unless I miss my guess, they'll likely throw up their hands on this one and then move on to a more pressing case."

"Don't let Tony ever hear you say that," Rafael said.

"If it were Tony leading the investigation, then we might have cause for worry," I said. "Unless he's gone back to work for the N.O.P.D. He hasn't, and we have little to worry about."

"Wish I was as sure as you are," Abba said. "I don't want to spend my next birthday in a prison cell."

"You won't," I said. "Unless . . ."

"Unless what?"

"You get drunk in a bar and start bragging about being in the orphanage just before it burned to the ground."

"People do that?"

"Criminals are their own worst enemies."

"Is that what we are?" she asked.

"No, baby. We weren't the ones that killed those people and then burned the place to the ground," Rafael said. "We are simply innocent onlookers to an awful act."

"Wyatt, is that right?"

"Like Raf said, we're as pure as the driven snow. Just lock up what happened at the compound in some recess in your soul and don't ever tell anyone."

"Jeez!" she said. "Any wine left?"

"Half a bottle, my dear. You're in luck, and so am I."

Rafael unscrewed the cap and handed it to her. Putting it on her shoulder, she drank until red drops dribbled down her long neck.

"What the hell!" she said. "Now I know how it feels to be a hardened criminal."

"No you don't," I said with a laugh.

Fog was rolling in from the river, a tanker's lights casting eerie moving shadows beyond the levee as we neared the French Quarter. We found a parking spot on a dark side street several blocks from Bourbon. The wine had apparently placated Abba's feelings of guilt because she was smiling after parking and locking the car.

"Hope ol' Nellie's still here when we return," she said.

"It's not just the car we have to worry about," I said. "Let's hope we don't get mugged before we make it back."

"Have faith," Rafael said. "God protects children and idiots."

"Is that a quote directly from the Bible, Padre?" I asked.

Rafael had brought along the jug of wine and was

well on his way to being fully inebriated. He took a healthy drink from the bottle before answering.

"If it's not, it should be."

"Amen, Padre. Please pass the wine," Abba said.

Fully affected by the cheap red wine, Abba and Rafael were feeling no pain. The swallow I'd taken had given me a slight buzz, and I remembered vividly why I'd become addicted. Since the dose was therapeutic and not for pleasure, I managed to put it behind me and not beg Rafael for another drink.

Lights appeared in the distance, and we began hearing music and noise emanating from the most famous street on earth long before we reached it. The first people we saw were a group of drunk college students, all with plastic go-cups brimming with their favorite alcoholic beverages.

"Since our bottle's not plastic, we better ditch it," I said. "Don't want to draw attention to ourselves."

Rafael took one last drink from the bottle and then handed it to Abba. They left it behind a trashcan before we turned onto Bourbon Street.

"Bet it won't be there in the morning," Abba said.

Rafael agreed. "At least with any wine left in it."

"How far is this knife shop from here?" I asked.

"It's close. Maybe in this direction," he said, pointing.

Mere days before Halloween, Bourbon Street was alive with people in costumes. Though several months yet until Mardi Gras, there was always an excuse for a party in the Big Easy, Halloween one of the biggest.

Barkers grabbed at our arms as we passed the open doors of the many strip joints. Music wafted from the saloons, mingling with crowd noise out on the sidewalk. Dozens of cheesy teeshirt shops beckoned us to venture inside and partake of their wares. Rafael stopped at a liquor stand on the sidewalk and bought two decorative plastic containers filled with their syrupy interpretation of a Pat O'Brian's Hurricane.

"I'll buy you one if you drink it," he said.

He laughed when I said, "Quit tempting me. You're supposed to be a man of God, and not the Devil."

Flashing neon illuminated the fog with an eerie glow, providing all the atmosphere anyone could need. The spooks, vampires, ghosts, and goblins on both sides of the street only added to that illusion.

"There's a witch," Abba said. "Wonder if it's the one we're looking for."

"That young lady is dressed in the popular manner in which we perceive a witch. The reality, I assure you, is quite different."

"You keep saying that," she said. "How so?"

"If we find the witch that burned Father Fred's compound, you will understand fully. Meanwhile, that's our destination up ahead."

Chapter 15

How Rafael had managed to differentiate the shop from all the others, we'd passed was a mystery to me. Since the teeshirts and cheesy souvenirs in the front of the establishment appeared no different, it gave me cause to wonder if he was too drunk to remember the shop's location. I needn't have worried.

A starkly dressed young woman behind a counter spanning the back wall greeted us with a frown and a nod. Her floor-length dress matched the long hair touching her bare shoulders: black with lime green highlights. A colorful tattoo, partially hidden behind a single gold earring, decorated her neck. From her nose, a matching circular ring dangled.

"Help you?" she said.

"I was here about a year ago," Rafael said. "You had a knife display."

"Still do. Far end of the cabinet," she said.

"I'm looking for something in particular: a Gothic dagger that possibly possesses magical powers."

The young woman's expression remained impassive. "All knives have magical powers. Some more than others."

Rafael waited for her to elucidate on her comment. When she didn't, he brushed off her lack of enthusiasm and began studying the cutlery housed in the far end of the display.

I became suddenly aware of background music being piped into the room through hidden speakers. Had the volume been loud, the discordant, head-banging song performed by Sid Vicious and the Sex Pistols might have seemed out of place. Instead, along with the commingled odors of scented candles and Nag Champa incense, it helped complete the little shop's illusion of dark mystery.

Rafael didn't seem to notice, his rapt interest focused on the display cabinet. Abba and I joined him. He soon returned his attention to the young woman.

"We brought a dagger with us. Would you mind taking a look at it?"

Retrieving the knife from the inner pocket of his parka, he handed it over the counter to the woman. Her expression never changed as she hefted the dagger and then handed it back to him.

"Very nice," she said.

"Can you tell us anything about it?" he asked.

"Such as?"

"Who is the person that crafted it?"

She stared at him for what seemed like thirty seconds before answering.

"I'm afraid I can't give you that information."

"Why not?"

"My shop is unique. Except for the teeshirts and souvenirs in front, you won't find the knives and swords we have here anywhere in New Orleans. Or, for that matter, anyplace else in the world. If you want to purchase a knife or dagger from this shop, then I'll be happy to help you. It's our policy not to give out the names of the artists and craftsmen that supply us."

"We don't want to buy anything from that person, we simply want to ask him or her a question about the dagger I showed you."

The young woman's frown and arms clutched

131

tightly around her chest shouted volumes that she wasn't impressed. Glancing on the wall behind her, I saw something that jogged my memory. The color of the woman's eyes and the shape of her ears also seemed vaguely familiar. Finally, it came to me.

"Are you Cyn Czarnecki?"

She stopped staring at Rafael and glanced around as if noticing me for the first time.

"Do I know you?"

"When I was much younger, I used to visit your father's shop on Royal."

"Oh?" she said.

"From what I remember, your dad was a collector of anything and everything that had to do with New Orleans."

"You have a good memory. My father's shop closed more than twenty years ago."

"You still have the sign," I said.

She glanced behind her at the old sign on the wall that said, Antique Guns & Swords, and smiled for the first time.

"Your memory is more than good, it's remarkable," she said. "I couldn't have been more than ten or twelve years old. How did you recognize me?"

"Your eyes," I said. "While our dads were pouring over the cutlery, I was looking at your eyes. I remember thinking how exotic they looked. They are still just as mesmerizing as I remember."

Though Cyn Czarnecki tried not to blush, she failed miserably.

"That's all very interesting," she said when she regained her composure. "The fact remains I don't give out the names of our artisans."

"Is he your husband?" I asked.

"How did you know that?"

"Just a guess," I said. "The dagger Rafael showed you, as you already know, is valuable. We'd like to return it to its rightful owner. We only wish to ask your husband who that person is and how we might find them."

"Is the dagger linked to a crime?"

"Of course not. If we thought it was, we'd have gone to the police instead of here."

She glanced around at the grandfather clock that was just beginning to chime.

"My night manager is running late. She'll be here any minute to relieve me. Do you have a car?"

"We've parked a few blocks away," I said.

"Wait for me at the corner of Claiborne and Esplanade. Follow me when I drive past."

"How will we know it's you?" I asked.

"I drive an old, black Bentley that's very recognizable. When you pull in behind me, flash your lights twice, so I'll know it's you. I'll take you to my husband's blacksmith shop."

The odor of incense and the reedy voice of Sid Vicious dissolved away as we exited to the Bourbon Street sidewalk. Ground fog, crowd noise and a strong smell of stale beer, strong pot, urine, and vomit replaced it. When we reached the dark side street where Rafael had abandoned the wine, we realized that he'd been wrong. The wine was still in the bottle as when he'd left it. They started back in on the wine on the way back to the Aztek. Twenty minutes passed as we waited for Cyn Czarnecki.

"Hope she didn't blow us off," Abba said.

"If she did, we'll pay her another visit tomorrow," I said.

"How in the world did you remember her after twenty years?" Rafael asked.

"When I saw the old sign behind the counter, it reminded me of her father's shop."

"You sounded more interested in her than the knives her father sold," Abba said.

"I was a teenager," I said. "Girls were my number

one interest."

"Remind me to call bullshit next time you compliment me," she said.

"It's still amazing to me that you'd remember her after twenty years," Rafael said.

"I told you, Padre, I never forget a face."

"How did you know she was married? She wasn't wearing a wedding ring. Even so, how did you guess her husband was the person that made the dagger?"

"Body language. She seemed like someone interested in signs and symbols. She wears her wedding ring on her middle finger. When I complimented her, she fidgeted with the ring. She did it again when I asked her about the person that made the dagger."

They stared at me as if I were an alien from another planet. There was little traffic on Claiborne and Abba glanced in the mirror.

"I'm still confused," she said. "Why did she suddenly change her mind and agree to take us to her house?"

"She may dress like a Goth, but she's born and raised a New Orleans girl. She recognized me. Her dad did business with my dad. They trusted each other, and now she trusts me. Simple as that," I said.

"Simple, huh?" Rafael said. "When you die, they should save your brain for research purposes because I've never met a person that reasons the way you do."

"Is that a compliment or a complaint?"

"Both," he said.

Rafael raked his hand through his thinning hair, and Abba shook her head before they grew silent and worked on polishing off the last of the wine. Twenty more minutes elapsed before a black Bentley passed slowly on Claiborne. The vanity tag on the bumper of the old but elegant Bentley said, Dagger Lady. Abba pulled in behind her, flashed her lights twice, and then followed her up Claiborne.

Dagger Lady soon turned south into the Faubourg Marigny district and continued almost to the river. Palm trees in front of the house imparted a Caribbean flavor to the old Creole cottage. Though the night was foggy and mostly starless, I could see the house had a fresh coat of blue paint that contrasted Nawlin's style with its yellow shutters. Abba parked the Aztek on the street, and we followed Cyn Czarnecki inside.

The house was nothing like I had suspected, more like something out of 1,001 Arabian Nights. Multicolored, diaphanous sheets draped from the ceiling, the smell of burning incense pleasant and almost enough to cover the faint odor of mold that couldn't be eradicated from the wooden walls. Music from a local oldies station emanated from an antique console radio in the corner. Cyn smiled when she saw me looking,

"We keep it on when we're away. Though we've never had a problem with break-ins, I believe the music might confuse thieves if they did get into the house."

"Probably a good idea," I said. "If you like eighties-vintage music, that is."

She nodded. "I hate it. The station only has about twenty-five songs on its playlist, and it gets monotonous. When I'm home, I turn it off and play my own music, at least until I go to bed."

"And your husband?" Abba said.

"He isn't into music. Come to think of it, we have so little in common I don't know what keeps us together, except that I love him and he loves me," she said, turning off the radio and replacing the eighties music with reggae.

"No Sex Pistols?" I asked.

"Our customers at the shop like it," she said. "Guess it puts them in the right mood to buy a knife. When I'm home, I prefer Bob Marley. Have a seat, and I'll get us something to drink."

A bong and other drug paraphernalia sat on the stained and burned coffee table in front of the threadbare couch where we sat. Cyn returned with a bottle of Southern Comfort, an ice bucket, and five tumblers.

"My dear, you were reading my mind," Rafael said.

"I don't need a glass. I don't drink," I said. "At least not anymore."

She lit up a joint, took a hit and handed it to me. "Puff of pot?"

"I'm fine," I said, passing the joint to Abba without partaking.

The smell of pot permeated the room as Cyn went to the kitchen, returning with a chilled bottle of mineral water.

"Skunkweed," she said. "Very potent."

"Is your husband here?" Rafael asked.

"His blacksmith shop is in the backyard. He'd keep the fire stoked twenty-four hours a day if I'd let him. I'll get him."

"Mind if I go with you?"

She nodded, took another puff from the joint, poured herself a shot of Southern Comfort over ice and then started for the back door. Grabbing the bottle of mineral water, I followed her.

Nothing but vacant lots occupied the land behind Cyn's house.

"Katrina did the trick on many of the houses and buildings closest to the river," she said. "Makes for a wonderful view and plenty of privacy."

"I love it. It's beautiful out here."

"We love it, too. Whenever I can get Rory to stop working for awhile, we sit in the swing on our back porch and watch the lights across the river as the sun goes down."

As if on cue, a tanker appeared through the

gloom, its running lights casting an eerie glow on the fog spilling over its bow. It wasn't the only peculiar thing I saw.

Red and orange flames flashed from the open windows and the large door of her husband's smithy, the discernible clang of metal resonating along with the sound of jazz coming from a music venue not far away. A man with a hammer was pounding red-glowing metal against the shop's anvil. He looked up and smiled when Cyn called his name.

"It's late," she said. "We have visitors, and it's time to stop for the night and come inside."

Chapter 16

I'd returned to the couch, sitting by Abba and Rafael when Cyn's husband appeared in the kitchen door. I had no idea how big he was until I saw him framed in the doorway.

Big was an understatement. He was massive. He had on a pair of steel-toed army boots with green argyle socks sticking out the top, a red kilt and nothing else. Though he didn't have the defined musculature of a bodybuilder, he looked powerful enough to tear down a wall with his bare hands. Cyn was grinning when she tried and failed to put both of her hands around his upper arm.

"This is Rory. He's my big boy, and I do mean big."

Rory's face was black with soot, and his teeth flashed when he smiled. He had a full growth of wiry beard and even wilder brown hair. When he kissed his wife, she made a face and pushed him away.

"You stink," she said. "Take a shower and change out of that awful kilt."

"Hello, everyone," he said with a wave. "I won't be long."

Rory's grin never disappeared as he kissed Cyn again before disappearing into another room.

"I think your husband could easily make it as a

professional wrestler," Rafael said as Cyn topped up his tumbler with ice and more Southern Comfort.

"My guess is the other wrestlers would be afraid to get in the ring with him," she said. "I saw him lift the front end of a Chevy off the ground once. He's a pussycat, though I have little doubt he could hurt someone if he tried."

I raised my hand. "Not I. Rory wouldn't have to try very hard. Is he Scottish?"

"What gave you your first clue?" she asked, barely able to keep a straight face.

"The kilt, though it was his brogue that gave him away."

"He was born in Glasgow. His parents moved here when he was a child. He can't seem to lose the brogue even though you'd think he was a Cajun the way he likes crawfish and gumbo. His last name . . . Our last name is Boyd."

Rory soon joined us. "I'm Rory. Welcome to Boyd Castle," he said, his voice deep and his brogue thick.

It made me wonder if, like Bertram, he heightened his accent around people he'd just met. Cyn waited until he'd shaken our hands, then invited us to have dinner with them. I was starved and apparently so were Abba and Rafael, all of us happy to oblige her.

We were soon sitting around their circular kitchen table eating gumbo and French bread. Abba wiped her mouth with a big napkin when she'd finished her last bite.

"Cyn, your gumbo is wonderful," she said.

"The best," I said.

"Count me in on that accolade," Rafael said.

"I know you're just nice. Doesn't matter because I love compliments," she said. "Anyone save room for key lime pie?"

We waited until Rory had finished his third bowl of gumbo, and then all had a slice of pie. Along with

139

the others, Rory was drinking Southern Comfort. Though I didn't ask her to, Cyn brewed a pot of strong Creole coffee and chicory especially for me. Our appetites sated, we returned to the comfortable couch in the living room.

"They are here to ask you about a dagger you made," Cyn said.

Rafael fished around inside his parka, producing the beautiful piece of cutlery, and then handed it to Rory.

Rory recognized it immediately. "Where did you get this?" he asked.

"We didn't steal it if that's what you mean," I said. "We think it belongs to a person we believe to be a witch. We wish to return it to her."

Rory's dark eyes blazed a hole through me as he stared for a very long moment before responding to what I'd told him. When I started to say something, he waved his palm and shook his head.

"This is Exethelon. It took me seven days to craft. There's not another blade on earth like it. It has magical powers, and even its name has some unknown, magical meaning."

He smiled at Rafael's next comment. "Cyn told us all knives have powers."

"Some more than others," he said. "Usually, the power they have is dependent upon the kiln in which they are fired and the expertise of the smithy. That is not the situation with this blade."

"Then please tell us what the situation is," Rafael said.

"No dagger has more power than Exethelon. You said you believe the owner to be a witch. She is much more than that. She is a powerful sorceress."

He glanced at each of us to see if we were smiling. None of us were. Rafael was the first to speak.

"You say this dagger you call Exethelon is magic.

It's been in my possession for several hours now, and I've had no indication of its magical powers."

"Did the sorceress give you this dagger?"

Cyn gasped when Rafael said, "We found it deeply buried in the heart of a dead man."

Rory's massive chest swelled when he inhaled before replying.

"Then the dagger served its purpose. It no longer belongs to the sorceress."

"To whom does it belong?" Rafael asked.

"The one who pulled it from the dead man's heart. Do you believe in destiny?"

"I'm a Catholic priest," Rafael said. "Of course I do."

"Then believe this. The person that pulled the dagger from the dead man's heart was predestined to do so. Though I have no idea what that reason is, I do know it must remain in that person's possession; at least until destiny deems it's time to pass it to another."

Rafael glanced at me. "Wyatt retrieved the dagger."

Rory, again, showed us his palm. "Tell me no more," he said.

He handed me the dagger. When I touched it, the same force I'd felt when I pulled it from Father Fred's heart surged up my arm. Abba gasped, and Rafael's jaw dropped when the dagger with the heroic name began to radiate a golden glow.

"Oh my God," Abba said. "I don't believe this."

"Believe it," Rory said. "I created this dagger using specific instructions from the sorceress. The runes on the blade have a secret meaning known only to her. I do not lie when I tell you they give the blade magical powers. Did you sense the power when you first touched the blade?"

I was silent for a moment before answering. "We exited the room when the floor and walls caught fire.

I was halfway down the stairs when an overwhelming urge caused me to return to the room. By the time I had the dagger in my hand, the smoke, fumes, and flames had grown almost intolerable. I couldn't see the door for the smoke. Some force in the dagger pulled me through the gloom and out the door, my skin barely scorched. I should be dead now, and I'm not."

"The dagger called to you. You had no choice but to possess it."

"I have a choice," I said, "Please, take it back."

"No," Rory said. "The dagger is yours, along with its magic. You must keep it until its purpose is served."

"And then what?" I said.

"Your duty will be complete, and ownership conveyed to another, for another purpose."

"But that's why we're here," Abba said. "We are looking for my sister. At least a person I'm beginning to think of like my sister. The witch, or sorceress, is the only person that can help us. Can you please tell us how to find her?"

"She can only be found if she wants you to find her," he said.

"How did she find you?" Abba asked.

"My father and grandfather were both smithys. In Scotland, their blades were considered the best of any in the world."

Rory grinned when Rafael said, "Your business doesn't seem like the type where you have to do much advertising."

"Rory has a waiting list that spans more than two years," Cyn said. "He's quite literally the best knife, dagger, and sword maker in the country; perhaps the entire world." She touched his hand. "That's how we met. He and his father sold my dad a sword many years ago."

"We were both quite young. I fell in love with

those eyes of hers the first moment we met," he said.

Though she punched his big arm, she didn't deny the attraction they both must have felt.

"You speak of the woman we thought was a witch as if she's some sort of mystical goddess," I said. "Surely she didn't just drive up in a car and ask you to make her a knife."

My comment made Rory guffaw. "Aye, Wyatt. You are correct about that."

"She didn't ride in on a broom, did she?" Abba asked.

"She could have if she had wanted to. The sorceress is a shape-shifter. She flew through the window of my smithy shop in the body of a pigeon. When I glanced around, she transformed into an enormous black woman dressed like an Antebellum field hand."

"I'm having trouble believing all of this," Abba said.

Rory was prepared for everyone's skepticism. "Then suspend your disbelief lassie, because what I'm telling you is true. She gave me specific instructions on how to construct the blade. She returned a week later, took the knife and left me with twenty pieces of gold."

"Surely, you're making this up," Abba said.

"I assure you that I am not. Cyn, show her the gold."

Cyn stood on her toes and reached for a cardboard box on an upper shelf of their bookcase. I could see it was heavy by the way she carried it. As we watched in amazement, she dumped the contents onto the coffee table. Rafael whistled softly as he reached to pick one up.

"These are Spanish gold doubloons, aren't they?" he asked.

"Looking bright as the day they were minted in the 1500s," Rory said.

143

"Are you sure?" Abba said.

"Pick one up. What else could they be? You can feel how heavy they are," Cyn said.

"How much are they worth?" Abba asked, hefting a single doubloon in her hand.

"A dead man's ransom," Rory said.

Before anyone else could comment, a beautiful black, long-haired dog came through the back door. After receiving head rubs from Cyn and Rory, he checked out Rafael, me, and finally Abba. His tail never stopped wagging.

"What's your name, pretty boy?" Abba asked.

"Slick," Cyn said. "He's a Gordon Setter."

"Looks almost like an Irish Setter," Rafael said. "Except slightly smaller and black instead of red."

"Gordon Setters are Scottish," Cyn said. "We rescued him from the pound."

"Who would abandon such a beautiful dog?" Abba asked, by now hugging the friendly animal.

"Unscrupulous breeders," Cyn said. "Only solid black Gordons are usually kept and bred. Those like Slick that are born with a white blaze on their chests are often killed when they are still puppies."

"Horrible," Abba said, giving Slick a motherly hug. "He is so beautiful. Why is it I've never heard of or seen a Gordon Setter before?"

"They're very active dogs. They need to run ten or more miles a day to be happy and healthy. Slick will climb over our fence when he feels like a run," Cyn said. "We've stopped trying to keep him penned."

"He runs down by the river until he gets enough exercise for the day. When he does, he always returns home," Rory said.

"Definitely not a dog for most city dwellers," Abba said.

Cyn put the doubloons in the cardboard box, and then back on the shelf. I still had the dagger. It felt warm in my hand and continued to glow.

"Are you telling us that you don't know where the sorceress lives?" I asked.

One of the front windows was open, and we could hear the sounds of boats on the river. A gust of wind blew the door ajar, and fog wafted in through the crack. Rory slugged his Southern Comfort, got up and closed it.

"I didn't say that," he said. "She lives somewhere in the Honey Island Swamp."

"That's a wild and treacherous place," I said. "How on earth can we find her if we don't have directions?"

"If she wants you to find her, then you will. If not, there's nothing more I can do for you."

Chapter 17

Eddie missed his favorite pillow, his neck sore when sun shining through a window awoke him the next morning. After showering and getting dressed, he padded down a long hallway, following his nose to the aroma of bacon and eggs. Everyone else was already at a long dining room table, drinking coffee and orange juice as they waited on him.

"Have a nice nap, sleeping beauty?" Frankie asked. "We thought you were going to sleep all day."

"It's not even eight o'clock yet."

"Everyone gets up earlier on the farm," Frankie said.

Adele had risen from her seat and led Eddie to an empty chair next to Josie and Jojo.

"Don't mind him," she said. "He can be an old bear until he's had his first pot of coffee in the morning."

"No problem," Eddie said. "That's something I can relate to. What's on the agenda for you girls today?"

"Lil and I are going to play a few sets of tennis and then relax at the spa; maybe have a massage."

"I'm in heaven," Lil said. "Tony and I tried out the hot tub last night."

"Good for you," Adele said. "How was it?"

146

"Wonderful. We're going to get one for our backyard."

"How about you, Tony?" Frankie said. "You like hot water?"

"In my life, I've been in plenty," he said.

Eddie was more interested in what Josie was doing. "What do you and Jojo have planned?" he asked.

"I'm homeschooling Jojo this year. When we finish for the day, I'll probably just cuddle up in bed and read a book."

"I'm jealous," Eddie said.

"Dad has lots of great books in the den."

"Wasn't exactly what I meant."

Everyone at the table, including Frankie, tried to ignore Eddie's comment. Josie just grinned and shook her head."

"You?" she asked.

"Tony and I are headed to the track to ask a few questions. Maybe we can go for another walk when we return."

"Maybe," she said.

Josie and Jojo were soon off to study lessons, Adele and Lil on their way to get dressed for tennis. Frankie was lacing his coffee with scotch, his attention somewhere else.

"Why the long face?" Tony finally asked.

"Cops arrested my right-hand man Bruno Baresi last night and charged him with murder."

"Who did he kill?" Eddie asked.

"Nobody," Frankie said. "This is a frame job, pure and simple."

"Let me rephrase my question; Who is he supposed to have killed?"

"Diego Contrado. Chuy Delgado's nephew."

Tony whistled softly through his teeth. "What kind of evidence do they have?"

"Circumstantial. They were both eating at the

147

same restaurant."

"Surely that can't be all they have," Tony said.

"They got other evidence."

"Like what?"

"Contrado was killed with Bruno's pistol."

Tony had to stifle a laugh. "Seems more than just circumstantial to me."

"The owner, Pinky Robinette, used to work for me. Lots of paisanos, and now the Mexican gang, like to eat and drink there. Pinky don't allow no violent behavior, and he makes all the boys check their guns at the door. Anybody there could have taken it and used it to kill Contrado."

"What else they got?" Tony asked.

"Bruno got a phone call and went outside to take it. It was about the same time Contrado was shot."

"Was it just a coincidence that Bruno happened to be at the restaurant the same time as Contrado?" Eddie asked.

"It was Friday. Bruno's a creature of habit. He eats at Pinky's every Friday night."

"Pardon me for saying so," Tony said. "Seems to me your boy is in a heap of trouble."

"Yeah, well you're gonna find out because I want you to talk to him and get his story."

"Instead of looking for the horse?"

"Why hell no! In addition to finding Jojo's horse. Can you handle it?"

Eddie answered for him. "Tony's the best criminal investigator I know. I'm pretty good myself, and I'm helping him. We can handle it."

Frankie took a sip of his coffee, stared at Eddie and smiled. "Maybe you got more moxie than I give you credit for."

"Thanks," Eddie said.

"That ain't all. Some of Delgado's men caused a stir at my nightclub over in Fat City last night."

"What did they do?" Tony asked.

"Pistol whipped one of my boys on his way out to the parking lot."

"How do you know they were Delgado's men?" Eddie asked.

"They was speaking Spanish," Frankie said.

"And?"

Frankie slammed his coffee cup on the table. "And nothing. They was Delgado's men. I don't need an affidavit to prove it."

"Eddie don't mean no harm," Tony said. "We're both on your side. He's just being a good investigator and asking lots of questions."

Frankie's frown disappeared as he pushed away from the table. "Sorry, I'm in a foul mood and there ain't a whole lot I can do about it."

"You got a reason to be upset," Tony said. "Stop worrying about Bruno and Jojo's horse. Eddie and me are on the job. We'll take care of things for you."

"Thanks, Tony. I feel better already. Now, I got work to do. Give me a report when you get back to the farm."

Tony and Eddie watched him disappear down the hallway.

When he was gone, Eddie said, "Now what?"

Frankie had left his bottle of scotch on the dining room table. Tony grabbed it and poured a liberal dose into his own coffee.

"Just my luck," he said.

Eddie took the bottle and laced his own coffee. "What?"

"A partner with a big mouth."

"We can handle this," Eddie said.

"Hope you're right about that," Tony said. "Let's get dressed and hit the road. We got lots of ground to cover and not much time to do it."

The quarter horse campaign had ended the previous day. When Tony and Eddie reached the track, all they found were a few trainers and lots of roustabouts loading trucks and trailers. Frankie had supplied them with stable passes which they wore around their necks on lanyards. They needn't have bothered.

Lil had made sure that Tony's khakis were tightly pressed. He wore no tee shirt beneath the magnificent palms swaying in a gentle breeze on his green Hawaiian shirt. He didn't miss the perennial tie he'd always had to wear as a homicide detective, though he liked the dark brown corduroy sports coat his kids had given him for his birthday.

Eddie's black and gold Saints parka was open enough to reveal his L.S.U. T-shirt. He liked to think his penny loafers with no socks and designer blue jeans made a fashion statement. The truth was, his job required the wearing of an expensive suit every day. Maybe why he enjoyed looking like a tourist from the west coast on his days off.

"Think you can find the stable Lightning Bolt was in?" Tony asked.

"I'm not senile."

Eddie didn't laugh when Tony said, "Yet, at least."

The stable where Lightning Bolt had been was empty, the door ajar.

"Not much here," Eddie said.

Tony poked his nose out the back door. "There's a dumpster back here. The trash hasn't been picked up yet. Go out front and watch the door."

"Why?" Eddie said.

"You be surprised what winds up in the trash. I'm going to dig through it and see what I find."

"Knock yourself out," Eddie said.

Twenty minutes passed when a man with a bottle of red energy drink in his hand pushed open the stable door to see who was there. Tony had finished his dumpster diving and was sticking something into his jacket as he reentered the stall area.

"You boys look lost," the man said. "Looking for something?"

The man's aviator sunglasses perched atop his red hair that was rapidly growing gray. He seemed to have a permanent grin beneath his untrimmed handlebar mustache.

"A friend of ours had a horse in that stall a few days ago," Eddie said. "We didn't realize the meet was over."

"Frankie Castellano."

"Yes, how did you know?" Tony asked.

"He don't usually run quarter horses. Caught everyone in the paddock by surprise when he entered a race with one."

"Bet he did," Eddie said, extending his hand. "I'm Eddie, and this is Tony. You work around here?"

"Jake Kratchit. I'm the stable superintendent."

"Sounds impressive," Tony said. "What exactly does your job entail, Jake?"

"Not much of nothing, at least between meets. When the thoroughbreds or quarter horses are running, seems like I'm busy twenty-four seven."

"Are you the person that assigns the stalls during the meets?" Tony asked.

"That and a whole lot more," Jake said.

Eddie pointed to the stall where Josie had shown him Lightning Bolt.

"Is that stall permanently assigned to Mr. Castellano when his horses run here?"

"Nope, I had to do some shuffling when the horse was added to the race."

"You didn't already know about it?" Tony asked.

"It was a last minute addition."

"Is that normal?" Eddie asked.

"Weren't nothing normal about it. Had everyone in the paddock wondering how this no-name horse

151

managed to all of a sudden have a favorable lane coming out of the gate."

"How did that happen?" Tony asked.

"Frankie Castellano. When he says frog, people jump. Ain't right, maybe. It's still as simple as that."

"People in the paddock were mad?" Tony said.

"Pissed off is more like it. You boys don't look like cops."

"Because we're not," Eddie said. "Insurance investigators. Trying to get a lead on what happened to Mr. Castellano's horse. Know anything about it."

"Not much around here I don't know."

"Then will you discuss it with us?"

"Why not?" Jake said. "I ain't got a dog in the fight. Buy me a cold beer, and I'll tell you what I know."

"You got it," Tony said. "I could use a cold one myself. Where to?"

"I'm pretty much done for the day. There's a neighborhood bar just outside the main gate called Big Sam's Firehorse Lounge."

"Yeah," Tony said. "Saw it when we came in the gate. Want to ride with us?"

"Got to lock up a few stalls first. Meet you there in about twenty minutes."

Chapter 18

Despite its grandiose name, Big Sam's Firehorse Lounge was little more than a ramshackle hole-in-the-wall bar frequented by track workers, visiting jockeys, and trainers. The quarter horse meet having ended, the place was empty of customers. Tony and Eddie sat at the bar and ordered cold mugs of Abita.

Big Sam was anything but. A former jockey, he stood nowhere near six feet tall, though his expanding waistline indicated he liked sampling his own wares. He was busy puttering in back when they came in. After pouring their beer, he returned to what he'd been doing and left them alone.

"What'd you find in the dumpster?" Eddie asked.

"Bottle of shoe polish. Probably the one used to dye the horse's blaze."

"I saw you stuff something in your jacket when Jake showed up. What else did you find?"

Tony produced a leather wallet from his pocket, opened it and showed it to Eddie.

"A passport and a one-way ticket to Belize."

"Let me see," Eddie said. "You think this means something?"

"Depends on who Wendell Swanson is. Maybe Jake can tell us."

"What else do you expect we'll get from Jake?" Eddie asked.

"Like he said, there's probably not much that happens around the paddock he don't know about. There are security cameras everywhere you look. My guess is, he don't want nobody knowing he's talking with insurance investigators. Probably why he wanted to meet us here."

"Fine by me, though it seems like a lot to go through in exchange for a cold beer," Eddie said.

Tony held up a crisp hundred dollar bill. "It's gonna cost us at least this much, and maybe more for whatever he tells us."

"He didn't seem like that type of person to me," Eddie said.

"Don't think so? I'm betting this ain't Jake's first rodeo, and that he realizes the value of information."

"And isn't afraid of Frankie or the Mexican cartel?"

"Not too scared to score an extra hundred here, there, and yonder," Tony said. "Even if what he has to tell us turns out to be a dud, at least we get a cold beer, or two."

"Amen, brother," Eddie said. "I'll drink to that."

Jake Kratchit came through the front door as Tony and Eddie were touching glasses. Big Sam stopped his puttering long enough to pour the stable superintendent a tall one.

"Let's sit in back," he said. "Big Sam's an old gossip and what I'm gonna tell you don't need to go no further than just us three."

"Right behind you," Tony said.

Tony and Eddie followed Jake Kratchit to a table in the back of the dark bar. The old wood floor had apparently spent time underwater because it creaked as they walked across it. The floor, along with the walls that desperately needed a fresh coat of paint, also had an under smell of mold. Eddie hoped it didn't launch him into a sneezing fit. Jake downed half his beer before breathing a word. After wiping his mouth with the back of his hand, he banged the glass on the table.

"Damn, that's good," he said.

"I told Big Sam to keep 'em coming," Tony said. He handed Jake the hundred dollar bill. "For your trouble. I know information don't come cheap."

Jake grinned, took the bill and stashed it in the pocket of his well-worn Western shirt.

"You coulda had me for twenty. Don't matter none cause I ain't giving it back."

"And I don't want you to," Tony said. "Tell us a few things we don't already know, and there's another Bennie in it for you."

Jake grinned again. "Then if I don't know it, I'll make something up. What would you like to hear?"

"You can start by telling us something about the jockey and trainer that were murdered."

"You sure you ain't cops?"

"Do we look like cops?" Tony asked.

"Not really. Eddie's hair is a little too long. Private dicks, maybe."

Big Sam showed up with a tray of beers before Tony had a chance to reply to Jake's comment. Jake didn't seem to need an answer as he took a big drink from his glass.

Big Sam showed Tony a thumbs up when he said, "Better bring Jake another. He's getting ahead of Eddie and me."

Jake finished his brew. "Thanks," he said. "I needed that. It's been one hell of a meet, with the murders and all."

"Tell us about it."

"Like I said, I didn't have much time to find Mr. Castellano a stall. Don't matter none, cause he ain't a person you want to say no to."

"That's a fact," Tony said. "Did you know the

155

trainer and jockey?"

Jake smoothed his handlebar mustache with a pair of dirty fingers. "I knew Wendell Swanson, the trainer. Don't know much about the jockey."

Tony gave Eddie a glance at the mention of the trainer's name. "What's the deal with Swanson?"

"Mr. Castellano don't usually race quarter horses, and he didn't have no quarter horse trainer. Swanson's been out of work for several years. An agent got him the gig with Mr. Castellano because he was the only trainer he could get on such short notice."

"Why has he been out of work?"

"Little problem he had while racing in New Mexico."

"Oh? Tell us about it."

"Racing officials are a mite more picky in New Mexico than they are here in Louisiana. They suspended Swanson for using a belly bomb on one of his horses."

"Belly bomb?" Eddie said. "What the hell is a belly bomb?"

"You boys don't hang around the track much, do you?" Jake asked.

"Apparently not," Tony said. "Tell us about it."

"Most trainers cheat, and they do it using PEDs, performance-enhancing drugs. Trainers aren't supposed to administer any drug to a horse twenty-four hours before a race. All except Lasix, that is, the anti-bleeding drug. Don't matter, though, cause all the trainers dope their horses anyways."

"Who is supposed to regulate such things?" Eddie asked.

"State racing boards."

"And they're not doing their job?" Eddie said.

Jake snorted, and then took a drink of the fresh beer Big Sam had brought him.

"Why hell no! If PEDs were as prevalent among

human athletes as they are horses, you'd see all sorts of records broken. The regulators just look the other way."

"These PEDs make that much of a difference?" Eddie asked.

"So many races are won by a head, or a nose, any little edge can make a big difference in the outcome of the race. You might not see it so much in lower class races. When it comes to big stakes, it's out of control."

"You have to be kidding," Eddie said. "Even the Kentucky Derby?"

"You know what the purse was for the winner of the last Derby?"

"Tell us," Eddie said.

"Almost a million and a half bucks. You think people won't kill for that kind of money?"

"And you say everyone in the stable area knows it?" Eddie asked.

"Most all jockeys use buzzers. Their trainers know they're using them. Hell, one top trainer has killed seven horses experimenting with different performance enhancing drugs."

"How does he get away with it?" Eddie asked.

"He's rich enough to hire as many lawyers as he needs. Accuse him, and he takes you to court and rakes you through the coals."

Tony sipped his beer. "Hard for me to believe that everyone cheats."

"If they want to win, they do. It ain't cheating if they don't get caught."

"What's this belly bomb thing?" Tony asked.

"Sometimes the trainer don't want his horse to win. He'll give his animal a big pill a few hours before the start of a race. When it dissolves, it gives the horse a giant stomach ache. If a horse ain't feeling a hundred percent, it won't run a hundred percent."

"Damn!" Tony said.

"Damn is right," Jake said. "And a belly bomb is

almost impossible to detect, or prove."

"Why would a trainer want his horse to lose?" Eddie asked.

"All sorts of ways to make a buck when you're a cheater. If the horse was the clear favorite and all the bettors expect him to win, they bet accordingly. It really shakes up the odds if he don't, and a longshot wins. Even better if two longshots come in first and second."

"That happen often?" Tony asked.

"Often enough. All the trainers know each other. When they think they need a new truck or down payment on a house, they collude with a buddy to make it happen."

"And organized crime?" Eddie said.

"In on it big time, and don't miss a trick. They just don't like it when they don't know what the outcome will be."

"How do professional gamblers make a living if there's so much cheating going on?" Eddie asked.

"They're like you; they buy information. If the money's right, there's always someone in the paddock that'll tell you what's about to go down."

Eddie drained his beer and motioned Big Sam for another round.

"If what you say is true and there's so much cheating going on, why hasn't somebody done something?"

"It's a dirty little secret that almost everyone in the racing business knows about. Who cares if somebody gets drunk and talks? The average Joe on the street either don't believe it or else don't give a shit. Kinda like those aliens in New Mexico."

"Speaking of New Mexico, why exactly did Wendall Swanson lose his job if regulation is so lax?" Tony asked.

"He was using a belly bomb to rig the outcome of a race. The problem is, the horse's owner was betting big for a win. When his horse finished dead last, he fired Wendall, and then turned him into the racing commission."

"Who was the owner?"

"Angus Anderson. He had Wendall banned from training for two years."

Tony gave Eddie another glance. "Anderson has that kind of power?"

"You shitting me? Mr. Anderson don't like to lose. Lucky for Wendall he just got him banned and didn't kill him."

Eddie thought it wise to not reveal their interest in Anderson.

"How did Wendall support himself during his absence from racing?" he asked, changing the subject.

"He knew the ropes and all the tricks. Became a handicapper. Not many days passed he wasn't either at the track or at an off-track betting facility. He liked to make exotic bets. He had a little system he thought gave him an edge, and he especially liked betting trifectas. You know what that is?"

"Picking the order of the first three horses," Tony said.

"Right," Jake said.

"What about the jockey?" Eddie said.

"Country boy from Oklahoma. Heard he was an up and comer. He'd won a few races up at the track in Sallisaw. Good looking young fellow named Kenny Smith. I met his widow when she came down to claim the body. Want to see her picture?"

Jake pulled up a photo on his cell phone and handed it to Eddie. It showed several men loading a casket into the back of an old Ford pickup. The young woman holding an infant was crying. Jake showed them a closeup.

"She's stunning," Eddie said.

"Pretty enough to be a movie star," Jake said. "Dirt poor, though. Boys around the track donated as much as we could to help her with the burial and all. The baby was only a year or so old."

"What's her name?"

"Jessica."

"What happened to her?" Eddie asked.

"Guess she went back to Sallisaw."

When Jake finished the last of his beer, Tony gave him another hundred dollar bill.

"Thanks for the info."

The track manager nodded, slapped Tony on the shoulder and started for the door.

"See you boys around," he said.

Eddie waited until they were alone, then asked, "What do you make of his story?"

"Don't know," Tony said as Big Sam delivered yet another round of beer.

Tony handed him a hundred and asked for the tab. Big Sam was turning to leave when Eddie called to him.

"Wait a minute, Big Sam. Did you know Wendell Swanson?"

Big Sam's expression never changed. "You blind? Can't you see my pictures behind the bar?"

It was impossible to miss the mostly black and white racing pictures not just behind the bar, but on practically every wall. Most of them were of a particular triumphant jockey taken in the winner's circle.

"Couldn't miss them," Eddie said. "Is that you in the pictures?"

"I was one of the highest winning jockeys until I fell and broke my back. I know all the track rats, including Wendall Swanson. He was in here the night someone shot him to death."

"Did you tell this to the police?" Tony asked.

"Course I did."

"Was he drinking alone?"

"He was drinking. He weren't alone."

"You know the person he was with?" Eddie asked.

"Don't know his name though I seen him in here before."

Tony glanced at Eddie to see if he was paying attention. Eddie was literally sitting on the edge of his chair.

"What'd he look like?" Eddie asked.

"Big Mexican dude with skull and crossbones tattooed on his knuckles."

"Thanks, Big Sam. Keep the change."

Big Sam nodded, and then sauntered away, returning to whatever he'd been doing behind the bar.

"Damn!" Eddie said. "You think the cops picked up on that little tidbit of information?"

"If somebody ain't paid them off to forget about it," Tony said.

"Let me see that passport," Eddie said.

Eddie thumbed the document and ticket in the plastic flap. Tony watched him as his dark eyes narrowed.

"What is it?" he asked.

"There's something else in here other than just the plane ticket and passport."

Chapter 19

The room had gone deathly quiet. When Slick whined and wagged his tail, breaking the tension, Rory gave his head a rub.

"What now?" Rafael asked.

"Visit the Honey Island Swamp," I said. "See if the witch will allow us to find her."

Rory grabbed the bottle of Southern Comfort, topping up everyone's glass. The reggae music had ceased, replaced by Wagner's Symphony in C major. The heroic music and dim lighting somehow fit the mood it seemed we'd all attained.

Rory's brogue had grown thicker when he stared straight at me and said, "You are risking your very life to enter the swamp to seek counsel from a very dangerous sorceress. This woman you are looking for must be very important to you."

"More than I've cared to admit, even to myself."

"How long has she been gone?" he asked.

"Two years. When her twin sister committed suicide, Desire vowed to become a nun and live the rest of her life cloistered in a nunnery."

"Sounds like Guinevere. Does that make you Lancelot or Arthur?"

"More like Sancho Panza," I said.

Rory wasn't finished with his twenty questions.

His next query caused me even more anxiety. The candle on the coffee table was melting, wax beginning to clump on the unpolished wood.

"How did Desire's sister die?" he asked.

I gazed at the flickering flame a long moment before answering.

"She jumped off the Crescent City Connection, into the Mississippi River. I tried to grab her wrist. She touched my hand, our eyes locked as she plummeted to her death."

Suddenly overcome by memories, emotion, and music, a sob rose up my throat and burst from my lips. I tried to catch my breath. My tears kept flowing. Cyn and Abba rushed to my side, each clinging to an arm. Rafael kneeled in front of me and began praying.

"I'm so sorry," I finally managed to say. "I've never told that story to anyone before now."

"It's all right," Abba said, embracing me. "You've kept it inside too long. It was time to let it out."

She handed me a crumpled napkin. I used it to wipe my nose, the salty tears burning my eyes. It wasn't the only thing I needed at that moment.

"Mind if I have a shot of whiskey?" I said.

"Wyatt, don't do it," Rafael said. "I beg you."

Rory poured a shot of Southern Comfort into a glass and handed it to me. I drank it with one swallow. When Rory offered me more, I waved him off.

"It was all I needed. I'm okay now."

"Can you tell me why you suddenly decided to look for Desire after two years?"

"Please, Rory," Cyn said. "No more questions. Can't you see how distraught Wyatt is?"

"It's okay," I said. "My story felt like a confession. Guess I'm still a Catholic because it was just what I needed. I even had a priest to hear me out."

"Are you sure?" Rory asked.

I nodded. "A night or so ago I saw an apparition. It was a funeral procession moving slowly beneath the room where I live. Early morning, streetlights were barely a dim glow through the creeping fog. I saw Desire riding alone in a white limousine. I also found this pendant that Desire's mother swears was buried with Dauphine, Desire's twin sister."

I handed the pendant to Rory, his expression grave as he turned it in his hand.

"To which convent did Desire go?" he asked.

"We don't know. She was very secretive about it, not even telling her mother."

"Then how did you get here?"

"Desire's mother Junie Bug broke her promise and peeked out the door when two people arrived for her. One was a man named Father Fred. It was his heart that I pulled Exethelon from. The other person was a woman named Sister Gertrude. We have reason to believe she knows the whereabouts of Desire. Sister Gertrude is the only clue we have left, and the sorceress is the only person that can tell us where to find her."

Rory cast his gaze at Rafael. "You're a priest. Can't you call around and find out where they took Desire?"

"Believe me, I've tried. I spoke with every Catholic convent in south Louisiana. No one I spoke to knew anything about Desire's whereabouts."

"Then maybe she's no longer in south Louisiana," Rory said.

"We have no idea if she's even still alive, much less the name of the convent or its location. It seems as if there's but one person left that can tell us for sure," Rafael said.

"You'll need a boat," Rory said. "The swamp is a maze of bogs, blind chutes, and giant trees some of which have never been cut. There are places in that swamp that are all but impassable. Few men know their way around even with a boat."

"I know someone that not only has a boat, he also has a fishing camp located right in the middle of the Honey Island Swamp," I said.

My pronouncement riveted everyone's attention.

"Tell us," Abba said.

"His name is Jean Pierre Saucier. He's a homicide cop in Chalmette. I met him a while back during a murder investigation a client hired me to do. I'll call him tomorrow."

"No, lad," Rory said. "We must leave tonight while the moon is nearly full."

"We?" Cyn said.

Rory stood from his chair and walked toward his bedroom door.

"I can not let them begin this quest alone," he said. "I have a dark feeling the journey will be extremely dangerous, and that they are definitely in need of my brawn. I am going to prepare myself. Call your friend with the boat."

"But it's after midnight," Abba said.

"Jean Pierre is the one person I know that won't mind a call at this hour," I said.

Rory disappeared into his bedroom while I punched in Jean Pierre's number on my cell phone. I'd finished talking when Rory returned dressed in a ceremonial kilt complete with sash and tam. A broadsword hung from the scabbard attached to his belt.

"What did your friend with the boat say?" he asked.

"We're meeting him at the entrance to the Chalmette Battlefield. He'll lead us to his fishing camp where we can spend the night and get an early start tomorrow."

Rafael gulped the rest of his Southern Comfort. "Though there's nothing in the world I'd rather do than continue with this journey, I'm afraid my work as a rent-a-priest must get in the way. My cruise leaves the Port of New Orleans for the Bahamas tomorrow. My employers will be upset if I'm not on it."

"Lass, this journey will be no place for a woman. You can take Rafael home. I will drive Wyatt to meet his friend with the boat."

"Not on your life," Abba said. "I started this search, and I intend to finish it. We'll drop Rafael off at his car, and then I'm driving us to Chalmette."

"I can not tell you how much danger this journey may entail," Rory said.

"And I'll have three strong men to protect me. I'm going, and I'm not taking no for an answer."

"How long will this journey take, and who will care for Slick while I'm at work and you're on your quest?" Cyn asked.

"We will need a brave dog," Rory said. "Slick will accompany us."

Cyn had an expression of resignation on her pretty face as she tossed her hands in the air and rolled her eyes.

"It'll all work out," I said.

Rafael was still apologizing when we dropped him off at his car.

"I wish I could go with you," he said.

"We couldn't have gotten this far without you," I said.

"Is there anything else I can do?" he asked.

Rory answered for me. "Say a prayer for us, Father. We are going to need it."

Not being an observant Catholic, I was uncomfortable when Rafael had us join hands and bow our heads. Abba had already given us her thoughts on religion. Though she took our hands, she was also rolling her big brown eyes. Rory wasn't so encumbered.

"Amen, Father," he said. "Every quest should

begin with a prayer to Almighty God." When Abba made a sarcastic face, he said. "You do believe in God, don't you?"

"Let's just say I'm an agnostic and leave it at that."

Hearing the less than subdued annoyance in Abba's voice, Rory let the subject drop as she pulled away from the curb and headed toward St. Bernard Avenue and Chalmette.

Jean Pierre and his big chocolate lab Lucky were waiting for us on the side of the road in his old red pickup. We piled out of the car so I could make introductions.

"Wyatt, my man, how the hell you doing?" Jean Pierre said, pumping my hand.

"Great, J.P. These are my friends, Abba and Rory."

"Jean Pierre Saucier," he said shaking their hands. "Girl, you about the prettiest woman I seen around Chalmette in I can't remember when." Grabbing her left hand, he eyed it for a wedding ring. "You two hitched?"

"Rory is, though not to me," Abba said.

"Is Wyatt your boyfriend?"

"Just friends," she said.

Jean Pierre turned his attention to Rory. With hands on his hips, he said, "Son, you about a big one. How much you weigh, anyway?"

"Two seventy-five," Rory said.

"Mardi Gras ain't for a couple of months. You on your way to a Halloween party?"

Rory didn't smile. "I'm Scottish if you can not already tell."

"Hell, mon, sorry about that," Jean Pierre said with a grin as he slapped him on the shoulder. "I'm a damn coonass if you can't already tell, and loving every minute of it."

Standing about six feet tall, Jean Pierre had

wavy hair and eyes as dark as Abba's. Slender of build, he was dressed in worn jeans and a Western shirt. Boots and Stetson completed his cowboy appearance.

He had the good looks of a French movie star. He knew it and used it to its full advantage. His jovial nature was hard to ignore, and both Abba and Rory were soon smiling at one of his many Cajun tall tales.

"You caught me just at the right time," he said. "I'm on vacation. Lucky and me was set to head to our camp tomorrow morning. I couldn't find nobody to go with me, so I'm glad you called. The place is in the middle of nowhere and can get kinda lonesome at night."

Feeling his gaze, Abba glanced away from his stare and looked at the two dogs, still circling each other and wagging their tails.

"Looks like those two hit it off," she said.

"That's my dog, Lucky. Hundred-forty pounds of pure love."

"That heavy? Oh my God!" Abba said.

"He's an eating machine," Jean Pierre said. "That's a fact. Now, Wyatt, tell me why it's so important for you to visit the Honey Island Swamp at this time of night?"

"Long story, J.P. We'll fill you in on the way there."

"Don't think you'll all fit in my old truck," he said.

"Do you live near here?" Abba asked.

"Couple miles away."

"We'll follow you there. You can leave your truck and go with us."

He stood for a moment in silence, shaking his head as he stared at her car.

"What's that thing called?" he asked. "Don't think I ever seen one like that."

"Because they didn't make very many. It's a

Pontiac Aztek," she said. "Best car on the road."

"If you say so, sweet thing. Hope it drives better than it looks."

"My name is Abba," she said. "Not sweet thing."

J.P.'s smile never disappeared. "Well slap my face," he said, tapping his cheek with his palm. "Didn't mean to insult you. You just so pretty, the words just flowed from my lips before I could choke them back. Forgive me?"

When he took her hand, she was unable to mask a smile of her own.

"You're a mess. Didn't your mother try to teach you better?"

"It almost put my poor mama in the crazy house trying to change me. She finally give up trying."

"I'll bet she did," Abba said. "Let's take the truck to your house before I have to be the one to slap that pretty face of yours."

Chapter 20

Abba broke all existing speed limits as she headed
north. I sat in the back with Jean Pierre, Rory
hunched in the front seat and looking uncomfortable,
and the two dogs in back. North of Slidell, J.P. leaned
over the front seat to give Abba directions.

"Better start slowing this buggy down. There's an
exit up ahead on the right."

The off-ramp led to a narrow side road that soon
began veering east.

"Who turned out the lights?" Abba asked.

J.P. chuckled. "Once we get across the bridge up
ahead, about the only lights, we're gonna see will be
the moon and stars. Too many clouds to see those
tonight."

Abba had greatly reduced her speed. When the
rear end of the Aztek slid in a puddle of water, she
slowed almost to a stop.

"Want me to drive for you, sweet thing?" J.P.
asked.

"No, and if you call me sweet thing one more time,
I'm going to put you out on the side of the road."

"Suit yourself," he said. "Just try to stay out of
the ditch. It's swampy on both sides of the road and
them monster gators in there are always looking for a
midnight snack. That ain't to mention the Swamp
Monster."

"Would you shut the hell up?" she said. "I'm nervous enough as it is without you making matters worse."

"Just trying to help," he said.

"How far is your camp?" I asked, interrupting their banter.

"About ten miles; the last two by boat. We'll have to leave your car at the dock," he said.

"Will it still be there when we return?" Abba asked.

"Ain't many thieves this far out in the middle of nowhere. I'll put a Chalmette police department sticker on your dash. Your vehicle will be fine till we get back."

Rory had fallen asleep and was snoring, opening his eyes when Abba pulled the Aztek to a stop at a lonely fishing dock. A single exposed bulb swayed in a gentle breeze as we unloaded J.P.'s equipment. Something was howling in the distance.

"Are there wolves in the swamp?" Abba asked.

"Don't know what that was," J.P. said. "A good friend of mine that does lots of camping around here says, there are sounds you hear at night you recognize, some you don't, and others you don't even want to know."

"You're making that up," she said.

"No ma'am, I'm not."

"Not to worry, lassie," Rory said. "I have my broadsword."

Rory was still dressed as a Scottish warrior with the sword hanging from his side. J.P. grinned and shook his head, though he was careful that no one other than I saw it.

We loaded the ice chests and other equipment onto J.P.'s twenty-foot pontoon boat. Once everyone including the dogs was aboard, he untied us from the old wooden dock, gave the boat a kick to start it moving, and then jumped aboard. Within minutes, he had the motor humming. He let it drift while he went to the front of the boat to light the two lanterns that would serve as our running lights. We motored into the foggy darkness, no one except J.P., and maybe the dogs, able to see more than ten feet or so in front of the boat.

"You know where we are going?" Rory asked.

"Get your panties out of a wad, big boy. I've done this a thousand times or more."

"Well, I can't see a thing," Abba said, having to raise her voice to be heard over the drone of the motor.

"There's some lawn chairs against the railing. Open them up, sit down, and relax. I know where I'm going. I'll get us there in one piece, I promise."

The steering wheel was near the back of the boat. Rory unfolded a chair and fell asleep almost immediately. Slick and Lucky lay at his feet and they had closed their eyes. Abba grabbed my elbow, pulling me to the front of the boat.

"Let's sit up here. I need to talk to you," she said.

"What's up?" I asked.

Though the motor was humming and we were all the way to the front of the boat, she spoke in a subdued voice, leaning closer so only I could hear.

"Who is this insulting clown that talks like a hick?"

"It's just an act," I said. "J.P. is no hick. He has a degree from USL in Lafayette. He served with honors in Afghanistan as a First Lieutenant. Lawmen all over the state know and look up to him."

"He's coming on to me like a sexist pig," she said.

"J.P. is not sexist. Womanizer, maybe. I promise you he respects women. He's obviously attracted to you and can't help himself."

"That's not good enough," she said.

"J.P.'s a lawman. He won't assault you, I promise."

"I'm not worried about him assaulting me. I just want to be treated with a little decency and not feel like a piece of bloody meat being waved in front of a wild animal."

"I'll have a talk with him," I said.

"I know we need him right now. I don't want to be a bitch about it."

"You have every right in the world to be concerned. I'll have a talk with him."

"You say he has a degree. What's it in, underwater basket weaving?"

"You wouldn't believe it if I told you," I said.

"Try me."

"The performing arts. You should hear him sing and see him dance. He's been an extra in lots of movies filmed around here. He's had more than one chance to do even more as an actor, though he's turned down every opportunity."

"And why is that?" she asked.

"You'll have to ask him."

"He's good looking enough to be a movie star, but then so are you, and you're not sexist."

"I've had my moments," I said.

"No, you haven't."

"No one's perfect; least of all me."

Apparently satisfied with my response, Abba grew silent, at least for a few minutes.

"I can't see a thing except for the flame from those two lanterns. You think he knows where he's going?"

"I've been with him in a boat much smaller than this, during a major storm, and when we had no lights at all."

"What happened?" she asked.

"The boat sank. We somehow made it to shore."

"That's comforting to know," she said. "I hope he's learned something because I'd hate to think about having to swim for shore. God only knows

173

what's out there."

"It was more than just a storm. We were in a hurricane. No one on earth could have navigated any better than he did. There's barely a breeze blowing tonight."

"And that's what bothers me. How can he see through the fog?"

"Stop worrying. If J.P. says he'll get us there safely, then I trust him, and so should you."

"Sorry I'm so negative," she said.

"It's okay."

"I'm tired, we've been drinking all day, and . . ."

"We saw dead people."

"I don't know why it should bother me the way it does," she said.

"We were at the scene of several violent murders. It's normal to feel upset."

I clutched her hand, and she didn't pull away. "It's just now really hitting me. Guess the excitement of the chase and all the alcohol had my senses anesthetized. Right now, my head is pounding, my stomach churning, and I feel like crap."

"We'll all feel better after we get some sleep," I said.

Abba grew silent, though she continued holding my hand. Thirty more minutes passed, fog rolling off the prow of the boat as J.P. cut the engine and nosed into a wooden dock. Hurrying past us, he secured us to the mooring spot with a rope.

Rory and the dogs awoke when the noise of the engine ceased. With the big ice chest under one arm and an Army green duffel bag under the other, he followed us off the boat, J.P. leading the way with one of the lanterns. The other he handed to me.

Though it was dark and the camp cloaked in moving shadows, I could see J.P.'s fishing camp was more than I'd expected. It sat on tall pilings that jutted up out of the water. The wooden structure needed a paint job. It was two-stories tall and much bigger than I'd thought it would be. A screened porch completely encircled the building, and the hinges creaked when he undid the latch and opened the door.

We followed him across an equally creaky porch to the front door of the house. Even though it was late October, the old house gasped when he pushed open the door and entered. J.P. sat the lantern on an old wooden kitchen table bare of even a splotch of paint, took the one I was carrying and handed it to Rory.

"The generator's in back. I haven't started it in a while. It's old and kind of touchy, and I may need some muscle to get it started. Can you help me, Rory?"

Abba and I glanced around the spacious old fishing camp as J.P., Rory and the two dogs disappeared into the darkness. An overhead light came on when we heard the sound of a gasoline motor. J.P. was smiling when he, Rory, and the dogs returned.

"This big boy's got a set of muscles on him. He cranked that ol' engine in one pull."

"This is quite a place you have, J.P.," I said. "I wasn't expecting anything this big."

"Way bigger than I need. For no more than I paid for it, I couldn't turn it down."

"How much was that?"

"Nothing. My uncle Johnny left it to me when he passed. Sleeps ten easy. Upstairs is all bedrooms. Mine has a porch overlooking the swamp. I collect rainwater in a cistern out back."

"Sounds like a smooth operation," I said.

"The tank's filtered to keep out the bugs. No hot and cold running water but I have a shower stall on the back porch.

"Mind if I use it?" Abba said.

"You bet you can, pretty lady. You'll feel lots

175

better, even if the water's only warm."

"Best news I've heard all night," she said.

"I see none of you brought a change of clothes. I got a closet full left by various people over the years. Everything's clean, and you don't have to worry about giving them back."

"Is that a Cajun thing?" I asked. "Bertram had loads of clothes last time I spent the night in his camp on Pontchartrain."

"How's that ol' Cajun doing?" J.P. asked.

"He never changes. As ornery as ever," I said.

"I need to get up to the city for a visit."

"Yes you do," I said.

J.P. pointed. "There's a chemical toilet through that door; not fancy, though it's reliable. The mosquitoes aren't bad this time of year. Everything is screened, including the veranda, so there's no bug problem as long as you stay inside. Well, except for a few roaches and such."

We followed him up the creaky staircase. As he'd said, there were plenty of empty bedrooms. Rory practically collapsed on one of the beds and was soon snoring loudly. After Slick jumped up beside him, J.P. closed the door, and then led Abba and me down a narrow hall.

"This is lovely," she said.

J.P. opened a hall closet, grabbing a handful of sheets and towels.

"Even have clean sheets," he said, tossing a fluffy towel to Abba. "The shower stall is on the porch in back. There's a bulb that works, and you probably want to check for bugs before you climb in. Like I said, the water's only warm, though I guarantee you won't freeze to death."

"I'm in heaven," she said.

"The camp is even air-conditioned. Don't need it this time of year. Just crack the windows. They all have screens to keep out the bugs and other critters."

"Thanks, J.P.," I said. "You're the best."

J.P. handed Abba a lantern. "Every now and then I get a coon or possum out there on the porch. They're friendly. Just shake your lantern in their direction and tell them to scat."

"And if they don't?" Abba asked.

"Just holler. I'll be more than happy to come help you out."

"No thanks. I'll take care of myself."

"And I'll bet you can, little lady," he said. "Not much of the night left. Get some rest. I'm going fishing before breakfast, and I'll let you sleep in."

Abba started for the shower, and I turned for one of the unoccupied bedrooms. J.P. tapped my shoulder, stopping me in my tracks.

"This doesn't seem like a school outing, and I have a feeling you haven't told me everything I need to know. Tomorrow, before we proceed any further, you need to explain what we're dealing with."

Chapter 21

Abba awoke to the aroma of scrambled eggs wafting up the stairway. She found an old cotton robe in her bedroom closet, put it on, started downstairs to investigate, and followed her nose to the kitchen. She found Jean Pierre standing in front of a four-burner propane stove, stirring something in a cast iron skillet with a wooden spoon.

"Smells wonderful," she said.

When J.P. turned around with a big Cajun grin, Abba saw his long apron decorated with a giant bottle of red Tabasco sauce."

"Morning," he said. "Sleep well?"

"The shower was wonderful, even if I had to share the stall with a big spider. Soon as my head hit the pillow, I was down for the count. I didn't realize how tired I was."

J.P. poured coffee into a cup from the metal pot simmering on one of the burners and placed it on the kitchen table in front of her. Retrieving a carton of cream from the big red ice chest, he sat it on the table along with a sugar pourer.

"Cream and sugar?" he said.

"I usually drink my coffee black. This looks extra strong. It probably needs a little lacing."

"If the spoon don't stand up in the cup, then it ain't real Cajun coffee."

"Why do you talk like that? Wyatt told me you have a college degree. Surely they taught English at USL."

"I'm a homicide detective. People affected by murder often conveniently forget everything they know. My patois gets me in lots of doors," he said.

"Why are you a homicide detective? Wyatt said you have a performing arts degree."

"Wyatt's not usually such a gossip," he said.

"I was cursing you for being such a sexist. He was taking up for you."

"Good for him. I'm not a sexist. I'm Cajun, and Cajuns like to flirt."

"Well, I'm Creole. I'm not used to it, so please stop."

Slick and Lucky bounded through the open door before J.P. could respond to her comment. After removing the skillet from the burner, he opened two cans of dog food and took it out to the porch to feed the hounds.

"I'm sorry if I've offended you. It's a cultural thing. Cajuns express themselves openly. If they like something, they tell you; if they don't like something they tell you. It was the way I was raised, and I'm too old to change."

Abba shook her head as she sipped the hot coffee from the metal cup.

"Why are you a homicide detective if you have a degree in the performing arts? There are plenty of acting jobs here in south Louisiana. Wyatt told me you've been an extra in several movies already."

"I enjoy making movies though it's not all I need in life. I'm a thrill freak. I like the danger and excitement that goes with detective work. I also like solving puzzles. The job is natural for me."

J.P. turned away from her and returned to the cast iron skillet on the propane stove.

"Who taught you how to cook?" she asked.

"My mama, aunts, uncles, grandparents, and my daddy. All Cajuns like to cook."

"A cultural thing," she said.

"That's right."

"What are you cooking? It smells wonderful."

"Eggs scrambled with crawfish, red and green bell peppers, onion, and a chopped up, seedless jalapeno, and a side of grits. Ready to eat?"

"I'd be lying if I said no," she said.

J.P. fixed a plate for Abba and one for himself. They were soon sitting at the table, enjoying breakfast like an old married couple, J.P. doctoring his already spicy eggs with Tabasco sauce. Abba didn't speak until she'd finished the last bite. Grabbing the coffee pot from the burner, she topped up each of their cups.

J.P. smiled when she said, "You know I'm black, don't you?"

"You may be African-American, but you ain't exactly black. Hell, I'm darker than you are."

"You have a tan. You obviously spend lots of time outside."

"I hunt and fish whenever I get the chance. Didn't sit too well with my ex."

"She didn't like your hunting and fishing?"

"Hated it. She wanted me home every night before dark. Kind of hard to do if you're a homicide detective."

"You like black women?"

J.P. laughed aloud. "I like all women. I just haven't found one yet that'll put up with me."

"I hear that," she said.

"What about you? You have a steady boyfriend?"

"I'm in college at Tulane. I'm going to be a doctor."

"You're smart and will make a good one," he said. "You'll have to work on your bedside manner, though."

"Will you shut up? Just about the time I reach the point where I'm starting to like you, you say something totally ignorant."

J.P. tapped his head. "Cajun culture," he said. "Can't change it."

Abba grabbed the dishes from the table and took them to the sink. He joined her when she filled the basin and began washing them.

"Thanks for your help," he said. "I'm used to doing for myself and Lucky."

"No problem. My mom died when I was young, and I always helped my dad with the chores around the house."

"Sorry to hear about your mom. How old were you when you lost her?"

"Nine," she said. "Cancer got her."

"Bet your dad was upset. Good thing you were there for him."

"He was crushed. It's going on twenty years now, and he still hasn't remarried. My dad is white. Mom was black. He didn't know he was white when they married."

J.P.'s eyebrows rose when he glanced at her. "You making this up?" he asked.

"Long story," she said. "Maybe I'll tell it to you sometime if I don't kill you first."

When they'd finished washing the dishes and tidying up, J.P. returned to the stove.

"Wyatt and the big boy will be waking up soon. Want to help me cook some more eggs?"

When Rory and I awoke and went downstairs, we found J.P. and Abba sitting on the covered veranda that encircled the house. The dogs were roughhousing over a bone, Abba giggling like a

181

schoolgirl and J.P. laughing at some joke we hadn't heard. Rory was gazing at breakfast waiting for us on the kitchen table and paying no attention to the two outside. They seemed startled when I stuck my head through the door to tell them we were up.

"We were wondering if you two were going to sleep all day," Abba said.

"I slept like a baby," I said. "Now, my stomach's growling."

"Abba and I already ate. You better get to the table and stake your claim before big boy eats it all."

Despite J.P.'s warning, I needn't have worried. There was plenty of food on the table, even for Rory's giant appetite. He was smiling when he finally finished eating and wiped his lips with a big checkerboard napkin.

"What now?" I asked.

"Let's sit on the deck," J.P. said. "Sun's out today for a change, and we can take in a few rays while you bring me up to speed about what we're dealing with here."

The deck jutted out over the water, and we got our first glimpse of the swamp in the daylight. At the same time, it was both magnificent and frightening. The water in front of J.P.'s camp was open. Cypress trees with bloated trunks grew in the shallow, coffee-colored water. A big gator was floating beneath us, apparently waiting for a treat from J.P. J.P. didn't disappoint, feeding him marshmallows stuck to the end of a long pole.

"Can't keep enough of these things around," he said. "Them gators do love their marshmallows."

"Who would have thought," I said.

A big fish broke the surface, sending slow-moving ripples across the still water. Blue herons circled overhead, and a crane was busy fishing in the shallows.

"Are the alligators dangerous?" Rory asked.

"Not unless you run out of marshmallows," J.P. said. "They ain't the only predators in this swamp. There's hogs, snakes, bobcats, black bear, and probably wolves and mountain lions."

"How big is the swamp?" Abba asked.

"Seventy-thousand acres. About half is a permanently protected wildlife refuge. It's in the middle of the Pearl River Wildlife Management Area. The whole thing is really huge."

"It's beautiful here," Abba said. "And so peaceful. No engine noise; only the sound of birds, wind, and water lapping against the dock."

"I spend as much time here as I can," J.P. said. "This swamp hasn't changed in a thousand years. There are places you can only get to in a boat, and others you can't get to at all."

"That's what worries me," I said.

"Better start from the beginning."

"It's a long story," I said.

"Don't matter none. We ain't going nowhere till I hear it."

"It has to do with a woman," I said.

J.P. glanced at Abba to gauge her reaction to his comment after he said, "Don't it always?"

"I was just starting to warm up to you," she said.

"Just kidding," he said. "Do I know this woman?"

"I don't think so. She was the daughter of a rich client of mine. I fell hard for her. When her twin sister Dauphine committed suicide, Desire vowed to join a convent and become a nun."

"Of course," J.P. said. "The Vallee twins. I remember the details from the news, and Bertram filled me in on what happened to you afterward."

"I flipped out, fell off the wagon, and went begging to an old flame. She took me in, though the relationship didn't last long. When she kicked me out, I came to my senses and sobered up. While I was away, Bertram got me a job from a Hollywood

183

producer filming in town. He hired me to investigate the murder of a prominent actor on Goose Island. It's where J.P. and I met."

"How long ago was that?" Abba asked.

"Not more than a couple of years."

"I would have guessed you two had known each other all your lives," she said.

"That case almost got us both killed," J.P. said. "People tend to bond quickly when their lives depend on it."

"What happened?" Rory asked.

The big Scot shook his head when J.P. asked, "Know what a rougarou is?"

"Neither do I," Abba said. "I'll bite. What is it?"

"A Cajun werewolf."

Abba and Rory waited for the punch line. There wasn't one. They both turned their attention to me.

"A story for another time," I said. "We need to tell J.P. about Desire."

"That's right," J.P. said. "Rougarous and Swamp Monsters can wait till later. At least rougarous. There may be Swamp Monsters running around Honey Island Swamp. I haven't heard of any rougarou sightings."

"We'll tell you later," I said when Abba protested.

"Later on when we're sitting around a glowing campfire," J.P. said. "Once you hear the story, it's almost a guarantee you'll cuddle up close to me tonight."

"In your dreams," Abba said. "Tell him about Desire, Wyatt."

I repeated the tale of waking up to the ghostly funeral procession, seeing Desire in the limousine, and then finding the pendant.

"The funeral procession filled me with fear that Desire is somehow in grave danger. Abba works for Desire's mother. We met when I visited Junie Bug to see if she shared my fears. She did and gave me the names of the two people that came for her daughter the day she left for some unknown convent. Sister Gertrude and Father Fred."

I showed him Exethelon.

The ceremonial dagger transfixed J.P.'s attention instantly. He whistled softly.

"This is a beautiful weapon," he said. "I don't believe I've ever seen such craftsmanship in a dagger."

"Rory made it. We looked him up last night because we hoped he could tell us who he'd made it for."

J.P. continued fondling the dagger as he turned his attention to Rory.

"Son," he said. "This is the finest piece of cutlery I've ever held in my hands. Remind me to take back all those nasty things I said about you. What do these engravings mean?"

"That, lad, I do not know. I made the dagger for a sorceress. She showed me drawings of what she wanted to be engraved on the blade. All I know about them is that they have a magical meaning, and the dagger itself is magical."

J.P.'s brow grew furrowed when he turned his attention to me.

"Tell me how you came to find this beautiful hog sticker?"

"I'd rather not say."

"What kind of happy horseshit answer is that?"

"You're a homicide detective. For obvious reasons, telling you the story presents a problem."

"You trying to say you found it at a murder scene?"

I nodded. "Murders we discovered while searching for Desire."

"Murders? How many and when did they occur?"

"Three victims. Last night. One of them was Father Fred."

"Impossible," he said. "There's nothing on the wire about a triple homicide last night."

"Good, then maybe Abba and I had a group hallucination."

J.P.'s eyes narrowed as he stared at me for what seemed like a minute but was probably no more than ten seconds.

"Okay," he finally said. "I'm pretty sure neither you nor Abba killed anybody. What worries me is why you didn't report it to the police."

"For the same reason, I'm having trouble explaining the situation to you. I don't want you to arrest us and take us downtown."

"Maybe you better explain to me why I shouldn't do just that," he said.

Chapter 22

The big gator finally gave up his wait for another marshmallow and disappeared into the shallow depths of the brown water. Overhead, a pair of bald eagles circled as I racked my brain for an explanation why we didn't call the police after discovering a murder scene.

"Our trail of information led us to an orphanage run by Father Fred. He was dead when we got there, Exethelon buried in his heart. Two guards were also dead and all the people staying at the orphanage gone."

"So why didn't you call the police?"

"The place caught fire and burned to the ground before we had a chance to."

"Who started the fire?"

"It combusted spontaneously," I said.

"I'll buy lots of shit. I ain't buying that," he said. "Someone had to start the fire."

"The sorceress," Rory said. "She is also the person who slew the three men and allowed the prisoners to escape."

"Prisoners? You said it was an orphanage."

"We have it on good authority that Father Fred was trafficking in human slaves. He and Sister

187

Gertrude bought and sold people like cattle. I believe retribution was the motive for his death."

"And this sorceress lives somewhere in the Honey Island Swamp? How do you know that?"

"I learned as much when she commissioned me to craft Exethelon," Rory said.

"But you don't know where in the swamp?"

"We were hoping you did," I said.

J.P. pulled a cell phone from his pocket and dialed someone. We listened to the one-sided conversation until he'd finished.

"The orphanage burned last night," he said. "You weren't lying about that. There were no bodies found by the investigators. You sure you saw three dead people?"

"Like I said, maybe Abba and I had a group hallucination."

"Abba?"

"Now that I think about it, it seems more like a dream," she said.

"Okay," he said. "I'll worry about what you just told me sometime in the future. How do we go about finding this sorceress?"

"I'll admit, I haven't a clue," I said.

Abba nodded. "Me either."

"Then where the hell do we start?" J.P. asked, looking at Rory.

"Exethelon," the giant Scot said.

J.P. rolled the dagger in his hand. "Maybe you better explain to me how that's supposed to work."

"Return it to Wyatt, and you will see," Rory said.

I felt the power of the blade once I again held it in my hand. J.P.'s expression changed to disbelief when it began to radiate a golden glow.

"What the hell!" he said.

"Wyatt retrieved Exethelon from the dead man's heart. It is now forever his, along with all the powers it possesses. Its magic will only work for him. It will lead us to the sorceress."

"You aren't exactly dressed for a trek through the swamp," J.P. said. "You and Abba look as if you're on your way to a day of sightseeing in the French Quarter. Rory's wearing a kilt, and none of you have boots. I can't let you go deeper into the swamp dressed like this."

"This is the way Wyatt and I were dressed when we left home yesterday morning," Abba said. "Needless to say we haven't had a chance to change."

"What do you suggest?" I asked.

"Postpone the trip for a day or so," he said.

"Impossible for me," Abba said. "I can't take off from work that long."

"Nor can I," Rory said.

J.P. looked at me and said, "Wyatt? You got a plan B?"

"Is there someplace close where we can buy what we need?"

"There's a little settlement about a mile from here: a few houses, a café, a general store, and even a liquor store. If your credit card's big enough, we can get boots, jeans, hats, and supplies, and just about anything else we need there."

"Why not?" I said. "I just cashed a big ticket at the track. I'm flush right now, and I have a credit card I've only used once or twice. Let's check out the settlement. If my plastic doesn't ignite first, I'll pick up the tab."

✥✥✥

Back in the pontoon boat and heading back in the direction from which we'd come the previous night, we began to see many mostly ramshackle fishing camps on both sides of the wide channel. We hadn't noticed them because it had been too dark when we'd floated past. When we rounded a sweeping bend in the river swamp, we got another surprise.

189

Large, beautiful and obviously expensive houses occupied the banks of an expansive pond that had formed in the sweeping meander. They all had impressive docks occupied by luxurious boats. There was also a marina with a dockside restaurant, and a filling station, complete with a colorful Shell sign, for boats.

"Does this place have a name?" Abba asked.

"Not really, though the locals call it Richville," J.P. said.

"Those lavish houses and their manicured lawns look out of place for a swamp," I said.

"At least a million bucks apiece," J.P. said. "Some rich developer must have bribed someone in power for the rights to put it here, and has made a fortune doing it."

"Must be nice to have that kind of money," Abba said.

As we drifted toward the public dock we heard the whomp, whomp, whomp of an approaching helicopter. It descended over the large houses and disappeared from sight behind the trees.

"Ain't no roads into Richville," J.P. said. "People that own these houses have to boat in like everyone else, or fly in for the weekend in their private chopper."

"Tough duty," I said.

"Looks like they're planning to have a grand old Halloween party from the looks of all the decorations," Abba said.

Abba was right. Carved pumpkins, scary witches, and frightening ghouls draped with fake blood, and spray-on cobwebs decorated the docks, luxury boats, roofs, and yards of the little settlement. A chill in the air, Spanish moss hanging from tree branches, and the mist rising up from the water helped enhance the effect of the creepy decorations.

After J.P. had moored the pontoon boat, he led us up the boardwalk, past the filling station to a grocery and general store. A young woman dressed in denim pointed to the clothes aisle.

"Hope they have jeans large enough for Rory," I said.

"They will," J.P. said. "The place is sort of pricey, as you might imagine, but they have a little bit of everything."

J.P. was right about the jeans and the prices. I practically choked when I saw the sales tags. It didn't really matter though because I had a totally unexpected thirty plus grand in my bank account. As we selected boots, clothes, backpacks, and supplies, the tab began to quickly add up.

I must have had a constipated look on my face because J.P. asked, "You okay?"

"Nothing like a little sticker shock to jolt you back to reality."

The total bill came to almost two thousand dollars, and I strongly considered taking a shot of Rory's Southern Comfort he'd purchased at the little settlement's well-stocked liquor store. As we motored away from the high-dollar settlement, I drank from a jug of lemonade instead.

Clouds had begun covering the sky as we motored down the river, back to J.P.'s camp. Rory, Abba, and I arranged the packed ice chests, tents, and other equipment I'd purchased as we did. After drifting to the middle of the big pond, Abba glanced up at a flock of storks flying overhead.

"What now?" she asked.

"Wyatt must spin the blade," Rory, looking like a giant logger in his new jeans and boots, said. "Where it points is the direction in which we should go.

They watched as I gave the blade a spin, rotating as fluidly as a gyroscope before finally stopping.

"That way," Rory said, pointing.

Two brown pelicans took flight when J.P. cranked the engine.

"Hope this ain't a wild goose chase," he said.

Abba and I weren't so sure either. Rory walked to the front of the boat, Slick at his heels. He stood gazing ahead at the water passage we followed, hefting his broadsword and occasionally stroking its blade.

The water passage we followed was more than a swamp, it was an arboreal jungle filled with giant cypress trees on both sides of the narrow waterway. Their bloated trunks, Spanish moss draping their limbs, were huge and ageless.

"It's beautiful," Abba said. "What caused this swamp to be here?"

"It's a river swamp," J.P. said. "Water level fluctuates depending on the rainfall. When the water's high, it covers the little islands in between the meanders. When it's not, the high ground stands a few inches out of the water and is covered with hardwood trees and aquatic plants that can tolerate occasional soakings."

"Quite an ecosystem," Abba said.

"There are river swamps all over the world. This one's extra big because there are two rivers instead of just one. The Pearl and the West Pearl are miles apart but parallel each other. No way to map the damn thing because the channels change every time the place floods."

Feral hogs peeked at us from the thick underbrush of shore, unmindful of the alligators sunning on the bank. We'd left the main channel several times, following narrow and shallow chutes through the swamp.

There was no roof on J.P.'s pontoon boat, the branches of the surrounding trees draping almost to the water's surface. When Abba suddenly screamed, J.P. threw the motor into neutral and rushed to the side of the boat where she was kicking and squirming.

Something was moving on the floor of the boat. Lucky and Slick had it cornered and were circling it, barking and growling. I could see it was a big snake.

"Get away from it," J.P. said. "It's a cottonmouth."

Brushing past the two dogs, he slid the snake over the side of the boat with the paddle he was carrying. The snake was heavy and made a big splash when it hit the water. I watched as it swam away, finally disappearing into a pile of mostly submerged brush. Abba was still shaking, hugging herself as she bounced up and down on her toes. J.P. hugged her.

"It's gone," he said. "No harm done."

"It dropped out of the trees, onto my shoulders. Scared the living hell out of me," she said.

"This thing's got a canvas top. It's not sunny but now's as good a time as any to put it up."

Rory and I helped him raise the boat's roof, and we were soon covered with a layer of canvas.

"Do those big snakes live in trees?" Abba asked.

J.P. shook his head. "No, but they can climb. When the temperature's cool they like to sun themselves on the low-lying branches. The roof will keep them off of us if this chute doesn't get too narrow and hang us up."

"What if it does?" I asked.

J.P. dug into a wooden storage box, fished out a machete and tossed it to me.

"If it gets any tighter and narrower, we'll have to start chopping our way through and hope we don't go aground."

"Not to worry, laddie," Rory said. "My sword is all we'll need."

To show us, he felled a sapling with one stroke of the big sword.

"Good, because I have a hunch we're going to need you before the day is over," J.P. said.

Rory moved his lawn chair to the front of the boat, the sword resting across his knees.

"Say no more," he said. "Aila and I are ready for action."

"You name all the weapons you make?" J.P. asked.

"Of course," Rory said. "Though they aren't all as magical as Exethelon, they're all alive and thus require a name."

J.P. maneuvered the boat slowly and cautiously as floating limbs, and other debris became ever more prevalent. When the passage grew tight, Rory would stand on the bow of the boat and chop down the vegetation impeding us. Still not fully recovered from the incident with the snake, Abba sat shivering near the center of the boat.

"You okay?" I asked.

"Nothing a shot of Rory's Southern Comfort wouldn't cure," she said.

"I heard that," Rory said. "Your wish is my command, fair lady,"

I caught the silver flask he tossed to me, opened the lid, sniffed the contents, and then handed it to Abba.

"Maybe this will help," I said.

It was late in the day when we finally exited the narrow passage and entered a wider and deeper pond. J.P. killed the engine and threw out the anchor.

"I've never been this far into the swamp," he said. "I'm sure that not many people other than us ever have."

With the motor dead, the birds and other wildlife were the only sounds remaining. It felt, quite literally, as if we were in the middle of nowhere.

"Hope you know the way back," I said.

"My phone's GPS does," J.P. said.

"Then please don't drop it overboard," Abba said. "We'd never find our way back through this watery maze of wildlife and creeping vegetation."

The day was dreary, darkened by persistent cloud cover. Abba shivered and pulled a light sweater over her blouse. Rory helped J.P. find something to eat in the ice chest. They arranged mustard, mayonnaise, cheese, and bologna, along with a loaf of bread, on a folding table.

"Better enjoy it now," J.P. said. "We won't be able to carry all this food and drink when we have to start walking."

"We're lucky you're with us," I said. "Otherwise we'd be wandering around with no food at all."

"And definitely no whiskey," Rory said as he saluted J.P. with his flask.

"Thank Wyatt, not me," J.P. said.

"How far do you think we've come?" Abba asked.

"Probably not far in a straight line," J.P. said. "Unfortunately the chutes and meanders don't trend in straight lines. I'd be lost as a goose if it wasn't for the dagger pointing the way."

Exethelon must have been listening to the conversation because it suddenly began spinning like a top. We watched until it finally slowed to a halt.

"What the hell was that all about?" J.P. asked.

"It doesn't seem to be pointing anywhere," Abba said.

"Give it another spin, Wyatt," J.P. said.

I reached for Exethelon. As if suddenly welded in place, it refused to move. The golden glow turned red and became hot to the touch, smoke beginning to rise up off the blade.

"Rory, what's it doing?" I asked.

He didn't need to answer. As we watched in awe, the magical dagger rose up off the floor of the boat as it rotated slowly. Thick gray vapor soon completely enclosed it into a cottony cloud that increased in size as it moved out over the water. We watched it move up a tiny creek that was feeding the main channel. J.P. shut the ice chest, retrieved the anchor, and then started the motor.

"This is as far as we can go in the boat."

"What now?" Abba asked.

"Tie up to a tree and then go the rest of the way on foot. Either that or turn around and go back to the house."

Chapter 23

Tony watched as Eddie unfolded papers he'd removed from Wendell Swanson's passport wallet and then spread them out on the bar.

"What you got?" he asked.

"A betting ticket, a page someone tore from a daily racing form, and an advertisement for a horse auction," Eddie said.

"I didn't see anything except the passport and ticket to Belize."

"The wallet has a hidden pocket."

"Let me see the betting ticket," Tony said.

Eddie handed it to him, waiting as Tony spent a moment studying the information on the square piece of paper.

"Well?"

"It's a four-horse trifecta box from a race that took place two days ago," Tony said. "The same race that Lightning Bolt won,"

"Makes sense," Eddie said. "The page from the racing form is for that race. Swanson circled four horses. The same four horses in his trifecta. How much did he bet?"

"His thousand buck trifecta cost him a cool twenty-four grand," Tony said.

"You certain about that?"

"It's printed right here on the ticket. Swanson boxed Lightning Bolt and the top three horses based on the morning line odds."

"He must have been pretty sure he'd win," Eddie said.

"Well, he didn't," Tony said.

Eddie continued to study the page torn from the racing form.

"Another long shot finished second," he said. "Guess who owns the horse."

"Chuy Delgado?"

"Close but no cigar. Angus Anderson."

"Damn!" Tony said. "Wendell's old boss busted his trifecta. Bet that must have pissed him off."

"And ruined his chances of retiring in Belize. He'd have won close to a million bucks if the race had ended the way he picked it."

"He should have stuck with a sure thing and bet on Lightning Bolt to win," Tony said.

"Leopards don't change their spots. Wendell saw his chance to retire like a king in Belize and took a swing for the fence."

"And blooped a stinker to short center field instead."

"Enough already with the baseball cliches. What do you make of it?" Eddie said.

"Maybe it was Swanson's idea and not Frankie's to put shoe polish on Lightning Bolt's blaze."

"You should ask him."

"It's on my list," Tony said.

"It could mean Swanson was in on Frankie's little scam. If so, it might be the reason he was murdered. What do you think?"

Big Sam sauntered up to the bar before Tony had a chance to answer Eddie's question.

"Thought you boys were on your way out the door. Need more beer?"

"I'm floating," Tony said. "Got anything to eat?"

"You'll find the best po'boys and muffulettas in town, dressed or undressed, right here at Big Sam's."

"That's a powerful claim considering you're talking about the best in all of Nawlins. Can you back it up?"

"No brag, just fact. Try one. If you don't like it, then it's on the house."

"And your oyster po'boy?"

"The best."

"Talked me into it. Bring me one of those po'boys, and I'll take you up on your bet."

"Make mine a muffuletta," Eddie said.

"You won't be disappointed," Big Sam said.

Eddie and Tony were soon working on their sandwiches as Big Sam watched with a smile.

"Well?" he finally asked.

"Best oyster po'boy I ever ate," Tony said. "My own mother couldn't have made one any better. I'll have to start coming here for lunch when I'm in the neighborhood."

"Ditto for me," Eddie said. "I have to admit, this is the best muffuletta I've ever put in my mouth."

"Served on fresh Italian bread with sesame seeds."

"Love the olive salad, and all the salami and provolone. It's great."

Tony wiped his mouth with a napkin after washing down his last bite with cold Abita. He shoved the notice of the horse auction across the bar to Big Sam.

"Know anything about this?" he asked.

"Course I do," Big Sam said after scanning the clipping from the newspaper. "Sallisaw quarter horse sale. A big regional event that's held every spring up in Oklahoma."

"Ever been?"

"Lots of my customers go every year. They know how to raise good quarter horses up in Oklahoma."

"What about Wendell Swanson? Do you know if he ever went?"

"Before Mr. Anderson fired him, the two of them never missed it. Wendell had a good eye for horses."

"How long ago was that?" Eddie asked.

"That he was fired?"

"Yeah," Tony said.

"About three years. Probably the same sale as the date of this notice."

"Let me see that?" Tony said, taking a closer look. "Wonder why he was holding onto a notice of a three-year-old sale?"

Big Sam shook his head as he turned to leave them alone. "No idea on that one. Yell if you need another beer."

"Must have been important to him to hang on to the sale notice all that time," Eddie said.

Tony reached for his cell phone. "Let me just check it out."

Tony spent the next five minutes on the phone. Eddie could tell by his frown that he wasn't gleaning much information.

"What?" Eddie asked when he'd hung up.

"Secretary I talked with wouldn't give me the time of day. She did mention one thing that's kinda interesting."

"What?"

"She told me the quarter horse auction three years ago set an all-time sales record. One Oklahoma bred horse went for more than a million bucks."

"Sounds like a lot for a quarter horse."

"Don't know. What's important is the name of the horse that sold for the million bucks."

"Tell me," Eddie said.

"Thunder Bolt."

"You gotta be shitting me," Eddie said.

Tony didn't reply to Eddie's comment, calling to Big Sam instead to bring them their tab. After handing the little man another hundred and telling him to keep the change, Tony downed the last of his beer and started for the door.

"Where are you going in such a hurry?" Eddie asked.

"Sallisaw."

"Oklahoma's a long way from here. What do you think you'll find that you didn't get on the phone?"

Tony was already out the door. Even though his legs were short, Eddie had to hustle to keep up as he hurried toward his Mustang in the shell and gravel parking lot.

"Well?" he asked as Tony was unlocking the car.

"The name of the person that paid a million bucks for Thunder Bolt."

Eddie climbed into the front seat. "You don't intend to drive, do you? If you are, it'll take us a day to get there and another day to return."

Tony tapped the brakes and pulled to the side of the street. "I better call Frankie."

Frankie picked up on the first ring. "Talk to me," he said.

"Eddie and I need to go to Oklahoma."

"For what?"

"Answers to important questions in our investigation."

"Oklahoma's a long way from New Orleans. How you planning to get there?"

"Fly to the nearest airport, and then rent a car, unless you got a better plan."

"Where are you now?"

"About a mile from the racetrack."

"Wait for me in the infield. I'll pick you up soon as my pilot gets the chopper warmed up and ready."

Frankie hung up before Tony had a chance to reply.

"What?" Eddie asked, having heard only one side of the conversation.

"Frankie's coming for us in his helicopter. Up for a wild ride through this fog?"

Eddie laughed and shook his head when he said, "Do I have a choice?"

"Get in. We're going back to the track."

After parking the car, Tony and Eddie hiked through the cloying fog to the middle of the racetrack. The place was deserted. At that moment, it seemed like the loneliest place on the planet.

"You've really been shoveling out those hundred dollar bills," Eddie said. "Hope Frankie pays well."

"Last case I did for him he ate my ass out because the bill I give him wasn't high enough. Lil and I took a trip to Italy on the money I made and still had lots left over."

"Must be nice," Eddie said.

"Frankie's got more money than he can say grace over. He only buys the best, and only hires the best people. I know you'll never go to work for him. If you ever did, he'd treat you like a king."

"I'd say he's more likely to whack me for dating his beautiful daughter," Eddie said.

"In case you haven't noticed, Josie has him wrapped around her little finger. How's your relationship going?"

Eddie laughed. "Absolutely nowhere."

"I have eyes. I know better than that."

"She has one hard and fast rule that's stopping us from going much further."

"And that rule is?"

"No sex outside of marriage and no divorce, not ever, for any reason."

The sound of a turbocharged engine interrupted their conversation. Frankie's Jet Ranger landed in a swirl of fog and flying debris. When the passenger door opened, Frankie signaled them to join him.

They lifted off in a blanket of thick ground fog, finally emerging into clear sky and then flying over a city that looked as if it were being engulfed by an angry cloud.

Frankie laughed when Tony asked, "Can we make it to Oklahoma in this crate?"

"And then some," he said. "Fill me in on what we're looking for in Sallisaw."

"They have a spring quarter horse sale at the track every year," Tony said. "I've got a buttload of questions I couldn't get answers for over the phone. I also have a question for you."

"Hit me with it," Frankie said.

"Was it you that had Wendell Swanson put shoe polish on Lightning Bolt's blaze?"

"I don't have a clue what you're talking about?"

"The white blaze on Lightning Bolt's face," Eddie said. "Wendell covered it with black shoe polish before your race the other day."

"Though I knew Wendell from seeing him at the track, he was just a temporary employee. If he knew about my plans for the horse, he figured it out on his own."

"Must have, because he bet a pile of money on the race," Tony said.

"How much?"

"Twenty four grand."

"He didn't bet it to win, or it would have mucked up the final odds."

"Then maybe that's the reason he bet the way he did. He boxed a four-horse trifecta. Another long shot busted the box. One of Angus Anderson's horses."

Tony and Eddie both grinned when Frankie said, "That cheating asshole. What are you two laughing at?"

"Don't you think that's like the pot calling the kettle black?" Eddie asked.

"At least my con was the winning con."

"Don't you have any remorse about all those poor bettors that lost money because of you?"

"I don't feel sorry for any of those slobs that buy a racing form and bet on the ponies maybe once a week, or every now and then. If they're too stupid to know the name of the game, they may as well dump their money down the toilet."

Frankie shook his head when Eddie asked, "What exactly is the name of the game?"

Frankie didn't immediately answer. They were already high above the clouds, flying over the rolling terrain of central Louisiana. Frankie broke out a bottle of scotch and poured them drinks before answering.

"Dog eat dog and may the best man win," he finally said. "Enough about that. What are we likely to find in Oklahoma?"

"Wendell had an advertisement in his passport wallet for the spring quarter horse sale in Sallisaw. Problem is, it was from three years ago."

"And?"

"We think Wendell and Angus Anderson, his boss at the time, attended the sale. One of the horses, namely Lightning Bolt, sold for more than a million bucks. We need to find out if Anderson was the bidder, or maybe even the buyer."

"You gotta be kidding me," Frankie said.

"No, we ain't," Tony said.

"Then Anderson would have recognized the horse before the race," Frankie said.

"Maybe not, since Wendell had covered Lightning Bolt's most prominent physical feature with a bottle of shoe polish."

Frankie gazed out the window as they passed over the city of Shreveport, and the eastern periphery of haunting Caddo Lake.

"I'm having trouble getting my head around this," he said.

"There already was bad blood between Swanson and Anderson," Eddie said. "Maybe when Anderson

204

found out Wendell had pulled a fast one on him, he had his big Mexican henchman whack him."

"That's just one of the questions we need answers for," Tony said. "We still don't have a clue if Lightning Bolt is still alive. If he is, how do we go about finding him?"

"What do you really think? Is the horse dead?"

"I don't have any hard and fast answers. My gut tells me he's still alive."

Frankie turned his gaze to Eddie. "What's your opinion?"

"I'm starting to think you need to cool it with the Mexican mob. They may not be responsible for the two murders."

"You know something you're not telling me?"

"We got a few things working. Some of them we didn't figure on," Tony said.

"How much longer till you know something concrete?"

"No investigation ever goes as fast as you think it should. We're right where we need to be. If Lightning Bolt is alive, Eddie and I will find him. If we do, Jojo will be one happy little boy. If we don't . . ."

"And you think we'll get the answers we need in Oklahoma?"

"Don't know," Tony said. "That's why we're on our way to Sallisaw instead of enjoying this scotch on your veranda."

205

Chapter 24

The headquarters for the yearly quarter horse sale in Sallisaw was at the track. Much as he'd done in New Orleans, Frankie's pilot landed the chopper in the infield. Their unexpected landing must have caused a stir. A police car, its blue lights flashing, and two police officers were waiting for them as they exited the chopper.

The two officers were complete opposites, one tall and the other short. The short officer's nametag identified him as Olsen. He had a weak chin, a pencil mustache, and a balding head. The taller officer with thick glasses never removed his hat or his hand off his revolver.

"What the hell do you think you're doing?"

Eddie grabbed Frankie's shoulder, looked him in the eye, and shook his head.

"Let me handle this. What's your problem, Officer Olsen?"

"I got no problem," he said. "You want to come down to the station and tell me what yours is?"

Eddie pulled his I.D. out of his wallet and showed it to him.

"We're with the Federal D.A.'s office. We're here on official business. You want to dial your superior and let me talk to him?"

"What kind of business?"

"That's privileged information. Now, we need to get on with our investigation. Can you give us a ride to the administration office?"

Officer Olsen blinked twice before speaking. "Sure, get in."

After dropping them in front of the administration building, Officers Olsen and his lanky partner drove away in a trail of dust.

"Pretty slick," Frankie said. "What would you have done if he'd asked to speak to your boss?"

"I'd have called Wyatt. He would have covered for me."

"And if Wyatt wasn't around?"

"Guess we don't have to worry about that, and those two saved us a quarter-mile hike."

"You're good," Frankie said. "I like it."

The administration building was a two-story, ell-shaped, flat-roofed structure that looked as if someone had built it on the cheap. Tony was almost through the building's front door when he stopped and turned around.

"Quit stroking it, you two. It's almost five. If we don't hurry, we'll have to stay here until tomorrow."

"How do you know where to go?" Frankie asked.

"From the address on the sales notice. This building. Room 105."

A middle-aged secretary with wire-framed glasses perched atop her head was straightening her desk, apparently in the middle of shutting things down for the day.

"May I help you?" she asked.

Eddie whipped out his I.D. again and showed it to her.

"We're with the Federal District Attorney's office. We have a few questions that need answers."

Her tone was indignant when she said, "I wasn't told of any impending investigation."

An older man that looked enough like the woman to be her brother stuck his head out of the office.

"Who is it, Velma?"

"These gentlemen are with the Federal D.A.'s office," she said.

"Oh? I'm Orville Pendergrass. How can I help you?"

"What's your position, Mr. Pendergrass?" Tony asked.

"Director of sales," he said. "Who are you?"

"Tony Nicosia," he said, extending his hand. "The two gentlemen with me are Eddie Toledo and Frankie Smith. Can we impose upon you for a few minutes of your time?"

"What's this all about?" Mr. Pendergrass asked.

"Nothing that pertains to you or your organization, I assure you. We just need your help in an ongoing investigation that we aren't privy to discuss with you," Eddie said. "Can we have a few moments of your time?"

"Of course," he said. "Velma, you can go home now. I'll lock up when I finish with these gentlemen."

"You sure?"

She smiled and started for the door when he nodded and said, "I'll take care of this. See you tomorrow morning. Please come into my office and have a seat."

There were only two chairs in front of Pendergrass' military-style desk.

"I'll stand over here," Frankie said, motioning Tony and Eddie to take the chairs.

"Now please tell me how I can help you?"

"We have a few questions about your yearly quarter horse sale, specifically the one you had three years ago. Do you have a list of potential buyers that attended the sale?"

"Of course we do," he said. "The sale is exclusive. Buyers come from all over the world, and we have to prequalify them before letting them bid on the stock."

"Mind if we have a look at your list?" Eddie asked.

"This will take a minute," Pendergrass said. "I already shut my computer down for the night."

"Sorry we're keeping you overtime," Tony said. "This shouldn't take long."

"No problem," he said. "I'm an old bachelor and take my meals at the diner in town. No one's waiting at home for me."

Pendergrass didn't respond when Tony said, "Sorry to hear about that."

When the computer finally booted, he pulled up a program and hit the print button. In a few seconds, the old printer across the room began to whirr. After it had spit out three pages, Pendergrass removed it from the printer and handed it to Tony.

"This list is in alphabetical order. I don't find the name of the person I'm looking for. Is it possible it got left off the list?"

"Not possible. If their name isn't there, then they didn't attend the sale."

"Do you have a list of the names of the horses and who purchased them?"

"Of course," Pendergrass said, printing the list without Tony having to ask.

"I see that a horse named Lightning Bolt was sold for a million one hundred thousand dollars."

Pendergrass smiled. "Yes, a record that still stands."

"And the purchaser was a man named Conrad Finston. Is it possible that this person Finston was someone else and using an alias?"

"Impossible," Pendergrass said. "Mr. Finston is a well-known breeder of quarter horses. We've dealt with him many times in the past. I assure you that it was he that purchased the horse."

"Do you have a list of the unsuccessful bidders?" Eddie asked.

"Not in this database," Pendergrass said. "Our resident auctioneer and his staff keep those records."

"Can we talk with him?" Tony asked.

Pendergrass glanced at his watch. "He'll be in his office, though at this hour he may be a little . . . How should I say this? In his cups."

Pendergrass nodded when Tony said, "So he's a drinker?"

"The finest auctioneer in Oklahoma," Pendergrass said. "Except for his little drinking problem."

"We'll muddle through it because we really need to talk to him," Eddie said.

"His office is in the sales barn. I'll accompany you."

The Sallisaw racetrack had hosted horse races until a failing economy had sent it into bankruptcy in 2010. Though never really world-class, the facility appeared far more than a large oval track with a few wooden bleachers. Now, the fading structure sat unused, a diva awaiting fans that had deserted her forever for a younger voice.

The stables, paddock area, and exercise paths were also empty, looking ghostly as the sun was already beginning to set in the western sky. They followed Pendergrass to a large sales barn, the only building in the entire facility with a fresh coat of paint. The sign over the door said, Home of the Annual Sallisaw Quarter Horse Sale.

The inside of the sales barn featured steel bleachers, a dirt floor, and the smell of manure. A microphone used by the auctioneer waited on a raised wooden dais. A row of wooden holding pens fronted one of the walls. Something was inside one, kicking and trying to get out. When a woman screamed, Eddie vaulted over the fence to help.

An obviously disturbed white stallion was turning in rapid circles as it kicked at the walls with its hind feet. An attractive young woman with ash blond hair draping her shoulders, and dressed in faded denim and a red Western shirt tied in such a way as to show off her bare midriff was pinned between the horse and the gate. She'd backed up as far as she could, and there was no place left for her to go.

Eddie quickly got between her and the stallion and began waving his arms and shouting. When the horse rose up on its hind legs, Eddie grabbed the rope dangling from the beast's neck and began easing him toward himself. He motioned the young woman with a cock of his head to get the hell out of the pen. Climbing the fence, she straddled it.

"Thank you," she mouthed to him before dropping to the other side.

Too busy trying to rein in the big stallion Eddie had little time to react to her pretty face and winsome smile.

"Whoa, big fellow," he said.

When he pulled close enough, he clutched the horse's bridle and began patting his neck. The white horse's demeanor calmed immediately.

"It's okay," he said.

A bow-legged man of short stature raced into the pen, took the rope, and led the horse away. He shook Eddie's hand when he returned alone. He was clad in manure-stained jeans and a torn Western shirt of unknown vintage. His leather cowboy hat was also old, oily and perched on his balding head. His clothes and breath reeked of whiskey.

"Son, you got a set of balls on you," he said. "White Lightning is one of the meanest stallions to come through this sales barn. He's already terrorized a couple of our handlers to the point that one of them quit."

"Why do you put up with that kind of behavior?" Tony asked.

"Cause he's a racing champ with a royal bloodline some buyers will pay a king's ransom for."

The little man smiled when Tony said, "Like Lightning Bolt?"

"White Lightning and Lightning Bolt are brothers. Makes sense to me that White Lightning's as good as his brother and someday he's gonna make some stud farm a bunch of money in fees. I'm betting I know right now who'll end up with him."

"And who would that be?" Eddie asked.

"Mr. Conrad Finston, the same person that bought Lightning Bolt."

"What makes you think that?" Eddie said.

"He's both a breeder and a collector. He buys every horse he possibly can that's conceived from that particular bloodline."

Pendergrass stepped in front of Tony. "Obadiah, these gentlemen are with the authorities."

The little man extended his hand to Tony. "I'm Ob Stuart," he said. "I'm not under arrest, am I?"

"Why hell no," Tony said, shaking his hand. "Like Mr. Pendergrass said, we just have a few questions to ask you."

Ob rubbed his chin as he assessed the way the visitors were dressed.

"You boys don't look like cops."

"We just made ourselves comfortable for the long flight here."

"Where you out of?" Ob asked.

"Washington," Eddie quickly said.

Tony gave him no further chance to continue his own line of questions.

"I'm Tony, the man that saved the girl is Eddie, and this man behind me is Frankie."

Ob gave Frankie an assessing glance. "You look familiar. Do I know you?"

"I get that a lot," Frankie said. "Guess I got a common-looking face."

"What's your last name, Frankie?" Ob asked.

"Smith," Frankie said, giving Eddie a sideways glance. "How much are you asking for White Lightning?"

"More than a cop makes in a lifetime," he said. "That's for sure."

"Guess you're right about that," Frankie said. "Just curious."

"Probably something like two million dollars considering what Lightning Bolt sold for as a colt."

"Lightning Bolt is the reason we're here," Tony said.

"I thought as much," Ob said. "We heard someone killed him down in Louisiana. Damn shame! One of the best quarter horses I ever seen. Believe me, I seen quite a few."

"Mr. Pendergrass told us who bought the horse. Do you remember any of the other serious bidders?" Eddie asked.

"There was only one," Ob said.

"You remember his name?"

"Sure do. Wendell Swanson."

"Was Angus Anderson with him?" Eddie asked.

Ob shook his head. "He was alone. As I recall, his last bid was nine hundred fifty thousand."

"Sure about that amount? It was three years ago."

"I remember because we'd already passed our all-time high bid. I was waiting on Wendell to be the first person to bid more than a million bucks. It was his bid. He stopped short by fifty thousand dollars."

"Why do you suppose that was?" Tony asked.

"Hit his limit, I guess," Ob said. "Strange, though."

213

Tony and Eddie exchanged glances. "What's that?" Tony asked.

"Wendell was bidding for Angus Anderson. If Mr. Anderson wants something, he don't let money stand in his way. Seems unlikely to me he'd bid nine hundred and fifty thousand and not a million."

"What are you getting at?" Tony said.

"The reason Mr. Anderson fired him."

"Which was?" Tony said.

"Not like some people say for giving Mr. Anderson's horses a belly bomb in New Mexico."

"What, then?" Tony asked.

"For my money, someone paid Wendell a wad of cash to stop bidding when he did. More than getting him fired, it might even be what got him killed down in south Louisiana."

"You think it was Conrad Finston who bribed Wendell to throw the auction?"

Ob put his hands in the air and took a step backward. "I never said that. I'm just an old drunk. Don't believe a word I tell you." He glanced at the Timex on his wrist. "Hope you boys are finished with your questions cause it's past my bedtime."

They watched him limp away through the back door of the sales barn.

"Not only is he a sot, but he's also a crazy old man," Mr. Pendergrass said. "Please disregard his innuendos concerning Mr. Anderson and Mr. Finston."

Tony nodded. "I don't believe a word he said."

"Neither do I," Eddie said.

"You are wise not to," Pendergrass said.

"Say, Mr. Pendergrass, that young woman seemed familiar to me. Who is she?" Eddie asked.

"Jessica Smith," he said. "The widow of Kenny Smith, the jockey murdered in New Orleans."

Chapter 25

The facility used an old Jeep to drive potential customers around the track area. It was already after dark when Mr. Pendergrass took them to the infield where Frankie's chopper awaited.

"Thanks for all your help," Tony said, shaking Pendergrass' hand.

"Glad to be of service," he said.

"Say, Mr. Pendergrass, what's the story on Jessica Smith?" Eddie asked.

"Dirt poor, on food stamps, and mucking stables to try and earn enough money to pay the bills for herself and her baby."

"Can't her parents help her?"

"Both deceased. She has distant relatives in California. Kenny met her there while he was racing. That's where she moved from after they'd married. Except for her baby boy, I'm afraid she's all alone in the world."

"Where does she live?"

"Kenny was an up and coming jockey and made good money while he was alive. Jessica has a little frame house not far from Main street. At least it's paid for, free and clear, from the money Kenny earned as the winning jockey in a stakes race in California."

Eddie fumbled for his wallet, pulled out two twenties and a ten and handed the bills to Mr. Pendergrass.

"Please give her this," he said.

"You don't have to do that. I assure you, she's a strong-willed woman and resents being thought of as a charity case."

"Then tell her it's a gift to buy Halloween candy with," Eddie said. "Either that or overtime money that she's earned."

"Thank you, Mr. Toledo. I will see that she gets it."

Pendergrass sat watching from the driver's seat of the Jeep as the chopper lifted off the infield and banked south, heading for New Orleans.

"I'm developing a new opinion of you," Frankie said when they'd reached altitude.

"How's that?" Eddie asked, holding his empty glass out as Frankie began dispensing scotch.

"You're brave, generous, and I like the way you handled those two cops. Both you and Tony think fast on your feet. I like that. How'd you learn to handle horses?"

"No clue. I've never been on a horse in my life," Eddie said.

"You're shitting me," Frankie said.

"Nope, I grew up in urban New Jersey. Only horses I ever saw were in parades."

"Then how the hell did you know how to handle that big stallion?"

"Don't know, other than I watched a million and one Western movies while I was growing up."

"I may have to change my opinion of you again," Frankie said. "That was dumb. You could have been killed."

"My mom always said if I had as much between my ears as I have between my legs, I'd be really dangerous."

"Your mother said that?"

"Not in those exact words, though that's what she meant."

"What about the rest of your family?"

"I have three sisters, two older and one younger. My dad died of a heart attack in his forties. I was the only male in the house growing up. It made me the man of the family, even when I was young."

"How's your heart?" Frankie asked.

"Solid as a rock. I must have inherited Mom's genes and not Dad's."

"That's good to know," Frankie said. "Where'd you go to school?"

Eddie laughed. "What is this, twenty questions?"

"Just curious."

"I have a degree in forensic science from Rutgers, and a law degree from the University of Virginia."

"Impressive," Frankie said.

"I worked for the F.B.I. after law school."

"Then how did you wind up with the Federal D.A.'s office?"

"Someone there must have liked me and pulled strings to get me transferred. I'm still not exactly sure how that came about, but it's worked out for me."

"Did you like the F.B.I. ?"

"I like investigation, and I help Tony every chance I get."

"What do you think, Tony? Is Eddie any good at P.I. work?"

Tony didn't answer. He'd fallen asleep, his eyes closed and his chin resting on his chest.

"Guess he can't handle his scotch like us," Eddie said.

Frankie smiled, tapped glasses with him, and said, "That's another thing I like about you."

"Wish your beautiful daughter liked me as much," Eddie said.

217

"I'm pretty sure she does," Frankie said.

"Why do you think that?"

"She told Adele."

Eddie had no reply for Frankie's declaration and decided to change the subject to something not quite so touchy.

"We got lots of information today. Wish I knew more about Conrad Finston." When Frankie made a face, Eddie said, "You know him?"

"Oh, I know him all right. He has a large horse farm in Florida. He breeds both thoroughbreds and quarter horses and owns the Finston chain of hotels."

"Wow, then he's mega-rich. Did you buy Lightning Bolt from him?"

"Not exactly," Frankie said.

"Maybe you'd better explain."

"I borrowed the horse."

"Does Finston know Lightning Bolt is missing?"

Frankie's wry grin melded into a grim expression. "He don't know yet that I borrowed the horse."

Eddie shook Tony's shoulder until he opened his eyes. "Wake up. Frankie just told me something I think you need to hear."

Still half asleep, Tony rubbed his eyes as Frankie repeated what he'd just told Eddie. Before he was half finished, Tony was wide awake.

"Let me get this straight," Tony said. "Finston's chief trainer lent you Finston's horse for one race so you could teach some chumps in New Orleans a lesson."

"That's right."

"Surely, Finston knows by now that his horse is gone."

"He owns lots of properties including a Swiss chalet in the Alps. He's there now and won't be back until next week. Jensen, his chief trainer, ain't about to tell him, and neither am I."

"Say we find Lightning Bolt, and that's a big if. Who you gonna give the horse to, Jojo or Finston?"

The chopper wobbled as the pilot flew it through a cloud. When they emerged, Frankie glanced out at the lights of a city below instead of immediately answering Tony's question.

"You think we got a chance Lightning Bolt is still alive?" he finally asked.

"Earlier today, I thought he was dead. Right now, I'm not so sure."

"And if he ain't?"

"If Lightning Bolt ain't dead, and that's still a big if, I'd bet good money he's in a stall right now at Anderson's horse farm," Tony said.

"What's your reasoning for believing that?" Frankie asked.

"Want me to tell him, Eddie?"

"You're on a roll," Eddie said. "Go for it."

Frankie freshened their drinks with more scotch and ice. "Yeah, Tony, tell me what I'm missing here."

"One of the main reasons we wanted to visit the sales barn was to find out if Anderson and Swanson went to the auction together. They didn't. Swanson was alone."

"So?"

"Wendell Swanson bid almost a million dollars for Lightning Bolt but stopped short, letting Finston outbid him. It tells me one thing and implies another."

"What?"

"Anderson had enough trust in Swanson to authorize him to spend a million dollars of his. It also means he wanted the horse real bad."

"Maybe a million dollars was his top bid," Frankie said.

"If so, then why didn't he bid that much?"

"Because Finston went over that amount before he had a chance to."

Tony shook his head. "You heard what Ob Stuart said. He could have bid a million but stopped short by fifty grand. Most importantly, he thinks it was the reason Anderson fired him."

"You may be right," Frankie said. "A few hundred thousand here and there is peanuts to a man like Anderson. His company spends billions drilling for oil in the Gulf of Mexico."

"Exactly," Tony said.

Even if he did fire Swanson for throwing the bid, what does it have to do with him having the horse now?"

"Anderson coveted that horse. Swanson knew it," Tony said. "Swanson also knew he would recognize the horse. That's why he covered his blaze with shoe polish."

"Anderson figured out he'd been duped and decided to get even with you," Eddie said.

"Then why did he have Chuy Delgado's son-in-law whacked?"

"Don't know yet. That's still a question we need an answer for," Tony said.

"Maybe he saw a chance to pin the murder on you," Eddie said.

"And then stole Lightning Bolt, and had his newspapers and wire services concoct a false story about his death," Tony said.

"And you think maybe the dead horse was a plant and not Lightning Bolt," Frankie said.

"Maybe, though it don't really matter," Tony said. "Big Sam, a former jockey believes Lightning Bolt is dead, and so does Pendergrass and Ob Stuart."

"It just don't make sense," Frankie said. "Why would he have someone killed for a horse that he can never breed or race again, or for that matter ever let anyone know that he has?"

"Don't know," Tony said. "Eddie and me intend to find out before we go making accusations."

"How you gonna do that?" Frankie asked.

Tony held his glass for Frankie to pour him some more scotch. "Don't know yet."

More than two hours had passed since they'd left Sallisaw. Now, they could see the ephemeral glow of New Orleans shrouded by cloud cover in the distance. It would soon be Halloween, the moon not yet full. Frankie yawned.

"It's getting late. Let's call it a day and go to the farm. I'll have the boys get your car in the morning."

"No can do," Tony said. "Eddie and I have one more place to visit tonight."

"Can't it wait until tomorrow?"

"Your man, Bruno Baresi's in jail, charged with a murder you say he didn't commit."

"I got lawyers working on it," Frankie said.

"Not good enough," Tony said. "Anderson's bodyguard, Lonzo Galvez was in a bar with Wendell Swanson the night he was murdered. We need to find out if he was also at the restaurant where Diego Contrado was killed. What's the name of the restaurant and who is your contact there?"

"Pinky's on Toulouse. Pinky Robinette owns the place and used to work for me."

"Still on good terms?"

Frankie smiled. "If he wasn't, he'd be running his restaurant in Mississippi."

After dropping off Tony and Eddie in the infield of the horse track, the chopper disappeared in a vortex of rotating ground fog.

"Shit," Tony said. "Visibility zero and the car parked a hundred yards from here."

"I hear music coming from one of the restaurants at the track. Follow me; I have good ears."

They made their way through the fog to the track parking lot where they finally found Tony's car.

"Thank God for the fog lights," Tony said as they

headed toward Pinky's on Toulouse."

"With this soup were in, we'll be lucky if the place isn't shut down for the night."

"Been like this almost a month now," Tony said. "It'll be open. Everybody's pretty much got it figured out."

"If you say so," Eddie said.

Tony was correct. Despite the surrounding fog, several cars were parked in Pinky's lot. The restaurant occupied an old two-storied building, a peephole in the antique front door as in speakeasy days. Light jazz emanated from the New York-style bistro when they opened it and entered. They walked down a short flight of stairs where a smiling woman greeted them.

"Two for dinner?" she said.

"Just drinks," Tony said. "Can we sit at the bar?"

"You bet," she said. "Have one for me while you're at it."

The small white tiles on the floor reminded Tony of a barber shop. Dark wood paneled the walls, and antique fans hanging from the molded ceiling moved in lazy circles. White tablecloths draped the twenty or so tables, a few of them occupied by smiling customers. The ambiance was relaxing, and Tony could see why diners would enjoy the atmosphere.

An antique wooden bar stretched across the back of the large, open room, the bartender dressed in a white tuxedo, his hair oiled and his handlebar mustache reminiscent of a bygone era.

"I'm Louis," he said with a smile. "What can I get for you gentlemen?"

"Dalmore and water," Tony said.

"Make it two," Eddie said.

"Ever try Monkey Shoulder?" Louis asked.

Tony shook his head. "Nope. What the hell is Monkey Shoulder?"

"It's a mixture of three different single malts.

Most everyone likes it. Want to try a shot?"

"Why not?" Tony said.

Louis filled two shot glasses from a bottle that said Monkey Shoulder. Tony and Eddie were both smiling after downing the scotch.

"That's great," Tony said. "Maybe my new favorite drink."

"Mine too," Eddie said.

"Don't get too attached," Louis said. "It's sort of hard to find."

"Then it sounds like we'll be coming back often," Tony said. "Not too many diners tonight."

"Ground fog," Louis said. "I'll be glad when this weather pattern passes. It's really starting to affect my livelihood."

"I hear that," Tony said. "Pinky around tonight?"

Louis' smile disappeared. "Who wants to know?"

Louis' smile returned when Tony pulled a hundred dollar bill from his wallet and handed it to him.

"Me and Ben Franklin here."

Chapter 26

A sudden chill swept through the swamp as we loaded our daypacks, tied the pontoon boat to a cypress tree, and then stepped onto the spongy earth of the high ground that stood only a few inches out of the water.

Once away from the main pool, the cypress trees began to disappear, replaced by hardwood trees stunted by the swampy earth in which they grew. There was no clear path through the trees and underbrush. J.P. wanted to brief us, so we gathered around him."

"There are no roads, and the only paths are animal trails. As you can see, it gets tight in places, so we'll be walking in single file. Slick and Lucky will go first and be our scout dogs. They'll alert us if there's trouble ahead. Rory, you walk point. Keep your sword ready and widen the path if necessary."

"Will do," Rory said.

"Wyatt, you follow Rory. Let the dagger point the way and direct him when we need to change course."

"What about the dogs?" Abba asked.

"They'll sense what we're doing and get ahead of us. You'll see. They're natural hunters."

Slick and Lucky were eager to get into the woods their tails wagging when Abba knelt and hugged them.

"What about me?" she asked.

"You follow Wyatt, and I'll bring up the rear. Any questions?" We stood there, shaking our heads. "Then let's move out," he said.

Lucky and Slick moved ahead of us, walking ten to fifteen feet ahead of Rory. I rested Exethelon in the palm of my hand, tapping Rory's shoulder whenever we needed to adjust our course. As J.P. had said, Lucky and Slick altered directions every time that we did.

"We're not going to get anywhere very quickly moving no faster than we are," Abba said.

"It is what it is," J.P. said. "Everybody, watch your step. It's slick, and there's snakes, hogs, and quicksand, hidden by the brush."

We halted abruptly after thirty minutes of steady walking when Slick barked once and stopped in front of us. J.P. signaled for us to stay in place as he went to see what they'd found. He wasn't smiling when he returned.

"There's a creek blocking our path. It's either wade across here, or else follow the bank till it narrows for an easier crossing."

"How far out of the way would we have to go?" I asked.

"No telling," he said. "Let's see if we can ford this baby right here,"

We followed him to the edge of the creek, about twenty feet across and filled with rapidly moving water.

"Now what?" Abba said.

J.P. gave me a glance and said, "Cowboy, can you still throw a rope?"

"Don't know," I said. "It's been a few years."

He handed me the lariat he kept attached to his belt.

"See if you can put the noose over that small tree

on the far bank."

"Not much room to maneuver," I said.

"Rory, use your sword and clear him some room to twirl the lariat."

J.P. didn't have to ask Rory twice. With a grin, the big Scot began felling the small trees until I had enough room to toss the lariat. My target was a dead tree, mostly devoid of branches. The others watched as I twirled the rope and let it fly, missing on my first attempt.

"I'm a little rusty," I said.

"Take your time," J.P. said. "We're stuck here till you get lucky."

I got lucky on my next attempt, the noose tightening around the dead tree. J.P. took the rope from me and gave it a healthy tug. After looping the rope around another tree, he handed it to Rory.

"I'll go first. Don't allow any slack in the rope."

"It won't get away from me," Rory said.

J.P. stepped into the water, probing the bottom with his walking stick as he went. It was deeper than it looked. When he reached the center of the creek, he slipped, his feet coming out from under him. He held onto the rope. After struggling to regain his footing, he managed to crawl out on the other side.

"It's moving faster than I thought. The creek bottom is slicker than owl's shit," he said. "Dogs next. Untie the end of the rope and tie it behind Slick's front legs. I'll pull him across."

Rory attached the rope to Slick, and then gave him a hug and a pat.

"Swim to J.P.," he said,

The beautiful black dog bounded into the water, caught up by the current almost immediately. Lucky was barking, and his tail wagging as J.P. pulled Slick out of the water, enduring another drenching as Slick tried to shake himself dry. He wiped water out of his eyes with the back of his sleeve before tossing the rope back to Rory.

"Now Lucky," he said.

The big Lab made the crossing with no problems. J.P. gave him a big pat and then tossed the rope across the creek.

"You next, Abba. I'm already drenched so I'll meet you in the center of the creek and help you across."

"It's cold," she said after wading into the water.

J.P. met her halfway. When she slipped and let go of the rope, he grabbed the collar of her shirt with one hand and held on to the rope with the other. They were both wringing wet when they crawled out on the other side.

"You next, Wyatt," J.P. said, calling to me.

As Abba had said, the water was cold and quickly filled my boots. I was up to my waist, the current at its strongest when I reached the center of the creek. J.P. extended a hand to help me out of the water.

"Okay, Rory."

The big Scot waded into the water. Taller than all of us, he made it across with little problem. J.P. stood on the bank, staring at the rope.

"Where are you going?" Abba asked as he waded into the creek.

"Can't leave the rope here," he said. "We may need it down the line."

We watched as he struggled across the creek to untie the rope. Hanging on to the loose end, he started toward us, losing his footing almost immediately. Rory was quick to react, grabbing the rope and pulling J.P. to shore. Tired and wet, he lay on the bank until he was through breathing hard and spitting up water.

There was a bit of a sandy beach, bare of trees and vegetation, where the creek made a turn. The sun was peeking through the cloud cover for the first time since we'd left J.P.'s fishing camp. J.P. sat in the sand, pulled off his boots, dumping water out of them.

"We need to build a fire and dry our clothes and boots, or we'll be covered in fungal growths before we get back home. We all have survival blankets in our packs. You can change behind those bushes."

After removing his shirt, he began collecting driftwood to make a fire.

Abba joined Rory and me as we pulled off our boots and dumped out the water. We soon had a roaring fire going, our clothes drying on spits around it. J.P. grinned as we sat near the fire, wrapped in our blankets.

"My hair's a mess," Abba said. "Wish I had a brush to get out some of these snarls."

"You're more gorgeous with snarls than most women are after leaving the beauty parlor," J.P. said. "Plus, you're sexy as hell with nothing on but that blanket."

"Don't get any ideas," she said. "I still don't like you very much."

"You'll get over it," he said.

"Since we're already situated and have a fire built, why not just stay here for the night?" I asked. "There can't be much more than an hour or so of daylight left."

"Because this little spit of land will be under water if it rains tonight. From the looks of those clouds, we'd better get dressed and on our way."

"I'm starving," Rory said. "Is there anything to eat around here?"

J.P. dug in his pack and pulled out four bags wrapped in cellophane. He tossed one to each of us.

"Trail mix," he said. "That should hold us until we can find a place to stop for the night."

With J.P.'s prodding, we were soon dressed and back on the trail. The creek behind us was but a fading memory.

"Thank God for the boots," Abba said. "Every

step I take I expect to have a snake jump out at me."

"We'll be okay. It's been getting cooler lately, and most of them are looking for a place to hibernate."

"Does it ever freeze here?" Abba asked.

"You bet it does," J.P. said. "More often than New Orleans because we're further north."

"I went on a swamp tour once," Abba said. "This is the first time I've ever left the boat."

"Let's hope it's not our last," I said.

"You could have gone all day without saying that," she said.

"Sorry. One thing I know; we couldn't have a better swamp guide than J.P."

Though the weather wasn't unusually cold, it was still seasonally cool. A flock of noisy cranes, on their way to their winter hibernation spot in the wetlands south of us, flew overhead. When a wild hog popped out of the underbrush, J.P. tapped it on the snout with his walking stick. We listened as it scurried back into the scrub.

Lucky and Slick kept most of the wildlife away from us, occasionally stopping to bark at a hog or possum. They were both having the time of their lives.

"It'll be dark soon," I said. "What's your plan?"

"We don't want to be wandering around in the dark. Let's hope we find a little swath of higher ground where we can spend the night without getting our feet wet."

"And if we don't?" Abba asked.

"We choose our best option, set up camp, and then start a fire."

"Good," Abba said. "I don't like sleeping in complete darkness."

J.P. said, "I was more worried about having a place to heat up our beans."

"I didn't forget the Southern Comfort," Rory said.

"I thought Scots were supposed to drink scotch," I

said.

"Never acquired a taste for it. Cyn got me started on Southern Comfort."

"I like it too," Abba said. "Wonder why Cyn likes it so much."

"Janis Joplin," Rory said. "She always had a bottle at every concert. Cyn adores Janis Joplin's songs."

"Me too," J.P. said. "She had quite a voice for a little lady."

We kept looking for J.P.'s little swath of high ground. As light grew dimmer, it started to become ever more apparent that we weren't going to find it.

"There ain't no good place to make camp," J.P. finally said. "We'll have to make do right here."

"Right where?" Rory said. "It looks exactly like where we just came from."

"Bitch, bitch, bitch," J.P. said. "We got no other choice."

"I'm standing in an inch of water," Abba said. "We'll be soaked before morning if we sleep on the ground."

"Hand me your pack," J.P. said, holding out his hand.

He rummaged through her daypack, removing something that vaguely resembled a ball of twine. When he unfolded it, we realized it was a hammock. There was also rope in the pack. As we watched, he strung the hammock between two small trees that stood about six feet apart.

Her pack also contained a sheet of plastic. Stringing a line over the hammock and between the two trees, he draped the plastic over it so that it created a roof. Almost finished, he hung a mosquito net under the plastic and over the hammock.

"Takes a little getting used to, but it'll keep us off the ground and free of pesky crawling bugs."

"And if it rains?" Abba asked.

"Nothing more relaxing than sleeping suspended in the trees and staying dry as rainwater drips off the plastic roof."

Chapter 27

Abba was less than convinced about our sleeping arrangements as she stared at the hammock J.P. had erected for her between two trees. It mattered little. The light was waning, and dark clouds had begun gathering. A flock of geese in a tight formation honked as they flew overhead.

"How do you get in that thing?" she asked.

"I'll help you," he said with a smile.

"That's okay. Like you said, I'll figure it out."

"That's enough of me playing den mother for one night," he said. "You two big boys can put up your own hammocks."

Rory pulled the hammock from his daypack and held it at arm's length.

"I do not know if this will support me," he said.

"Trust me," J.P. said. "It's strong enough for even someone as big as you are. You've used your survival blanket already. Don't matter how light they are. You know they'll keep you warm. Now, let's snap to it because it looks as if it's going to rain."

Rory clicked the heels of his boots together and saluted smartly.

"Yes sir," he said.

J.P. grinned and saluted him back. "Now you got the right idea. Soon as we get our hammocks installed, we need to gather some wood. Rory, you find us some big pieces. Abba and Wyatt, you two gather the kindling."

"Where do we go to the bathroom?" Abba asked.

"Behind a bush, no further than twenty feet from here. You each got a roll of toilet paper in your pack. Make it last."

"And if we don't?" Abba said.

"Plenty of leaves in the swamp to use. Just don't grab a handful of poison ivy."

Before long, there were four hammocks erected in a semicircle. J.P. had an even larger sheet of plastic and made a roof over all four hammocks. He arranged more plastic on the ground so we'd have a place to sit without getting too damp. When we'd finished, J.P. stood, hands on his hips, surveying our work.

"Not bad for a bunch of cub scouts," he said. "This is our base camp. Long as we're here, don't ever get out of sight of it. Am I understood?"

He laughed and shook his head when all three of us came to attention and saluted him.

We'd gathered a stack of wood and kindling just in time and had a nice fire going near the edge of our plastic roof. As darkness encroached on the swamp, the clouds opened up, and it began to rain. It brought with it more than a chill. Suddenly cold from the perceptible drop in temperature, Abba hugged her arms tightly to her chest.

As J.P. had said, our survival blankets were light and warm. After eating cans of beef stew and beans, we cuddled up around the fire with survival blankets draping our shoulders. Abba, Rory, and J.P. were drinking Southern Comfort. I made do with water from my canteen. I was enjoying the solitude, and the sound of rain on the plastic when Abba made a comment that caused us all to laugh.

"If we really were scouts, and you were our den mother, you'd be telling us a ghost story right about now."

"Wouldn't be no story," he said. "I'd be telling you a true tale that'd make chills climb up your spine. My hammock is barely big enough for me. Don't matter none cause you'd be begging to crawl in beside me."

"You're so full of shit," she said.

"Want to hear the story?" he asked.

"I'm not a little girl. It'll take more than a corny story told around a campfire to scare me."

"You grew up in New Orleans. Surely you've heard of the Honey Island Swamp Monster."

"I've heard of lots of things. That doesn't mean I believe them," she said.

"You can believe this one because everything I'm gonna tell you is true."

The little patch of high ground J.P. had managed to find for us was no more than a few inches higher than the surrounding ground. It was apparently all we needed as rainwater began flowing around our little island. Flame from the fire flickered when a clap of thunder sounded nearby.

"Hope we don't get struck by lightning," Abba said. "I'd hate to miss hearing your tall tale."

J.P. had brought an extra blanket for Lucky and Slick. They'd curled up on it, not far from the fire. Both were already soundly asleep. Lucky began to snore as J.P. took a swig from the big flask of Southern Comfort they were passing around the campfire.

"Some people seem to think the Swamp Monster first appeared in the sixties. That's not true. It's been in this swamp since long before that."

"Indians?" I asked.

"Not quite that far, though all the way back to when the French first began to settle New Orleans. This entire region was forest and swamps. The first settlers wanted high ground on the river, and that's what they found at the site that is now New Orleans."

"Lad, what are you smoking?" Rory said. "Everyone knows that New Orleans is below sea level."

"Is now," J.P. said. "Not then. Parts of the French Quarter are still above sea level."

"Then may I ask what happened?" Abba asked.

"Before they built the levees, New Orleans flooded every spring. The floods brought silt from up the river. Swampy land naturally subsides but the spring silt adjusted for it. When they built the levees, the floods mostly stopped, and so did the influx of silt."

"I thought you were going to tell us about the Swamp Monster," Abba said.

"I'll get to it. What's your hurry? Got someplace you need to go?"

"Just asking," she said.

"My point is that this whole part of south Louisiana was swampy back in those days. The mosquitoes and poor drainage resulted in epidemics of malaria and yellow fever. France was having a hard time convincing settlers to move here, so they started bringing over prisoners, prostitutes, and social misfits. Three of those misfits were the cause of the Swamp Monster."

J.P. paused as thunder sounded overhead, heralding an even stronger influx of rain. Slick scooted closer to Lucky, the big lab who was sleeping soundly through the storm.

"Don't stop now," Abba said.

J.P. shook the flask Rory had handed him. "You two are drinking too fast. This baby is half-empty. We'll have to turn around and go home when that happens."

"Do not worry," Rory said. "I have yet another full flask in my daypack."

"Good for you," Abba said.

"Thank Wyatt," he said. "He paid for it."

235

I could only shake my head. "Nothing worse than an alcoholic having to pay for someone else's whiskey," I said.

"Tell us about the misfits," Abba said, ignoring my comment.

"Three brothers and the person they'd brought with them: a slave."

"Slavery is abhorrent," Abba said. "I don't understand how people were able to treat other humans the way they did."

"That's the point," J.P. said. "This particular slave wasn't quite human."

Abba was quick to take offense. "That's a horrible thing to say. It's just an excuse so the people enslaving them could justify their cruelty and lack of empathy."

"Don't get your panties in a wad. This particular slave wasn't black. More like a creature almost seven feet tall with yellow eyes, big teeth, and brown hair over most of her body. Even on her face."

"You mean like a bear?" Abba said.

"More like a caveman, or in her case, cavewoman."

"How did she come to be a slave to these men?"

"These brothers would have been in prison, and rightfully so if they had stayed in France. France released them from prison to help populate the new colony. They bought this female from someone aboard the ship they arrived in."

"And she was a slave to those people?"

"They'd found her when she was young, living in a cave in southwest France. They raised her as a slave, beating and abusing her, and keeping her chained in a basement when she wasn't working. They named her Lucy."

"How cruel," Abba said.

"As bad as they were, the brothers were worse. They not only beat and abused Lucy they also used her as a sex slave."

"That is simply detestable," Abba said.

"The brothers dealt in human misery. They had acquired a huge black man everyone called Prince that they'd trained as a boxer. When he wasn't fighting, they kept him caged in the same room as Lucy. She spoke some guttural language no one understood, and Prince was the only person that could communicate with her.

"Do you know why they called him Prince?" I asked.

"Because of the tribal tattoos all over his body. He was supposedly from West Africa. People that knew about such things said it was a mark of royalty. Don't know if he was, but he answered to the name."

"How did he get to New Orleans?" Rory asked.

"Slave traders found him wandering near the coast. He was alone, a broken and grieving man."

"Does anyone know why?" Abba asked.

"Supposedly, a warring tribe had massacred his family and burned his village while he was away. He was still in a state of deep depression when the slavers captured him and took him by slave ship to the West Indies. He eventually arrived in chains in New Orleans.

"And the brothers bought him?" Abba asked.

"He was big, very dark-skinned, and evil looking. Gambling was big in the colony, and they saw the potential to box him. They had trouble at first because he didn't want to fight."

"At first?" I said.

"He finally came around. They started by starving him and then using a bullwhip and the threat of death. In those days, a fight didn't end until one of the fighters was either dead or else beat to a bloody pulp. The brothers began making lots of money with him. Didn't matter none because he always ended up pretty beat up himself. Lucy was there to tend his wounds and nurse him back to health. He never lost until . . ."

"Until what?" Abba asked.

"He came up against someone he knew from Africa: his own son." Abba's hand went to her mouth. "Prince recognized who he was in the ring against. His son did not. The giant African refused to hit him. The crowd was going crazy, demanding that the son, a man as big as Prince, though lots younger, kill him. He came close to doing just that."

"But he didn't?" Abba said.

"Prince was comatose in the center of the ring, blood all over the place. The crowd thought he was dead. He didn't move when the referee threw a bucket of water on him.

"The three brothers lost their asses, and they were pissed. When they realized he was still alive, they thought about killing him themselves. Thoughts of a rematch changed their minds. Lucy was still awake, waiting for them, when they threw him on the dirt floor beside her, not bothering to chain him."

"Oh my God!" Abba said. "What did she do?"

"Her kind couldn't really cry. She started making a sound that sounded like chirping. It was her way of crying. She had Prince's big head cradled in her arms. Thinking he was dead, she was rocking him like a baby. Somehow, through his stupor, he heard her, opened his eyes, and smiled. It was then that Lucy snapped."

J.P. grew silent as rain continued to fall and thunder rocked the hardwoods around them.

"Continue with your story, lad," Rory said.

"Lucy laid Prince gently on the floor, then reached behind her, and yanked her chains from the wall. The room they lived in was a shed behind the main house. The three brothers were drunk, still angry as hell, and licking their proverbial wounds. They were all fit men in their own right. It didn't matter because Lucy killed all three of them, beating them to death with the chain still attached to her wrist.

"Her anger continued to rage, long after the men were dead on the floor. She tore a slat from a chair, stuffed it between her wrist and the manacle, and proceeded to twist the metal until it broke. She tossed the bloody chain on top of the men, ripped a blanket from one of the beds, and then returned to the shed for Prince.

"They escaped through the darkness, Lucy carrying Prince in her big arms. They didn't stop until they reached the Honey Island Swamp."

"How do you know all this?" Abba asked. "Surely you're making it up."

"My uncle's best friend was an Indian that had grown up in the swamp. He'd heard the story from his family. The Indians protected Prince and Lucy until the day they died."

"Prince survived?" I asked.

"Not only did he survive, but he and Lucy also had many children before they died. Like their mama, they were big, hairy and had yellow eyes. The legend of the Swamp Monster began when someone spotted one of these creatures."

"You think they're still out there?" Abba asked.

J.P. nodded. "You can't hear them over the sounds of the storm. Before we leave the swamp, I promise that you will."

239

Chapter 28

Following a brief demonstration by J.P., we were all able to get into our hammocks with little trouble. Despite having my doubts, I'd fallen asleep almost immediately. It was still raining when we awoke the following morning.

"Now what?" Abba asked.

"We don't have rain slickers, so we stay here until the storm passes."

"And if it doesn't?" she said.

"We'll give it a few hours and then worry about it," J.P. said.

"What about breakfast?" Rory said. "I am starving."

J.P. grinned and said, "Want me to call room service?" Duly chastised, Rory didn't answer. "There's more trail mix in our packs and also packages of beef jerky."

Abba yawned and pulled her blanket tightly around her shoulders.

"I need to go to the bathroom," she said. "How can I do that without getting drenched?"

J.P. handed her a sheet of plastic. "Use this to cover yourself the best you can. The fire has gone out, and we got no more dry wood to start another. Get your clothes wet and they might stay that way for awhile."

"At this point, I don't care," she said.

"Yes, you do. We're in a swamp, and staying dry is a basic part of field hygiene. We have to do it or risk infections, fever, and fungal growths."

"Surely, we'll be back home before that becomes a problem," she said.

"Don't bet on it. Everything grows faster in the swamp. Get an infection, and it don't take long for a fever to get critical."

"So what do you suggest?"

"Stay beneath the plastic as best you can, and don't get wet," he said.

We all managed to stay dry during our trips into the bushes. The dogs were restless, venturing into the rain briefly to do their business, and then shaking themselves dry when they'd returned. J.P. had brought them a small bag of dog food. After eating, they returned to their blanket.

It was peaceful sitting under the plastic roof, listening to the gentle sound of falling rain. I dozed off for a bit. When I awoke, I saw Abba and Jean Pierre, sitting close and smiling as they chatted. J.P. was the first to notice that I'd awakened.

"Good day for a nap," he said. "Rory joined you. He snores louder than Lucky."

"I'm not very alert in the morning without at least one cup of java," I said. "Bertram always has a fresh pot brewing behind his bar. It has spoiled me."

He tossed me a jar of instant coffee, a plastic cup, and a spoon.

"Kind of crappy tasting, but it'll give you a jolt of caffeine. Abba and I are already on our second cup," he said.

"Thanks," I said as I mixed some of the powder with water from my canteen. "Beggars can't be choosers. Think the rain will ever stop?"

"Let's hope it's sooner rather than later."

J.P.'s instant coffee didn't dissolve well in the tepid water from my canteen. It did give me the jolt he'd promised. Lucky and Slick, like Rory, were asleep on their blanket and not worried about coffee, or the rain.

"Abba's been telling me a little about herself," J.P. said.

"You must be a good homicide detective," she said. "I don't believe I've ever known anyone as nosy as you."

"I'm still curious about something," he said.

"What?"

"I understand why Wyatt is here. You seem to have as much invested in finding Desire as he does. Why is that?"

"A long story," Abba said.

"It's raining, and I got no place to go."

"It's also complicated."

"Is that so, Wyatt?" he asked.

"Very complicated," I said, tossing him the jar of instant coffee.

"Tell me," he said. "I'll try to keep up."

"I don't know. It's sort of private."

"Does Wyatt know?"

"Not because I told him. He figured it out while working on a case."

J.P. turned and gave me a glance. "He'll never tell me," he said. "He still thinks he's a lawyer. Please tell me."

"My dad's name is Vincent Gigoux. His real name is Vincent Vallee. Junie Bug's husband was Gordon Vallee. His real name was Gordon Gigoux."

"Good God almighty," J.P. said. "Your dad is the person that was switched at birth with Gordon Vallee. Why hasn't he ever come forward? The Vallee fortune is huge."

"He's a proud man. He didn't earn it, so he doesn't feel right claiming it. He's also a building contractor and has done very well in his own right."

Abba shook her head when J.P. asked, "Does Junie Bug know who you are?"

"I went to her house thinking I was going to tell her. She thought I was there to apply for a job as her assistant. I needed a job, and Junie Bug pays very well. I've come to like her and realized I could never tell her."

"Damn!" he said. "That's a big cross to bear."

A thought crossed Abba's mind, and she began to smile. "Know what's funny?"

"Tell me."

"Dad and Junie Bug have so much in common it's a shame they'll never meet. They are both exceptionally good-looking; Junie Bug loves the arts; my dad is an amateur artist; Junie Bug's been in several movies; Dad acts in dinner theater and has had several bit parts in locally filmed movies."

"Why not fix them up?" J.P. said.

Abba laughed aloud. "It would never work."

"Because?"

"Neither of them would consider meeting the other."

"Tell Junie Bug you want her to meet your new beau. Tell your dad the same thing. Have them meet you at some atmospheric little bistro that plays soft music beneath muted lights."

"It might just work," Abba said. "What happens when I don't show up with a new beau?"

"Don't do that. I'm an actor unless you've forgotten. I'll play the part."

Abba stared at J.P. a moment. "You'd just be acting?"

J.P. grinned. "Of course I'd be your beau. You're the most gorgeous woman I've met in many a moon."

"You are so full of shit," she said, turning away and crossing her arms.

"Stop being so selfish and think of your dad and

Junie Bug. Don't they deserve to meet each other?"

"Of course, but . . ."

"But what? You dislike me so much that you'd deny them their happiness?"

"You never stop, do you?"

"What?"

"You don't care about either my dad or Junie Bug. You just want to get into my pants."

"A double date's not a lifelong commitment," he said. "Is it?"

"I might consider going on a double date with you, but only because you're an actor, and because except for Wyatt and Rafael, you're the only other person in the world that knows about Dad and Junie Bug."

"You could ask Wyatt to take you on the double date."

I tossed my hands in the air. "Don't get me involved in this. I'm not playing."

J.P. put his hand on top of Abba's, and she didn't move it away.

"Sounds to me like this ol' Cajun boy is your only choice. What do you say?"

Rory snorted and rolled over before Abba could answer. J.P. and I laughed, and despite herself so did Abba.

"Okay," she said. "Sounds like a plan, if we ever make it out alive from this God-forsaken swamp."

"Good," I know just the place to take them."

She wrenched her hand away from him and pointed her finger at his nose.

"It damn sure doesn't mean I'm going to sleep with you. Is that understood?"

She almost slapped him when he said, "Hell, girl, I don't see how I'd ever get much sleep anyway if I was in bed with you."

It was early afternoon when the storm passed, and we broke camp. When we started walking, my legs were sore, and I realized how long we'd been on our feet the past two days.

Light sweaters for everyone were just a few of the things we'd purchased at the little settlement. Now, it was considerably colder than when we'd entered the swamp, and I was glad for the one I was wearing. The sky darkened, and ground fog became ever more prevalent the farther we hiked. Soon, the swamp around us took on a surreal atmosphere. When some creature howled in the distance, J.P. called us to a halt.

"What's the dagger doing?" he asked me.

"Hasn't moved since we left camp."

"Let's take a break," he said. "We need to make sure that thing is working before we traipse around here like chickens with our heads cut off."

None of us had a watch. We all had a surprise coming when Abba checked her cell phone.

"I'm not getting a signal," she said.

We reached for our phones. "Nor am I," Rory said.

"Me either," J.P. said. "Wyatt?"

"Nope. What now?"

"Hope that the dogs know the way back to the boat," he said.

"And if they don't?" Abba asked.

"Wait until the clouds clear and then traverse our way out using the sun and stars," I said.

"You have to be kidding?" she said.

"I've got a backup," J.P. said. From his daypack, he pulled an old-fashioned compass and showed it to us.

"I never go hunting or fishing without it."

"You know how to use that thing?" Abba asked.

"I was an infantry officer in the army. You can bet I know how to use it," he said.

"Good," she said. "I was starting to get scared."

"Then stay scared," he said. "It'll keep you on

your toes." He waved off the flask of Southern Comfort when Rory offered it to him. "No more whiskey until we camp for the night. We're deep in the swamp, and there's no telling what we may encounter. We need to be on top of whatever comes our way."

An eerie blue glow and dampening of sound are what came our way. They accompanied the misty haze that seemed to engulf us. The mental sensation it produced was surreal and made me feel as though I was in a waking dream. Unknown creatures suddenly began howling in the forest around us, jolting me back to reality. Once again, J.P. signaled us to halt.

"Take a look at this," he said.

We gathered around him, staring at the compass in his palm. The dial was spinning out of control.

"That can't be good," I said.

"The dagger," Abba said.

Exethelon was aglow, pulsating from a light gold aura to an angry red.

"We must be nearing the house of the sorceress," Rory said.

Abba was clutching J.P.'s arm, frightened by the strange howls that had only grown louder.

"This is insane," she said.

"Just a hallucination," J.P. said. "I never heard anything like that in my life. Those howls aren't real."

"Then why are we all hearing them?" she asked.

"Maybe it's a dream," I said. "Though I'm not sure whose dream it is."

"What creatures are making that noise?" Rory asked. "I have never heard anything like it. Not even in the haunted Scottish moors."

"Whatever they are, they're making my skin crawl," Abba said. "Is it the Swamp Monster, and is it possible there's more than one?"

The two dogs were also spooked. They'd returned from the trail and stood near, growling as they scanned the forest around us.

"Beats the hell out of me," J.P. said. "Wyatt put the dagger on the ground and let's see what it does."

Exethelon continued to glow and pulsate as I placed it on the damp earth. It sat there a second and then began to rotate, slowly at first. When it finally came to a stop, it pointed at a cobblestone pathway that had suddenly appeared in front of us.

"Oh my God!" Abba said. "Was that here a second ago?"

"No, but maybe it's the path we need to follow."

"If we're not dreaming," I said.

"If we are, we'll have to wake up sometime," J.P. said. "Let's move out."

We made good time for the next hour as we traversed the pathway that had appeared from nowhere. We also began seeing other things that seemed totally out of place.

"It's a mirage," J.P. said.

I wasn't so sure as I stared up at Jackson Square, St. Louis Cathedral and the Pontalba Buildings, in the sky above us.

"I've never seen a mirage," Abba said. "What's causing it?"

"Strange atmospheric conditions," J.P. said. "New Orleans is nearby. That's why we see it."

"Not so fast, lad," Rory said. "Take a look now."

The vivid French Quarter image was gone, replaced by buildings in another grand city.

"You know where it is?" J.P. asked.

"I do," Rory said. "It is Glasgow, Scotland."

"Something or someone is playing tricks on our minds," Abba said.

We were still looking at the mirage of Glasgow when Slick and Lucky began barking. We hadn't noticed that they were ahead of us and had gotten out

247

of our sight.

"Stay put," J.P. said. "I better check this out before we go any further."

He was gone no more than a few minutes when he appeared through the fog on the trail in front of us.

"What is it?" I asked.

"Wait and see for yourself. You're not going to believe it," he said.

Chapter 29

Music in Pinky's bistro segued seamlessly from the Roaring Twenties to early New Orleans jazz as the bartender named Louis took the hundred-dollar bill Tony held out to him. After twisting the end of his handlebar mustache, he stuffed the money into an inner pocket of his white tuxedo.

"Hate to disappoint," he said. "Pinky's not here tonight. Maybe I can help."

"When's he coming back?" Tony asked.

"Not till tomorrow," Louis said.

Seeing Louis wasn't going to return the hundred he'd given him, Tony decided to ask him a few questions.

"Did you know the man who was killed here the other night?"

"You cops?"

"Do we look like cops?"

"Off-duty cops, maybe."

"We ain't cops, off-duty or otherwise. Eddie and me have a few questions, and I got more bennies for you if you can answer them. Capiche?"

"Pinky don't like the help talking about the customers."

Tony fished another hundred from his wallet and held it on the bar in front of Louis.

"Pinky ain't here," he said.

Louis took the money, stuffing it into the same pocket as before.

"Like I said, business has been slow for the past month, and I need to pay some bills. What was your question again?"

"Did you know Diego Contrado?"

"Yeah, I knew Mr. Contrado. Came here a lot. Sometimes in the middle of the day. Always sat at the bar, same place as you two."

"Was Angus Anderson ever with him?"

Louis hesitated a moment before answering. "Sure. They were business associates and met here all the time."

"Associates and not friends?"

"They talked business. Horses, mostly." Louis grinned. "Every now and then they'd talk about women."

"But Anderson wasn't here the night Contrado was killed?"

Louis hesitated again. "I didn't say that. They were here earlier. They argued. Mr. Anderson was mad as hell. Stomped out of here like a crazy man. Didn't even bother clearing his tab."

"What did Contrado do?"

"Just laughed. Called Mr. Anderson a loco gringo."

"Did you tell this story to the police?" Tony asked.

"I never talked to the cops," Louis said.

"Oh? How did you get out of that?"

"Pinky spoke to them for me."

Eddie gave Tony a glance. "What about the cook, the waitresses, and the rest of the staff? Did the cops question them?"

"They only talked to Pinky. He told them what they needed to know. You fellows need another Monkey Shoulder?"

"Keep them coming," Tony said.

"This bottle's empty," Louis said. "I'll get another from the back."

When they were alone at the bar, Eddie pulled out a notepad, writing something in it.

"What?" Tony said.

"The names of the cops that interviewed Pinky. Making a note to remind me to call Tommy and find out who they are."

"On the take," Tony said. "You can bet on that one. Sounds like they already knew who they were going to charge for Contrado's murder."

"Tommy's going to earn his keep before this one's over with," Eddie said. "Oh, and remind me to tell Frankie about Monkey Shoulder."

"The best decision you ever made hiring Tommy," Tony said.

"Hope you're right, and I hope you don't run out of hundreds.

Tony had no time to reply as Louis returned with a fresh bottle of the exotic scotch, pouring each of them fresh drinks. Music in the bar had changed again, this time to ragtime piano. Fog wafted through the front door when a handsome man in a blue pinstripe suit and an attractive woman in a black designer dress entered the bistro. Tony and Eddie didn't notice.

"What was Anderson and Contrado arguing about?" Tony asked.

When Louis held out his palm, Tony crossed it with another hundred-dollar bill.

"I didn't catch the entire conversation," Louis said. "Just bits and pieces."

"Then give me the gist of it."

"They were arguing about a horse. Apparently, Mr. Contrado had sold one to Mr. Anderson. For some reason, Mr. Anderson wasn't too happy about it. He wanted his money back. Mr. Contrado wasn't having none of it and laughed at him. If you know Mr.

Anderson, then you know he don't like to be laughed at."

"I'm half starved," Tony said. "Can we get something to eat here at the bar?"

"You bet," Louis said. "I'll get a couple of menus and be right back."

When they were once again alone, Eddie asked, "What's your take on this pile of shit we're stepping in?"

"Don't know. I wouldn't think someone would kill a good bud, but then there was Cain and Abel, so you can't rule it out."

"Hell, Tony, it didn't sound to me like they're buds. Like Louis said, more like business associates."

"Hard for me to believe a man with Anderson's stroke would be involved in any way with the Mexican Cartel."

"Why not?" Eddie asked. "Their money spends like everyone else's."

"Right about that."

"Who'll we ask about the horse?"

"Frankie, I guess," Tony said.

"Or Josie, in case we're talking about quarter horses. She seems to know more about them than Frankie does."

Tony was soon eating a French dip, Eddie a Reuben. Louis was polishing a glass nearby in case Tony had more questions and more hundreds. He didn't have long to wait as Eddie held up his empty glass.

"I only have a few more bennies left," Tony said. "Can you answer a few more questions."

"Hit me with them," Louis said, holding out his hand.

"You know Bruno Baresi?"

Louis nodded. "In here most every night."

"You think it was him that killed Contrado?"

Louis twisted his mustache as he shook his head. "He didn't do it."

"How do you know that?" Eddie asked.

"Couldn't have done it because it was one of the rare nights he wasn't here."

"The police report says Contrado was killed with Baresi's pistol. How do you explain that?"

"Police must have got it when they arrested him. They didn't find it here."

"Sure about that?" Tony asked.

"Like I said, Mr. Baresi was someplace else."

"You seem pretty sure about that. How do you know?"

"Because he was with his girlfriend, my sister Donna. They were on a sailboat out on Pontchartrain."

"If he has an alibi, then why is he still in jail?" Eddie asked.

"Bruno's old lady. She don't know he's got a girlfriend. He's more afraid of her than going to prison."

"How do you know that?" Tony asked.

"Like I said, he's been going with my sister Donna for more than a year now. He bought her a new Lincoln and an expensive condo over by the river. Not much I don't know about Bruno, including his underwear size."

"And his wife don't know?" Tony asked.

"If she does, she hasn't let on," Louis said. "Bruno sure ain't gonna tell her."

"What about Lonzo Galvez, Anderson's bodyguard. Was he here?"

"He's never far away from Mr. Anderson. He usually waits in the kitchen. The cook and the girls feed him, and I take him drinks."

"Did he leave with Anderson?" Tony asked.

"Always does," Louis said. "He don't ever get too far away from his boss."

Tony handed him another hundred. "Bring us one more round and then clear our tab," he said. "We gotta get outa here." Louis was walking away when he added, "And add a fresh bottle of Monkey Shoulder to the tab. We'll take it with us."

Eddie had closed his eyes as soon as his rear end touched the front seat of Tony's Mustang. They were halfway across the Causeway before he opened them again. The fog was rising up off the water and starting to pour over the road.

"Sorry," Eddie said. "I didn't realize how tired I was until I closed my eyes."

Tony didn't take his eyes off the narrow road in front of them. "Been a long day already, and barely even ten yet."

"And we still need to talk with Frankie and Josie when we get back to the farm. Hope I don't fall asleep while we're getting the third degree."

"Or in bed with that pretty daughter of his."

Eddie laughed. "Not much chance of that. Like I said, she told me last night she doesn't believe in sex outside of marriage."

"That can't be good for you," Tony said. "You don't believe in sex inside of marriage."

"Funny. I believe in marriage. I'm just not ready for it yet. Maybe I'll be when I'm forty-something."

"By then, your hair will be thinning and your gut thickening. Young, pretty women won't give you a second look. Just something to think about."

"Whatever," Eddie said. "If I married Josie, I'd probably have to quit my job. Too much of a conflict of interest."

"If you marry Josie, you won't need your job. Frankie will see you, and her have everything you ever need."

"I hope you don't run out of hundreds. No wonder you're such a crack investigator," Eddie said.

"Like I told you earlier, Frankie gives me a big retainer whenever I start a new job for him. I convert about two grand of it into hundreds. Money buys everything, Frankie says. Tell me if you need more. Just don't let a nickel hold up a dollar."

"Be nice if all clients were like that," Eddie said.

"Most of them are. They hire me because I get them results. That's the bottom line."

"And Frankie?"

"My best client. If I'd had an endless supply of bennies when I was a homicide detective, I could have solved the city's murder problem for them."

"I feel your pain," Eddie said. "What now?"

"We did good today, and I'm pretty sure we got most of the puzzle pieces covered. Right now, we just don't know how they all fit."

"At least one piece is still missing."

"Which one?" Tony asked.

"If Anderson had Contrado killed because of a horse, how does that little tidbit of information jibe with our investigation?"

"Was wondering about that myself. Maybe they were arguing about Lightning Bolt," Tony said.

Eddie shook his head. "Not according to Louis. He said it was over a horse Contrado had sold to Anderson. That precludes the possibility that they were talking about Lightning Bolt."

"We both know that the big stallion is somehow involved," Tony said.

"And that whoever killed Contrado has obviously paid off the police," Eddie said.

"Anderson is the mayor's first cousin. Who better to orchestrate a cover-up?"

"And use his media empire to skew the news to confuse the public and the police as to what's really happening. I think we have our killer. Baresi's just the fall guy."

Tony nodded. "Frankie's lawyers will get Bruno off the hook, though it sounds like he won't have such an easy time explaining to his old lady about his girlfriend."

"Something else we don't have an answer to," Eddie said.

"Only one?"

"Let's just say for giggles and grins that Anderson did steal Lightning Bolt. What does he intend to do with him? He can't race him, and he doesn't seem like the sentimental type."

"He can't breed him, either," Tony said. "Unless he plans to use him to fill in for another horse."

"Not likely. He couldn't get the kind of stud fee a horse of Lightning Bolt's caliber would command, even if there weren't the matter of DNA. I also doubt he has a grandson to give him to."

It was too cool for the air conditioner and too hot for the heater. Humidity was high both outside and inside the car. Tony flipped on the defroster and turned up the fan to clear the haze on the inside of the window.

"Anderson has wanted Lightning Bolt since he was a foal," he said. "Maybe bad enough to kill for him."

"Not his style," Eddie said. "We know his motive for killing Contrado could have been his horse sale gone bad."

"And he was pissed at Frankie for fixing a race he thought he'd already fixed."

"But why did he steal Lightning Bolt?" Eddie said.

By now, visibility on the Causeway was greatly reduced. Tony adjusted the brightness of his fog lights and slowed the car to a crawl.

"Guess that's the sixty-four dollar question," he said.

Chapter 30

No one was asleep, not even Jojo, when they reached Frankie's horse farm. Not only was everyone still awake, but they were also waiting in a group on the front porch. When Eddie stepped out of the car, Jojo ran over and hugged him. Eddie ruffled his dark mop of hair.

"How you doing, Tiger?" he said. "Don't you think it's a little past your bedtime?"

"Mama and Papaw said I could stay up till you got home."

Eddie squeezed the boy's shoulder. "I'm glad you did."

Josie was right behind Jojo, smiling as she gave Eddie a sensual kiss. Almost too sensual. He glanced at Adele and Frankie to gauge their reaction, surprised to see that they were both smiling.

He, Josie and JoJo strolled to the porch, arm-in-arm. When they reached it, Josie gave Jojo's bottom a friendly swat.

"Eddie's home now and it's bedtime for you," she said.

"Goodnight, Eddie," Jojo said with a wave as he followed his mother into the house.

Frankie continued to smile as he glanced at his expensive gold Rolex.

"I was beginning to wonder if you two were going to make it back tonight. I came close to sending out some boys to look for you. Everything okay?"

After Lil and Tony had exchanged a kiss and hug, Tony handed the bottle of Monkey Shoulder, wrapped in a brown paper bag, to Frankie.

"Everything's fine. Eddie and I brought you something," he said.

"What is it?" Frankie asked as he pulled the bottle out of the bag.

"Some damn good scotch," Tony said. "How you doing, Adele?"

Like Frankie and Lil, Adele had a drink in her hand. It didn't stop her from hugging both Tony and Eddie.

"Great. Are you two hungry?"

Sensing Adele had cooked up something especially for them, Tony didn't tell her about the sandwiches they'd eaten at Pinky's.

"I can always find room for anything you cook. You know that, Adele. Whatcha got?"

"Spaghetti and meatballs. Pancho's secret recipe," she said. "Haven't made it in a while and Frankie's been after me to do it."

"Thank you, Adele, and thank you, Frankie," Tony said.

"How about you, Eddie?" Adele asked. "You hungry?"

"You kidding? I'm always ready for the best Italian spaghetti and meatballs in New Orleans," he said.

"Great," Adele said.

"If I could find a woman that cooks like you, I'd have been married years ago. You know what they say; the way to a man's heart is through his stomach."

Adele's smile quickly disappeared, and so did Frankie's.

"Good. It's waiting on the stove," Adele said before he had a chance to ask if he'd said something wrong.

Tony also noticed the reaction to Eddie's comment and tried to bail him out.

"I'm betting Josie can cook with the best of them," he said.

"Adele's giving her a few lessons," Frankie said.

"Hey, there's more to a good relationship than just good cooking," Eddie said.

"That's a fact," Frankie said, slapping his shoulder as his smile returned.

Eddie wondered about Frankie and Adele's reaction at the mention of cooking. He forgot about it when they entered the ranch-style kitchen and smelled the wonderful aroma of Adele's famous spaghetti sauce.

Josie joined them, returning from Jojo's bedroom. Wrapping an arm around Eddie's waist, she gave him another hug and kiss. As before, Adele and Frankie just kept smiling.

"The girls opened two bottles of Chianti. Myself, I want to try this scotch with the weird name," Frankie said.

Adele punched his arm. "I already know you're going to have some of both," she said. "You always do."

"You know me too well, don't you?" he said. "Maybe that's why I love you so much."

"Just one of the many reasons," she said. "I also give a mean back massage."

"The best. Everyone grab a chair. I'm anxious to hear what Eddie and Tony learned after making me go to the house."

"You were welcome to come along," Tony said.

"I know," Frankie said. "I enjoy watching you boys work, and I almost did. The little lady here always wants me to come home at a decent hour."

259

"You know you love it," she said.

"Baby, you bet I do," he said, giving her bottom a friendly pinch. "As much as I want to hear what happened, there'll be no discussing business while we eat. After dinner, we'll sit on the porch, and you two can catch me up on what you learned today."

Between bites of pasta, Lil reached over and squeezed Tony's hand. "I'm so glad you're not a cop anymore," she said. "You were never home early. Always more like four in the morning."

"We were both younger then," Tony said. "I hope I never have to leave home in the middle of the night again to oversee a homicide investigation. Those days are behind me."

"What about the other night?"

"A once in a blue moon event. Tommy needed my help, and I was happy to give it to him. Where's Patchy?"

"I swear you care more about that dog than you do me."

Tony got tomato sauce on her face when he leaned over and kissed her cheek.

"You know that ain't true," he said.

"Patch and Silky are asleep at the bungalow. There's a doggie door, and they both love the place. I wish you weren't working so you could enjoy it with us."

Tony bent his head closer to her and held his voice down so that Frankie wouldn't hear him talking about business.

"Eddie and me are close on this one. Might even have an answer for Frankie as early as tomorrow. Then we'll have plenty of time to enjoy this place together. Frankie's already told me that he and Adele expect us to stay another week after I solve the case for him."

"Good because I just love it here. Adele and I rode horses today, played tennis, and then went swimming in the heated pool. We even had a massage from a professional masseur. I'm so tired, I'll probably fall asleep the minute my head hits the pillow."

"We'll see about that," he said.

Slightly tipsy after two glasses of Chianti, Lil didn't even try to stifle a giggle.

Frankie's good mood continued, bolstered by Adele's pasta and the bottle of Monkey Shoulder. He didn't let the bottle get far away, and he carried it with him when they sauntered out to the partially covered deck.

The night was cool, and the fog gone for the moment, wafted away by a gentle breeze. Someone had lit the large fire pit, and they found places to sit on the couches and chairs that circled around it. Tony closed his eyes, almost nodding off when he and Lil sank into one of the comfortable porch couches.

"Oh no you don't," Frankie said, topping up his scotch. "No one goes to sleep until I hear your report. What you got for me?"

"Let me get Eddie over here, and we'll tell you," Tony said.

Eddie was paying no attention to Frankie or anyone else except Josie. He was sprawled in a big recliner, Josie draped across his lap and playing with his hair.

"Hey, break it up you two," Frankie said, grinning. "You two ain't married yet, and we need Eddie's input over here."

Josie bounded out of Eddie's lap, sat in her dad's and gave him a hug.

"Spoilsport," she said.

Before Josie could return to the recliner, Eddie moved over to the couch, sandwiching Lil between him and Tony as the word yet reverberated in his head.

"Does anyone need me to top up their scotch or

wine before we get started?" Frankie asked.

Not waiting for an answer, he began topping up all their drinks. When the bottle of Chianti ran dry, he opened another.

"Now," he said. "If everyone's situated on drinks, I want to hear about your trip to Pinky's."

"Pinky wasn't around," Tony said. "Didn't make any difference because our bartender was plenty talkative. We learned a bunch."

"Tell me," Frankie said.

"First thing we found out was Angus Anderson, and Diego Contrado had drinks at the bar the night Contrado was murdered."

"Makes sense," Frankie said. "They was together at the track bar the night of the race."

"Apparently, everything wasn't so hunky dory with them. They had an argument at Pinky's that made the bartender very uncomfortable. Anderson got so mad, he stomped out of the restaurant. He left Contrado alone at the bar, mumbling under his breath, according to the bartender."

"What were they arguing about?" Frankie asked. "Did he know?"

Tony sipped his scotch and leaned forward, out of the grasp of the comfortable couch.

"Something about a horse Contrado had sold to Anderson," he said. "Supposedly, the deal went bad, and Contrado refused to give Anderson his money back. The bartender didn't know any of the details."

"Figures," Frankie said. "Those two are always at the track together. Makes sense that they had dealings in the horse business."

"Any ideas on the horse they were arguing about?" Tony asked.

"Those two love quarter horses. I only keep up with thoroughbreds. Josie may know something."

She was already searching the internet using her cell phone.

"If there's something on the net about it, I'll find it," she said.

"What else?" Frankie asked.

"The bartender gave us an alibi for Bruno Baresi," Tony said.

"Like what? My five-hundred dollar per hour lawyers haven't found anything yet."

"Figures," Eddie said.

"What's your problem with expensive lawyers?"

"Maybe I just wish I was one," Eddie said, grinning."

"That's not your only reason," Frankie said. "Tell me why you really feel that way."

"In my experience, white-collar law firms have little reason to solve their client's problem only to get off the sugar tit. They usually keep sucking until you finally have to wrench them loose."

"If what you say is true, then what should I do about it?" Frankie asked.

"If it were my money, I'd fire them and hire a couple of hungry hundred-dollar per hour lawyers."

"All lawyers are supposed to act professionally. Especially those in the law firms I hire."

"No matter how much they charge an hour, they're all human. In your case, I say they haven't even tried to do you a good job."

"How can you be so sure of that?"

"Because it took Tony and me less than two hours to learn Bruno wasn't at Pinky's the night Contrado was killed."

"Impossible. Bruno would have said something by now, not to mention the cops found his pistol near the murder scene."

"Planted," Tony said.

"You'd better explain," Frankie said.

"Crooked cops conducted the investigation, and it was a farce," Eddie said. "The only person they interviewed was Pinky. Louis, the bartender, says

Bruno was on a sailboat on Pontchartrain with his girlfriend."

"How would he know that?" Frankie asked.

"Bruno's girlfriend is his sister. According to him, he even knows the size of Bruno's underwear," Tony said.

"Then who's side is Pinky on, and why hasn't Bruno told this to the lawyers?"

"Don't know who's side Pinky is on other than it's not yours," Eddie said.

Frankie's smile had disappeared. "I'll worry about Pinky later. Tell me about Bruno."
Bruno's more afraid of his old lady, according to Louis than a charge of first-degree murder," Eddie said. "Want me to have a come to Jesus talk with your fancy lawyers for you? We'll have Bruno out of jail tomorrow."

"Likely soon to be divorced Bruno, or maybe even murdered by his old lady," Tony said.

Still focusing his attention on Eddie, Frankie ignored Tony's comment.

"You'd talk to the lawyers for me?" he asked.

"Sure I will," Eddie said. "Sounds like they need to be taken down a notch or two and I'm just the man to do it for you."

"You're on," Frankie said. "If Bruno didn't pull the trigger, then who killed Contrado?"

"Lonzo Galvez," Eddie said. "Angus Anderson's bodyguard. The same person that took your trophy from Wyatt and me. The same trophy found at the murder scene of your trainer and jockey."

"Angus is politically connected. I doubt he'd ever be charged, much less convicted of murder. At least not in Orleans Parish."

"We're working on the political corruption aspect of New Orleans at the Federal D.A.'s office," Eddie said. "Problem is there are so many crooks in city hall, we're having a hard time figuring out where to start."

"Nobody knows that better than me," Frankie said. "Around here, you just gotta play the game. You want to do something about it, you got to start at the top and work your way down."

"That's what we're figuring out," Eddie said.

"What about Lightning Bolt?"

"Eddie and I think he's probably at Anderson's horse farm. Just a gut feeling because we have no proof."

"Even if Lightning Bolt is still alive, we wonder why he would want the horse," Eddie said. "Unless Anderson needs a pet because he can't race or breed him."

Josie wasn't paying attention to the conversation as she worked the digits on her cell phone, searching the web.

"I found something you're just not going to believe," she said.

Chapter 31

A damp breeze had begun blowing up from the south, the fog beginning to disappear. It was soon replaced by gentle rain, its fine mist dampening the edges of the covered deck. Lil leaned closer to the fire pit to warm her hands. Adele hurried inside, returning with sweaters for herself, Josie and Lil.

"Baby, don't keep us in suspense," Frankie said.

"Maybe this is what we're looking for. Baja Racing sold a champion quarter horse to Angus Anderson three months ago for almost six million dollars."

"You got to be kidding. How much did you say he paid?" Tony asked.

"Just under six million bucks," Josie said.

"Who is Baja Racing?" Eddie asked.

"Just a sec and I'll find out." After another quick search, she said, "A corporation, though it looks like Diego Contrado is the primary stockholder."

"Bingo," Tony said. "Good work, Josie."

"The horse's name is Lightning in a Bottle," she said. "And listen to this."

"What?" Tony and Eddie said at the same time.

"I checked the pedigree section of the quarter horse association's website. The horse Angus Anderson bought from Baja Racing is a full brother—same sire, same dam—to Lightning Bolt."

"So what?" Frankie asked. "Those two buy and sell horses every day. It might not mean anything."

"Maybe not," Eddie said. "It's still one hell of a coincidence that the two horses are full brothers."

"Maybe he likes the bloodline," Frankie said.

Something about the tone of Frankie's voice made them both reluctant to answer his questions. Josie wasn't afraid of her father and asked something of her own.

"Then why did Anderson want Contrado to return his money?" Josie asked.

"Baby, I don't have a clue," Frankie said.

"Anderson's horse farm is no more than five miles from here," she said. "Let's take a look at his stables. Now's a perfect time."

"Probably not a bad idea," Tony said.

"I'm in," Eddie said.

Josie was beaming. "We'll need dark clothing. We have black sweatsuits with hoods at the spa."

"Baby, you're not going anywhere," Frankie said.

"And why may I ask not?"

"Too dangerous. The cartel has men out there, even at this hour. That's not to mention you could get shot trespassing on Anderson's property."

"I'm the only one that knows the way to Anderson's farm. Since I was the real estate agent that sold it to him, I know the location of every barn, stable and house on the place, and I also know what Lightning Bolt looks like."

Frankie downed his glass of scotch in one swallow. "What do you intend to do if Lightning Bolt is there; steal him and then ride him home?"

"Sounds like a perfect plan to me," she said.

"Not a bad idea," Eddie said. "I'll ride him."

"Bullshit!" Frankie said. "You've never even been on a horse and you damn sure ain't starting out on a crazy dangerous stallion like Lightning Bolt."

"Don't look at me," Tony said. "I never been on a horse, either."

"Good, then no one is going tonight. I'll take some boys over tomorrow and get the horse myself."

"No you won't," Josie said. "Anderson's place is probably an armed camp right about now; same as Murky Bayou is. They'll stop you at the front gate. If you ever manage to get in, the horse will be gone when you reach the stable. Then, what will you tell Jojo?"

"Speaking of that, I got something I need to fess up to."

"What?"

"I didn't really buy Lightning Bolt, I borrowed him from someone I know. If we get him back, then I need to return him to his rightful owner."

Her dad's answer confused her, and she took a moment to say, "Can't you just explain the situation and then buy Lightning Bolt from him?"

"Baby, you don't understand. The man who owns him is one of the few people on earth that has more money than me; lots more money than me, and Lightning Bolt is one of his prized possessions."

She thought for a minute and then said, "You're good at fixing things. You always did when I was growing up. Can't you fix this for me and Jojo?"

"I'm sorry, Baby. I wish I could," Frankie said.

"Let's get the horse and then worry about it," Eddie said. "I have an idea that might work."

Josie clutched Eddie's hand. "If you can manage that, you'll be my hero, and Jojo and I will love you forever."

꿏꒭

Josie was having none of her dad's warnings. Dressed like ninja warriors, she, Eddie, and Tony were soon on their way to Angus Anderson's farm. The rain had stopped and the ground fog was rapidly returning.

The area was hilly and all but the main road to the horse ranch constructed of dirt. Josie knew every backroad in the parish and directed Tony to a hill overlooking the large farm.

"Kill your lights before you reach the top of the hill," she said.

"How am I supposed to know when to stop?" he asked.

"I'll tell you."

Before reaching the top of the rise, they began to see the lights of the horse farm. Josie pointed at a large building down the hill.

"The one with all the lights is the security building," she said. "That's where they view their security cameras and dispatch people to patrol the place. There's only one guard at the front gate."

"You sure?" Tony asked.

"I told you, I was the real estate agent that brokered the sale. I had the farm on the market for almost a year and visited it more times than I can count. Believe me when I tell you that I know it like the back of my hand."

"How do you intend to enter the property without being seen?" Tony asked.

"A dirt road that doubles as a firebreak circles the farm. There are no lights or security cameras in the open fields in the back portion of the farm. You stay here. Eddie and I will hike in."

"More power to you," he said. "My knees are repaired, but I'm not ready to test them with a hike like you're talking about."

"I don't know about Eddie. I jog almost every day. For me, it'll be a piece of cake."

Eddie wasn't so sure. "I'd feel better about it if I hadn't drunk half a bottle of Monkey Shoulder. At least I'm loose. Wish we had a flashlight."

Tony reached into his glove box, found a small flashlight and handed it to Eddie.

269

"I never go anywhere without it," he said.

Eddie slipped it into the pouch of his black sweatshirt. He and Josie had darkened their faces. When they pulled the hoods over their heads, they looked like Special Forces troops. Eddie's head was throbbing, and he didn't feel much like an elite soldier.

"Either of you have an aspirin?" he asked.

Tony handed him a bottle from his glovebox and gave him his flask of scotch to wash it down.

"Maybe I just need a little hair of the dog instead of these aspirins. How about lending me your flask?" he said.

"Your ass," Tony said. "You had a chance to bring some of your own. Here, take a good belt. Don't forget to leave some for me."

Eddie drank until he started coughing, and liquor dribbled down his neck. Josie just shook her head.

"Don't take all night." When Eddie belched, she said, "Maybe you better forget about what I said about loving you forever."

Ignoring Josie's rebuke, Eddie returned the flask to Tony. "I'm good now. Let's do it."

Damp fog washed over them as they left the warmth of Tony's car and started down the hill toward the dirt road that encircled Anderson's horse farm. Visibility was almost nil and the going slow. When Josie bumped into the fence, she knew that they were where they needed to be.

"The back pasture is on the other side of the fence, the stable area just beyond a practice track. It's about a half mile to the barns. You up for it?"

"How are we going to stay on course. I can barely see you, much less a half mile in the distance."

"There's a fence that divides this area into two pastures. One is for the stallions, the other for mares and their colts. It goes all the way to the railing on the practice track. We'll follow the outside fence until we reach it."

Eddie and Josie climbed over the fence and began following it. The inside dividing fence they were looking for was farther away than Josie had thought. The ten minutes it took them to reach it seemed like an hour.

"Here it is," she said.

"I was starting to get worried."

"Don't. I know where I'm going."

"At least we don't have to worry about someone spotting us," he said. "the only problem is, how are we going to get Lightning Bolt out of here, even if we find him?"

"We'll lead him out the same way we came in," she said.

"How will we get through the fence with him?"

"There's a back gate." She dangled a large keychain in front of him, close enough so that he could see. "Farms like this often have multiple locks so all the different people that require access can enter when they want. Unless they removed my lock, and I doubt they did, I still have a key."

"Slick," Eddie said. "You real estate people are on the ball."

"And don't you forget it," she said, stopping to give him a kiss.

Their embrace lasted longer than either of them had expected. Josie didn't even try to stop him when his hand wandered a little too far down her back. Finally, she shoved him away.

"Enough," she said. "We have a job to finish."

"Sorry," he said. "My mind was wandering."

"So was mine. We'll have time to take care of other business when we complete the task we're working on now."

Eddie didn't ask her what she meant by her comment, his imagination working overtime as he followed her through the thick soup. They soon reached the railing of the exercise track, and Josie crawled through. With some difficulty, Eddie followed after her.

"The railing will lead us to the stable area," she said.

"Then what?"

"They keep all the horses stalled in the main barn at night. The studs have their own area and are isolated from the rest of the horses. That's where we'll look."

"What about security cameras?" he asked.

"I know where they are. We'll be okay, as long as we don't bump into a security guard."

It wasn't far from the main entrance of the practice track to the barn. A red light began blinking when they opened the door and entered. Josie began punching numbers on the flashing keypad.

"Hope they haven't changed the code," she said.

There was a single beep, and then the light on the pad returned to green.

"Damn!" Eddie said. "Glad you have a good memory."

"I don't," she said. "I programmed it with the same code I use on all my listings. Anderson's people apparently never changed it."

"Sniggling little oversight," he said. "Sounds like Anderson needs to fire his security force and start over."

"It's not just Anderson," she said. "Most people never reprogram the keypad that opens their garage. Bet I can get into half the garages in New Orleans by punching in 1-2-3-4."

The interior of the large barn was dimly lit. It didn't matter because the visibility was ten times better than outside the barn. Eddie marveled at the craftsmanship that had gone into the structure and could only guess how much it had originally cost to build. He didn't have long to wonder as they departed one portion of the barn and entered another.

"This is where they keep the stallions standing stud," Josie said.

A gold plaque bore the name of each stallion occupying a stall. There were also pictures of the horses, either racing or else in the winner's circle. A short bio gave the horse's lineage, race record, and lifetime winnings. As they moved from stall to stall, looking for Lightning Bolt, Eddie could see that Anderson had acquired an impressive stable of champion studs that he apparently charged an equally impressive stud fee for.

"I found something," Josie said.

"Lightning Bolt?"

"His brother's stall."

"Lightning in a Bottle?"

"Yes, let's check it out."

They entered the spacious room that housed the horse. The big stallion munching on oats raised his head when Josie and Eddie walked up to the railing on his stall. The first thing they saw was the distinctive blaze on his face.

"Good God, it's Lightning Bolt," Josie said.

"What's he doing in Lightning in a Bottle's stall?"

"We can worry about the answer to that question later," she said. "Right now, we need to get a rein on him and then get the hell out of here."

Eddie found a rein on the wall and was watching her slip it over the horse's head when a big hand grabbed his shoulder. Even in the dim light of the stall, he could see the skull and crossbones tattoos on the knuckles of the hand.

When someone said, "Looking for something?" he didn't have to see the man's face to know who it was.

Chapter 32

Eddie flinched when he saw Lonzo Galvez's hand resting on his shoulder, and then heard his voice. He had little time to react as Anderson's big Latino bodyguard wheeled him around and backhanded him, the blow knocking him back against the railing of the stall. Galvez didn't wait to see if the blow had knocked him out as he opened the door to Lightning Bolt's stall and went after Josie.

Suddenly wide-awake, the big stallion became animated and began bucking and kicking. Thinking Galvez was after him, he kicked the man in the shoulder with his dangerous hind hooves.

Galvez recovered quickly and began circling the periphery of the stall, trying to stay away from the hooves of the bucking stallion. Josie could see Eddie lying comatose on the hay-strewn floor. Seeing something hanging on the wall that she recognized, she grabbed it, hiding it behind her back.

Lightning Bolt continued raising havoc, wildly whirling in circles, bent on kicking something or someone. Josie managed to keep the horse between her and Galvez as she maneuvered her way to the stall door. Galvez wasn't far behind her.

Eddie was lying on the ground, one leg beneath him and his head canted at an odd angle. Josie barely had time to touch his scalp when Galvez exited Lightning Bolt's stall. His fists clenched, a scowl contorted his face as he charged toward them. When he got there, he quickly got a surprise.

Josie had grabbed an electric prod, a device for helping to control the dangerous stallions when they became unruly. When Galvez reached her, she stuck the prod between his legs and pulled the trigger.

Lonzo Galvez was big, strong, and mean. It didn't matter. When Josie shocked him with the electric prod, he dropped to his knees like a sack of cement. He wanted to get to his feet but couldn't. His legs and his entire body had turned to the consistency of jelly. Not waiting for the shock to wear off, Josie broke the prod on his head, and then began trying to beat him senseless with what remained. Eddie grabbed her arm and stopped her.

"Don't kill him," he said. "He's out like a light."

Sirens were sounding, and security lamps were flashing all through the barn.

"We don't have much time," he said. "Let's get Lightning Bolt and get the hell out of here."

"Are you okay?" she asked.

"Just a sore jaw and a little whiplash. At least I'm better off than he is."

Josie tossed what was left of the electric prod to the stable floor. "Those things should be banned, though I'm glad for that particular one," she said. "How can we calm down Lightning Bolt? He's going crazy in there."

Eddie didn't answer, entering the big horse's stall and approaching him with caution.

"It's okay, boy. I'm not going to hurt you."

Something in Eddie's voice calmed the big stallion. After grabbing the reins, Eddie patted the side of Lightning Bolt's head and led him out the open door of the stall. Josie jumped on his back, not waiting to ask.

"Hop on," she said.

"Not yet. Someone needs to open the front door."

"Then hurry. We don't have much time."

Security personnel was entering the front of the barn as Josie, Eddie, and Lightning Bolt exited the rear door. Grabbing Eddie's hand, she helped him up behind her on the horse. Lightning Bolt recoiled when he walked out into the rolling fog bank. Though they had no saddle, they somehow managed to stay on the big animal's back when he raised up on his hind legs.

The gate to the practice track was open, and Josie raced Lightning Bolt through it. A late October wind had picked up and was beginning to blow away the fog. Through the still hazy darkness, they could see the railing on the far side of the track. There was no exit other than the one they'd entered. The shouts of angry men echoed behind them.

"What are you going to do?" Eddie asked when they reached the railing.

Josie didn't answer, turning the horse and running back a hundred feet or so before stopping. Wind was whistling through the railing, the rolling fog mostly gone. She and Eddie could clearly see the dozen or so men running toward them.

"Hang on," Josie said, giving Lightning Bolt's rear a swat.

Eddie grabbed hold, his arms latched around Josie's waist as they raced toward the railing. He'd seen quarter horses run many times but had never, until that very moment, had any earthly idea just how fast they were.

As the railing approached, he closed his eyes. They both held on as the big stallion went airborne, clearing the railing with room to spare. She didn't slow him down until they'd reached the back gate.

"Damn!" he said. "I didn't know quarter horses could jump like that."

"Me either," she said.

She slid off the horse, opened the gate, and waited until Eddie had trotted Lightning Bolt through it. He gave her a hand, and she jumped up behind him.

"You drive," she said. "I have a call to make."

Tony answered his cell phone on the first ring. "What's up?"

"Eddie and I have Lightning Bolt. We're heading toward the farm. Anderson's bodyguard recognized us. From the lights and the shouting coming from Anderson's place, I'd say there's a small army heading toward Murky Bayou."

"What do you want me to do?" Tony asked.

"Call Dad and tell him to alert the cavalry. And Tony, tell him to please hurry."

When they reached the edge of Frankie's farm, Eddie raced the big stallion through the phalanx of Black Tahoes lining the dirt road bordering the entrance. Josie jumped off into the arms of her dad.

"You okay, Baby?" Frankie asked.

"Just barely. Look behind you."

An armada of white Suburbans came racing up the road behind them. Seeing the wall of Tahoes, the drivers of the vehicles began falling in line beside one another in an empty field across the way. Angus Anderson exited a Suburban. Shielded behind one of the vehicles, he began talking through a bullhorn.

"Frankie Castellano, you wop horse thief. Give me back my stallion."

Frankie had his own bullhorn. "Or what?"

"Spend some hard time in prison. You know who my cousin is."

"Probably better than you do."

"Unless you give my horse back right now, you're going to soon find out, not to mention that pretty daughter of yours is in deep shit."

"What about my daughter?" Frankie said.

"She almost killed one of my men with a horse prod. Give me the horse, and I won't press charges."

Before Frankie had a chance to reply, a row of Black Navigators began driving up and parking beside the Suburbans. Soon, there was a semicircle of expensive SUVs across the road from the entrance to Frankie's farm.

Men armed with shotguns and automatic weapons began filing out. A Latino man with his own bullhorn exited one of the vehicles and started talking. It was Chuy Delgado, headman of the Mexican crime cartel.

"Castellano, you and me got a score to settle. Now, you're gonna pay for killing my son-in-law."

"I didn't kill nobody. Until last night, I thought it was you that killed my jockey and trainer. Now I know you didn't do it and I know who did. The same person that killed Diego."

Chuy Delgado didn't immediately respond. "Who?" he finally said.

"Your good buddy Angus Anderson."

"You're a lying sack of shit," Delgado said. "Anderson didn't kill nobody."

"Then why did he have my horse? His newspapers reported it was killed, along with my two men. I'll bet he told you the same thing."

"He's a liar," Anderson said on his bullhorn.

"Am I? My daughter just found the horse at Anderson's ranch and rode him home. What do you think Anderson and all his men are doing here?"

"Show me the horse," Delgado said.

When Frankie grabbed Lightning Bolt's reins, Josie stopped him.

"You're not going out there. They'll kill you the minute they see you. They won't kill me. I'll show them the horse."

"No you won't," Eddie said, snatching the reins out of Frankie's hands.

278

Before they could react, he sprang up on
Lightning Bolt and rode him into the circle of
headlights. He didn't stop until he was directly in
front of Delgado's car.

"There's not another horse in the entire world
that looks like this one. Recognize him?"

Delgado walked out of the shadows, straight up
to where Eddie and the horse waited and touched the
bolt on his forehead.

"Where did he come from?" he asked.

"Like Frankie said, Josie and I just liberated him
from Anderson's farm."

"What was he doing there?"

"The name on the stall we found him in was
Lightning in a Bottle. As you probably know, that
horse is Lightning Bolt's full brother."

"So what?"

"Same DNA, that's what. Since you and your
son-in-law sold Lightning in a Bottle to Mr. Anderson,
my guess is you knew he was shooting blanks. When
Contrado refused to give Anderson his six million
bucks back that he'd paid for the horse, he had him
killed. Then he had Frankie's trainer, and jockey
killed and stole Lightning Bolt. He faked the horse's
death and replaced Lightning in a Bottle with
Lightning Bolt. As you can see, he was hoping like
hell you and Frankie would cancel each other out."

"How do I know you speak the truth?" Delgado
said.

"Have the dead horse's body exhumed. This, as
you can clearly see, is Lightning Bolt. The dead horse
is his brother, Lightning in a Bottle. Anderson killed
your son-in-law, Frankie's jockey and trainer, and his
own horse to get even with you and Frankie."

"I want to take the horse just to make sure what
you say is true."

"No way," Eddie said. "This horse is state's
evidence. He stays with Mr. Castellano. You got a

problem with that?"

Angus Anderson was standing in clear view of Chuy Delgado. Delgado gave him a burn-in-hell look before returning to the back seat of the lead Navigator. He peeled off down the road followed by a caravan of similar-looking vehicles. Eddie rode over to where Anderson was waiting.

"In case you don't already know, I'm a Federal D.A. I'm filing Federal murder charges against you tomorrow. Your cousin and all of your influential relatives will be powerless to help you. If I were you, I'd pack my bags before then and go someplace where they can't extradite you."

Anderson's Suburbans were driving away, Frankie's men cheering when he rode back to where they waited. Frankie was the first to shake his hand when he dismounted the horse.

"Like I said before, you got a set of balls on you."

Josie had her arms clamped around Eddie's waist. "I am so proud of you," she said. "How did you know the dead horse was Lightning in a Bottle?"

"I don't, at least for sure. Tony and I talked about it, and we decided he wanted Lightning Bolt long before he bought Lightning in a Bottle. Wendell Swanson likely sealed his own fate when he took a bribe instead of buying the horse at auction like Anderson had wanted him to."

"What'll I do now?" Frankie said. "Return the horse to Conrad Finston, or give him to Jojo?"

"Neither," Eddie said. "Like I told Anderson, Lightning Bolt is state's evidence. Tomorrow, when Jojo wakes up, there'll be a pony waiting for him. His own pony."

"But I told him he could have Lightning Bolt," Frankie said.

Eddie held up a hand and shook his head. "We don't always get everything we want. Jojo's an intelligent young man. Take him aside and explain to him why he can't have Lightning Bolt. He'll understand. I promise you that he will."

"You seem pretty sure about that," Frankie said.

Eddie looked him straight in the eye and said, "Trust me on this."

Frankie's big smile returned, and he slapped Eddie's shoulder. "Then let's go to the house and celebrate."

Through the conversation, Josie's arms had remained wrapped around Eddie's waist.

"The only place this man is going right now is to bed with me," she said. "And don't even think about trying to wake us up early tomorrow because we're not answering the door."

Chapter 33

J.P. waited on the trail until we'd joined him. The path had led us to a small clearing in the hardwood forest, in front of us the strangest house imaginable.

A lifelong resident of New Orleans, I'd seen many large live oaks. There were several such trees in City Park, their drooping branches covered with Spanish moss and resurrection fern. They were ancient, maybe centuries old. The tree in front of us was even larger, older, and stranger.

The tree pierced a ramshackle, wood-framed house. Trunk and branches skewered the wooden structure, the resultant symbiosis somehow breathing life into the walls, roof, shuttered windows, and doors of the house. In short, the tree and the house were one.

The cobblestone path ended at the red front door, the old paint job flaking around the edges. The shutters were yellow, the walls light blue, reminding me of the many color schemes in the French Quarter.

The colors of the house weren't the only things that caught my eye. Everywhere I looked, the greens were greener, browns browner, and so on. The colors of everything around prompted me to think that maybe someone had slipped me some LSD. The others were equally awed.

"What in the living hell!" J.P. said.

Around the house and tree grew a wild garden of vines, creepers, and so many colorful nightshades and other wild blooms that their perfume was almost intoxicating. Foxes, rabbits, squirrels and other animals played on the grass in front of the house, and birds of vivid colors flew in the blue sky above us. Nothing seemed normal.

"It's like a fairyland cartoon," Abba said. "It wouldn't surprise me if an elf scurried across the path in front of us. What is this place?"

"We've crossed over," Rory said.

"You mean we're dead?" Abba asked.

Rory didn't answer.

"We ain't dead," J.P. said. "At least I'm not."

"It does seem like we're in another world," Abba said. "What do we do?"

"Knock on the door," I said.

Without waiting for the others to follow me, I walked up the path and knocked. A pale little man with a pencil mustache and smarmy smile opened the door. A French accent flavored the words pouring from his mouth.

"Please come in. We have been expecting you."

I motioned the others to join me before following him. We entered a room far larger than the outside of the house implied. A very large black woman clad in a yellow floor-length dress that seemed from another era stood behind a table, her palms flat on its surface.

On her head, she wore a matching tignon, a turban-like headcover free women of color were required to wear during the Pre-Civil War Era in New Orleans. It was soon apparent that she wore the tignon because she liked it and not because someone required her to. When we'd entered the room, she glanced up from what she'd been doing.

"I'm Tubah Jones," she said. "We've been waiting for you."

"You knew we were coming?" I asked.

283

"From the moment you pulled Exethelon from the wizard's heart and started the fire."

I glanced at J.P. to gauge his reaction to her remark. I could tell by his inquisitive glance that it had caught his detective's attention.

"Yes, I pulled the dagger from Father Fred's heart, the fire already burning."

"Exethelon, as you now know, is magical. You were destined to pull it from someone's dead heart. It became yours the moment you entered the room."

"Even so . . ."

She stopped me with a wave of her hand. "You thought it would be better for you if the building and everything in it burned to the ground."

"I'll admit the thought crossed my mind. Doesn't matter because I never would have done it."

"Exethelon senses your every wish and reacts accordingly. Though you didn't know you started the fire, the simple truth is that you did."

I opened my mouth to defend myself. Realizing I could never prove or disprove to anyone what my thoughts were at a particular time, I simply closed it and shook my head.

"You didn't know about the dagger's power when you first touched it. Now that you do, I fully expect you will act accordingly."

"Of one thing I'm pretty sure," J.P. said. "Wyatt didn't kill Father Fred or the two guards."

"No he didn't," she said. "They were killed by a dark spell I cast on them."

"You admit to murdering them?"

"Do you intend to take me into custody and then charge me with casting a spell?"

"You either murdered them, or you didn't," J.P. said.

"When you were young, did you ever tell your mother you wished she were dead?"

"If I did, I didn't mean it," he said.

"What if she had died? Would you have been responsible?"

J.P. thought a moment before answering. "There's a difference between saying something in a moment of anger and casting a spell that kills somebody."

"If I admitted that I killed someone by casting upon them a magical death spell, do you believe a judge and jury would find me guilty?"

"Probably not," he said.

"The man you call Father Fred and his two guards were evil. They committed more atrocities than you'd ever believe, and were the embodiment of pure malevolence. I didn't kill them. I simply cast a spell that resulted in their deaths. Trust me when I tell you that the world is a far better place now that they're gone."

"What happened to the prisoners they kept at the old orphanage?" I asked.

"Released and transported to safety," she said.

"Transported?"

Her nod was the only answer to my question.

"Wyatt and I met a man who was a victim of Father Fred," Abba said. "He told us the false priest was a slaver and a cannibal. We haven't talked to J.P. about it. He doesn't know how evil Father Fred was. Wyatt and I do."

"But you're not here because of Father Fred."

"We're looking for a young woman. Rory told us you might know where we can find her," Abba said.

Rory nodded when Tubah Jones said, "I'm very impressed with your craftsmanship. I'm over two hundred years old, and I've known many sword makers during my lifetime. You are the best of them all." She returned her gaze to Abba. "I know of the young woman of whom you speak. I also know where she is."

"Will you share that information with us?" I said.

285

"You are here because I need your help. I have a problem I cannot solve alone."

"Then please tell us," I said.

"In due time. Are you hungry?"

"Starved," Abba said. "All we've had for awhile is trail mix and jerky."

"Good," Tubah Jones said. "The table is ready in the kitchen."

She led us through the house that seemed to have endless rooms. Much like her dress, the kitchen reminded me of one from Antebellum New Orleans. The table was large and could easily have accommodated twenty or more people. Made of wood, it looked as if it were an antique or a replica of an antique.

Bowls of steaming food waited for us on the table; potatoes, carrots, and practically every vegetable dish imaginable. There was no meat. Tubah Jones explained.

"We who live in this house are all vegetarians. I hope you don't mind."

"Everything smells wonderful," Abba said. "Who else lives here?"

"My husband Boris and I have many children. You saw some of them playing in the front yard when you arrived."

"We saw no children," Abba said.

As if on cue, a boy and a girl, clowning and having a good time, entered the kitchen. When the girl pushed the boy, he transformed before our eyes into a cocker spaniel puppy and began barking at her.

The girl transformed into a kitten, cuffed the cocker with a paw, and then ran out of the kitchen, the puppy chasing after her. I blinked, not believing what I had seen. J.P., Abba, and Rory could only stare at the door through which they had disappeared.

"Boris, the children and I are shifters," she said.

She laughed when J.P. said, "You mean like a werewolf?"

"If we wanted to be," she said. "It's dark outside and the night's cold. Let's go in by the fire."

"It can't be dark yet," Abba said.

Tubah pulled back a curtain so that we could see outside.

"Oh, but it is," she said.

The room had thick rugs on the floor, overstuffed chairs and couches, and a fireplace nearby with a crackling fire warming the air. We gathered around Tubah who was apparently intent on telling us something.

"You are here because you are seeking a young woman. She is alive, at least bodily, though just barely."

"Please tell us where to find her," I said.

"She is with Sister Gertrude in the convent known as Sisters of the Mist. Desire, like all the other prisoners, kept there, is in grave danger."

"Desire is a prisoner?" Abba asked.

Tubah nodded. "The convent is a place of evil, the young women taken there under false pretenses. Desire, like the others, thought she was joining a sisterhood to serve Christ as a cloistered nun. Now, those women are prostitutes and nuns of the Devil. Desire's situation is even worse."

"The convent is a whorehouse?" J.P. asked.

"Run by Sister Gertrude; the other Sisters of the Mist vampires."

"You have to be kidding," Abba said.

"I'm not."

"How is Desire's situation worse than being forced into prostitution?" I asked.

"She is also a host to the vampires. They feed on her blood. She has been slowly slipping away since she arrived at the convent. Her mind has all but left

287

her, and that is quite possibly her only salvation at this point."

"You have to help us save her," I said.

Tubah shook her head. "No, you have to help me. That is why I summoned you here. The convent is as large as a castle and even surrounded by a large moat. It resists even my darkest magic and is all but impenetrable."

"Why is this castle so important to you?" Abba asked.

"As I said, the convent is a place of pure evil. It's built atop the gate to hell, and the entrance to hell itself lies in the dark basement of the castle."

"I'm having a hard time believing this," Abba said.

"Believe it. A boulder blocks the gateway and keeps the demons of darkness in the netherworld. Every one-hundred-sixty years, on the night of All Saint's Eve, this changes."

"What happens?" I asked.

"If no one blocks the boulder from being moved, demons are released and havoc ensues. This country has yet to fully recover from the harm caused the last time this happened."

"The Civil War?" I said.

"It could have been averted peacefully. It resulted in the most American deaths ever for a single war; almost as many as all the other wars combined."

"And if the demons are released tomorrow night?"

"I can only imagine," she said. "Will you help?"

"I'm in," I said.

"Me too," J.P. said.

"As am I," Rory said.

"Count me in," Abba said.

"If the castle is impenetrable, then how will we get in?" J.P. asked.

Instead of answering his question, she asked, "Do you believe in destiny?"

"Sure," he said.

"As Rory told you before you left New Orleans, this is a quest. Each of you has a purpose, and each must make a vital decision before All Saints Eve ends tomorrow at midnight."

The window was partially open. Something was howling in the swamp beyond the house.

"What creature is making that noise?" Abba asked.

"One of the People. Would you like to see?" Tubah said.

"Is it dangerous?" Abba asked.

"Not if I accompany you."

She led us outside, into the darkness. There was neither fog nor rain, only the golden light of the fullest moon I'd ever seen. Hundreds of white, saucer-sized moonflowers had bloomed, their perfume filling the air. The howling stopped, though something was rustling in the bushes beyond the house.

"Barzoom," Tubah said. "Show yourself."

None of us was prepared for the creature that exited the bushes.

"Oh my dear God!" Abba said, taking a step backward as her hand went to her mouth.

Chapter 34

When the creature stepped from the bushes, my own eyes probably grew as large as J.P. and Rory's did. Like Abba, we all backed up a step.

"Do not be afraid," Tubah said. "He won't hurt you."

The big fellow stood every inch of eight feet tall, stooped, lanky, and muscular. A thatch of brownish-gray hair sprouted from the rear portion of his large head and draped down his hairy back. His fingers and toes were human-like and featured long nails. His big eyes were yellow and accentuated a mouth filled with fangs and highlighted bone structure causing him to look permanently angry.

Though he was anything but human, his legs and torso were human-like, and thinly covered with hair. Almost no hair covered his extra-long arms, and the bare skin accentuated his bulging muscles. The creature called Barzoom was quite naked, and it was obvious he was a male. He dropped to one knee in front of Tubah, bowed his head in respect, and touched her hand.

"These are the brave souls I'm entrusting you to protect," she said.

After rolling his big yellow eyes, he gave us a glance and nodded. When he opened his immense jaws, a high-pitched wail emanated from deep in his barrel chest.

"Rise, and return to your people," she said. These warriors leave at dawn for the castle of the Sisters of the Mist."

Without a sound, he melded into the darkness. After he'd returned to the underbrush surrounding Tubah's house, he began the unnatural howl we'd heard in the swamp. Others like him joined in the chorus. Though I'd seen the creature up close that was making the sound, its eerie howls caused the hair on the back of my neck to stand on end.

A moment passed, and then J.P. asked, "Is he the Swamp Monster?"

His question brought a smile to Tubah's mouth. "You are one of only a handful of individuals that has ever seen one of the People up close. But don't worry; no one will ever believe you."

"Hell," J.P. said. "I wasn't six feet away from him, and I'm still not sure I believe my own eyes. One thing, though."

"You have a question?"

"Every report I ever heard about the Swamp Monster said they smelled to high heavens," J.P. said.

"Much like skunks, they have scent glands," Tubah said. "The foul odor is emitted when they feel they are in imminent danger. You do not want to be anywhere near when that happens."

"I'll take your word for it," J.P. said.

"Let's return to the fire, and I'll brief you on what you need to do to save Desire, and to stop the incursion of demons from hell."

Late fall weather outside Tubah's house had chilled me to the bone. The crackling fire felt like heaven as I sank into an overstuffed chair. J.P. and Rory shared a couch, and Abba sat on the stone ledge in front of the fire, warming her hands. Rory broke out the flask of Southern Comfort.

291

"Mind if I have a nip?" he asked.

"Only if you don't plan to share," she said.

The whiskey flask was soon changing hands. Tubah didn't speak until everyone, including her, had drunk from it. Finally, she handed it to me.

"No thanks," I said. "I'm an alcoholic, and don't drink anymore."

"Because of my magic, tonight is different. We have many important things to discuss, and it's best done if everyone is intoxicated. But do not worry. I promise you will suffer no lasting effects from the alcohol."

I took the flask and had a drink, the whiskey soothing my nerves like a dear old friend as it warmed my throat. I was quickly in an almost forgotten state of euphoria as I returned the flask to Rory.

"You each have a specific task to perform," Tubah said. "If you fail, the mission will fail. Fate will call upon each of you to make an important and tortuous decision. How you resolve the problem will affect you as a person forever."

Abba said, "It all sounds so ominous. What exactly do you mean?"

"You'll each know what it means when it happens."

"Then tell us what each of us needs to do," J.P. said.

"You, Jean Pierre, have an important role to play. You won't be accompanying the others to the castle."

"But they need me," he said.

"The task you perform will either result in a successful mission or doom it to failure. Are you ready to hear what it is we need you to do?"

"Yes ma'am," he said.

"The Convent of the Sisters of the Mist is located so deep in the swamp that no man can ever find it. On Halloween night all that changes."

"Tell me," he said.

"Though vampires populate the castle, Sister Gertrude is human. Well, at least almost human. As was Father Fred, she is also involved in slavery, the sex trade, and every evil aspect of human trafficking."

"And the castle?" I said.

"Little more than a brothel. Like Desire, Sister Gertrude forces her victims to help act out her clients' perverse fantasies. Some of them, like Desire, provide sustenance for the vampires."

"But she's still alive?" I said.

"She has suffered dearly, her body in an advanced state of decline. She has changed so drastically that you may have a difficult time recognizing her. She is, however, very much alive."

J.P. could see how much Tubah's description of Desire's condition was upsetting me and thankfully changed the subject.

"How do her clients find their way to the castle?" he asked.

"Sister Gertrude owns an exclusive gentlemen's club on Bourbon Street that caters to much more than the viewing of naked ladies. An interspatial portal connects the club and the castle."

"What does it have to do with Halloween night?" Abba asked.

"Every year, Sister Gertrude hosts the Vampire Ball on the night of All Saint's Eve. The ball takes place at the castle, and the guests are transported there."

"And you want me to be one of the gentlemen transported through the portal," J.P. said.

"All of Sister Gertrude's regular clients attend the ball. Management also invites certain high rollers

293

who happen to be in the club. It is up to you to make sure that you are invited."

"Hell, this sounds more like fun than a job," J.P. said.

"Believe me when I tell you that the monsters you will be dealing with are deadly serious," Tubah said. "If Sister Gertrude's people think you are a plant, they will kill you."

"Got it," J.P. said, his smile disappearing.

"The ball is a masquerade affair befitting of Halloween. You will be in costume. I will see that you get to the club. Getting an invitation to the Vampire's Ball is dependent on your acting ability. It is one of the reasons you were chosen, and I have no doubt that you will succeed."

"What happens when I reach the castle?" he asked.

"The party will be in progress, every conceivable act of sexual debauchery on full display."

"Good," he said. "I've always been a fan of sexual debauchery."

Tubah grinned as she said, "Your reputation precedes you. You must battle your primal urges and ignore the revelry taking place around you for the good of the mission."

"I'll do my best," he said.

"Amid the confusion and pandemonium, you should be able to make your way to the front gate. Open it, and then lower the drawbridge over the moat."

"Sounds easy enough to me," J.P. said.

"Not so easy. Like the Vatican, Sister Gertrude has her own version of a Swiss Army, hers comprised of rogue mercenaries, killers, and half-human trolls. They don't partake in the festivities and will be on the lookout for intruders. If you are discovered, they will kill you."

"How much time will I have?" he asked.

"Very little," Tubah said. "At midnight, the gateway to hell will open, and demons will begin pouring out. You'll have less than an hour to accomplish your task."

"Say I'm successful opening the door and lowering the drawbridge. Then what?"

"Rory," Tubah said. "You have perhaps the most important job."

"Tell me," he said.

"You must channel your inner-Scottish warlord because you will be leading the People tomorrow night. I am not exaggerating when I say that only you and they can save the world an untold measure of hardship and death. Are you up to the task?"

"My broadsword Aila and I will do our best," he said.

"That is all I can ask. You and the People will be waiting. When the gate is open, and the drawbridge crosses the moat, you will likely have to fight your way into the castle. You'll find the soldiers of the Swiss Guard are fierce fighters. As fierce as they are, they are nothing compared to what you will encounter when you reach the basement."

"What about Abba and me?" I asked.

"You will enter the castle with Rory and the People. When you find where they keep Desire, you must rescue her and then lead her to safety."

"I'm not much of a fighter," I said.

"We shall see," she said. "Amid the bedlam of the masked revelry, perversion, and battle, you should be able to spirit her out of the castle."

"What about the other victims?" I asked.

"That is part of the question that only you can answer," Tubah said.

"What else?" J.P. asked.

"Sleep, if you're able to. Tomorrow, you leave at dawn."

It was still dark when Tubah and Boris awoke us. It was the first time in my life that I'd ever woken up from a night of drinking without having a hangover. A good thing I didn't know Tubah's secret and wasn't tempted to return to my former alcoholic ways. Tubah fed us breakfast while she gave us last minute instructions. Slick and Lucky were wagging their tails, perhaps in anticipation of what they sensed was about to happen. J.P. gave Lucky a head rub.

"You will require a costume, Jean Pierre," Tubah said.

The moment the words were out of her mouth, J.P.'s camos magically changed into a tuxedo, complete with a green, feathered mask. He reached into his tuxedo jacket and pulled out a diamond-studded money clip.

"Damn!" he said. "There are thousands of dollars in this wad of cash."

"Only an illusion," Tubah said. "But not to worry. Sister Gertrude's minions will only see what they think is real money."

"Will I need all of this?" he asked.

"Maybe even more," she said. "If you do, it will appear."

"Hey, I already like this gig," he said. "I can do some damage flashing around this kind of money."

"Exactly what you do not need to do. Tonight, you will see things you won't believe and be tempted to join in the revelry. Resist your temptation, or the mission will fail, and innocent people will die."

"I'm hip," he said.

Tubah nodded. "Boris will show you the entrance to the portal."

"You won't need me for the next eight to ten hours. What will I do until then?"

"Wait patiently beside the fire. Drink coffee. Take a nap. You will be in grave danger from the moment you set foot in Sister Gertrude's club, so prepare yourself mentally for the trials that await you."

Before Boris could lead him away, I shook J.P.'s hand. "Good luck," I said.

Rory also shook his hand. Abba hugged him and began crying, her tears dampening his shoulder.

"We'll all get through this just fine," he said, kissing her forehead. "And don't forget about our date." He scratched Lucky's ears. "You take care of these people until I join you."

Once J.P. was gone, Abba wiped her eyes.

Seeing the smile on my face, she said, "What?"

"Nothing," I said.

Tubah interrupted us, probably saving me from more of a reprimand.

"Boris will lead you to the castle. It's not that far away from here, though you would never make it without his help. It is time, and you must go now."

We were dressed in our camos the same as when we had arrived at Tubah's house. Rory wasn't happy about it.

"If I'm going into battle, I'd prefer doing it in my own Scottish battle garb," he said.

"Before you enter the castle, I will make it so," she said.

"What about Abba and me?" I asked.

"I will change your hiking clothes into costumes. Until then, the clothes you have on will be better suited for a trek through the swamp."

"Then I guess we should leave now," I said.

"Yes. Once you are gone from here, I will no longer be able to provide much assistance. From this point on, everything relies on your instincts, a certain amount of good luck, and destiny."

"You said that with an ominous tone," Abba said. "Is there something you aren't telling us?"

"Just this: if you are destined to fail, you will. If you are destined to succeed, you will, but . . ."

"But what?" Abba said.

"Sometimes, we sculpt our own destinies."

Chapter 35

Dressed in camo, combat boots, and jungle hats, Abba, Rory, and I left the house of the sorceress. Boris led the way, though not as the little man with the smarmy smile we knew. He'd transformed into a large gray wolf, and his menacing presence proved somewhat disconcerting.

Though his appearance bothered us, it wasn't as bad as Lucky and Slick's reaction when he transformed in front of them. They began growling, preparing to fight when Tubah worked some magic on them. Though they sniffed noses with Boris, their body language indicated they weren't happy about having him around.

Long before we'd gone a mile, morning sun had begun rising over the hardwood trees behind us. The brightness didn't last long. Ground fog, starting first as wispy strands of vapor, began forming clouds that turned our trail into a ghostly pathway.

Slogging through the fog proved a slow process. Rory learned as much when he banged headfirst into a tree branch and almost knocked himself out. The muddy ground made our trek even more treacherous, Abba and I both slipping and falling on our rears.

Lucky and Slick had finally grown used to Boris and followed closely behind him as he hurried

through the thick soup. When gentle rain began
dissipating the curtain of cottony moisture, we were
once again able to see. Abba wasn't happy about the
rain dripping down her neck.

"Tired?" I asked.

"Aren't you? Sloshing around in this muck is
wearing me out."

"I'm glad I'm not the only one that it's
bothering?" I said. "You okay, Rory?"

"Aye, though I am probably the first Scotsman
that has ever gone on a quest through a Louisiana
swamp."

His comment caused Abba to smile. "At least
you're not wearing your kilt."

Our banter had caused us to slow even more.
Boris soon doubled back to find us, howling to voice
his disapproval of the rate at which we were moving.
Rory took a drink of Southern Comfort and then
tossed the flask to Abba.

"Not much left," she said. "Want the last swig?"

"Not me," I said. "Tubah's not here, and I'm
taking no chances that her spell has worn off."

"Then you finish it," she said, returning the flask
to Rory.

We continued along the trail, trying to ignore the
rain soaking our clothes, and puddles of water
dampening our socks and causing our toes to squish
around inside our boots. It was hard not to notice that
the trees were even larger than before, making me
wonder if we were the first humans to trod this path.

Boris never slowed, and we had to hurry to keep
him in sight. I was gawking instead of watching
where I was going and almost bumped into him. He'd
transformed back into human form, Lucky and Slick
looking confused as they stood by his side.

"We are moving too slowly," he said. "At this rate,
we won't make it to the castle in time."

"I don't see how we can go any faster," Abba said. "I can barely see more than a foot or so in front of me, and I've already busted my ass twice."

"Humans move far too slow. You need to be transformed," he said.

"Into wolves?"

Boris nodded.

"Can you do that?" I asked.

"I cannot. Tubah can."

"Tubah isn't here," Abba said. "How can she help us?"

"She is watching us at this very moment," he said. "The dogs must also be transformed, or there will be problems."

"What do we need to do?" I asked.

"Be aware that when your bodies change so will your minds. You will become wolves and not just humans in the bodies of wolves. Prepare yourself because for some, what you are about to experience can be a life-changing shock."

Before I could ask another question, the hair on my arm began morphing into thick, gray fur. It wasn't just the hair on my arms undergoing alteration. My bones began popping as the structure of my entire body began to change: hands and feet into paws, my mouth into a muzzle filled with dangerous fangs, and my human brain changing into the heart and soul of a feral wolf.

Abba squealed, and the dogs yelped as they began experiencing the same phenomena of transformation. When the alteration was finally complete, we circled each other, snarling and nipping. Boris dove into the middle of us.

We quickly learned that he was the alpha and the leader of the pack. It didn't take him long to establish his authority. I yelped and backed away when he nipped my tail and sank his teeth into my rear end. When Rory and Abba charged to my

301

assistance, Boris' bared fangs and lunging growls quickly cowed them. Lucky and Slick already knew who was the boss and circled the fray, waiting for the inevitable results.

His authority established, Boris raced away into the underbrush. We howled and followed him. When he disappeared for a moment in a hanging mass of vines and creepers, we thought he'd abandoned us. Once we entered the arboreal tent, we saw that he was waiting.

Boris hadn't lied when he told us that our transformation would be a life-changing experience. Reality as I had known it had suddenly disappeared. It started with my perspective of everything around me.

No longer was I six feet tall. Now, I was running on all fours, seeing the world around me from a vantage point of only three feet off the ground. The effect on my psyche was astonishing.

I could suddenly smell things I'd never smelled, hear things I'd never heard, and sense things that would have frightened the life out of me had I not also acquired the heart of a wolf. It didn't dawn on me that no human had ever even imagined the path we were following.

Fairy-like phosphorescence, lighting the darkness of what seemed a well-worn animal path, sparkled like a Christmas tree. The roof of the vegetal tent barely topped our heads. If I'd been thinking like a human, I'm sure I would have wondered if the People had an alternate route to the castle that they were taking. Thinking like a wolf following a pack, the thought never crossed my mind.

The dirt floor of the arboreal pathway was wet, dozens of paw prints marking our course. The multitude of scents was almost overpowering, though we saw no other animals, bears, snakes, or otherwise. When we exited the tunnel, thick fog quickly enveloped us. Boris stopped, circled us once, and then howled. Abba, Rory, the dogs and I joined him.

We didn't need to have Boris in our sight when he took off up the trail. We only had to follow his strong scent. If there were any animals in our way, they gave us a wide berth. It was raining again. I was running in a pack of wolves, and mere words can't explain the visceral excitement, intensity, and breathless awe I was experiencing.

My heart continued to race as we followed Boris down creek beds, through almost invisible paths through bramble bushes, and every obscure shortcut that possibly only he knew to the castle of the Sisters of the Mist.

The forest grew thicker, the trees taller. He finally stopped in front of one of the largest trees I'd ever seen. It was hollow, and we followed him into its interior. The lighting was dim though it was no detriment to our elevated senses. As we watched, he began to transform from wolf to human.

All of us began reverting to our former selves, Abba, Rory and I human, Lucky and Slick back into canines. At least that's what we thought at the moment. As we huddled in the darkness, we quickly realized we were all quite naked.

"Stop staring at me," Abba said, covering her breasts with her arms.

"Sorry," I said.

We weren't naked long. Apparently still with us, Tubah restored our camo fatigues and boots. They were once again clean and dry. Boris was peering up at the inside of the hollow tree.

"I have never seen such a place," Abba said. "Where are we?"

"Not far from our destination," Boris said.

Abba was correct. The hollow tree had the look and feel of an enormous wooden cathedral. When my eyes adjusted, I could see the circular stairway that disappeared into the darkness as it ascended. Boris produced a torch, its flame providing eerie illumination as he began climbing the narrow stairway.

"We are no longer beasts of prey," he said. "We must ascend this stairway or be in danger of being eaten by animals larger than us."

"What animals are you speaking of?" Rory asked. "Only the Swamp Monster is bigger than me, and they're on our side."

Boris grinned though he didn't answer Rory's question.

"It's huge inside here," I said. "This tree must be gigantic."

"Not so big," Boris said. "Tubah has changed us into elves so that we can use this tree as a vantage until darkness comes.

"I am no elf," Boris said.

"Neither am I," Abba said. "I don't feel small at all."

"Your dogs think you are," Boris said.

Lucky and Slick had begun their transformation outside of the hollow tree. Even ten feet below us, they looked enormous. When they saw us, they began barking.

"They no longer recognize us. They can rest in the hollow at the base of the tree and will be fine until we return. No more questions. We need to keep climbing."

My legs grew weary as we followed Boris up the spiraling stairway. I was out of breath when he reached a ledge near the very top of the tall tree and finally drew to a halt. Through a hole, we could see a large clearing in the swamp and the spires of a majestic castle. The growing mist and cottony clouds failed to mask the impressive edifice.

"It's so beautiful," Abba said. "I can't believe this place even exists. Is it . . . ?"

"The castle of the Sisters of the Mist," Boris said. "It is about a hundred yards from here to the entrance. The drawbridge is the only way to cross the moat. We wait here until Jean Pierre lowers it."

"Tubah has the power to transform us into wolves and elves," I said. "Why does she need us to enter the castle? Can't she just cast a spell and accomplish her purpose?"

"Though Tubah is a powerful sorceress, her powers end outside the castle walls," Boris said. "There are guards in the turrets surrounding the castle, and that is why you must wait until after dark."

"How much longer will that be?" Abba asked.

"We made excellent time once we transformed," Boris said. "It won't be dark enough for several more hours."

"Will the darkness be enough to mask us when we cross the open area?" Rory asked.

"With the surrounding trees and thick mist, the swamp becomes almost pitch black after dark. Sometimes the guards set bonfires to light the castle's perimeter. Tonight is All Saint's Eve, and surveillance will be lax. With luck, you should be inside the gate before they know you are there."

"And if not?" I asked.

"You'll die in a hail of arrows before you reach the gate," he said.

"That's not a pleasant thought," Abba said. "What'll we do until it's time to go?"

Boris produced a silver flask from the pocket of his jacket and handed it to Rory.

"We are not inside the castle walls, Tubah's magic still strong. She sent something for you."

Rory opened the flask and took a drink. "Hello, Southern Comfort," he said. "I wondered if I'd ever taste your sweet lips again."

"It is much more than whiskey," Boris said. "It is imbued with magic and meant for all of you. Unlike alcohol, it will hone your senses, make you think more clearly, and assist you in completing your mission."

I glanced at Boris when Rory passed me the flask. "Are you sure about this?" I asked.

"You have my word," he said. "Now, you must rest and recuperate from our trek. Drink whiskey and wait until dark when Jean Pierre lowers the gate and allows you and the People to enter."

"And you?"

"I will wait here for your return until shortly after midnight. If you are not here by then, I will assume the mission has failed, and that you are all dead."

"What else?" I asked.

"Say a prayer for Jean Pierre. His life is in great danger, and it is very possible he will die before he's ever able to open the gate and lower the drawbridge."

Chapter 36

J.P. had dozed off from boredom while waiting for darkness to fall. He awoke when Tubah shook his shoulder.

"Time has come," she said. "Are you ready?"

"As I'll ever be."

"You'll do just fine," she said. "Just stay focused on what you are trying to accomplish, and don't let any of the beautiful women you're going to meet, influence your decisions."

"I've never had an easy time with that one," he said.

"Tonight is different. Many people are counting on you. One more thing," she said.

"Yes?"

"The window of opportunity you will have to lower the drawbridge is small. You will be sorely tempted to try to do more. You must not."

"Please explain."

She shook her head. "I have told you more than I should have."

Tubah refused to answer any more of his questions, leading him instead to the door of the interspatial portal, and then watching as he pulled the mask over his face. When the door shut, leaving him in total darkness, he became light-headed. For a fleeting moment, he thought he might have to throw up. He didn't. When he opened the door, he was on Bourbon Street.

Mardi Gras in the French Quarter is wild, Halloween on Bourbon Street maybe even wilder. Hundreds of costumed revelers filled the festive thoroughfare, drinking, singing, and dancing. The revelry quickly caught up to J.P. The entrance to Sister Gertrude's gentleman's club was several blocks away as he pushed slowly through the crowd.

No city celebrates Halloween like New Orleans does, and there are none quite as imaginative at creating unusual costumes as natives of the city. A young woman dressed as a harem girl caught J.P.'s eyes. He also caught hers. Making a beeline to him through the crowd, she ripped off his mask and kissed him.

The male companion of the inebriated young woman grabbed her arm, pulling her away through the crowd. On any other night, J.P. would have been disappointed. Tonight, he simply shrugged and started away again through the mostly drunken crowd of costumed zombies, witches, and pirates.

High Rollers was the fitting name of Sister Gertrude's club, the barker at the door letting everyone know beforehand that the cover charge to enter the establishment was a hundred bucks. J.P. paid the cover charge and tipped the door attendant another hundred. Sounds of loud music, the smell of strong alcohol, and the sight of near-naked women greeted him when he entered the club. A smiling waitress with a thick thatch of blond hair greeted him.

"I'm Opium," she said.

"That's a new name on me. Why do they call you that?" he asked.

"Maybe because I'm so addictive, and every man's fantasy," she said. "What can I get you to drink?"

Opium's costume was little more than a pink nightie worn over a black G-string and mesh stockings, complete with red garters that matched her mask.

"Southern Comfort on the rocks," he said. "And make it a double."

"Never had a customer order one of those," she said.

"Just started drinking it myself, and it's kinda growing on me."

"I'll need a credit card," she said.

"Never carry one when I'm out on the town. I got plenty of these," he said, handing her a hundred dollar bill.

"Guess that'll work," she said. "I'll ask my manager."

"You do that, sweet thing. Tell him I got a thousand with his name all over it."

"I'll tell him," she said.

He pinched her bottom when she turned toward the bar to order his drink.

"That'll cost you extra," she said.

"Then don't worry. My money's burning a hole in my pocket."

After returning with J.P.'s drink, Opium rewarded him with a sensual kiss and flash of her breasts. Before she could walk away, he stuffed a handful of hundreds into her nightie.

Fittingly for Halloween night, the bar's motif was the color red. Red, rotating spotlights cast a supernatural glow on the walls, ceiling, and floor of the establishment. A fog machine beneath the dance floor periodically shot clouds of mist around the naked dancers. Loud, head smashing, heavy metal music blasted from giant speakers.

J.P. elbowed his way past the men sitting around the raised stage and began tipping the two dancers with hundred dollar bills. A man in a pinstriped suit soon pushed through the crowd and tapped his shoulder.

"Hey, bud, we need to have a little talk," he said.

"You bet," J.P. said. "Just give me a second to give these pretty ladies a few more hundreds."

The man in the suit had oiled hair, a pencil-thin mustache, and a broken front tooth. He wasn't smiling as he led J.P. to a dimly-lit hallway, stopping by a fake potted plant.

"You can't stay here unless you got a credit card," the man said, his voice stern.

J.P. flashed his thick roll of cash. "You don't take real money in this place?"

"We keep a running tab. Can't do that without a credit card," the man said.

J.P. just grinned and shook his head. "No problem," he said. "I'll just head down the street to Bootleggers. They and their girls don't mind taking real money."

When J.P. turned to leave, the oily man called to him.

"Wait just a second. Why the hell don't you have a credit card?"

"Maybe you should ask Gertrude," J.P. said.

"You know Sister Gertrude?"

J.P. nodded. "Doesn't everyone?"

"I'll just call her and see."

"You do that," J.P. said. "Tell her Jean Pierre Saucier will be spending his money at Bootlegger's from now on."

"Never heard of you," the man said.

"And I bet you wouldn't recognize Bill Gates if he walked up and shook your hand."

"You ain't Bill Gates," the man said.

"Nope, I'm J.P. Saucier."

Before J.P. could take a step for the door, the man grabbed his elbow.

"I hate to bother Sister Gertrude. She's sort of busy tonight. Stick around. We'll take your cash this time, though next time you come in, you'll need a credit card."

J.P. stuffed a hundred dollars into the oily man's coat pocket. Opium was waiting nearby, watching the exchange. She smiled when the man gave her a nod. She was still smiling when she took J.P.'s hand.

"I was worried old prune face was gonna kick you out for not having a credit card," she said. "Against club policy, you know. He gave me the high sign, so I'll be taking care of you the rest of the night."

"Great," J.P. said.

"Follow me," she said. "You're special tonight. You're gonna have your very own fantasy room."

She led him to a second level overlooking the main bar. Wispy curtains of blue and purple silk formed the private room, a table, and couch the only furniture. J.P. sank into the couch, Opium piling into his lap. He was already well on his way to being sexually aroused when two scantily clad dancers joined them.

"This is Nightshade and Belladonna," Opium said.

"They sound dangerous," J.P. said.

"We are dangerous," one of the women said. "Hope you have plenty of money on you because we're the two best table dancers in town."

J.P. reached for his roll of cash. "Prove it," he said.

He soon had rotating dancers keeping him company whenever they weren't on the dance floor. Though he had no watch and there was no clock on the wall, he was on his third Southern Comfort and knew he had been there awhile. He was starting to worry when a woman he hadn't seen before arrived at the table.

The dancer sitting on the couch beside him got up and let the woman replace her, not saying goodbye as

311

she slipped out of the silk curtains. The others quickly followed suit, leaving him alone with the attractive woman.

"I'm Batgirl," she said.

"Hi, Batgirl, I'm J.P. I love your costume."

Batgirl smiled, showing him her blood-red fingernails that matched the color of her lips when she used them to caress his wrist. Red hair highlighted her black latex bikini and calf-length, spiked heel boots, and splayed over her bare shoulders. Her eyes were a shade of green he'd never before seen and reminded him of a cat's.

"The girls say you're a big spender," she said.

Just to show her she wasn't mistaken, he stuffed a hundred into her bra.

"Shouldn't Batgirl be wearing a mask and bat ears?" he asked.

"I have something better," she said.

"Like what?"

"These," she said, opening her mouth to show him a perfect set of vampire fangs.

"Those look real," he said.

"Because they are, and so are these," she said, pulling down her bra. "Ever had sex with a gorgeous, red-headed vampire?"

"Can't say as I have, though I'd like to," he said.

"How about having an orgy with ten beautiful vampires?"

J.P. removed his mask and grinned. "Baby, that sounds like heaven to me. Where is this party? I want to be there."

"Not in heaven. I can promise you that. And there won't be any angels hanging around either."

"Sounds kinky," he said. "Tell me more. I'm interested."

"Thought so," she said. "What's your favorite perversion?"

"I'm Catholic," he said. "I always thought it

would be kinda cool to have sex with a nun. Not just any nun, but one as gorgeous as a movie star."

Batgirl showed him her fangs when she smiled and nodded. "How would you like to have sex with the most beautiful nun in the world?"

"Now, you're talking my language," he said. "Where do I sign up?"

"The owner of this nightclub hosts the Vampire Ball at her castle every year on Halloween. Only the elite are invited to attend."

"Who do I have to kill to get an invite?"

Batgirl grinned. "No one. You just need lots of money."

"I got plenty of that," J.P. said. "How much we talking about?"

Below them, the music had stopped briefly as one of the dancers finished her set to the applause of appreciative men sitting around the dance floor. After scooping the pile of wadded cash off the stage, the naked dancer grabbed her tiny outfit, took a bow, and strutted away behind a dark curtain.

"Ten grand, for starters," Batgirl said. "That amount doesn't include sex with the nun."

"I've got a wad of hundreds here but not that much," J.P. said.

"Maybe that's why you need a credit card," Batgirl said.

J.P. was glancing at the roll of hundreds in his hand when a flashy credit card appeared bearing the name J.P. King.

"I didn't want to use this," he said, handing her the card.

She took it and started away. "I'll run this first. Hope you got a giant line of credit."

"Me too," he said as he watched her disappear behind the flowing curtain.

She returned with a smile on her face. "You're golden, Mr. King. Your credit card is unlimited."

"The only kind I have," he said, stuffing several hundred-dollar bills into her bra. "Hell, if this party is everything you say it is, I hope it don't catch fire and burn. Tell me more about this beautiful nun."

"Her name is Desire. She was a supermodel, and I'll bet you've seen her picture on a magazine cover."

"You gotta be kidding," he said.

"No, I'm not. She's an honest-to-God nun. For the right price, she'll do anything you want her to do."

"How much?" he asked.

"She's the most expensive piece of ass you've ever had, or will ever have again," she said.

"You got me drooling just thinking about it, sweet thing. Tell me how much."

"Twenty grand," she said. "And that's just for her."

"Girl," he said, "Put it on the card and give yourself a big tip. I can hardly wait. How do I find this beautiful nun?"

The heavy chain Batgirl slipped over his head had a golden doubloon attached. Stamped on the doubloon was the picture of a nun. Beneath the picture were the words Vampire Ball.

"She's on the third floor of the castle where Sister Gertrude keeps her sex slaves."

"Desire's a slave?"

"Bought and paid for. Believe me when I tell you that no sane person would willingly perform the perverted sex acts some of the men require her to do. Unless they were frightened out of their minds that someone would punish them severely if they didn't."

"Guess that's her problem and not mine," he said.

"You just bought yourself the fantasy of a lifetime," she said. "Keep the necklace around your neck. One of the attendants at the ball will see the doubloon and take you to Desire."

"I got a big appetite," J.P. said. "What else you got?"

"Desire's your wildest wet dream," Batgirl said. "There's more, though, if you have any bullets left in your gun."

"Will you be there?" he asked.

"Before the night is over," she said. "When I arrive, I'll find you."

"How do I get to this party?"

She took his hand, led him through the noisy and crowded bar to the same hallway where he'd spoken with the manager. She pointed to the door at the end of the hallway.

"Through that door," she said.

"Sure you're not coming with me?"

"Like I said, I'll be along after I get off work."

"You sure?"

Drawing close to him, she kissed his neck. "I keep my promises," she said opening the door for him.

As he had in Tubah's interspatial portal, he grew light-headed when Batgirl shut the door behind him. The sensation lasted only a moment. Loud music and the cacophony of hundreds of revelers swept over him when he opened the portal door.

Chapter 37

J.P. had a hard time believing his eyes when he exited the interspatial portal. He'd attended lavish parties held in Garden District mansions, and Mardi Gras balls hosted in giant ballrooms. Nothing prepared him for the outlandish theme party he'd stepped into.

The ballroom was enormous, the ceiling in places fully three stories above the stone floor. There was no electricity, only the flickering light of a dozen candle-powered chandeliers and crackling fire from several massive stone fireplaces.

Priceless Persian rugs covered the floor, expensive tapestries draping from the walls of stone. A smiling woman dressed as a serving wench met him at the door.

"Welcome, my lord. I see you are wearing a gold doubloon around your neck."

"Yes," he said. "I haven't seen this many masqueraders since I was in college and snuck into the Rex Ball."

"We have quite a turnout tonight," she said. "I am Guinevere, your hostess. Your every wish is my command. And I truly mean every wish. The kinkier it is, the better I'll like it."

"Anything?"

"Whatever your heart desires."

The long braids in Guinevere's flaxen hair draped over her shoulders. The emerald green sheath she wore matched the color of her eyes, and was low cut and revealing. It barely covered her shapely derriere.

"Open your mouth," he said.

She smiled, baring her teeth in a manner that clearly showed her vampire fangs.

"You like?" she asked.

"You bet I do," he said. "Give me a quick tour, and then I'll decide what my pleasure is."

She pointed to a row of wooden benches brimming with an array of food befitting a feast. Serving wenches wandered around the tables, refilling pitchers of wine and food bowls. J.P. hadn't eaten since breakfast, and the aroma made his stomach growl.

"Sister Gertrude always prepares a magnificent feast for everyone to enjoy. Are you hungry?"

"Starved," he said.

"Would you like for me to find you a seat at the table?"

"Wish I had time. I got other things on my mind right now."

"I'll bet you do," she said, her smile showing her fangs. "There's an empty couch by the fireplace. We could shed these clothes and get to know each other better."

"In the middle of all these people?"

"Look around. We wouldn't be the only ones partaking in a bit of sexual depravity."

Even though shadows masked much of the castle's large interior, J.P. could easily see to what Guinevere was alluding.

"Whoa!" he said. "I like my sex in private."

"Then you're not as kinky as I thought. Most everyone at this party enjoys viewing and being viewed."

"And you?"

"Baby, you'll never have sex as wild as you're about to have with me."

On a large stage, a magnificent orchestra was playing Mozart's Violin Concerto No. 3 in G major. Involved in gluttony or various acts of perversion, no one seemed to notice. There were also armed guards dressed like Spanish conquistadors, complete with body armor, helmets, spears, and swords, stationed at the doors and stairways.

"Sweet thing, you got me licking my chops. What's with the soldiers?" he asked.

She clasped her long arms around her chest, her smile changing into a pout.

"I thought you had your mind on me and not a bunch of soldiers," she said. "Did I forget to put on my perfume?"

Putting his arms around her waist, he kissed her neck. "No way," he said. "I was just wondering if those ugly galoots are bouncers."

"This castle is Sister Gertrude's private Vatican, those men her Swiss Army," she said.

"What the hell for?" he asked.

"Never know when a riot might break out."

"Ugliest bunch of soldiers I ever seen," he said. "They don't even look human."

"Because they're not."

"Then what the hell are they?" he asked.

"Mercenary trolls, giants, and ogres," she said. "Don't even look at those dudes sideways. They're so mean they'd kill their own mothers."

"How many are there?" he asked.

"Don't know for sure. At least two dozen."

Sister Gertrude's guards did look dangerous. Though not as big as the Swamp Monsters, they all bore spears and swords and looked as if they knew how to use them. J.P. pinched Guinevere's ass.

"Let's go find that beautiful nun. You up for a

threesome?"

"Now you're speaking my language, baby," she said. "You had me believing for a minute I'd drawn a dud for the biggest party of the year."

"Don't you worry sweet thing. I got big plans for you tonight."

Guinevere and J.P. negotiated their way through the wild party. An armed troll stopped them at the base of the stairs. He let them pass when Guinevere showed him the doubloon.

Up the stairs, the giant chandeliers were missing, replaced by candles that left the halls in smoke, flickering shadows on the walls, general dimness, and the hallway chilly. Noise from the party below had died away before they reached the third floor of the castle.

"Sister Gertrude keeps all her sex slaves on this floor. Desire is her favorite. When customers aren't drooling all over her, the old bat's usually in her cell using and abusing the one she considers her prize possession."

"I've never seen Sister Gertrude. What does she look like?

"Big, and I don't mean fat. Probably seven feet tall."

"You're kidding?"

"No, I'm not. The only thing short about Sister Gertrude is her temper. She backed down a troll once. Lifted him off the ground by the neck, and then squeezed his jugular till his eyes bulged."

"She killed a troll?"

"Threw him against the wall and cracked his head open, though she stopped short of killing him."

"Sounds pretty mean," J.P. said.

"Mean, big, and ugly, though she pays well. No one that works for her ever wants to leave." She giggled. "She's also a witch, and a harpy, and would probably turn us into toads if we ever tried."

"I thought she was a Catholic nun. I also have it on good authority that she's human."

"My ass! She's no more human than the trolls and ogres, and no more a nun that I am. Nun of the Devil, maybe. She likes mocking the church. She's not religious, I promise you."

"What the hell's a harpy?"

"You won't believe me if I tell you," she said.

"Try me."

"When Sister Gertrude angers, she transforms into her real persona."

"Which is?"

"A monster with the face of a woman and body of a raptor, with talons so sharp and deadly, she can claw you to pieces with them while she pecks out your eyes with her beak."

"You're shittin' me!"

"Don't ever piss her off, or you'll find out for yourself."

"I met Bat Girl at High Rollers," he said, changing the subject.

"Bat Girl and I are besties. She'll be at the party when she gets off work."

"She told me," J.P. said.

"Maybe we can all have a good time together."

"Maybe."

Guinevere stopped in front of a wooden door with a tiny viewing slot. "This is Desire's room."

"You got a key?" he asked.

She smiled and showed him the key to the cell on the gold chain she wore around her neck.

"Master key for all the cells," she said. "Sister Gertrude and I are the only two people that have one."

The heavy wooden door pushed open with a groan, light from a dozen candles scattered around the room greeting them when they entered. The only furniture was a bed and J.P. could see someone was in it. Touching her shoulder, he shook it gently.

"Desire, is that you?"

When she turned over and stared into his eyes, her appearance startled him. J.P. had never met the young woman, though had seen her picture many times on various magazine covers. She was widely considered one of the most beautiful women in the world.

He stepped back in shock, barely able to hear her when she asked, "Do I know you?"

"I'm J.P.," he said. "A friend of Wyatt's."

"Wyatt?"

"Wyatt Thomas."

Desire extended her hand. "Please come closer. I can't see you."

J.P. took her hand and bent close enough to her that she could see his face. As Wyatt had said, her hair had gone completely white. Her cheeks were gaunt, skin pale. There were vampire marks on her neck. Her bare arms were raw from recent bindings. Her voice was weak, and he had a hard time hearing her, even when he drew close. One of the candles in a holder on the wall sputtered and went out.

"Wyatt, is that you?" she asked.

"I'm J.P.," he said.

She sank back into her pillow, tears appearing in her eyes.

"I thought for a moment . . ."

Guinevere was watching their exchange intently. J.P. stood and grabbed her hand.

"Change of plans," he said. "You got me to thinking about you, me, Desire, and Bat Girl. Let's wait till she gets here. All this smoke is getting to me, and right now, I need a breath of fresh air. Can you take me outside for a bit?"

"Guests aren't allowed outside the castle walls," Guinevere said.

"You told me my wish was your command.

321

Nothing I'd like better right now than to get into that slinky little dress of yours right in front of the main gate and do it with a bunch of those ugly trolls and ogres watching us."

Guinevere's smile reappeared. "That does sound kinky. I've wanted to have sex with a troll since I arrived here."

"Hell yeah," he said. "If there's a guard at the front gate, I'll invite him to join us." There was a cord, whips, and other sexual paraphernalia lying on the floor beside the bed. Grabbing a rope, he said, "Lead the way."

"There's a secret passage," she said. "We can get to the front door through it without having to make our way back through the crowds. It's dark so we'll need candles."

They grabbed burning candles, finding the secret passage behind a tapestry hanging on the wall in the hallway. A mouse scurried under their feet when they entered the darkened passageway.

"It's narrow, damp, and slippery," she said. "So watch your step. You'll be no fun with a broken leg."

The tunnel smelled of must, mold, and candle smoke. The air was stale. Something sounding like a high-pitched scream echoed through the dark passageway.

"What the hell was that?" he asked.

"Bats," she said. "Don't be afraid. I'll protect you."

"I'll bet you will," he said, pinching her ass again.

"Better watch it," she said. "Or I may have to have you right here in the dark on this damp stone floor."

"If we don't get to where we're going pretty soon, I'll take you up on it."

The tunnel became steeper as it spiraled downward. At least there were steps. They finally reached level ground and Guinevere began searching

322

for the exit.

"It's been a while since the last time I took this tunnel. Can't quite remember where the exit door lever is."

J.P. was getting antsy when a door in the wall slid open. They were quickly outside the castle, and it was dark.

"We girls rarely come out here," she said. "When we do, we usually go through the castle's main entrance."

"Where is that?" he asked.

"Around the corner. The barracks and mess hall for the soldiers are beyond the main entrance."

"What time is it?" he asked.

"You taking medicine?"

"Just wondering how much longer before midnight."

"Another hour or so," she said. "You'll know because there's always a big fireworks display."

"Then we better get on with it. Where are the guards located?"

"Those turrets on either side of the front gate to the castle," she said.

"How many men?"

"Don't know," she said. "Why?"

"One of them is all we need. I don't want to invite their whole crew."

"Volmak, the officer in command, is a friend of mine," she said. "He and I've been planning to get naked together for a while. I'll see if he'll send the others inside for a break."

"You think he will?"

"Baby, he may not be human, but he's definitely a male. If I can get him alone for a minute or so, I'll have him eating out of my hands."

"You're getting me excited thinking about you getting him excited," J.P. said.

J.P. stayed in the shadows as she ascended the

stairs to one of the turrets. He needed a weapon. The only thing he could find was an oak barrel stave. Like a baseball bat, he swung it once to gauge its heft. Satisfied that he could do some damage with it, he hid it behind his back.

Before many minutes had passed, four soldiers descended from the turrets. They didn't see him in the shadows, pressed against the castle wall, as they disappeared around the corner. Guinevere soon exited the turret, leading Volmak, a big troll by the hand. He met them with a big smile.

"Pleased to meet you. You speak English?"

Volmak stood several inches taller than J.P. and looked as solid as the walls of the castle. His frowning expression never changed when he grunted and nodded that he understood.

"Good, since I'm the one paying for this fantasy, I want you to strip this pretty girl naked, tie her arms and legs with this rope, and then put her over your knees. Think you can handle it?"

Volmak grunted before ripping the emerald dress right off Guinevere's body. She was ecstatic when he grabbed her braided hair, holding her with it as he secured the rope around her arms and legs.

"Stuff something in her mouth so she can't squeal, and then give that pretty little bottom of hers a good spanking."

Volmak grunted as he bent her over his knees and began spanking her. J.P. was behind them. Pulling the barrel stave from the shadows, he used it to take a full swing at the troll's big head.

Chapter 38

When J.P. crashed the barrel stave into the back of Volmak's head, he quickly realized the blow had barely fazed him. He nailed him again when he turned, this time swinging with his legs set, and with the full weight of his body. When the troll didn't fall, J.P. thought he was in trouble. He wasn't.

Volmak's eyes closed and he toppled over backward, onto the ground. Guinevere struggled as J.P. retrieved the key to Desire's room from her neck, patting her bare butt as he did.

"Sweet thing, leaving you here is just about the hardest thing I ever done, though right now I got bigger fish to fry."

After a quick look around to see if anyone had witnessed the incident, he left Guinevere bound on the ground as he sprinted to the front gate, found the big crank that opened it and began turning it furiously. When the drawbridge hit the ground on the other side of the moat with a thud, he ran across it, a candle in his hand, and began shouting.

"Rory, Barzoom, the gate's open. Hurry up!"

As he gazed into the darkness, the clouds parted as a full, yellow, Halloween moon began illuminating the plain between the castle and the trees. Figures began to emerge from the shadows. It was Rory, and the Swamp Monsters followed closely by Wyatt, Abba, Slick, and Lucky.

Rory was in full Scottish battle regalia, Aila, his big broadsword, in his hand.

"Whoa," he said. "They can't go in there like that. Where are their weapons?"

"They fight with staffs," Rory said

The Swamp Monsters were dancing up and down, pounding their wooden staffs into the dirt, and making high-pitched unearthly sounds as they stoked themselves for the ensuing battle.

"Sister Gertrude has her own army. I promise you they ain't gonna drop their weapons and run," J.P. said.

"Contain your fears, or they will fell you before the first blow is ever struck. I am ready to fight to the death, and so are these fine lads."

"All right then," J.P. said. "Let's get across the moat before someone raises the drawbridge and closes the gate on us."

The thundering herd followed J.P. into the castle's courtyard.

"The entrance to the castle is around the corner," J.P. said. "There's a big costume party on the ground floor, most of the participants too drunk or drugged to put up any resistance. Sister Gertrude has about two dozen armed trolls and ogres that you'll have to fight your way through before you can get into the basement."

"How will we find it?" Rory asked.

"There's a staircase that winds up to the upper floors, and down to the basement. There are guards at the stairs. You can't miss it. What about the dogs?"

"Slick and Lucky will come with me," Rory said. "I have a feeling deep in my soul that I will need them before midnight arrives."

J.P. knelt down and gave Lucky a hug. Lucky licked him and wagged his tail when he said, "Take care of that big Scot, you hear?"

Rory shook his hand, and then turned to the Swamp Monsters, issuing a Scottish war cry. Barzoom and the others began their eerie wailing, and then followed Rory and the two dogs to the castle's entrance.

"Do you know where to find Desire?" I asked.

"There's a secret passage we can take to the cell where they keep her. Wyatt . . ."

"Yes," I said.

"Don't flip out because you ain't gonna recognize her."

"What have they done?" Abba asked.

"Everything except take her very soul," J.P. said. "And I'm not so sure they haven't accomplished that as well."

"Can we get in once we get there?" Abba asked.

"I got a key to the door," J.P. said. "We'll have to find some candles first because the passageway is pitch dark."

We found candles in holders on the wall in the hallway leading to the passage. A secret door cloaked behind a tapestry opened after J.P. had manipulated a hidden lever.

"There are bats and rats in this passageway. Try not to freak totally out," J.P. said.

"I hear them," Abba said. "This place is creepy as hell."

"You ain't seen nothing yet," J.P. said.

Abba's assessment of the secret passageway was right on point. It was dark, dank, and musty. Bats flew past our heads, Abba's hands held high to keep them from getting tangled in her hair.

"Thank God!" she said when we'd finally exited into the flickering light of the third-floor hallway.

She and J.P. entered after opening the door to Desire's cell. I waited in the hallway, not knowing after hearing J.P.'s description if I could take seeing the woman that had once filled the large void in my heart. J.P. and Abba were at her bedside, and my feet finally began to move.

I wondered if Desire would recognize me. She sat up in bed, dispelling those doubts when she clasped her willowy arms around my neck. Like a frightened child embracing their mother, she held on, as if ending the grip would be her death.

When I stroked my hand through her wild hair, I wondered what horrors she'd endured, and if she would ever be the same again. That was assuming we would succeed in rescuing her. I had only a moment to ponder my thoughts as Sister Gertrude walked through the door.

The huge woman dressed in nun's garb glared at me. When she pointed and spoke, I realized it was an expression of pure hatred.

"You!" she said. "Release my precious doll."

As Desire tightened her grip, I felt every rib in her wasted body. She couldn't stop trembling as her tears dampened my neck. Sister Gertrude's face contorted into an even uglier frown. When she bowed her head and raised her arms, her habit disappeared in a puff of smoke. For only a moment, she stood naked until her human body began to transform.

Unable to believe their eyes, Abba and J.P. backed against the wall as Sister Gertrude's arms became wings, her face, and body morphing into the beak and talons of a giant raptor. With Desire's arms still clutching my neck, I could barely move as the giant bird with the face of a monstrous woman shrieked and attacked. I had but a split second to respond to the creature's assault.

Out of nowhere, Exethelon appeared in my hand. As the enraged harpy charged toward Desire and me, the magic dagger flew from my grasp, burying itself deeply into her heart.

Sister Gertrude's Swiss Army met Rory and the Swamp Monsters with instant resistance as they entered the castle. Guests began screaming, pulling on their clothes and trying to flee. The well-trained cadre of trolls, giants, and ogres had no such inclination, raising their weapons and attacking the intruders.

As the ballroom rapidly became a noisy battleground, the masquerade party dissolved into a chaotic scene of mass hysteria. It was quickly apparent the under-armed Swamp Monsters were at an extreme disadvantage.

After what seemed an eternity of intense combat, Rory, the dogs, and the Swamp Monsters were no closer to the entrance to the basement than when the battle had begun. Slick and Lucky crouched with their fangs bared, protecting Rory as he continued to swing his big sword.

Even armed with only broad staffs, the overmatched Swamp Monsters were holding their own against the fierce attack of trolls and ogres. Bodies lay bleeding on the castle floor, including two of the Swamp Monsters. It wasn't going well when the second wave of Swiss Army soldiers came streaming through the front door of the castle. Barzoom had fought his way to Rory's side.

"Holy Mother of Christ!" Rory said. "It is almost midnight, and I have to make it to the basement. Can you open a path for me?"

Barzoom nodded and began swinging his broad staff with redoubled intensity. Trolls and ogres dropped in his wake as he began clearing a path to the stairs leading to the basement. Rory was by his side, the two dogs guarding their rear. Against greater odds, they somehow made it to the stairs. Rory clutched Barzoom's big wrist before descending the circular stairway into the castle's basement.

"God save us, lad," he said. "I'll take it from here.

329

Your men need you back upstairs."

Sounds of battle died behind them as Rory, Slick, and Lucky raced down the narrow stairway. They found the door to the basement ajar, intense light radiating through the crack. Rory hit the door at a full run, tripping and tumbling down a short flight of stairs leading to a circular room.

A huge granite boulder sat in the center of the small room. Rory grabbed his sword and picked himself off the ground. The great stone was moving. Soon, arms, legs, and creepy tentacles began protruding from the base of the boulder. Using his weight and strength, he attempted to keep the stone plug over the hole. Slick and Lucky stood barking as he struggled to keep shut the door to hell.

Unspeakable fiends, evil spirits, and demons finally managed to push the boulder aside and began streaming up from the fiery depths below. Rory backed away toward the stairs, cutting down demons as they exited the hole. The two dogs stood beside them, ripping at flailing limbs of frenetic demons.

A stench of death pervaded the basement oozing with demon's blood as Rory, Slick, and Lucky stood at the base of the stairs, blocking the onslaught pouring from the depths of hell. Not knowing if he could hold his position, he looked at the dogs, gave the basement door a glance, and then shook his head. After crossing himself, he began attacking the demons again with renewed passion.

An expression of horror and disbelief appeared on the face of the harpy when Exethelon pierced her heart. Clutching the hilt with both hands, she sank slowly to the floor. As life seeped from her body, she transformed back into a human. J.P. felt the dagger's power surging up his arms when he pulled it out of her heart.

"Exethelon is yours now," I said. "Let's get the

330

hell out of here."

I wrapped Desire in a blanket, carrying her as I followed Abba and J.P. back into the hallway. We waited on him as he used the key to open all the doors on the floor.

"Sister Gertrude is dead," he said. "We have to get out of here."

Though all the former prisoners looked in better shape than Desire, they were in obvious shock as they exited their cells and joined us in the hall. J.P. took a moment to address them.

"There's a battle waging downstairs. Let's all stay together, and I'll lead you through the fighting to the portal that will deliver you to safety."

Abba stayed close to me, stroking Desire's hair, trying to comfort her as we started down the stairs. Desire felt so light that I had no difficulty carrying her. Sounds of battle accosted our senses when we reached the ballroom. Screams and wails of dying and wounded fighters met us when we made it to the base of the stairs.

"That open door up ahead is the interspatial portal. It will take you to a strip joint that exits on Bourbon Street."

"You must come with us," Abba said, clutching his wrist.

"I don't see Rory or the dogs. They must be in the pit. I'm going to rally the Swamp Monsters and lead them down there."

"No, they may already be dead. If you go, they'll kill you too," she said.

Instead of answering, J.P. embraced her. Abba was crying when their kiss ended.

"Since that may be the first and last time I ever get to kiss you, I wanted to make it a good one." He turned to walk away, stopping, as if he'd forgotten something. "Wyatt, take good care of those two girls."

J.P. waded into the battle in the main ballroom. An experienced combat officer who'd seen plenty of action in Afghanistan, he quickly assessed the situation, realizing the Swamp Monsters were getting the worst of the exchange.

Guinevere had given him incorrect information. Sister Gertrude's Swiss Army was much larger than she had told him. The Swamp Monsters were outnumbered at least four to one. While they were presently holding their own, he knew he had to do something to change the course of battle.

Barzoom turned when J.P. yelled his name. J.P. grabbed his nose and made a face.

"Stink 'em out!" he said above the din.

Barzoom understood instantly. The foulest odor J.P. had ever smelled soon began filling the room. Sister Gertrude's Swiss Guard began gagging, rubbing their eyes, grabbing their throats and dropping their weapons.

Haze drifted in the air of the large ballroom, trolls, and ogres running for the door. In the military, J.P. had experienced gas attacks. Nothing prepared him for the horrible effects of the Swamp Monster's foul odor. He was about to run for the front door himself when he saw one of the trolls hadn't deserted the fight. He was standing behind Barzoom, preparing to lop off his head with his sword. Drawing upon some inner strength he didn't know he had, he launched Exethelon at the troll.

Sister Gertrude's warrior fell over dead as Exethelon found its mark. Barzoom wheeled around. When he saw the dagger, he grabbed the hilt and pulled it out of the dead troll. In an instant, a golden glow began emanating from the blade. J.P. lurched forward, joining him, wrenching the sword out of the fallen troll's hand.

When J.P. raised the sword in a salute to Barzoom, and they touched blades, his eyes stopped burning. The weapon took on the same golden glow as Exethelon's. Realizing what had just occurred, he began picking swords up off the floor and tossing them to the remaining Swamp Monsters. Forming a semi-circle around Barzoom, they extended their swords as he touched each one of them with Exethelon. All the blades were soon aglow. The Swamp Monsters began to dance and howl.

"Too early to celebrate," J.P. said. "The magic dagger is yours now. Lead us to the basement. We have a world that needs saving, and it may already be too late to do it."

J.P. and the Swamp Monsters raced down the stairs to the basement door. From the sounds of battle coming from behind it, they knew Rory, and the dogs were still holding the demons from hell at bay. When Barzoom burst through the door, Rory came tumbling out. He was bloodied and bruised but came up fighting.

Seeing that Rory was down, the demons from hell began pouring through the door. When they did, the Swamp Monsters attacked, and the fight was on. The big Scot's eyes opened when Barzoom touched Aila with Exethelon. Bounding to his feet, he sprang into battle, his sword slashing with newfound strength.

"Help me, lads," he said, calling to the Swamp Monsters.

The stairway down to the pit of hell was narrow, only allowing one person at a time to pass. Barzoom and Rory were leading the way, slowly pushing the demons back down the stairs.

"Find Slick and Lucky," Rory called to J.P. "They're hurt. Don't let the demons drag them to hell."

Rory's words incited the Swamp Monsters, and they began fighting even harder. They had just driven the last demon into the pit when J.P. found Slick and Lucky.

Blood oozing from numerous lacerations covered their fur. They both looked dead. J.P. left them to help Rory and Barzoom lift the giant boulder and drop it on the gateway to hell. The circular basement grew suddenly quiet. Then a howl went up. The Swamp Monsters began dancing and pounding the floor. Rory was dancing with them until J.P. grabbed his arm.

"You did it, big fellow. The world is safe for hundred-sixty more years, and it's all thanks to you and the dogs."

J.P. shook his head when Rory said, "Where are Slick and Lucky?"

Chapter 39

Abba was in tears as we loaded everyone into the portal and shut the door behind us. Several of the young women we'd just rescued grew light-headed and passed out. Dozens of patrons of Sister Gertrude's gentlemen's club looked at us in shock when we exited the portal.

"Get out of our way," I said when an angry man in a pinstriped suit got in our faces.

When he didn't immediately respond, I shoved him against the wall and kept walking, through the front door and into the madness of Halloween on Bourbon Street.

Past midnight, we could clearly see the fireworks exploding in the sky over the river. For the first time in many days, the ground fog had disappeared. Sister Gertrude's former sex slaves began clapping and cheering. One of the young women melted away into the crowd.

"Wait," Abba said, calling to her. "Don't run away. We can help you."

Another soon followed her. Before long, they'd all disappeared into the cluster of masked insanity rampant on the world's most famous street. Abba started to cry.

"They are survivors," I said. "They'll be okay.

335

Right now, we have to get Desire to a doctor."

"A doctor may restore her body. Nothing will ever restore what that horrible Sister Gertrude stole from her."

"What are you talking about?" I asked.

"Her soul. Oh, Wyatt, what are we going to do?"

"Get her to a doctor first and worry about her soul later. We're losing her. I can feel her slipping away."

Abba jumped when someone touched her shoulder. When he spoke, his African accent was unmistakable.

"Thank God I've found you," he said.

"Lando, is that you?" I asked.

It was Lando Impeke, the caretaker of St. Roch's Chapel. We could see his snowy hair and broken tooth when he pulled the mask up over his head and smiled.

"Yes, I've been searching for you since darkness fell. Thank God you're alive."

"How did you know we'd be here?" I asked.

"I knew. Let me see the girl."

I pulled back the blanket from Desire's face, and Lando touched it with the stump of his right hand.

"She's barely breathing," I said. "We need to take her to a doctor."

"Her body will survive," he said. "It is her soul that needs saving. We must take her to St. Roch."

"That's crazy," Abba said. "She needs a doctor, not your religious mumbo-jumbo."

Lando gazed up at me. "My car is a few blocks away. I am here for a reason. Even if you do not believe me, take a leap of faith."

We pushed through the masked crowd on Bourbon Street, happy revelers unaware of our plight. When we reached a quiet side street intersecting Bourbon, Lando led us into the darkness. As the noise behind us began to die away, Abba continued to sob and to grumble.

"This is insane," she said. "There's nothing to gain by going to St. Roch. You don't believe this man's malarkey, do you?"

"You've seen things over the past two days you would never have believed," I said. "Now, I believe Lando was on Bourbon Street for a reason. If he thinks he can help Desire, then I'm going to let him try."

Though her grumbling ceased, her tears did not. Even several blocks from Bourbon Street, we could still hear the crowd noise in the distance, and see colorful prisms of light exploding in the sky. After some difficulty piling into Lando's shocking pink Volkswagen, we left the French Quarter on our way to the nearby St. Roch Cemetery.

Lando parked outside the locked gate, light from the full moon shining down on the entrance as we exited his old beater. Desire was lifeless in my arms as he unlocked the gate. When he did, they swung open, a metallic clang beckoning us to enter. The moon illuminated our path as we approached the statue of the little girl.

"Remove the blanket and lay her on the statue," Lando said.

I didn't know if Desire was still alive when I laid her atop the statue of the sick girl lying in bed. If she was still breathing, her breath was so faint as to be imperceptible. As she lay prone on the statue, Lando knelt beside it and began to pray. I watched, waiting for a miracle that didn't occur. Undeterred, Lando glanced up at Abba.

"Help me," he said.

"I can't. I don't believe what you're attempting will do Desire a bit of good."

Lando was short, barely reaching Abba's shoulder. He stood and clutched her hand.

"This is as much about you as it is Desire. Can

you explain the moon and stars?"

"I don't need to explain them. I can see them and know they are there."

"What about the places you cannot see? Do they not exist?"

"Of course they do," she said.

"How do you know?"

"You're just trying to confuse me," she said.

"What is a shadow, or the reflection of a reflection? Where does a wisp of vapor go when it disappears in the blue of the sky?"

"Stop tormenting me. I don't have all the answers."

"Then quit trying to analyze what you do not understand. Allay your doubts and let faith flood into your soul. What you are about to witness has but a single explanation. Take my hand, my only hand; kneel with me and help me pray."

I didn't know if he'd convinced Abba, or if she were simply humoring him. Whichever, she took his left hand and knelt in front of the statue. Lando had begun reciting a short prayer, saying it repeatedly. Abba finally joined him, her voice low at first and then with greater intensity.

"Please, God, restore this woman's soul."

Raised a Catholic, I'd heard of miracles occurring all my life. I'd never witnessed a miracle and didn't expect to witness one as I gazed at Desire draped across the statue in front of me. As Lando had said, it didn't much matter what I believed.

As I watched, a golden light washed over the trio. Desire's eyes popped open, and the color of her hair began to change. When she stared up and saw me, she began to smile.

"Wyatt, is that you?"

Lando dropped us off on the street in front of Bertram's bar. We found the establishment filled with masked patrons. Bertram was working feverishly to fill the orders of beer, wine, and whiskey. He stopped when he saw us straggle through the front door.

"Good God almighty!" he said. "I was beginning to think you two was dead. Is this . . . ?"

"It's me, Bertram," Desire said, giving him a long hug.

"Baby, you look pretty as a picture. Where you been?"

"I have no idea," she said. "The last thing I remember is leaving Mom's house. Have you seen her?"

"She was in here last night," he said.

"Is she . . . ?"

"Doing just fine, though worried as hell about you."

"She shouldn't worry. I'm with friends, now."

"Anybody need a drink?" he asked.

"You have Southern Comfort?" Abba asked. "I've grown partial to it the past few days."

"Honey babe, I got most any kinda alcohol you can think of. Let's go to the bar. I'll make some room for you."

A couple of regulars sitting at the end of Bertram's bar smiled when he comped their tabs and sent them home. We were soon on stools across from the Cajun bartender, Abba, between bites of gumbo and sips of Southern Comfort, recounting the all but unbelievable things we'd experienced the past few days.

"Yeah, yeah," he said. "Have some more whiskey."

"We're going up to my room and crash," I said after a glass of Bertram's lemonade and two bowls of his spicy gumbo.

"That mangy cat of yours must have known you were coming. I ain't been able to get her to leave the

339

room all day."

"Good," I said. "I've missed her."

As we pushed through the ensuing Halloween party to the stairs, Abba began to sob.

"J.P., Rory, and the dogs are dead. I just know they are."

"Bull shit!" I said.

Desire hugged her tightly and also began to cry. I hugged them both.

"Wyatt, I don't think I can take this," Abba said. "What'll I do?"

Desire squeezed her hand and said, "Have faith."

Abba continued to cry as we climbed the short flight of stairs to my room. Her phone began ringing when we reached the door.

"My phone's working," she said.

"Then answer it," I said.

It was J.P. Abba wiped away her tears when she heard his voice.

"I've been so worried," she said. "Are you okay?"

"Couldn't be better. I'm sitting here at my camp with Rory."

"Thank God!" she said.

"Rory's as drunk as a skunk and singing bawdy Scottish songs. Hell, he may as well be, cause he smells worse than skunks. Guess maybe so do I."

"What happened with the demons from hell?" she asked.

"Don't know how they did it, but Rory and the dogs managed to keep them at bay in the basement till me, Barzoom and the other Swamp Monsters got there to help them. The Swiss Army dropped their swords and ran when the Swamp Monsters let loose their stink. Barzoom used Exethelon to give the fallen swords magical powers. Between their skunk odor, magic swords, and Rory, we managed to herd the demons back to hell, and then plugged the hole."

"What about the dogs?"

340

"They were all but dead when I found them in the basement. Neither one of them opened their eyes the whole way back to Tubah's house. Rory was crying like a baby, and maybe so was I."

"Are they dead?"

"Why hell no they ain't dead," J.P. said. "You think Tubah Jones was gonna let two heroes die? She gave them some concoction that revived them. They're bandaged up like a couple of accident victims, but their tails are wagging, and they are both going to make it."

"Thank God!" she said. "I've been so worried."

"The Swiss Army is gone. Last I seen of what was left of them, they was holding their noses and hightailing it through the swamp."

"And the vampires?"

"Guinevere, the vampire girl that had the key to Desire's cell, knew where Sister Gertrude kept all her ownership papers. She's now the owner of High Rollers and is hiring all the other girls. Said the first thing she was going to do was fire the mouthy manager nobody likes."

"Vampires on Bourbon Street?"

"Hell, girl, what else is new?"

"And the castle?"

"That's the strange part," he said. "As we was leaving, a thick cloud covered it. When it disappeared, the castle was gone."

"You mean like it was never there?"

"Exactly what I mean. Barzoom took the dagger, and he and the Swamp Monsters disappeared back into the Honey Island Swamp. Now, it all seems like a dream to me."

"Maybe it was," she said.

"How are you, Wyatt and Desire?" he asked.

"We're okay, Desire back to her old self."

"How?" he asked.

"Long story," she said. "I'll tell it to you when we

both have more time."

"Good," he said. "You haven't forgotten about our date, have you?"

"Wouldn't miss it for the world," she said.

When I opened the door to my room, Kisses jumped into my arms. I was as glad to see her, as she was to see me. Abba, Desire, and I were exhausted. We collapsed on the bed and fell asleep without bothering to undress. Kisses spent the night on my chest. She didn't awaken me, I had no fitful dream, and we slept peacefully through the entire night.

Next morning, Bertram was polishing a glass behind the bar when Tony Nicosia came through the front door.

"What's happening, Bro?" Bertram asked. "Survive Halloween okay?"

"Barely," Tony said. "Got any scotch in this place?"

Bertram grabbed a bottle of Dalmore from beneath the bar. "Your favorite," he said.

"Not anymore," Tony said. "Got any Monkey Shoulder?"

Bertram removed his trapper's cap and scratched his head. "What the hell is Monkey Shoulder?"

"Scotch," Tony said.

"You'll have to drink Dalmore till I get you some."

"That'll work," Tony said. "Seen Wyatt?"

"He's upstairs in bed with two pretty women and that cat of his."

"Except for the cat, it sounds like they may be having fun," Tony said."

"Just sleeping. When I peeked in on them, they still had on all their clothes. Where's Eddie?"

"We've all been staying at Frankie Castellano's horse farm north of Covington while Eddie and me was trying to solve a little problem for him."

"And?"

"Everything's copacetic," Tony said. "Frankie thinks me and Eddie set the moon. He and Adele are taking me and Lil to Italy with them next month."

"And Eddie?"

"You hadn't heard?"

"Heard what?"

"Eddie and Frankie's daughter, Josie are a number now. Adele and Frankie are planning the biggest wedding this parish ever seen."

"Oh?"

"Frankie's going to make Eddie his chief counsel. He'll be second in command of his whole operation. He's also going to give him and Josie his horse farm as a wedding present."

"What's Eddie think of all this?"

"He left early this morning to run an errand and ain't heard about it yet."

Bertram poured himself a shot of Cuervo. "Eddie's never gonna settle down with one woman. He ain't wired that way."

"He don't have much choice," Tony said. "Frankie will have him skinned alive if he trifles with Josie's feelings. He'll learn to love it. He just has to change his ways."

Chapter 40

It was growing dark as Eddie parked his black sedan in front of a tiny wood framed house about a block from the main street of Sallisaw, Oklahoma. As he got out of the car, he saw that a young woman was sitting alone on the front porch swing. She continued to swing as he walked up the broken sidewalk to the porch.

"Jessica Smith?" he said.

"Do I know you?"

"I'm Eddie Toledo. I met you a day or so ago."

Her eyes grew wider when he walked out of the shadows, and she got a good look at his face. Bounding out of the swing, she stepped off the porch and clutched his hand.

"You're the man that saved my life in the horse barn."

"I could see you were in danger."

"You're a hero."

"Anyone would have helped."

"No they wouldn't have," she said. "Thank you so much, Eddie."

"Just glad I was there when you needed me."

"You thirsty? I got ice tea in the kitchen."

"Sounds great," he said. "Please don't go to any trouble."

"No trouble. Wait in the swing. I'll be right back."

Rusty chains supported the old wooden swing hanging from the ceiling of the porch, their metallic creaks harmonizing with traffic sounds on the nearby highway. Jessica returned with a pitcher of iced tea and two tumblers. After pouring them a glass of tea, she scooted beside him.

Her simple yellow dress didn't cover her knees, the brown cotton sweater she wore her only concession to the night chill in the air. The swing being small, their bodies touched. Even in the dim light of a nearby streetlamp, he was close enough to see how pretty she was. She smiled when she noticed him noticing.

"Why are you here, Eddie?" she asked.

"I have something for you."

Taking a slip of paper from his shirt pocket, he handed it to her.

"What is it?" she asked.

"A cashier's check made out to you."

"This can't be mine," she said. "No one owes me thirty-three thousand dollars."

"I promise you, it's yours," he said.

"Where did it come from?"

"Your deceased husband, Kenny. He placed a bet on the last race he rode in. This is his winnings, and it belongs to you."

Tears began forming in the corners of her eyes. "This can't be. I must be dreaming."

"It is, and you're not," Eddie said.

Jessica put her arms around him, resting her head on his shoulder.

"You drove all the way from New Orleans to give this to me?"

"I had the day off," he said.

"Thank you, Eddie. You don't know what this means."

"I think I do.

"No, you don't. I just broke into my piggy bank and found three dollars and seventy-five cents in quarters, nickels, and dimes. It's all I have in the world. I didn't know how I was going to feed my baby this week."

"What's your baby's name?"

"Stevie Ray. Named him after a guitar player cause I'm hoping he grows up with talent enough to make him rich and famous."

"You hungry?" he asked.

"I've been eating ramen noodles for a week now."

"We could go someplace nice and get a steak."

Jessica wiped her eyes and smiled. "Stevie Ray's asleep. I can't go anyplace."

"I could get something and bring it back," he said. "What are you hungry for?"

"When I have a few extra dollars, I get fried chicken they sell at the convenience store."

Neon lights of the combination convenience store and filling station beckoned from across the street.

"I'll walk over and get us some. Anything else you need?"

"Uh . . ."

"What?" he said. "Tell me what it is. I'll get it for you."

She giggled. "I'm almost out of baby formula. Little Stevie was breastfeeding until my tits dried up. Formula is so damn expensive, even the cheap kind."

Jessica was smiling when he returned from the convenience store with two grocery bags in his arms.

"What in the world? Did you buy out the store?"

"Potato chips, chicken, beer, and baby formula. I'd go back if I missed something else that you need."

They sat on the porch swing, eating chicken and potato chips, and drinking beer.

"It's getting late," he finally said. I better get going. It's a long drive back to New Orleans."

Jessica touched his wrist, gazed for a moment

into his eyes, and then stole a quick kiss.

"Please, this is the best night I can remember for so long. I don't want it to ever end. Can't you come inside and stay for just a bit longer?"

As the front door shut behind them, Eddie heard the horn of a semi motoring past on the highway. It sounded far away, deep and mournful, like a jazz funeral marching through the French Quarter.

End

About the Author

Born on a sleepy bayou, Louisiana Mystery Writer Eric Wilder grew up listening to tales of ghosts, magic, and voodoo. He's the author of eleven novels, four cookbooks, many short stories, and Murder Etouffee, a book that defies classification. His two series feature P.I.s adept in the investigation of the paranormal. He lives in Oklahoma, near historic Route 66 with wife Marilyn, four wonderful dogs, and two great cats. If you liked *Sisters of the Mist*, please check out the French Quarter Mystery Series and all of Eric's books.